Critical Acclaim for Patricia Scanlan

Fina...

'Humor, glitz, ror...
This tale of one won...
herself will have readers ....
and the author'
Publishers Weekly

Foreign Affairs

'Warm, Irish saga of friendship, love and the
travel industry'
She Magazine

'A romantic, gritty saga'
Today

'Her books are crammed with glamour and sex, love
and jealousy, friendship and bitter enmity, all in an
Irish setting, though her characters are regular
globe trotters too'
Image

Apartment 3B

'Maeve Binchy is going to have a serious challenger as
the Queen of Irish fiction'
Dublin Evening Press

'A thumping good read . . . Skilfully and simply written'
Dublin Evening Herald

Also by Patricia Scanlan
and published by Bantam Books

Foreign Affairs

PATRICIA SCANLAN

Finishing Touches

BANTAM BOOKS
TORONTO • NEW YORK • LONDON • SYDNEY • AUCKLAND

FINISHING TOUCHES
A BANTAM BOOK : 0 553 40945 X

Originally published by Poolbeg Press Ltd, Dublin, Ireland

PRINTING HISTORY
Poolbeg edition published 1992
Bantam edition published 1996

Copyright © Patricia Scanlan 1992

Set in Stone Serif by Richard Parfrey

Bantam Books are published by Transworld Publishers Ltd, 61– 63 Uxbridge Road, Ealing, London W5 5SA, in Australia by Transworld Publishers (Australia) Pty Ltd, 15– 25 Helles Avenue, Moorebank, NSW 2170, and in New Zealand by Transworld Publishers (NZ) Ltd, 3 William Pickering Drive, Albany, Auckland.

Printed and bound in Great Britain by Cox & Wyman Ltd, Reading, Berkshire.

This book is dedicated to you, dear reader

Acknowledgements

In all thy ways acknowledge Him and
He shall direct thy paths
Thank you, God, for directing my path.

So many people have helped and supported me in the writing of this book. I'd like to take this opportunity to thank them. Thanks to:

My Irish publishers Poolbeg Press; my American publishers, Dell; my agent, Chris Green; my publicist and friend, Margaret Daly; my London publicists, Gina Sussens and Briony Harrison.

All the writers who have given me advice and encouragement: Maeve Binchy, Deirdre Purcell, Ita Daly, June Considine, Alice Taylor, Anne Schulman and Sean McMahon

Those who advised me as regards careers: a solicitor friend, Donie Wiley, Aoibhinn Hogan of the Beauty Shop, Mary Street, and Paddy Crosbie, interior designer.

David Stone and Pauline and Ann in Liverpool, Annette Tallon, Janet Rooney, Ciara Melligan and Anne Kirwan

The staff of Finglas Library

Helen and Gerry McCartney for lending me their mobile home in Wicklow to start this book

And especially my family and friends, who gave me such loyal support. For neglecting you so dreadfully while this book was being written, I can only apologise, and promise that I'll be all yours—until I start the next book!

PROLOGUE 1991

THE INVITATIONS

CASSIE

No wind can drive my bark astray
Nor change the tide of destiny.

❦

Oh Mary we crown Thee with blossoms today,
Queen of the Angels and Queen of the May.
Oh Mary we crown Thee with blossoms today,
Queen of the Angels and Queen of the May.

Cassie Jordan paused while sandpapering a dado rail, to listen to the words of that old, long-forgotten, much-loved hymn of her childhood. My God! she hadn't heard it in years. *That* brought back memories.

Cassie sat back on her hunkers and took a little rest. She would just do this last piece of rail before finishing up for the night. Tomorrow was going to be a long day—all her furniture and equipment was to be installed—so she had promised herself an early night. A nice cup of milky hot chocolate, a quick glance at the newspapers while listening to the rest of *Late Date,* and then she'd sleep like a baby.

She was sleeping much better these nights. She was still not free of all the shackles of guilt, resentment and unhappy memories, but she was working on it! If Barbara, her sister, wanted to spend her life in a bitter feud, that was entirely up to her. Barbara had resented Cassie ever since they were children and it had spilt over into their adult lives, Cassie reflected, as she got a fresh piece of sandpaper and started rubbing more vigorously than was necessary.

Well, the invitations had been sent out and would

have been received by now. She sighed. It would be interesting to see who in the family would come to the official opening of her new interior design business. She had invited them all, even Barbara and Ian. John and Karen would be there, supportive as always. Would Barbara let bygones be bygones, and would Ian, the brother-in-law Cassie so despised, come with her? Would Martin, her younger brother and Jean, his wife, who had interfered so much in what was really none of her business? Would her sister Irene bother to get in touch from Washington? She hoped they would. Life was too short to hold grudges and she had no intention of letting the past ruin her future. She was going to get on with her life. And what a life it was going to be.

A tingle of excitement ran through her. Starting her own interior design business was going to be the greatest thing! The correspondence course and all the studying were paying off. Although the official opening of **Finishing Touches** was next week—the premises were only just ready—her interior design business had been getting off the ground for the previous six months. It was one hell of an achievement and she had orders on her books right up to the end of next year, from clients all over Dublin city and county! Word of mouth was a great thing. And nothing gave her such a high as when she designed a room or worked out a colour scheme or found the perfect vase or lamp or picture. It was lovely to see something dark and dismal transformed to light and airy by her creative talents.

Sighing happily, she ran her fingers along the rail. It was smooth as a baby's bottom, just right.

Well, at last she had made her dream come true, despite all the opposition. David had kept her going, though, Cassie smiled to herself. David Williams had been the candle in her darkness for the last few years. Solid and dependable, he had come into her life when she was at her lowest ebb, seen her at her absolute worst and, despite it all, had fallen in love with her. And what joy that love gave her. David might be eleven years older than her, but he was the sexiest man she had ever met, with his piercing blue heavy-lidded eyes and that sensuous Welsh voice that she could listen to for ever, especially when he was whispering endearments to her during their lovemaking.

"Cassie, where did you find him? He's absolutely gorgeous. I could listen to him for hours!" Laura Quinn had raved after she met David for the first time. Laura, a high-powered solicitor, was not easily impressed, and Cassie had smiled in amusement at her friend's enthusiasm. Laura had carved out a career for herself in the legal world and become a partner in the solicitors practice where she had worked since the days of her apprenticeship. She was one of the best friends a girl could have and Aileen O'Shaughnessy was another. Just thinking of Aileen made Cassie laugh. She was as mad as a hatter, even now, but a truer friend could not be found.

Aileen's sister, Judy, was coming to work with Cassie. She hadn't worked a day since her marriage to the wealthy Andrew Lawson but she was finally going to become a career woman, much to Andrew's dismay. Judy was going to do PR, reception, and assist Cassie with the buying side of things. And she certainly had the contacts. There wasn't a shop in Grafton Street and its environs that she wasn't known in. Andrew Lawson's wife used her credit cards with gay abandon. As she once confided to Cassie, "I was born to shop!"

Stepping out of her overalls, Cassie ran a finger through her rich chestnut locks. She'd better get her hair done. After all, it was going to be her special day. Sitting in the small bay window of the landing of her little house, she looked out at the almost motionless waters of the Broadmeadow Estuary. She had been so lucky to get this house by the sea and she loved Malahide with its colour and charm and small-town friendliness. She had been right to sell up and move from Port Mahon, even though it was not very far up the coast. This was the place to start her new life.

David would stay the night of the party. That would be something to look forward to. They'd discuss the evening, who had come and who hadn't and what he thought of this one and that one. His dry, witty observations would make her laugh. David was a shrewd judge of character. Then they would make love in her big brass bed and she would fall asleep in his arms.

But for tonight, Cassie was content to be alone with her thoughts, watching the moon glimmer on the estuary, wondering who would come to her party.

THE FAMILY

A fool is too arrogant to make amends; upright
men know what reconciliation means.

Proverbs, 14:9

Barbara Jordan Murray was in a foul humour as she slogged away at an article that should have been on a magazine editor's desk at noon that day. Upstairs the children were arguing, despite the fact that it was after eleven and her little girl had to get up for school in the morning. "Ian, for God's sake will you do something with them!" she snarled at her husband, who was in the adjoining room looking at wrestling on the sports channel. A resonant snore was her spouse's thoroughly unsatisfactory response. Barbara gritted her teeth and bent her head to her work.

She was writing an article on families, and who knew more than she about that subject? "Don't talk to me about families," she muttered to herself, as she lied through her teeth and wrote that a united family such as her own was the greatest blessing.

That Cassie! The nerve of her! Sending them an invitation to the launch of her interior design business. A business that was set up with ill-gotten money that by right should have been shared out among the whole family. If Cassie Jordan thought she was going to worm her way back into their good graces after her outrageous behaviour, she could just think again. What an opportunist Cassie was. Barbara wouldn't put it past her sister to have bribed the judge in the court case. And that arrogant Welshman, David Williams, was in cahoots with her.

But *she'd* find a way to deal with Mr Smarty David Williams. The pen was mightier than the sword, as she had found out many times. No better woman for the hatchet job than Barbara Jordan Murray.

Only recently, hadn't she reviewed a first novel by a male colleague in a way that had the so-called literati rubbing their hands with glee. Privately, she had enjoyed the book immensely. But to admit to enjoying a *thriller* would be the kiss of death. People looked up to her. She had to maintain high standards. Her opinions counted for something. A good review from Barbara Jordan Murray meant high sales. Not that her filleting of Christopher Brand, her colleague, would affect *his* sales. People just went out and bought that pulp! It was galling. Here she was, writing excellent prose daily, and Christopher Brand had sat down and dashed off a trashy thriller that was number one in the bestsellers and looked like making him undeservedly rich. If only the publishers to whom she had sent her own novel, *The Fire and the Fury,* would get in touch! They'd had the manuscript for months! Barbara knew it was a literary masterpiece, she just *knew* it. Barbara Jordan Murray was a perfect name for a potential Booker Prize winner! And that's exactly what *The Fire and the Fury* was. David Williams and Christopher Brand could go take a hike.

Barbara smiled as she pictured herself making her gracious acceptance speech. Kristi Killeen, her arch-rival in journalism, would be spitting with rage. Kristi was a mere hackette gossip columnist, Barbara preferred to call herself a "diarist." She was also editor of the women's page of *The Irish Mail*! That really stuck in Killeen's craw!

Another delightful thought struck her. David Williams's eagerly awaited biography of Margaret Thatcher was due to be published later in the year and

she would be waiting! She'd *excoriate* him! No matter
how good his book was—and his biographies were usually
superb—he was in line for the worst review of his life.
What joy! Whoever said revenge was a dish best served
cold knew precisely what he was talking about.

"David Williams, you'll get what you deserve," she
murmured. Cassie would be fit to be tied. She was
absolutely crazy about the man. Barbara had to admit he
was sexy. Those eyes! The way they studied you. And
that mouth! So firm, yet sensual. Barbara felt a warmth
suffuse her. When she needed inspiration for the love
scenes in her book, she always pictured David. She was
the fire to his *fury*. Desire ripped through her. Angrily,
she banished his image from her mind. She couldn't
stand David Williams. Cassie Jordan was welcome to him.
He'd be there at the party, to be sure, with his overpowering, disturbing presence. Well, let him. What did
she care? *She* wouldn't be there.

No doubt John and Karen would go to Cassie's bash.
They were the greatest pair of arselickers. Well, Martin
and Jean surely wouldn't go and Irene was in America,
so Cassie would just have to do without most of her
family for her big night. She would find that they were
not slow about turning their backs on her, just as she
had turned her back on them.

A thunderous crash shook the light above her head.
"Jesus, Mary and Joseph, if I go up to you two, I'll wallop
you with the wooden spoon!" she yelled. Her threat had
the desired effect. Barbara didn't believe in corporal
punishment as a rule, preferring to reason with her
children—that was the "in" thing—but tonight she was
in no humour to reason with anyone. In the background,
Ian's snores reached a climax. Thank God he was tired,
she thought wearily, as she typed the last full stop. He

wouldn't be looking for sex tonight. No doubt David
and Cassie were making passionate love somewhere.
Well, if Cassie Jordan thought for one minute that
Barbara was going to let bygones be bygones she could
think again.

The only thing was that if she went to this launch
she'd see David again. It was so long since she'd seen
him. She could wear her new Gianni Versace strapless
ice-pink number that had nearly had Kristi Killeen
swallowing her false nails in envy when she'd seen it on
her at that big charity bash in The Royal Hospital,
Kilmainham.

Maybe she'd go; maybe she wouldn't. She'd see.

❧

Karen Jordan added the hot chocolate to the boiling
milk, let it simmer for a minute and poured it into two
mugs. She could hear John removing his wellingtons in
the back porch. Excellent timing, she smiled to herself.
Her husband had been doing a final check for the night,
making sure no foxes, cats or dogs could get at the hens
and that the temperatures in the glasshouses were just
right. He had been up since six that morning and she
knew he would be tired. She was tired herself.

Her husband arrived in to the kitchen, wiping his
hands. "Saw Cassie earlier on. She was on her way to
Malahide," he informed her as he kissed her on the cheek,
took his mug of steaming chocolate and followed her
into the sitting-room.

"How is she? All excited, I suppose?" Karen asked as
she cuddled up beside John on the sofa.

"Yeah, it's great for her, isn't it?" Cassie's brother
smiled down at his wife.

"If anyone deserves success, she does," Karen said

reflectively. She really admired her sister-in-law. Cassie had been through the mill these last few years and at last it looked as though all her hard times were over. Thank God John and she had stood by her all the way. At least they would always have a clear conscience about that. That Barbara and Irene could treat their own sister the way they had was unbelievable. But then, where money and land were concerned, nothing was sacred. She had seen it in her own family when her Uncle Jerry died and the family had fallen out over the will. Her father and his brother didn't speak to each other now.

Karen sighed. The minefield of families was enough to tax even the most diplomatic and tolerant of people. When she looked at her children playing happily together, she often wondered if they would end up at one another's throats the way her in-laws and her father and uncle had. It was a depressing thought.

"I'm looking forward to Cassie's party. We haven't had a night out in ages," John smiled down at his wife as he settled her more comfortably in the crook of his arm.

"I wonder if Barbara will come," Karen mused, taking a sip of her hot chocolate.

"Well, if she does, it will be because her nosiness gets the better of her," John retorted. There was no love lost between brother and sister. Barbara's egotism sickened John, who hadn't a selfish bone in his body.

"I don't think Irene will make the trip, do you?" Karen stretched luxuriously. This was her favourite time of the day, when the children were fast asleep and she and John could talk in peace.

"It might put her out too much. You know Irene," John said drily. "I wonder if Martin and the martyr will come."

"Oh John!" Karen reproved, giggling at her husband's description of his sister-in-law, Jean.

"I've just had a baby and I'm ex*hausted.*" John exactly mimicked Jean's breathless way of speaking. "I couldn't *possibly* go to a launch unless I have a foreign holiday to get over it."

Karen gave a hearty chuckle. Just as well they could laugh about their relations. Otherwise they'd go crazy.

"'*Mortin*'—I love the posh way she says Martin— "'Mortin, your sister Cassie has invited us to her party, but I don't think we should grace her launch with our presence. It would give her actions the seal of approval. And **Finishing Touches** is something we *definitely* don't approve of. And besides, Barbara would never speak to me again. Don't you agree, Mortin?'" John was in full flow. Jean just begged to be mimicked, with her girlish air that hid a will of iron.

Karen was snorting with laughter. "Give over, John. I'm going to spill this chocolate!"

"Sorry," he grinned, taking the mug from her.

Karen grinned back. She was crazy about her big bear of a husband. "I love you."

"I love you too," he echoed, bending his head and giving her a long, lingering kiss.

"Let's have an early night," she suggested, eyes twinkling as she surfaced for air.

"You wanton, wicked woman...Let's!"

"I'll just check the baby," Karen murmured as they climbed the stairs, arms entwined. She peeped into the darkened bedroom. Eighteen-month-old Tara lay wide-eyed, smiling up at her mother. An unmistakable smell reached Karen's nostrils. "Oohh, Tara!" she groaned, scooping the baby up and heading for the bathroom. John was washing his teeth.

"Do you want me to change her?" John asked, beaming down at his adored daughter.

"No! You go and warm up the bed for me," Karen instructed, whipping off the baby's nappy.

"Sure thing, mein boss!" John departed the bathroom, saluting.

Tara gurgled appreciatively. "Ma ma," she smiled at her mother and Karen's heart melted. "Da Da, La La." Her mother was getting her whole repertoire. La La was everybody else whose name she couldn't manage.

"Go night night for mammy," she said sternly, gently laying her daughter in her cot when she was finished. Tara was full of beans; she'd never get her off to sleep. Just for tonight, she'd give her a bottle to settle her down. She wanted a nice bit of nookey with her husband when they were both in the humour for it. It wasn't easy with two children and John's demanding work.

Swiftly, she prepared a bottle for the baby and settled her down. She brushed her teeth, gave herself a quick wash and flew down the landing to their bedroom. A familiar, rumbling sound assaulted her ears and she opened the door to find her dearly beloved out for the count, his musical snores raising the rafters.

"John...John!" she whispered hopefully. Not a stir. She hadn't the heart to wake him. He worked so hard for his family and he needed his sleep. Just her luck that he had fallen asleep on her tonight. Sighing deeply, she slipped into her nightdress, slid into bed beside him, switched off the bedside lamp and put her arms around her sleeping husband, murmuring, "I'll get you in the morning."

"You can go if you want, Martin. Don't let *me* stop you," Jean Jordan said huffily, as she flipped through the latest issue of *Hello* and wished mightily that she had Princess Di's figure and money.

"It might be a good time to let bygones be bygones. That's all I'm saying," Martin remarked diffidently, settling into one of the luxurious cane chairs in their conservatory. The conservatory had cost him an arm and a leg, but Jean hadn't given him a bit of peace until he had got it done. Now she wanted to get a patio and ornamental pool in the back garden. Barbara had some sort of gazebo thing and Jean couldn't bear to be outdone. Each of them was always trying to get one up on the other, despite the fact that they were so friendly, and it was costing him a fortune. He wasn't earning big bucks, despite what Jean might think. He was perfectly happy with the house and garden the way they were but when Barbara got something new, Jean got fidgety. He wanted to go to this do of Cassie's, to put the past behind him and start afresh. After all, Cassie *was* his sister and he felt that what had happened had all been a big mistake.

Cassie had spoken to him sharply a couple of times in the past for not doing more about the house for his mother. He had been furious, of course. It was easy for her to talk; she didn't have a wife and family to support, and a mother-in-law who clung to them like a leech. Despite the fact that she had two sons of her own, it was to Martin that Jean's mother turned whenever she wanted anything done in her house, and she *always* had something that needed doing. She came to dinner every Sunday and they took her shopping every Thursday night. He felt bad about not having been able to help a bit more at home, but he was permanently up to his eyes and, besides, Jean would have ended up with a face on her if he had spent too long at his ma's.

"You're very forgiving all of a sudden!" His wife interrupted his musings. "Could it be the fact that you're hoping Cassie might throw a bit of business your way, now that she's set up this interior design carry-on?" Martin was an electrical contractor.

"Trust you to think of something like that," he retorted. "Is Barbara going?" he asked, wishing that Jean would get back to her magazine, so he could have a snooze. He'd had a hard day at work. Then he'd had to put the kids to bed because Jean had her period and was feeling rotten. *Now* he had to listen to this earbashing. He should have stayed single!

Jean snorted. "Indeed she's not going. I spoke to her on the phone today and she wouldn't dream of it. You should know better than to ask."

"I was just wondering. You know Barbara...she'd go to the opening of an envelope," he grinned, amused at his little joke. Jean gave him a withering look.

"If you want to go to this thing tomorrow night, go! Just don't expect *me* to come with you, Martin Jordan," Jean said furiously, gathering up her *Hello* and marching *into* the lounge, leaving Martin sorry he'd ever mentioned it in the first place. Maybe he *would* go, and he'd bloody well say to his wife that he never criticised her family the way she criticised his. He had rewired her mother's home for nothing, and never a word about it, and her bloody brothers were as bad, expecting him to drop everything every time they needed a new socket put in. Only last week he had spent an entire night putting up wall-lights for one of them. Four hours' hard work because he'd had to chase walls. And what did he get for it? Two bloody pints, that's what. The louser. But dare he say anything to Jean? She'd go into a huff for a week. He was getting a bit sick of it. Well, he was seriously thinking of going to his sister's party, and if Jean didn't like it, she could lump it.

❦

Irene Jordan was one totally pissed-off lady. Prowling around her Washington condo she lit yet another Marlboro, dragging the smoke deeply into her lungs. How could Dean do this to her? After all this time! Men! They were shits! She had been sure he would marry her.

Her lower lip trembled, tears glittering in her big blue eyes. What would she do if Dean decided he wanted a younger mistress, or even worse, now that he was finally free, a younger wife? It just didn't bear thinking about. After all, Irene was nearly thirty and out there in the vastness of the USA, there were plenty of gorgeous nubiles eager to take her place. She was treading on very thin ice making her demands. But dammit, Dean just couldn't walk all over her. Not after she had spent the past four years bending over backwards to please *him*. Being the perfect mistress, the perfect companion! Senator Dean Madigan was having his cake and eating it.

It wasn't easy being a mistress. True, she had this lovely condo, and a new car, and he gave her a generous allowance so that she could visit beauty salons and gyms to keep herself looking the very best. True, he took her to places she had only ever dreamt about: cruising in the Caribbean, skiing in Aspen, surfing in Malibu. Life with the Senator had opened up a whole new world to her. But—and it was a big but—there was no security in being a mistress. And what Irene Jordan craved more than anything else in the world was security. The thought of being alone and fending for herself had always filled her with dread.

What Irene really wanted to do was to marry a nice rich man who would look after her and protect her from the big bad world. Her brief experience of working for a living in a nine-to-five job in Dublin County Council was the most horrific time of her life.

It had been her mother's idea that she visit her wealthy cousin Dorothy in Washington. But Irene had to admit that things were not looking good right now. She sighed deeply. What she wouldn't give to be a child again and to have Nora taking care of all her fears and worries. Her mother had been her great protector. Irene knew that compared to the rest of her family she had been spoilt rotten. She had been Nora's pet. But those days were gone and she had to depend on herself. Well, she had the condo, but that wasn't home—not really. She wished she were more like her sister Cassie, strong and independent. Imagine being thirty-six and not even married! And not worried about it either! Imagine setting up your own business, working fourteen hours a day! If only Irene could be like her, she'd have no problems. Well, she wasn't, and that was that. There was only one Cassie in the world.

Should she go to the official opening of **Finishing Touches**? Irene sighed, lighting up another cigarette and getting a split of champagne from the fridge. She supposed she should. Cassie had always been kind to her and only Cassie knew her awful secret. She didn't know what to do; she was far too upset over Dean to make a decision about going anywhere. To think she had wasted four good years on him, when she could have been playing the field. But she'd been so sure he would marry her when he was free. Well, it wasn't over until it was over; she could still hope that he would pop the question. In the meantime, she could be on the look-out; after all, she was very attractive and men were always coming on to her. The Senator was forever having to remind them that she was his lady. No more! If someone with prospects came along, Senator Dean Madigan could either marry her or go take a running jump. Defiantly, she rang up Dorothy and told her to round up a few eligibles for the weekend. Irene Jordan was on the hunt again, Washington watch out! In the meantime, she would enquire about a seat on Concorde. Dean was so rich he could hardly quibble about the price of a little old ticket—and if he did, tough. Irene had just about had enough. The Senator would soon find out that he couldn't take her for granted any longer! Cassie sure as hell wouldn't put up with being treated like a doormat. From now on, neither would Irene!

THE FRIENDS

Think where man's glory most begins and ends,
And say my glory was I had such friends.

WB Yeats

Aileen O'Shaughnessy wiped a bead of perspiration from
her brow as she waited for the director to yell cut so that
she could rush on set to powder the leading man's face
before shooting resumed. Algiers was the hottest location
of the many she had worked on since taking up her
career in the film world. It was a move she had never
regretted.

Right now, though, she felt she wouldn't be a bit
sorry to get back to the studio in London. Filming was
due to end in two days' time, all going well and if the
director didn't have a nervous breakdown—which was
becoming more of a possibility every minute.

Still, her tan was coming along very nicely, she
observed with satisfaction. Barbara would be envious.
She wondered if Babs would come to Cassie's bash. Cassie
had written to tell her that she had invited Barbara and
the rest of the family. Frankly, Aileen thought she was
mad! Aileen didn't believe in forgive and forget, well,
not with someone like Barbara. If Judy, her sister, had
behaved to Aileen as Barbara had behaved to Cassie, she
would never have anything to do with her again. In fact
she'd be lucky to be alive! Aileen was a redhead and had
a temper to match. It came in handy on occasions! Cassie
could do with having more of a temper; her trouble was
she was far too soft.

Aileen fanned herself in the intense heat. She was
dying to get home for a few days. Not dying to see her

mother, exactly. Angela O'Shaughnessy would whine and moan but Aileen had learnt not to take any notice. No, Aileen was dying to see Cassie and Laura. She had a little surprise for them. Aileen grinned, imagining their reaction to her news.

The three of them had been friends since their schooldays and had no secrets from one another. How enriched her life had been by such friendships. There was Barbara alienated from her sister by pettiness and envy. She didn't know what she was missing by shutting someone like Cassie out of her life.

Mind, she'd make a great film character! She and Kristi Killeen, gossip columnists *extraordinaire*. Hedda Hopper and the other one—Aileen couldn't think of her name; oh yes, it came to her—Parsons, Louella Parsons, had nothing on them! She wondered how *The Fire and the Fury* was progressing. What a film that would make. No doubt Barbara would want to play herself!

They'd had such a laugh when Judy told Cassie and Laura and her about Barbara's bodice-ripper which was masquerading as literature. That had been a lovely lunch, full of gossip and chat and gales of laughter. Although Aileen loved her job and really enjoyed travelling to exotic locations, even if they were a bit hot, she missed the girls.

She was so looking forward to Cassie's party. Now *that* would be a night to remember! She could feel it in her bones.

"Aileen, get your ass on set!" the director yelled.

"Keep your toupee on, dear!" Aileen smiled sweetly, strolling over to the leading actor, powder-puff at the ready.

❧

Laura Quinn sighed in exasperation as she scanned the notes on the Brickman file. Already she had discovered two errors in the draft deed that she was reading. Typing errors. It just wasn't good enough! Her secretary was becoming far too casual and she would have to speak to her about it. Accuracy in legal documents was of the utmost importance. She didn't want any of her department's deals held up because of typing errors. William Bennett Solicitors had a good reputation to maintain and Laura was damned if the side were going to be let down by her division.

A partner in one of the biggest legal firms in the city, Laura was in charge of the conveyancing department. It was a position she had achieved through grit and determination and she was especially proud because she was one of only three female partners in the huge firm.

She closed the file, put it in her Gucci briefcase, a present from her husband, Doug, and yawned mightily. She was terribly tired. All she wanted was to crawl into her kingsize bed and sleep her brains out. Unfortunately, she and Doug were throwing a dinner party for some clients of hers the next evening and she had a lot of preparations to do. The more she got done tonight the better. She set to work preparing a marinade, with swift economical movements, poured the marinade over the duck and put it in the fridge, with a sigh of relief. One chore done. Now to prepare some choux pastry. She had meant to buy some when she was in Marks and Spencers and completely forgot. This pregnancy was affecting her memory as well as everything else! In that respect Cassie was lucky. At least she didn't have children to worry about while she was getting Finishing Touches off the ground.

There were times Laura found it tough going com-

bining motherhood and a career, and with this new baby
coming along it was going to be even harder. Maybe
she'd resign and get Cassie to employ her the way she
had employed Judy. Laura grinned. Now, that would be
fun, working with Cassie. She was such a pet. After all
these years, they were still great mates. The way Cassie
had taken charge of her life again after all the hardships
and hassle she had endured impressed Laura so much.
She was certain she'd never have coped with what Cassie
had coped with. And then, despite her family, to set up
Finishing Touches. The girl deserved a medal. Well,
Laura would be there, cheering, on her big night. What
time was it? Twelve o'clock, and she was finding it awfully
hard to keep her eyes open. She was too tired to wait up
any longer for Doug, so she went upstairs and got into
bed. She must remind Doug to keep the night of Cassie's
launch free. Between them, her husband and she would
soon need a social secretary to manage their business
entertaining. It got a bit wearing at times, but that was
the price of success. Right now, Laura wasn't sure if it
were worth it. She was just dropping off to sleep when
her husband slid noiselessly into the room without
switching on the light. He undressed and got into bed
and put his arms around her.

"I'm awake," she murmured.

"We clinched the deal, Laura. It was a great night's
work but I'm bushed." Doug yawned.

"Me too!" said his wife. "Where did you go?"

"The Trocadero, and guess who was there?"

"Barbara!"

Doug smiled in the dark. "I asked her if she were
coming to Cassie's launch party."

"Oh you brat!" laughed Laura, cuddling closer to her
husband.

"What did she say?"

"Oh she was very snooty, as only Barbara can snoot. She informed me that she wasn't sure but she thought she had a prior engagement and she'd have to check her Filofax!"

"She would! I wonder will she come, though. Would she have the unmitigated gall? I think Cassie was crazy to invite her. She's *much* more forgiving than I could ever be."

"It would make for a very interesting evening all round if she *did* come, I'll tell you that for nothing!" grinned her husband. "If David doesn't throttle her, Aileen will."

"It would serve her right, the bitch!" murmured Laura and promptly fell asleep, much to her husband's disappointment.

❦

"Judy Lawson, you're a selfish, uncaring daughter. The least you could do is call in and see your poor mother. You know I'm not a well woman. But now you've gone up in the world, what do you care? You don't want to lower yourself by visiting me in my poor little semi." Angela O'Shaughnessy, Judy's mother, was in full flow at the other end of the phone.

Judy raised her eyes to heaven as the whining voice droned on and on. Just because she hadn't had a chance to call home this week Angela was on the phone moaning. Was her mother never satisfied? Judy popped in several times a week. Usually, if *Coronation Street* or *Emmerdale Farm* or *Knot's Landing* were on, she was told to be quiet until it were over. There were times she might as well not visit, for all the conversation she got out of Angela. And what was this bull about being too grand to visit her mother's semi-detached house? Angela was always giving her little digs just because Judy lived in a luxurious apartment in Sutton. Was she supposed to feel guilty because she had married a man with money? If only she had the nerve to turn around and tell her mother to shut up, and then hang up. After all, she was thirty-five, too old to be taking this crap.

"I'm sure you don't treat Andrew's mother in such an offhand manner." Angela was really getting into her stride now, her voice getting shriller as the façade of frailty slipped.

Well, she could moan, Judy decided, because once she started working with Cassie, she wouldn't be able to drop in quite as often and Angela had better get used to the idea. Judy had run around after everybody else for long enough. Now she was going to do something *she* wanted to do, despite Andrew's disapproval. And why would he approve? she thought. She had always been there to take care of him and the kids, to find his car keys and his briefcase when they went missing, to look glamorous and entertain his clients and friends.

"But what about the kids?" Andrew had demanded angrily after he had tried to buy her off with a trip to Paris for a shopping spree. It suited him, of course; it was a rugby weekend.

"They'll be fine," Judy retorted. "Ross is in school and Alice will be starting playschool. And Mrs Moore will be here." Mrs Moore came in every day to help out. Tomorrow, Judy was going to drive over to Diffusion, the fabulous boutique in Clontarf, and treat herself to a few smart business suits.

She wanted to be a real asset to Cassie, to prove to her friend that she could do the job. Cassie needed all the help she could get. They had been friends for so long now. It was funny the way things went. Judy had been friends with Barbara before she had got to know Cassie. It wasn't until they all shared a flat together that she had really become friends with Cassie, much to Barbara's chagrin. There had been some mighty arguments in that flat. Judy grinned at the memory. Of course Barbara had never forgiven Judy for the final row which had caused Judy to end up sharing a bedroom with Cassie rather than Barbara. To think they were sisters! Cassie and Barbara were like chalk and cheese. You could always depend on Cassie, whereas Barbara thought nothing of doing the hot-potato act if it suited her. She'd hardly come to Cassie's launch. Well, in the long run, she'd be the loser.

No doubt the divine David would be there. What a gorgeous man he was. Perfect for Cassie. Judy sighed, wishing that she and Drew were as close as Cassie and David. But her husband was always out. Flitting here and there. Entertaining clients. Going to rugby matches, playing squash. Drew had never subscribed to the notion that marriage was a partnership. She sighed again, deeply.

"Are you listening to me?" her mother demanded furiously, reminding Judy that she was still on the phone.

"Of course, Mother. But I'm afraid I have to go now. Andrew will be home soon and I want to pop his dinner in the microwave. I'll see you some evening next week."

"Next week!" shrieked Angela.

"Next week," said Judy firmly, hanging up the phone. Smiling at her bravery, she walked towards her bedroom to decide what she would wear to Cassie's launch. If Drew didn't come, well, too bad. She was a woman of the Nineties now; she could walk into a party alone.

❧

DAVID

*Nothing is so strong as gentleness, and nothing is
so gentle as real strength.*

Ralph W Sockman

The last few chapters were always the worst, the grind
almost over, the end in sight. David Williams sighed as
he typed up the chapter heading "The Resignation." More
of a push than a resignation, he reflected, as his fingers
flew over the keys of his word processor. Margaret
Thatcher's going had certainly been ignominious. But
then, that was politics for you.

He typed steadily, referring to the files of notes on
his desk as he required them. David had been working
on this biography for the previous two years and was
ahead of the posse. It didn't stop his publishers from
putting on the pressure, though, and he was beginning
to feel extremely weary.

It was at times like this that he understood why his
marriage to Danielle had broken up. He found it hard to
live with *himself* when he was nearing the final stages of
writing a book.

Cassie had coped with it, but then Cassie Jordan was
no ordinary woman. David smiled thinking about her.
Meeting Cassie Jordan had been the best thing that ever
happened to him, that and buying his little haven in
Port Mahon. Was it fate that had brought him to her
home town? God knows. All he knew was that he loved
this beautiful gutsy woman and she loved him.

The chiming of his grandfather clock startled him
out of his reverie. Eleven-thirty already and he still had
a couple of thousand words to go to get his quota in. As

soon as his manuscript was safely in the hands of his editor, he was taking Cassie away for a week, at least. If he had his way, he'd take her away for six months, but this business of hers was consuming her and if he got her to agree to a week's holidays, he'd be lucky. She had been through a hell of a lot and God knows she needed the break. Still, he had never seen her look so well. That awful drawn pallor was gone and her eyes sparkled with enthusiasm and vivacity, now that she had determined to put the past behind her and said to hell with Barbara and the rest of them.

David's mouth tightened into a grim line as he thought of Barbara and the grief she had caused Cassie. Barbara Jordan Murray was a bitch who thought she was a top-notch journalist, when in reality she was just a third-rate hackette writing for a third-rate excuse for a paper. If she didn't make him so angry over her treatment of Cassie, David would have found her amusing. She was pathetic, really, with her airs and graces. Cassie might forgive her for her past behaviour but David knew *he* wouldn't. Nobody treated Cassie the way that woman had and got away with it. If she *were* at the launch of **Finishing Touches**, although he doubted she would be, David would be keeping an eye on her. She knew better than to take him on and he fully intended to keep things that way. From now on, Cassie Jordan was going to do whatever she wanted with no interference from members of her family. He'd make damn sure of that.

🙟🙟🙟

BOOK I

1969–1978

CHAPTER ONE

Oh Mary we crown Thee with blossoms today.
Queen of the Angels and—

"Girls! Girls! *Girls!*" Mother Perpetua's stentorian tones belied the little nun's frail appearance. The entire class of 3S gave a great communal sigh.

Mother Perpetua harangued the thirty girls standing on the steps of the stage in front of her. "You're like limp lettuce-leaves. For goodness sake, girls, put a bit of enthusiasm into it. I had 2H here an hour ago and they were superb. You're not going to let a class of second years do better than you, surely!"

Cassie suppressed a yawn. Today she just wasn't in the humour for choir practice.

"Catherine Jordan, am I *boring* you?" the choir-mistress snapped.

"No, Mother," Cassie said hastily, not wishing to draw the wrath of Mother Perpetua down on her. Mother Perpetua was one of the most feared nuns in Saint Imelda's College.

"Well, straighten up, girl, and stop yawning. And that goes for the rest of you, too." She waved her baton imperiously. "Listen to how I want the second line sung. Queen of the Ang...els...Draw it out, please."

"Queen of the Ang...els," 3S sang dutifully.

"That's better!" approved Mother Perpetua "Once again from the beginning."

Not again, thought Cassie wearily. They must have sung the hymn twenty times already and she was heartily sick of it. It was so warm in the concert hall. The noonday sun shone in through the stained-glass windows, dappling the heads of 3S in a rainbow of pinks and greens and purples. The heat was making them even more lethargic than they would normally be on a Friday. Usually Cassie loved Fridays. Choir before lunch, after lunch a double cookery class and religion with Sister Eileen, who was their favourite nun. Then they were free for the weekend. Hearing the bell go at four-fifteen on a Friday was wonderful.

A trickle of perspiration dampened Cassie's neck where the collar of her cream cotton blouse was bound by her blue school tie. Opening the top button, Cassie loosened her tie a little. That was better. It was an awful nuisance having to wear a tie. It must be terrible for men having to wear them all the time. At least she could get rid of hers after school. A bee droned lazily against one of the windows and the heavy scent of lilac and wall-flowers wafted in on the breeze. She was looking forward to her stroll around the nuns' garden with Laura, her best friend. It would be so much nicer than being stuck in here with the sun shining on their red faces, watching Mother Perpetua waving her baton around pretending she was Leonard Bernstein or some other great conductor.

Laura had looked terribly worried that morning and had been late for school, which was most unlike her. Cassie knew something was up. "What's wrong?" she asked, as discreetly as she could. "You've a face as long as a fiddle."

As Laura took her place beside her friend during French, she whispered, "Something's happened. I'll tell you at lunchtime. I don't want the rest of them to know." Poor Laura, she thought; she was always having hassle at home. Where Cassie was the eldest in her family, Laura was the youngest in hers. Both positions brought their own problems. Ah well, she would hear all about

Laura's latest problem in an hour or so.

Five sharp rings of the bell interrupted Cassie's reverie and grins of relief passed along the three lines of ten pupils on the steps of the stage as the girls recognised Mother Perpetua's call sign. What a stroke of luck, her getting a call in the middle of class. It so rarely happened.

"Girls, I have to leave you for a few moments. Please excuse me and remain quiet until I return."

"Yes, Mother," they chorused.

They obeyed her command for five minutes and then, stretching limbs, they started chattering happily as they let off steam. Aileen O'Shaughnessy, the class wit, and one of the most popular girls in the school, leapt off the stage, fastened her cardigan under her chin in imitation of a veil and picked up Mother Perpetua's baton. "Girls, you're like limp lettuce-leaves," she announced in perfect mimicry of the little nun. "Straighten up, please. Button those cardigans!"

"Like this, Mother?" giggled Margy Kane, buttoning her cardigan on to that of her neighbour.

"What other way does one button one's cardigan?" Reverend Mother Aileen enquired haughtily as, giggling and skitting, the rest of them followed suit until they were all attached. "Now, girls, I know it's a little out of season but I think we should sing our class anthem."

A wild cheer greeted this pronouncement as, with a frenzy of baton-waving, Reverend Mother Aileen began to conduct and the class began to sing.

> 'Tis the season to be jolly
> Tra La La La La La La La La,
> Stuff Perpetua's hole with holly,
> Tra La La La La La La La La...

"More enthusiasm, girls!" screeched the mad conductor, twirling below them, the sleeves of her cardigan waving wildly around her head.

"*'Tis the season to be jolly,*" the rest of the class yelled, giving it their all, thoroughly enjoying themselves. Cassie, jolted pleasantly out of her weary stupor, was singing as loudly as any of them. Even Laura, attached to her by her cardigan buttons, was laughing heartily beside her.

"*Stuff Perpetua's hole with holly,*" they bellowed lustily, so intent upon their fun that they did not see the petite figure of the nun slip through the big mahogany doors at the end of the concert hall.

"How dare you! *How dare you!*" Mother Perpetua trembled with anger before them. Aileen halted in mid-twirl, her mouth an O of dismay. The others stood stunned, trying to smother their horrified giggles at the sight of Aileen, with her cardigan around her head, baton frozen in the air as she stared at the furious nun.

"You brazen hussy, Aileen O'Shaughnessy. But what can you expect from free education? It's the likes of you and riff-raff like you, the dregs of society, Aileen O'Shaughnessy, that's what you and this..." She turned to face the rest of the class. "...this crowd of juvenile delinquents are. You are not fit to wear the uniform of Saint Imelda's. Guttersnipes! Guttersnipes, the lot of you. Up to the big parlour with you. We'll see what Reverend Mother has to say about this!"

In the horror of the moment, forgetting that they were attached to one another by cardigan buttons, the class of 3S made to leave *en masse*. Blue buttons popped all over the floor as bodies became entangled and Mother Perpetua, almost apoplectic with temper, stabbed at those nearest her with the baton she had grabbed from Aileen.

Ten minutes later thirty girls stood under the cold eye of Reverend Mother Patrick, the principal of Saint Imelda's.

"Aileen O'Shaughnessy, as you seem to be the ringleader you will repeat for me the...ditty...you were singing when Mother Perpetua caught you."

"Me, Reverend Mother!" protested Aileen, with wide-eyed innocence.

"You, Miss O'Shaughnessy."

Cassie bit her lip at the sight of Aileen looking as though butter wouldn't melt in her mouth. She was petrified she was going to laugh, even though they were all in serious trouble. Beside her, she could feel Laura trembling with the effort not to break into hysterical giggles.

"I couldn't, Reverend Mother," their classmate said.

"Why not, pray?" Reverend Mother Patrick enquired coldly.

"I've forgotten the words," Aileen said weakly.

"Repeat it!" came the stern command.

"It's a bit...vulgar..."

"Immediately, if you please."

Taking a deep breath, Aileen stood up straight, and, ever the actress, flung her head back and with perfect diction repeated every word right down to the final tra la la. 3S listened in horrified admiration. A muscle jerked at the side of Reverend Mother Patrick's mouth, but otherwise her face seemed carved out of stone.

"Disgraceful. I'm shocked! Shocked at such vulgar unladylike behaviour. That girls of Saint Imelda's should behave as you have is unthinkable." Her gaze swept over the class like a cold shower. "You will apologise to Mother Perpetua and carry out whatever punishment she gives you and you will, all of you, come to school tomorrow morning. You will spend the morning in complete silence, studying in the library. Another offence like this and you will all be expelled. Dismissed!"

Despondently the girls of 3S filed out, aghast at the thought of spending a precious Saturday morning in school. They were even more devastated to find that they had to write out the words of the hymn they had been singing one hundred times. That was Mother Perpetua's punishment.

In the big parlour, Reverend Mother Patrick wiped the tears of mirth from her eyes. She had never seen Perpetua so angry. That Aileen O'Shaughnessy was a hilarious character, just the sort to give the bumptious choir-nun a run for her money. Pride comes before a fall and Mother Perpetua had plenty of pride. No wonder the girls made up such parodies. Heaven knows what they said about *her*. Reverend Mother Patrick had been running a school long enough to know that girls would be girls. Composing herself, she glided out of the big parlour, then began to walk as briskly as dignity would allow. *The Woman in White* by Wilkie Collins was being dramatised on the radio and she had been following it. It was coming to an extremely exciting part that she didn't want to miss. Glancing right and left, she saw the corridors were empty. With a sigh of satisfaction Reverend Mother Patrick slipped through the door that divided the school and convent and headed up to her private sitting-room.

❧

The nuns' garden was a haven of tranquillity. The lilac and cherry-blossom were in bloom and along the pathways beds of pansies and a host of other flowers lifted the heart. The cares of the world always seemed to be left behind when one entered the nuns' garden. No one would ever dream of larking around there—that was an unspoken rule in Saint Imelda's. Boisterous behaviour was fine in the schoolyard and classrooms but the nuns' garden was a place of peace where the nuns walked around saying their Rosaries silently to themselves, the only sound the rhythmic clicking of the big wooden beads as they slipped through their fingers.

It was lovely out there at lunchtime that day. Usually Cassie and Laura went straight out to the basketball or volleyball courts to have an energetic game before classes resumed, but today, by common consent the two girls made in the direction of the nuns' garden, their shoes echoing along the polished wooden corridor that led from the refectory. In common with the whole of Class 3S, Cassie and Laura were very fed up about having to come to school the following morning to carry out the punishment for Mother Perpetua, but Cassie sensed that what was bothering Laura was much more serious than even this great disaster.

They emerged into bright sunlight and walked slowly towards one of the wooden seats that dotted the garden. The wood was warm against their thighs as they sat down and Cassie felt a sense of peace envelop her as she always did in this lovely place. In a way she didn't want to hear Laura's bad news here. It took the good out of her little haven.

She dismissed the thought. After all, Laura was her best friend and best friends shared everything. "What's the matter, Laura, you look dreadful?" she said solicitously, turning to her raven-haired friend. Laura was so striking with her jet-black hair and startling blue eyes. Cassie always felt so untidy beside her glamorous friend. Her own chestnut curls had a mind of their own and

Laura's extra few inches made her uniform hang on her like a model whereas Cassie, being smaller, felt that hers looked like a sack.

"At least you've got boobs," her friend was always reassuring her. "All I've got is two fried eggs! And I'll be fifteen next year. *Quel désastre!*" Laura liked to speak bilingually.

Now she said fiercely. "Jill's going have a baby."

"Oh God!" Cassie was shocked. She hadn't expected this at all. Jill was Laura's elder sister. Their idol. Jill lived in a flat in Dublin and worked at the airport as a car hire rep. She was the ultimate in glamour. On rare occasions, as a treat, Cassie and Laura were invited to spend a night in her flat, where they ate lovely foreign food like lasagne and garlic bread and could smoke without fear of being caught by their parents. To live in a flat in Dublin and go to dances and pubs and stay up every night until all hours was Cassie's and Laura's dream and they spent many happy hours plotting their immensely exciting future. Listening to Jill telling them about the party that she went to and how she met a gorgeous hunk in Nikki's night club or had dinner with a pilot in the International Airport Hotel was better than the excitement of any novel. They couldn't wait to do the same themselves. And now here was their heroine, pregnant and unmarried. A fate worse than death in Ireland. It might be 1969 in the rest of the world, and free love and easy living might be the new thing, but here such news was a disaster. All the gossips in Port Mahon would have a field-day.

"Close your mouth and stop catching flies," Laura snapped irritably when Cassie failed to respond.

"Sorry!" murmured Cassie. No wonder Laura was upset. This was terrible news. Mrs Quinn would be going mad. Her own mother wouldn't be a bit pleased, either. Nora Jordan didn't approve of young girls going to live on their own in Dublin, and Cassie knew she was in for a rough ride when she left school and wanted to move to the city with Laura. This would only increase the difficulties ahead. Cassie would certainly never again be allowed to sleep over at Jill's flat after this news was made public.

"Sorry I barked," Laura said sheepishly.

"That's OK," Cassie reassured her. She'd known Laura for ages and didn't take any notice of the occasional abrupt remark. "Anyway, you've got reason to bark. How are things at home?"

"Ma's taken to the bed and Da has told Jill never to set foot in the house again. Mick went and got drunk and crashed his car into the pillar in the drive and I'm just sick of the whole lot of them!" Laura said mournfully. "It's not a bit fair!" she burst out. "Mick goes around getting drunk every weekend. He's crashed the car so many times but he's let get away with it at home and just because Jill's going to have a baby she's been kicked out. It makes me sick!" Her face was red with rage. Mick was her elder brother. "If Mick came in and said he'd got a girl into trouble do you think he'd be told never to set foot in the house again?" Laura was nearly crying now. "He would not! They wouldn't talk to him for a while and then it would be forgotten about. The double standard just makes me sick! Da makes no allowances for us girls and the lads get away with anything. God, I wish I were working and earning my own money. I'd be out of there so fast you wouldn't believe it."

"Do you want to come over and stay the night with me?" Cassie asked, feeling nothing but pity for Laura. Knowing what a tyrant Mr Quinn was, she could just imagine the state of poor Jill and the awful atmosphere in the Quinn household. "We can come to school together tomorrow," she added a little glumly, remembering the fate of their precious Saturday morning.

"Thanks a million, Cassie. I'd love to, if your mother won't mind."

"Of course she won't," Cassie assured her. "And I'll make you some hot chocolate with cream and flake in it."

Laura smiled wanly. "You're always great in a crisis, Cassie. I don't know what I'd do without you. Oh Cassie, you should have heard my da! He called Jill a slut and he roared and ranted the way he always does and I just hate him." She burst into tears at the memory.

"Shhh, don't be upsetting yourself," Cassie soothed, putting an arm around her weeping friend's shoulder. "It will pass over. He'll come around."

"No he won't," sobbed Laura. "He's a big bully and once he's got his knife into someone, it's there for good. He always holds grudges and he'll never forgive Jill."

Privately, Cassie had to agree that her friend's assessment of her father was extremely accurate. Peter Quinn was the rudest, most ignorant, most self-centred man, and he ruled the family with a rod of iron. To him, women were second-class citizens. He treated his wife and daughters as minions, expecting them to dance attendance on him and his sons. Laura, who was as strong-willed as he was, had a terrible time trying to cope with the unfairness of it all. Growing up in a generation where women were finally beginning to be treated as equals, she despised her father's male chauvinism and railed against it.

Cassie thanked God for giving her a father like Jack Jordan. Her father was the complete opposite to Laura's and Cassie loved him with all her heart. A genial, good-humoured, quiet man, Jack treated his sons and daughters as equals. He always had time to talk and listen to them and took a great interest in all their affairs. Much as he loved them all, Cassie knew in her heart and soul that she was her father's favourite. Each evening after she had done her study, her father and she would tramp the fields for an hour or two. She would tell him of her day and he would tell her of his as he puffed contentedly on his pipe. Jack loved the countryside. His farm was his pride and joy and although the hours were long and the work was hard, he provided well for his family and never a word about it, unlike Peter Quinn, who was always going on about how hard he worked and how much his children had to thank him for.

"Stop crying, Laura. It will be all right, honestly," Cassie said worriedly. It wasn't like Laura to break down. Usually she was such a strong character. She really was at the end of her rope. "Here's Miss Fagin," she went on urgently, spying their maths mistress bearing down on them. "If you don't stop she'll want to know what's the matter."

Laura hiccupped. "You'd better stop hugging me. She'll think we're a couple of lezzers. You know her and her warped mind."

Cassie giggled. "It might give her something else to worry about other than that the square on the hypotenuse is equal to the sum of the squares on the other two sides. Just look at her; she even looks like a triangle on legs."

Laura snorted. "Cassie Jordan, what a thing to say! But you're absolutely right! I've never noticed it before."

"Good afternoon, girls," the triangle on legs said, giving them a keen look as it passed by.

"Good afternoon, Miss Fagin," responded the girls politely, getting up from the bench. They went to the games room and had a game of table-tennis, which Cassie kindly allowed Laura to win, and then the great bell rang around the school and droves of blue-uniformed figures headed for their various classrooms to begin the afternoon's classes, like ants scurrying around an anthill.

As she put the finishing touches to her disgusting-looking carrageen mould in the school kitchen, Cassie cast a glance at her friend. Laura was cleaning the work-surface with a vague faraway look in her eyes, and Cassie knew she was thinking of the trouble at home. Well, at least tonight she could relax and forget about it. If only Barbara were going to spend the night with her friend Judy, it would be perfect. Then Laura could sleep in her sister's bed and Cassie wouldn't have to make do with the camp-bed. Of course, if Barbara knew Laura was staying, she'd probably stay at home for spite.

Cassie sighed. Her younger sister could be such a little madam, always wanting to do what Cassie was doing, always looking for notice. And she was such a tattle-tale, ratting on Cassie to her mother about Cassie and Laura and a few of the others being caught smoking in one of the boarders' bathrooms. It was Sister Eileen who had caught them, all ten of them, puffing away in the tiny bathroom, three of them sitting in the bath, four of them sitting on the edge of the bath, one sitting on the cistern of the loo, and the other pair sitting on the loo itself. Wreaths of smoke circling around their heads, they sat giggling and gossiping and puffing contentedly, ties loosened and uniforms in glorious disarray. Sister Eileen, who had a nose like a bloodhound and ears like an elephant, had heard the stifled giggles and smelt the smoke as she was walking past. Usually nuns and teachers were not to be seen on school corridors during lunchtime. They preferred the peace of the convent and staff-rooms as they recharged their batteries before returning to the afternoon fray. But now, flinging the bathroom door open, Sister Eileen stared grimly at the scene confronting her.

Margy Kane got such a fright that her cigarette smoke went the wrong way. She started to choke and Cassie had to thump her several times on the back. The others tried to extinguish their fags and the inhabitants of the bath struggled to climb out. In the midst of this uproar, Barbara, Cassie's sister, a second year student at the school, and her friend Judy, happened to be passing. Barbara, listening to Sister Eileen coldly tell the miscreants to follow her to the big parlour, was disgusted, her pinched little face wrinkling in disdain. Barbara, being the goody-goody that she was, wouldn't dream of smoking and was always threatening to tell on Cassie. So far she had refrained, but Cassie knew this time for sure Barbara would tell, because Cassie, fed up with her sister wearing her clothes and putting them back in her wardrobe dirty, had bought herself a padlock and locked her wardrobe door. Barbara had been furious and had been dying to get her own back ever since. The smoking episode had been a golden opportunity.

Sister Eileen had lined them up in front of her in the big parlour. "I am in two minds as to whether I should report this to Reverend Mother. It is absolutely outrageous and disgraceful behaviour. And not what is expected from the girls of Saint Imelda's. You wouldn't get the girls from Thompson and Maitland behaving in such a common fashion."

Thompson and Maitland was the nearby Protestant school and their exemplary behaviour was always held up to the Saint Imelda's girls. Mind, the Thompson and Maitland lot had confessed, one day they had been over on a courtesy visit, that the Imelda's girls were always held up as examples to them, so they all agreed to take no notice of such pronouncements.

"And furthermore, apart from the disgraceful disrespect to the uniform, have you girls no regard for your health and the state of your lungs?" the nun demanded to know. Philippa Feely was so upset at being caught that she burst into tears.

Sister Eileen was umnoved. "Oh, stop snivelling, Madam Feely. It's a bit late for that now! I want an essay on my desk tomorrow morning from all of you, on the dangers of smoking. Dismissed!" She turned on her heel and swept out, her crisp white habit flapping in the breeze.

"You should have seen their faces," she reported to a crowd of laughing sisters, later that evening in the convent. "If you had seen the contortions of Jane O'Hara trying to get out of the bath, with her socks at half-mast and her tie knotted up under her ear." Jane O'Hara was a gangling six-footer. "Don't ask me how I kept my face straight," she grinned as the other nuns laughed.

The smokers could not believe their luck. Sister Eileen was a brick for not reporting them to the Reverend Mother and that would have been the end of it had Barbara kept her mouth shut. But it had been too good an opportunity for revenge and she couldn't get home quickly enough to tell her mother. Nora had not taken so lenient a view as Sister Eileen, and Cassie had been stopped from going to the youth-club dances for a month. When Laura's mother met Mrs Jordan in the street and wanted to know why Cassie wasn't at the dances, Nora had informed her of the reason and Laura too had been stopped from going. One day, Laura swore, Miss Goody Two-Shoes was going to get what was coming to her. From then on, she called her Blabbermouth Barbara, much to the younger girl's disgust, for secretly Barbara was in awe of Laura with her striking good looks and air of supreme self-confidence.

The best thing to do, Cassie decided, was to say nothing about Laura staying until after Barbara had announced she was going to stay with her friend Judy. It would be too late for her to change her mind then.

CHAPTER TWO

"Why are you going to school on a Saturday morning?" Nora Jordan asked suspiciously. "Is this a punishment?" Cassie had visions of being prevented from going to the next youth-club dance so reluctantly, she had to fib.

"It's just a bit of extra study before our exams," she explained.

"Does Barbara have to go in?"

"Oh no," said Cassie hastily. "It's only because we're third years."

"It's also because we'll be missing some days next week for our school retreat," Laura added smoothly. Cassie stared admiringly at her friend. Laura was always able to think on her feet. That response was so plausible, her mother would have to believe it.

"Oh yes," Nora nodded, as she basted the stuffed sea-bass, already golden-brown, that she was going to serve for dinner. The smell of it made Cassie's mouth water. She was starving. "And who is giving you the retreat this year?"

"We don't know yet. All we know is that we've to go to the Priory at nine on Monday morning, and we don't have to wear our uniforms." Cassie was so relieved that her mother had accepted Laura's explanation without question. She was really looking forward to the retreat. Two days off school. Last year they had had a gorgeous priest, Father Paul, and they had all fallen madly in love with him.

"Wouldn't it be great if we had Father Paul again?" Laura echoed her thoughts.

"Mmm..." Cassie agreed enthusiastically, helping herself to stuffing while her mother was distracted, straining the peas.

"Cassie, would you set the table for me, like a good girl?"

"Where's Barbara?" Setting the table was Barbara's job. Cassie's job was to wash up after the dinner. But invariably Barbara was not to be found when it was time to set the table and Cassie ended up doing it.

"I don't know where she is. If you're going to make a fuss I'll do it myself," Nora said crossly in her martyr voice.

Cassie sighed. It was always the same. Barbara was a lazy little bitch and she got away with blue murder.

"Come on. I'll help you," offered Laura briskly, going to the drawer and getting a handful of place-mats. "How many for dinner?

"Mam, Dad, John, Barbara, Martin, Irene, you and me," Cassie said, counting on her fingers. "Eight." She counted out eight knives, forks and spoons and followed Laura into the dining-room.

"Which table-cloth?"

"The embroidered one. I'll get it," Cassie said grumpily, pulling open the door of the sideboard with more force than was necessary. "It's just not fair!" she muttered. "That one gets away with everything." Cassie flung the table-cloth across the long polished wooden table. "It's not that I mind setting the blasted table. I'd prefer to do that than the washing-up. She's even got an easy job. It's the principle of it. I don't see why just because I'm the eldest I have to do everything," she moaned as she began laying the table.

"At least John and Martin do a bit," Laura observed. "Just look at me. Once Jill left I had to do everything. Da doesn't think boys should have to do housework." This was true, Cassie conceded. Laura really had it tough at home. At least Nora insisted on the whole family doing their share, even if Barbara did her best to get out of it.

"Well, how are the terrible twins?" Cassie's father enquired, as he walked into the dining-room from the kitchen.

"Hi, Pops!" Cassie immediately brightened up as she affectionately kissed her father on the cheek.

"Hi, Mr Jordan," Laura said cheerfully, kissing him on the other cheek. Laura really loved Mr Jordan. He was a very kind man and always had time to talk to her and have a bit of crack with her, unlike her own sourpuss of a dad.

"What's this about you having to go to school tomorrow? Your ma was saying you've to do extra study or something?"

"That's right," Laura said demurely, saving Cassie the trouble of telling her father a fib.

"My eye," said Jack Jordan. "What were you up to this time?" He knew the girls of old. Cassie and Laura laughed. They knew Jack wouldn't give out to them. He was always entertained by their escapades. He chuckled as they told a censored version of their carry-on with

Mother Perpetua, refraining from giving exact vulgar details of their ditty.

"God help those poor nuns!" said Jack with mock solemnity. "Saint Trinian's had nothing on you lot. Young ladies, my hat!" The girls giggled. They loved it when Jack teased them.

❦

Barbara appeared at the dining-room door. She ignored the two older girls completely.

A thin, scrawny girl, with fine mousy hair and non-descript blue eyes, even at the age of thirteen Barbara had an air of self-importance about her. She was forever out to impress and loved to be the centre of attention. Bossy by nature, it galled her that Cassie was the elder, even though it was only by a year. And Cassie's friendship with Laura really infuriated her. What was really wrong with Barbara was a big dose of envy. When she watched the two older girls having fun, listening to the Beatles and the Rolling Stones and going into Dublin to stay over with Jill, darts of jealousy like hundreds of tiny pinpricks would torment her and as she watched them leave for the city, she fumed. *She'd* make them sorry one day.

Barbara's favourite way of making them sorry was to imagine that she was suddenly stricken with a fatal disease. Her funeral would be the biggest Port Mahon had ever seen. Almost six years before she had watched the funeral of President Kennedy and although she was very young, she had been deeply impressed. Once, when she was nine, she had put on her mother's black lace mantilla, gone to the parish cemetery and stood at her grandfather's grave, pretending she was Jackie Kennedy. She had pretended so hard she had made herself cry.

Barbara loved her imaginary games because in them she was always the heroine and she was always in charge. She would have a magnificent funeral in Port Mahon. The army would be there, the police, the Red Cross, anybody who wore a uniform. The priests would say wonderful things about her. About how kind she was and what a terrible tragedy it was that she had died so young of such a painful disease that had been so bravely borne.

Chief among the mourners would be Cassie and Laura, broken-hearted with grief and remorse over the way they had treated her. "My dear little sister," Cassie would cry, "please forgive me. Forgive me for treating you so badly!"

Barbara would be nearly in tears as she imagined this scene. She couldn't decide which was her favourite day-dream, her funeral one or the one where she was Beth in *Little Women*, when Beth got scarlet fever and Cassie/Jo was desperately worried. Really, she was so good at imagining things she was going to be either an actress or a writer when she grew up. In the meantime, she was doing her best to get a duplicate of the key to the padlock that Cassie had used to lock her wardrobe door. If she could just get her hands on it for an hour or two and bring it to Mr Nolan in the hardware shop to get a second one cut, that would be perfect. Barbara knew that Cassie had bought some new clothes a few Saturdays before. That was another thing that bugged her. Cassie was allowed to go into Dublin on the train and go shopping with Laura. When Barbara was going shopping, her mother accompanied her, and it wasn't the same thing at all. Next year, when she was a third-year student, she could go into town with Judy, Nora promised. In the meantime, Nora had quite a say in what Barbara bought and that did not suit her. If Nora had been with Cassie,

her sister would never have been allowed to buy the
latest outfit she brought home from Dublin.

Cassie had bought the most beautiful denim mini
and two gorgeous ribbed polo-necked jumpers. Exactly
what Twiggy or Jean Shrimpton would wear. Barbara
would *kill* to be able to wear that denim mini to the
disco that Saint Joseph's, the boys' secondary school,
were holding in two weeks' time. Well, she had two
weeks to get that key and get it she would.

Standing at the dining-room door, Barbara noted with
satisfaction that the table had been set. That was perfect
timing. Barbara hated setting the table. In fact she hated
all housework and tried to get out of it as much as she
could. Usually quite successfully. She saw that Laura
Quinn was staying for dinner. That was enough to put
anyone in a bad humour. If Laura called her "Blabbermouth Barbara" once more, she would really thump her.
Deep down, Barbara wished heartily that she looked like
Laura Quinn. With her jet-black hair and model-thin
figure, she was the height of elegance and her clothes
were always so with-it. Laura really had taste and style,
something that Barbara longed to imitate. Ignoring the
two older girls, she directed her gaze at her father. She
wanted to go to the junior disco tonight and it was
better to ask Poppa first because her mother might say
no outright. If Jack said yes, as he usually did, Nora was
more inclined to agree.

❦

"Poppa, can I go to the junior disco tonight and stay
over at Judy's?" Cassie heard her sister Barbara ask her
father. Typical of Barbara to appear when the table was
set.

"I don't see why not, Babs," Jack Jordan said agreeably.

"Ask your mother and then tell John to cycle down to the shop and get the evening paper for me. Isn't it great about Apollo 10? Nine miles from the moon's surface. What a feat, girls! What a feat! There'll be men on the moon yet!"

"And women!" interjected Laura, ever the feminist.

"Oh of course, Laura," agreed Jack, winking at Cassie.

Cassie smiled. Barbara left the room to announce to her mother that Jack had said it was all right for her to go to the disco and sleep over at Judy's. She couldn't care less about the Apollo space programme. Who the hell wanted to live on the moon? But Cassie was interested, as interested as Jack, and since the launch of Apollo 10, she and her father had watched and discussed the developments as they went on their evening walks. *Star Trek* was Cassie's absolute favourite programme and Jack was another fan. Mind you, he didn't like it for the same reason as Cassie, who rather fancied Captain Kirk. Laura was crazy about Mr Spock. Tonight, with Barbara out of the way, they'd be able to watch it in peace. Barbara thought it was pure nonsense and loved to show her superiority by making scathing remarks about people who watched silly programmes about aliens with pointed ears. Barbara preferred *The Forsyte Saga*. But then, she thought she was so literary.

In the distance Cassie could hear her sister ordering their brother John to go for the paper. "Get lost, I'll go when I'm ready," was John's spirited retort and Cassie grinned. John wouldn't put up with any crap from Barbara.

❦

That's telling her! John assured himself as he did a wheelie out the backyard, pretending to be Batman on his way

to the scene of a crime in Gotham City. He didn't mind
going for the paper. It was one of his jobs. He just hated
it when Miss Barbara told him to go for it. Who did she
think she was? A grown-up or something! If Cassie asked
him to go she usually gave him a few pence to spend on
himself. Cassie was OK for a girl. When she caught him
and Martin smoking down at the boat-shed, she had just
given them a clip on the ear and never said a word about
it to Mam and Pops. If it had been Barbara they would
have been sunk. Barbara was always going on that she
was a teenager. So what! Big deal! She was only three
years older than him. It was great that he was getting tall
now. She wouldn't be able to boss him around for much
longer. They had been having an argument the other
day and he had managed to give her a clout that had
made her screech. That would teach Miss Barbara to
annoy him again.

John smiled to himself as he cycled along the lane.
A lovely breeze blew in off the sea and he wondered if
his Uncle Joe would take him fishing soon. He was
starving. He could murder a packet of Perry crisps or a
Trigger Bar. What a thought. Cassie had whispered to
him that Laura was staying the night although he wasn't
to mention it to Barbara. That would be a bit of fun.
Laura was great gas. He called her Lanky Laura and she
always called him the Pest! Still, he liked Laura; she too
often gave him a few pence when she stayed over. He'd
ask Cassie to give him a hand with his sums and then
he'd have the whole weekend to spend solving crime.
He and Martin might play *Mission Impossible* down at
the boat-shed tomorrow. Cassie was quite good at sums,
for a girl. She was very good at explaining things. If you
asked Barbara anything she just called you a dunce and
walked off with her head in the air. She and that hoity-

toity Judy. They'd want to watch it, that pair! Batman knew they were agents of Catwoman and he was planning something special for them. He had been training his Batmouse for ages and the next time Judy stayed over with Barbara they were in for a bit of a shock. Ha Ha!

Something glinting in the sunlight caught his eye and he came to a halt with a squeal of brakes. Just as well he was riding his Bat bike. He looked around cautiously. It could be a trap of the Joker's. Robin the Boy Wonder, alias his brother Martin, was nowhere in sight to come to his assistance should he need help, so he moved with caution. A quick look. "Oh good!" said Batman to himself as he picked up a penny. He'd be able to buy himself a penny-bar. It would keep him going until dinner. Whistling cheerfully, he remounted his trusty bike and continued in the direction of Gotham City!

❧

Standing at the sink, up to her wrists in soapy water, Cassie washed each pot as her mother finished dishing up the dinner from it. At least it was peas and carrots today. If there was one thing she loathed it was a cabbage saucepan. She always preferred to get as much of the washing-up done as possible before sitting down to her dinner; knowing that she had a pile of dirty saucepans facing her always took the good out of her meal. Boy, was she starving! Nora was dishing up the roast potatoes, putting the crispiest ones on Irene's plate. Irene was such a pet. Nora would let her get away with anything. Cassie smiled as she saw her seven-year-old sister playing two balls up against the side of the house, her little blonde pigtails swaying crazily as she hopped around singing in her lispy voice:

Plainy a packet of Rinso
Uppy a packet of Rinso,
Downy a packet of Rinso.

She was doing the required actions with the balls. Irene was such a skinny little thing, with her spindly legs. You would think by the way Nora treated the youngest of the family that Irene was delicate, but all that was wrong with her was that she was a bit timid. And half of that was her mother's fault, Cassie reflected, as she got to grips with the greasy roasting-dish. After all, it was a bit much, her mother still collecting her from school as if she was a baby. Lots of Irene's classmates walked home through the town in the same direction and they didn't even have to cross the Dublin road. All she had to do was turn left off the main street, walk down Fisherman's Lane and then she was on the coast road, with a footpath the whole way to the farm, which was less than a mile away. Mam would have to let Irene stand on her own two feet some time. She wouldn't even go to sleep without a light on. None of the rest of them had got away with that!

"Cassie, will you bring in the dinners for me?" her mother asked. "That one there," she indicated a heaped plate, "is your father's, and that's Laura's." Nora smiled at her eldest daughter. "I'd be lost without you."

Cassie smiled back at the tall dark-haired woman standing at the cooker. Her mother was a fine-looking woman. After five children and years of hard work, her hair was only lightly flecked with grey. Her skin, untouched by make-up, was soft and unlined and her brown eyes sparkled with strength and good humour. A robust, active woman, Nora managed with ease to look after her family, assist her husband and be involved with the local community. Her mother was a very capable woman, Cassie acknowledged, as she called Irene and Martin in out of the yard and carried the two dinner-plates into the dining-room.

"Great, I'm famished," said Jack, rubbing his hands as he seated himself at the top of the table.

"I'll never eat all that!" protested Laura as she gazed in awe at the steaming plate that was placed in front of her. Despite her model-thin figure, she had a healthy appetite, but she wasn't used to such big helpings. Besides, her mother was not the world's greatest cook.

"Don't worry, John and Martin will help," Cassie reassured her as she headed out to the kitchen to get some more plates.

"Is John home yet? Put his in the oven," her mother instructed, as she passed by her carrying a tray with four dinners. "Just get your own, Cassie. Barbara! Martin! Irene! Dinner's on the table," Nora called. As Cassie prepared to put John's plate in the oven, the crunch of tyres on gravel informed her that her brother had arrived. His timing was always impeccable where food was concerned!

Dinner was a lively affair as usual and Cassie smiled as she saw Laura discreetly place a roast potato on each of John's and Martin's plates, much to their delight. After dessert, when the boys and Irene excused themselves to go and watch the cartoons before the news, Nora said to Jack, "I believe you've given Barbara your permission to go to the junior disco and stay at Judy's."

Barbara smirked self-importantly.

"I did, love," Jack agreed.

"Make sure you're home by eleven-thirty," Nora said firmly.

"Aw Mam! That's not fair!" Barbara protested. "Cassie is allowed to stay out until twelve."

"Cassie is a year older than you, Barbara. Don't argue, like a good girl." Nora stood up from the table. "I'm off to my ICA meeting. Jack, Joe left some fresh crabs in today if you want to cook them for supper. Laura is staying the night with Cassie so you can all have a sandwich."

Oh yum yum, thought Cassie in delight, although she was as full as an egg after her dinner. If there was one thing she loved it was crab-meat. Her Uncle Joe was a pet. Nora's brother, he fished his trawler out of Port Mahon and kept the family supplied with fresh fish.

"I'm going to have a bath before I go out if anyone wants to use the loo," announced Barbara, highly miffed at being told in front of Laura to be in by half-eleven. The indignity of it! Spoken to as if she were a child! She was half-inclined to say that she would come home instead of staying at Judy's so that Laura and Cassie wouldn't have the bedroom to themselves. But it was too late now to change her plans.

"Just a minute, young lady!" her father addressed her.

"Yes, Poppa," Barbara said coolly. She was not in a good humour.

"Your sister had to set the table, and that's your job, isn't it?"

"Yes, but I had to play a tennis match and that's why I was late. I'm in the league at school," Barbara explained, edging out the door.

"Well, I think it wouldn't kill you to finish the washing-up. Cassie has the saucepans all washed. Fair is fair, after all," Jack said firmly.

Barbara was fit to be tied! "But I'll be dead late," she wailed.

"Ten minutes and you'll have it all done. And bring

me in a cup of tea when you're finished," Jack ordered, winking at his eldest daughter. Cassie grinned at Laura. What a treat, not having to wash up. It wouldn't kill Barbara for once.

"Don't forget *Star Trek*," her father reminded Cassie as he went into the sitting-room to watch the news.

Barbara was furious. "You had no business setting the table. That's my job and I don't see why I have to do this bloody washing-up. It's not fair!"

"Mam asked me to set the table because you weren't here, as usual, so don't annoy me," retorted Cassie.

Barbara clattered plates and cutlery together.

"Don't *you* annoy me, Cassie Jordan!"

"Oh, shut up, Barbara, you do damn all anyway. It's always left to me to help around the house, so doing the washing-up won't kill you for once. Come on, Laura, let's go in and watch TV."

"Just go to hell," snarled Barbara, marching into the kitchen with a load of dirty crockery, which she dumped, none too gently, into the sink.

An hour later, Cassie, her father, Laura and the boys watched, thoroughly engrossed, as Captain Kirk, Mr Spock and the crew of the USS *Enterprise* engaged three Romulan ships in a nail-biting battle. Barbara appeared at the door. "Tsk...such rubbish!" she remarked with an air of supreme superiority. "I've just put the sheets of my bed in the washing-machine, so don't turn it off by accident. I'll see you tomorrow." She left, a trail of Lily of the Valley perfume wafting after her.

Little bitch! thought Cassie in annoyance. The only reason she had put her sheets in the washing machine was so that Cassie would not be able to sleep in her bed. Fortunately, Cassie had a sleeping-bag. That would do fine. Miss Barbara would never know that she had slept on her bed. It would be better than the camp bed, and Laura could sleep in peace in Cassie's. Typical of Barbara to be so spiteful.

CHAPTER THREE

After watching their favourite television programme, the girls took themselves off to the dining-room, where, with much moaning and groaning, they proceeded to write out their punishment lines. Their aim was to have it done before Nora got home. If Nora saw them writing lines, she'd know something was up.

They lay in their twin beds that night, sipping their hot chocolate and cream. Laura gave a huge sigh. Cassie, enveloped in a sleeping-bag on Barbara's bed, looked over at her friend. "Are you worrying about Jill?"

"Yeah, Cassie, I just feel so sorry for her. Da was such a bastard. I wish I could do something to help her. But what can I do?"

"You can stand by her. At least she'll know she can depend on you," Cassie said firmly. "Why don't we go to Dublin as soon as we get out of school and spend a few hours with her tomorrow? Do you think she'd like that?"

"Oh Cassie, that would be great. Are you sure you don't mind coming? Are you sure you don't mind about her being pregnant?"

"Don't be daft, Laura. Who am I to mind? I just hope to God it never happens to me, that's all. Not that there's much chance. Here I am, fourteen and manless," she reflected mournfully.

"Are you sorry you broke it off with Andy?" Laura asked sympathetically.

"Well, I am and I'm not," Cassie said seriously. "It was nice having someone special and having someone to bring you to the pictures and the disco. You know yourself." Laura nodded. She was currently dating Brendan Connolly, best friend of Andy.

"I just blew a fuse when I saw him kissing Denise Atkins down at the boat-shed the night of the barbecue."

"It was a great barbecue," Laura enthused. Catching Cassie's outraged expression she said contritely, "Sorry!"

"Denise Atkins! For God's sake! Can you believe it? She's done it with everybody she's dated," Cassie said in disgust.

"That's probably why Andy was kissing her," Laura said drily.

"Yeah," agreed Cassie glumly. "Andy has sex on the brain."

"Haven't we all?" retorted Laura tartly. "Even Perpetua, Mother Patrick, and the triangle on legs, our esteemed maths mistress, go to bed at night and think of sex. It's human nature, my dear."

Cassie laughed. "Could you just imagine Miss Fagin in the throes of ecstasy? She wouldn't know whether she was horizontal or perpendicular."

"Switch out the light and go to sleep or we'll never get up in the morning," Laura instructed. "It's after one and I'm going to have a nice horizontal dream with Steve McQueen. Goodnight, Cassie."

"'Night, Laura," smiled Cassie as she switched out the light.

❧

Sitting in the library yawning the following morning, Cassie sighed. It had taken her ages to get to sleep. To tell the truth she was still smarting over Andy Callan's betrayal of her. She had thought things were good between them. They got on great and enjoyed the same things, and even though she wouldn't let him do much more than kiss her, he had seemed happy enough until little tart Atkins had set her eye on him and he had gone running. Cassie had to admit that her pride was well and truly bruised. It had been hard going to the last two discos to watch the pair of them dancing, wrapped around each other. But she had held her head high and pretended she was having a good time and Laura and Aileen and the rest of the gang had been most supportive. Cassie knew that Denise would sooner or later set her eye on someone else and Andy would be dropped. Denise was notorious for doing that to guys. She was the *femme fatale* of Port Mahon. Well, Andy was welcome to her and she was welcome to Andy, Cassie had decided, as she tossed and turned trying to get to sleep while Laura slumbered peacefully.

She yawned again. It was so hot in the library as the thirty of them sat pretending to study under the arctic eye of Mother Perpetua. Resting her forehead on her hand, Cassie closed her eyes for a moment. Actually, with her head bent and Laura's tall back at the desk in front of her, Mother Perpetua couldn't see her. Cassie settled herself more comfortably. Only an hour to go, thank God. She could have a snooze on the train to Dublin.

"Would you like a pillow, Catherine Jordan?" A loud voice seemed to be coming from somewhere nearby. Cassie grunted and kept her eyes closed. She was so deliciously relaxed, she didn't want to wake up. She must be having a nightmare or something but she could swear Mother Perpetua was bellowing at her.

"Wake up, you lazy lump of a girl!" Cassie opened a bleary eye to discover that she was having no nightmare. Mother Perpetua was indeed standing over her bellowing, as the rest of the class giggled delightedly, relieved that they were not at the centre of this new drama with the fiery nun.

"Sorry, Mother!" Cassie shot upright. Ahead of her she could see Laura's shoulders shaking with laughter. Typical!

"Do you think you are in a holiday camp? What kind of behaviour is this for a Saint Imelda's girl? God has sent this class as a cross for me to bear," Mother Perpetua hissed furiously. A smothered snort from the desk in front drew her attention.

"Is something amusing you, Madam Quinn?" she said, in a tone that would have terrified Hitler.

"N...no, Mother." Laura struggled for control.

"Kindly stand up when I speak to you," snapped the nun. Laura stood. Aileen O'Shaughnessy, seeing that things were getting hot, pressed the bridge of her nose, held her breath and, a second later, there was a satisfactory spurt of blood. The class heaved a sigh of relief. Good old Aileen and her trusty nose-bleeds. They had got them out of many a tight spot.

By the time Aileen's nose-bleed was over, the time had come for the erring class to be dismissed. Mother Perpetua was more than glad to see them go. This lot were the bane of her life, the worst class she had encountered in thirty years of teaching. There were times she even thought they were getting the better of her. If she had not been afraid that Aileen O'Shaughnessy's nose would start to bleed again, she would have kept them for an hour longer as an extra punishment. Mother Perpetua did not like the sight of blood and felt a little weak. After lunch she was going to lie in her room and take a valium. The doctor had told her she was having a troublesome menopause and had prescribed the tablets for her. Perpetua rather liked them and allowed herself one as a treat now and again when the going got tough. Well, the going had been tough today, God knows. She might even take two!

Outside in the balmy early summer breeze 3S removed cardigans and wandered down the drive. "Jeepers, I thought Perpetua was going to have a blue fit. You should have heard the snores of you, Cassie." Aileen shrieked with laughter.

"I wasn't snoring, was I?" Cassie was aghast.

"You sure were, honey. Great big rumbling ones!" grinned Laura.

"Oh crikey!" Cassie muttered.

"Never mind. Perpetua forgot all about it when I turned on the big gusher," Aileen soothed her.

"Hey, listen! Thanks a million for making your nose bleed," Cassie said.

"You're welcome. I'll see you Monday at the retreat." Aileen winked.

"See you Monday," agreed the other girls as they parted at the gates of the school. Cassie and Laura went for a quick sandwich in the town and then caught the train for Dublin. They bought Jill a bunch of flowers from a street-trader on the way from Amiens Street and when she saw them she was very touched. They took her for tea in Bewley's and did their best to cheer her up.

❦

"You look fantastic, Cassie. Where did you get the skirt?" Margy Kane stared in admiration as the girls congregated outside the Priory the following Monday morning.

"I got it in Penneys. Do you like it? You don't think it's too short?" Cassie did a little twirl, delighted with herself. She knew she looked good in her new outfit.

"Oh it's fab, Cassie! It suits you. I wish I had the legs to wear a really short mini," Margy said enviously.

"It's great we don't have to wear our uniforms, isn't it? It's like being on holidays. Wouldn't it be brilliant if we had Father Paul for the retreat. He was super last year. You could say anything to him." Cassie was peering into the distance, looking for Laura. The main street was busy with people heading to work. Shop windows were being washed, deliveries were being made and the enticing aroma of coffee and bacon from a nearby café scented the fresh sea breeze and made Cassie hungry.

"Pity we haven't time to nip in for a bacon butty," Margy said regretfully.

"Hmm. Don't tempt me. Still," Cassie brightened, "we'll get biscuits and tea at eleven." She caught sight of Laura striding down the main street in a pair of tight denim jeans and a clinging white T-shirt. She looked sensational.

"Hiya," she grinned at Cassie.

"Hi, Laura, you look really good," Cassie greeted her friend.

"Do you think Father Paul will like this. I'm hoping to make him think twice about remaining a priest for ever," Laura laughed, eyes twinkling wickedly.

"Girl, when he sees that outfit he won't have a chance," giggled Cassie, who was looking forward immensely to the next two days. It was a great break away from school and routine and although it was supposed to be a spiritual affair, 3S had every intention of getting as much fun and entertainment out of the two days as possible.

"Here's Aileen." Laura waved madly at Aileen, who was on the other side of the street. "When we get in, we'll all get seats together, so we'll need seats for the four of us, Rose, Ger, Martina, Bernie and Pat. That's nine. OK?" ordered Laura, the organiser.

"Hi, gang!" smirked Aileen, who had just been whistled at as she crossed the street. She was dressed to kill in a white mini-dress and a pair of white leather boots, her eyes heavily kohled. She could have been mistaken for Mary Quant.

"Get a load of that!" gasped Margy.

"Do you think Father Paul will appreciate it?" Aileen raised an enquiring eyebrow as she basked in their admiration.

"There'll be a mass exodus from the priesthood once we hit the Priory," predicted Laura.

"O priests of Port Mahon, your hour has come," announced the giggling Mary Quant clone. Her expression changed to one of horror as she spied a familiar little figure marching briskly in their direction. "Jesus, here's Perpetua! Let's get the hell out of here."

With a hasty scramble they rushed through the gates of the Priory and ran up the steps to the door. Sighing with relief, they entered its cool marble foyer, where they were greeted by a smiling priest.

"Welcome, girls. Room Eight on the corridor to your left. You probably remember it from last year."

"Yes, Father, we do. Thank you." Aileen recovered her composure and led the way, hips swaying provocatively. They trooped into the room and greeted the dozen or so classmates who were already there. Swiftly,

Cassie arranged the nine chairs they were saving for the whole of their gang and Aileen plonked herself on one and drew a packet of cigarettes out of her bag.

"I'm gasping for a fag!" she drawled.

"Do you think we're allowed to smoke?" Margy's eyes were popping out of her head at this display of daring.

"Why ever not? We're not in uniform. We're third years, Margy! We must act it," lectured the sophisticate in white as she lit up and inhaled deeply. "This is the life, girls! This is the life! By the way, Cassie, Judy and Barbara had a tiff." She grinned at Cassie. Aileen was Judy's elder sister and was well aware of the state of affairs between Cassie and Barbara.

"Really! What happened?" Cassie was intrigued. Aileen took another pull of her cigarette.

"Well, seemingly, they were at the junior disco and Barbara left Judy alone for most of the night because Paddy Lowe was chatting her up."

"That little geek! God, I thought even Barbara had more taste than that!" Cassie said in disgust.

"Well, anyway," Aileen resumed her story. "I heard them arguing the following morning and Judy, who never says boo to a goose, you know, told Barbara in no uncertain terms that she didn't like being used and dropped and that she wasn't going to put up with it any longer. I felt quite proud of her, actually."

"Good for Judy!" Cassie agreed. She liked Judy O'Shaughnessy, who unfortunately was completely under Barbara's thumb. Well, maybe not any longer. Now that she was making a stand maybe the worm had turned. And good enough for Barbara, too! She'd have to learn that she couldn't go around treating her friends like dirt, or before long she wouldn't have a friend left.

Aileen laughed. "Barbara was really taken aback that

Judy had stood up to her for once and said what was on her mind. Then she left in high dudgeon."

"I'll bet she did," remarked Cassie, knowing her sister of old. "I wonder how long the tiff will last?"

"Oh not too long, I should imagine. Isn't there a junior disco at Saint Joseph's soon? All should be well by then." She arched a delicate eyebrow and nodded towards Cassie's skirt. "Oh, and I'd keep an eagle eye on that skirt, if I were you. It sounds suspiciously like the one Barbara is planning to wear. I just happened to overhear them talking."

"Oh is it now? Well, we'll see about that," said Cassie grimly. Barbara would go to any lengths, padlock or no padlock. Just as well Aileen had mentioned it. Forewarned was forearmed.

A commotion at the door heralded the arrival of the rest of the gang and there was much ooohing and aaahing as they all admired each other's outfits. "Are we allowed to smoke? Oh good," said Rose, immediately lighting up.

"Are we getting tea and biscuits before we start?" Martina asked hopefully.

"Personally, I'd prefer a G&T," replied the incorrigible Aileen.

"Or Father Paul," murmured Laura.

"Ohhhh yessss!" There was a ripple of agreement.

As the girls sat down and made themselves comfortable, the air of anticipation was almost palpable. They were all dying to see Father Paul again. He had made an enormous impression on them last year, with his film-star good looks and understanding personality. They had all been looking forward to this retreat for ages.

A small, thin, bespectacled priest came through the door and stopped short in shock. The fug of smoke

intermingled with twenty different perfumes almost
made his glasses steam up. Father Maurice Darnell had
sinus problems! A frown creased his brow as he gazed
around him in dismay. He had been right to be worried
about taking this retreat. The message had come from
Saint Imelda's that they particularly wanted 3S to have
a retreat with the emphasis on the spiritual side of things.
Looking at that creature in the white get-up, who was
smoking like a chimney, Father Maurice could tell that
there was absolutely nothing spiritual about her. Or the
other one with her skirt up to her buttocks, or the one
in the skin-tight jeans.

Two days with this lot! What had he done to deserve
it? Across the room he could see one girl putting on a
great slash of red lipstick; another held out her hand
while a companion varnished her nails. It was worse
than being in a beauty salon! Clearing his throat, he said
with an air of extremely false *bonhomie*, "Good morning,
girls."

He was ignored. The din of chatter swallowed up his
greeting. Father Maurice continued gamely. Nervously
raising his voice an octave, he tried again. "Good
morning, young ladies."

The girls nearest the door heard him and turned to
look. A hissing of "sshhh!" raced around the room, until
finally there was silence. The girls rose to their feet to
greet the priest. "Good morning, young ladies. My name
is Father Maurice. I'll be giving you your retreat for the
next two days." A gasp greeted this announcement.
Father Maurice made his way to the table and chair at
the top of the room. "If you would desist from smoking
until break-time please," he requested briskly, flinging
open a few windows *en route*.

"First we will say a prayer, putting ourselves in the

hands of the Lord above for the duration of this retreat."
He prayed most earnestly as the girls looked at each
other in profound dismay. Then he said, "You may sit."

The members of 3S subsided into their chairs, quite
deflated. "Today our lecture and discussion is going to
centre on the Ten Commandments. You may take notes
if you wish."

Silence greeted this pronouncement. Father Maurice
wiped his brow. Well, at least the creatures were silent.

It was a welcome relief for the class when the tea-
trolley was wheeled in, two hours later. Galvanised out
of their lethargy, 3S fell upon the goodies as the Israelites
had fallen upon the manna in the desert.

"You horse, Jane O'Hara," Aileen was heard to say.
"Stop guzzling all the chocolate biscuits. Look at her,
she's got three chocolate ones!"

"I have not!" howled an outraged Jane. "I'm just
bringing two over to Miriam and Paula."

"Here, give us some of those, Margy Kane. Don't be
so greedy," said someone else.

"Shag off and get your own." Margy battled through
the crowd with a plate of biscuits for the gang clutched
to her large bosom.

"Girls! Girls!" Father Maurice gulped in horror at the
savagery of the hordes around the tea-trolley.

"I don't want one of those crappy plain ones. Are
there no fancy ones left? Excuse me, Father." A stout girl
elbowed him out of her way and dived on the last plate
of biscuits. Father Maurice fled.

"He's so *boring*," groaned Cassie as she drank her tea
and ate one of the biscuits Margy had bravely procured.

"Perpetua's revenge!" growled Laura, who was
desperately disappointed not to have the chance to flirt
with Father Paul.

"Did you see the way he skipped over the Sixth Commandment, the little coward!" said Aileen with disdain. A glint came into her eyes.

"I know." She smiled devilishly. Leaning over, she beckoned them to draw closer and to shrieks of delight told them of her plan, which she proceeded to put into action as soon as the retreat was resumed after lunch.

"Are French kissing and heavy petting sins if they are done with love?" she asked the priest.

Father Maurice nearly fell off the chair with dismay. It was the question-and-answer session after the morning's lecture on the Ten Commandments. The creature in white with the black stuff around her eyes was standing up.

"Lovemaking in the confines of a marriage blessed by the sacraments is never a sin, as long as the partners respect the sanctity of their bodies. Outside of marriage it is, of course, sinful behaviour." There! He'd handled that fine, he assured himself.

"If it is done with love?" persisted Aileen. "After all, God gave us the gift of love. Surely we should be able to make love without guilt, as it is, after all, a gift from God?"

"I think you are confusing lust with love, my child. Lust is one of the seven deadly sins," Father Maurice said coldly.

Laura stood up. "Don't you think the church's stance on contraception is hypocritical considering the fact that they allow natural methods? Surely the aim is the same. To prevent conception. What's the difference between natural and artificial methods if the ultimate aim is the same?" she pounced triumphantly.

"I suggest you read Pope Paul VI's encyclical on birth control. You will find that it explains the church's position and you will get the answer to your question. It is far too involved a question to get into here. We must move on," Father Maurice said unhappily. Another day and a half of this lot! It was an unbearable thought.

"Well, I still think it's hypocritical," retorted Laura coldly. "It's just splitting hairs, if you ask me."

Nobody's asking you, you little madam, the priest wanted to snarl, but he restrained himself heroically.

"Splitting sperm would be more like it," drawled Aileen. 3S guffawed!

"Young ladies! Please!" Father Maurice said weakly, shocked by their vulgarity. With a sinking heart he saw that another one was standing up.

"Do you think," said Cassie, "that women should be ordained?"

"I most certainly do not," said Father Maurice piously, more to himself than his audience. "I think if God had wanted women to be priests he would have ordained them when he ordained the twelve apostles."

"But don't you agree that the church treats women as second-class citizens?"

And rightly so, thought the beleaguered priest, if the carry-on of this lot was anything to go by. The day women entered the priesthood would be the day he was gone. Forty years of avoiding them had not endeared the species to Father Maurice. "I certainly don't think any such thing. Men and women were created differently. Each sex has a specific role to play in life. God loves all his children equally."

"Do you think that priests should be allowed to marry? After all, some of the twelve apostles were married. And surely it would give them more experience of the problems faced by married couples, such as contraception?" Cassie was only getting into her stride.

"I think we should stick to questions and answers regarding our discussion of this morning. None of you has asked me any questions regarding, say, the missing of Mass. Profanity. The honouring of your father and mother." Father Maurice tried to steer the conversation to more innocuous matters. Aileen's eyes glinted with devilment. She stood up once more.

Father Maurice paled. Not her again!

"Speaking of fathers and mothers, how can the church justify interfering in the private lives of married couples?"

He couldn't take any more! He'd had enough of these she-devils. He'd plead illness. Anything to get away from them. They didn't know the meaning of the words "young ladies." The savagery of them at that tea-trolley. The questions they were asking. What were they teaching in secondary schools these days? French kissing! Contraception! They were only fourteen! He hadn't known anything about such matters until he had gone into the seminary. Father Maurice wrung his bony little hands together, glaring at Aileen, who stood waiting for her answer.

The arrival of the second tea-trolley of the day saved his bacon. Interfering between married couples was forgotten in the mad dash to the biscuits. Father Maurice hoped they choked on them. God forgive him. He would have to go to confession to seek absolution for the thoughts of hatred that surged through him at this very moment. Let somebody else take them on tomorrow. He'd had enough. He left them doing battle at the trolley. After half an hour, when he figured it should be safe to return, he appeared at the door and told them they could go home, as the retreat was finished for that day. There were howls of delight and he had to step aside smartly or he would have been crushed to pieces in the mad scramble to get out the door. Crazy hoydens, that's what they were. God grant he'd never meet their like again.

The following day, much to the dismay of Class 3S, there was neither discussion nor question-and-answer session. They had a Mass followed by a morning of silent reflection. After lunch they were shown a film of the works of the order in the third world.

They had never been so bored in their lives and it was almost a relief to get back to school the following day.

Mother Perpetua was waiting for them.

"You girls are a disgrace to this school," she ranted. "I saw you! Oh yes, I saw you. Dressed like trollops...like common hussies, hanging around the gates of the Priory. You, Miss Quinn, in your tight T-shirt and you, Miss Jordan, in a skirt that left nothing to the imagination. And as for Aileen O'Shaughnessy! Words fail me! Fail me! I have no control of you outside of school but," she paused for effect and stared at them with her little beady eyes, "I'm going to keep a tight rein on you, 3S. You'll be young ladies by the time I'm finished with you."

Thank God there are only a few weeks left and then we'll be free of her for practically three whole months, Cassie comforted herself as she made her way home after listening to Mother Perpetua's tirade. She was really looking forward to her summer holidays. In June and July she was going to work full-time in the sweetshop in the town where she sometimes helped out on Saturday mornings, and in August she and Laura were going to go on a day-trip to the Isle of Man. After that they were going to spend a week in Wicklow in a mobile home owned by Laura's aunt. They were looking forward to it so much. A holiday by themselves to do as they pleased! What absolute bliss.

Then Nora had earmarked her to help to wallpaper the sitting-room and paint the kitchen. Cassie didn't mind the idea of that at all; in fact she rather looked forward to it. During the boring days of the retreat, she had filled a notebook with drawings of houses and sitting-rooms and bedrooms. It had passed the time very pleasantly to sit and draw and work out colour schemes. She really enjoyed doodling. Art was definitely her favourite subject. Miss Carey, her art teacher, was very encouraging and told her she had good colour sense. If only Nora would let her decorate the bedroom in pink and grey. It would be really lovely. But of course, Barbara had objected and said she wanted it done in blue! Blue in a north-facing bedroom. A complete disaster! Warm colours were what was required and she had seen the most beautiful idea in a book on interior design that she had got out of the local library. Maybe if she let Barbara borrow the denim mini to go to that dance, she might let her have her way with the colours...

Barbara was thrilled with the offer of the mini. "Thanks, Cassie, you're brill!" she exclaimed.

Cassie laid down the conditions of the loan. "You can have it if you let me decorate the room in pink and grey."

"Can I have the purple ribbed polo-neck?" Barbara demanded.

"OK," Cassie said grudgingly. Typical of Barbara to twist the knife.

"You can decorate the room in mauve and scarlet then, for all I care."

Cassie was delighted.

The last few weeks of term slipped by uneventfully enough. 3S were putting in some serious study for their exams. They didn't want bad reports going home, that was for sure. They knew that Perpetua's comments on their report cards would be damning. But by and large, the rest of their teachers had no trouble from them, and the one bad comment might be overlooked among the list of eight or nine on the report card.

Next year they would not be able to take things so lightly as they would be doing their Intermediate Certificate, the first important exam of their schooldays. It would be the end of the free and easy days they were enjoying as third years. She had really enjoyed this year at school, Cassie decided, as they all trooped into their classroom on the day they got their holidays. Their term exams were over and most of them felt they had done OK, so they weren't stressed or worried about them. Mind, Aileen had made a terrible bloomer in her Honours English paper, confusing Keats and Shelley. And Miss Ryan had told her if she kept her mind more on her studies and less on entertaining the class she'd be better off. Aileen had been annoyed by the ticking-off and had stuck a note on the back of her English teacher's black gown saying in large red letters: *I'm Randy.*

Miss Ryan had walked through the main corridor and taken two classes before anyone in authority copped it. There had been delicious uproar at the discovery! Poor Mother Perpetua didn't understand quite what the fuss was about until someone explained it to her. She retreated to her bed that afternoon and took two and a half valium! Needless to say the culprit was never been found and everyone had to stay back after school for two hours. But it was worth it, all were agreed!

As the final bell of term went, a huge cheer reverberated through the entire school as the young ladies of Saint Imelda's danced and sang and charged down the driveway to freedom and a whole summer of bliss.

CHAPTER FOUR

Nora was always going mad at the untidiness of the bedroom shared by Cassie and Barbara. Cassie had been allowed to decorate it in pretty shades of pink and grey and she was so pleased with her colour scheme that for a while she made huge efforts to keep it tidy, despite Barbara's complete refusal to cooperate. But that was over two years ago now and Cassie's resolve had gradually weakened. One Friday, when Cassie arrived in from school, tired and fed up after a hard day, she found her mother in a bad humour. Nora just exploded.

"Your Aunt Elsie is coming tomorrow and staying for a week and I don't know how many times I've asked you to tidy up that bedroom of yours. The pair of you should be ashamed of yourselves. The place is a kip. Well, I can tell you one thing, Miss! You and Barbara had better get that room tidy tonight. And you needn't think you're going out, either. *You* can clean the brasses for me and that other one can do some of that pile of ironing."

"Ah Mam!" protested Cassie, stung by the unfairness of it all. Her part of the room was reasonably tidy. Most of her clothes were hanging up, apart from a pair of jeans or two and her windcheater. Barbara, on the other hand, had more stuff on her bed and on the floor than she had in her wardrobe. Nora occasionally did a hit-and-run clean sweep of the place, much to Barbara's consternation.

In most other ways, their mother was pretty easy-going, but when Aunt Elsie decided to come and visit, the entire Jordan family suffered. Aunt Elsie was Nora's eldest sister. She was unmarried, strict and humourless, and her house was like a little palace. Only a foolhardy speck of dust dared make an appearance in that spick-and-span abode; if it did it was instantly annihilated. Of course, it was all right for Aunt Elsie; she had nothing else to do but polish and clean, unlike her sister Nora, who had a family to look after, and who also helped her husband to run a farm. *She* didn't have time to worry about every speck of dust that appeared in the Jordan household. Yet always when Nora heard that her sister was coming on a visit, the house was turned upside-down and inside-out as a marathon spring-cleaning got underway. Even Jack dreaded his sister-in-law's visits as he saw his wife becoming harassed and agitated. Elsie was very quick to pass remarks and would not hesitate to comment on anything that caught her eye. She had once chastised her younger sister for having a slightly crooked hem on the gingham table-cloth that covered the kitchen table. Invariably Elsie would make some comment that would leave Nora angry and upset and she would be even more determined to make sure that her sister found no fault with the place on her next visit.

The news of an impending visit by Aunt Elsie cast gloom on the entire family, Cassie most of all because she was always called upon to do the lion's share of the cleaning. At times like this it was a real pain in the neck being the eldest. How could her mother be so mean as to stop her going to Kate Rooney's birthday party just because Barbara had left their room in a state as usual.

"I'll tidy up the room and do the brasses before I go out," Cassie said quickly, getting the Brasso out of the press under the sink as a sign of her goodwill.

"Did you hear what I said, young lady?" Nora was not to be trifled with. "No one, not you, not Barbara, not John, is going out tonight. This house has to be cleaned from top to bottom. And judging by the state of your rooms, you'll all be lucky to get to bed!" she said irritably.

"But Mam!" wailed Cassie. "It's Kate Rooney's seventeenth birthday. She's the first in the class to be seventeen and Laura and Aileen and all the gang will be there." Cassie forbore to mention that Donie Kiely was going to be at the party as well. She was crazy about him and she felt he was equally interested in her.

"Laura and Aileen don't have Aunt Elsie coming to stay. And I'm sure that their rooms are not like tip-heaps. Don't argue with me, like a good girl. I'm far too busy. Leave those brasses and get your room cleaned first, please."

"It's mostly Barbara's mess! For crying out loud! It will take me only ten minutes to clean my part." Cassie was starting to lose her temper.

"Don't speak to me in that tone of voice, Miss!" her mother warned.

"Well, I'm sick of having to do everything around here and I'm sick of getting the blame for Barbara's mess. It's just not fair and you're being totally unreasonable. I'll be the only one not at that party tonight!" Cassie's eyes glittered as she glared at her mother.

"I don't want any more of your cheek, Cassie, and let that be an end to it." Nora was as annoyed as Cassie as she turned back to peeling the potatoes for the dinner. With tears misting her eyes, Cassie slammed the kitchen door behind her and flounced along the hall towards her bedroom at the far end of the bungalow. She was *sick* of living in this house. It was always the same. Was Nora one bit grateful for all the housework Cassie did for her, week in, week out? Just because she was the eldest there was no reason to treat her like a slave! Cassie slammed her bedroom door behind her, wallowing in self-pity.

The party tonight was going to be a real rave-up. Kate Rooney's parents were very liberal; they were going into Dublin to a meal and they told Kate they trusted her. They even allowed her to invite boys to the party. And Donie Kiely was invited. Cassie had fancied him for ages. She often saw him at the Saturday-night disco. He was always looking at her and smiling at her. Tonight could have been the night they clicked. And now Nora had put her foot down and Cassie was going to be stuck at home like Cinderella. It just wasn't fair! Didn't her mother realise that she was going to be seventeen herself in a few weeks. Practically into her twenties. She shouldn't be treating her like a child any more because she most definitely *wasn't* a child.

Cassie glowered at her reflection in the wardrobe mirror. Soft chestnut curls with glints of auburn framed a well-defined face. Cassie had great cheekbones, all the girls at school said so. Her hazel eyes, flecked with green, ringed by silky dark lashes, were her best feature. Her mouth was too big, she thought glumly, her button-nose a disaster. She supposed her figure wasn't too bad: a neat bosom, a nice curvy waist, slim hips and legs that were shapely from all the basketball she played. It was certainly not the body of a child. Laura's father, Peter Quinn, was always giving her funny looks and finding an excuse to touch her. He really gave Cassie the creeps. Laura had told Cassie in disgust that her father read dirty magazines. It didn't surprise Cassie in the slightest!

She had planned to wear her new trousers and a very sophisticated grey-and-red jumper that she had bought in the sale in Roches. Now, thanks to blooming Aunt Elsie, Nora and Barbara, she wouldn't get the chance.

Well, things were going to change. She was going to start asserting herself more. After all, she was practically grown up. The first thing she was going to do was to tell her mother she wanted to swap bedrooms with Irene. Why should Irene get away with having her own bedroom? She was the youngest. Surely it was Cassie who was entitled to a bedroom of her own. Then, with her own room, she would be able to keep it perfectly tidy and Nora would finally realise that it was Barbara who was the main culprit as regards untidiness.

Irene probably wouldn't be too happy about moving but that was just tough. Her young sister had a small room just across the hallway. In it, she resided with dozens of soft cuddly toys, which were lined up neatly on shelves. Irene, a dainty little blonde who was timid and shy, also had a streak of stubbornness. If she dug her heels in and said she didn't want to move, Nora would say that was all right and leave her where she was. She was very protective and was always making a fuss of her. Irene loved being made a fuss of, especially when she got one of her asthma attacks. She would quite happily stay in bed, wrapped in her mother's quilted dressing-gown, playing away with her toys, delighted to be missing a day of school, while Nora prepared tasty little treats for her in the kitchen. "Irene's a bit delicate," Cassie often heard her mother tell friends. Delicate, my foot! she thought. None of the rest of them had been allowed to stay at home from school half as much as Irene. But she could understand why Nora treated Irene the way she did. As a baby she had nearly died from pneumonia, and ever since, Nora had taken the utmost care of her little girl. There was something about Irene that made people want to protect her. Maybe she was a bit mean wanting to make her share a bedroom with Barbara.

"There, you see! You're doing it again!" Cassie spoke crossly to herself as she hung up her jeans. "Making things easy for Irene! Why should Irene have things made easy for her? Why shouldn't I make things easy for myself? I am a person too!" She glanced over at her Desiderata poster. *"You are a child of the universe,"* she hummed. *"No less than the trees and the stars you have the right to be here..."* Laura had given her the poster for her sixteenth birthday last year and Cassie really treasured it. Yes, indeed, she decided, she had as much right to her own bedroom as Irene had, and once Aunt Elsie was gone she was going to ask about it. In her mind's eye she began to decorate it. Pink and grey, her favourite colours, but she would make sure that it didn't look too like her present bedroom. Fashions in interior design were changing all the time. She would put a border on the wallpaper and have a pink candlewick bedspread with small grey scatter cushions on the bed. She'd paint the door, skirting-boards and windowsill grey as well, to contrast with the pink walls. She had seen a beautiful room done like that in a magazine in the doctor's waiting-room. She had liked it so much that she had surreptitiously torn out the page and brought it home with her to put in her folder.

Cassie always kept a folder into which she put articles and ideas that appealed to her in magazines. When she was working, she was going to buy a house of her own and decorate it exactly the way she wanted to. Without being big-headed about it, she knew she had a talent for design. Her art teacher had advised her to go to art college, but Nora was not in favour of it. Cassie's next choice was to study architecture and she intended putting her name down for a place in the College of Technology, Bolton Street in Dublin. Of course she'd have to get the grades in her exams. She had done very well in her Intermediate Certificate, and so far she wasn't doing too badly with her studies. Fortunately, she enjoyed her subjects, apart from science, so it wasn't an awful chore to do a bit of swotting now and again.

Honestly, you'd think Nora would even appreciate that, she reflected, as she started picking up Barbara's clothes, which lay strewn at the foot of her bed. Barbara and Martin always had to be reprimanded for not studying hard enough. The more Cassie reflected on her current situation, the more aggrieved she felt and the more put-upon she became in her own eyes. In a thoroughly bad humour, she lifted all Barbara's clothes off the floor and flung them onto her divan. What a mess Barbara's clothes got into! A key fell out of a jeans pocket. Cassie's eyes widened. That looked like her padlock key. She flew over to her wardrobe and fitted the key in her lock. It fitted! But how odd. Just five minutes ago hadn't she opened the lock with the key she kept on an elastic band around her wrist? The little bitch! She'd got a copy made somehow. Just wait! Cassie fumed. Just wait until that one got home.

❦

Barbara didn't get home until after seven. Her class had been in the city on a cultural visit to museums and art galleries. Cassie had had to set the table and do the washing-up, although John had dried for her. Cassie had asked her father to try and change her mother's mind about the party and Jack had promised he would speak to her. Her parents were going out for an hour to attend the wake of an elderly neighbour. In the meantime, Cassie, hard at work doing the brasses, planned what she would say and do to Barbara.

Barbara breezed in full of the joys of spring, ravenous for her dinner, about half an hour after Jack and Nora had left. "I want a word with you," Cassie declared, holding open her palm, on which reposed the duplicate key.

Barbara paled slightly but immediately recovered her composure. "What's that? The key to your chastity belt?" she drawled sarcastically.

Cassie felt her temper flare. "You know very well what it is, you smart little sneak," she said furiously, all her resentment erupting. "I'm just sick of you and your sneaky little ways. And it's all thanks to you and your untidiness that I can't go to Kate Rooney's birthday party tonight. I got blamed for the mess of the bedroom and it's all your fault. I'm sick, sick, *sick* of you!"

"And I'm sick of you, Cassie Jordan!" Barbara echoed, rather taken aback by her sister's vehemence.

"How low can you get? Stealing the key to my wardrobe!" Cassie was shaking with temper. She had to restrain herself from shaking her sister until the younger girl's teeth shook.

"Well, if you weren't so mean with your clothes! If you were any sort of a sister you'd share! Aileen O'Shaughnessy always shares her clothes with Judy. She's a proper sister, not like you. All you care about is yourself."

"I beg your pardon!" snapped Cassie, outraged.

"It's true," retorted Barbara bitterly. "You never let me have your clothes. You never let me go places with you. Aileen is much nicer to Judy than you are to me. You're just mean and selfish and I'm glad you're not allowed to go to your stupid old party."

Cassie was flummoxed! Barbara thought Aileen was a better sister than she was! Well, really! And she wasn't the slightest bit abashed about being caught with a duplicate of the padlock key. If that wasn't just typical of Barbara, she thought in utter frustration. Someone must have told her that attack was the best form of defence. And typical of herself even to feel a twinge of guilt! For heaven's sake, she was the one who was sinned-against. Now don't get soft, she warned herself. Stick to your guns. Taking a deep breath, Cassie turned to her sister and said coldly:

"Barbara, the issue here is not whether Aileen is a better sister than I am. The point is that you did the sneakiest thing by stealing my key and getting a copy, which shows you haven't the slightest bit of respect for me. If you had any respect for my clothes and took care of them, I certainly would have lent them to you, but putting my clothes back dirty in the wardrobe is just not on, Barbara! So that's your own fault. And I don't think it's one bit fair that I get the blame for the mess of the bedroom when at least I make the effort to keep my half of the room tidy and you have the place looking like a slum. And I think it's really mean of you, if you want to know," she added more heatedly. "And I badly wanted to go to that party."

"Oh, just go and get lost, Cassie Jordan. You're always picking on me!" Barbara retorted furiously, raging at being caught and slightly shocked at the fury of her usually agreeable elder sister.

"I'm not always picking on you, Bar—"

"You are so!" Barbara's voice took on a high-pitched note. "Always. You treat me like dirt!"

"*I* treat *you* like dirt!" Cassie exploded, getting really mad. "Would you cop on to yourself!"

"Oh, leave me alone," sniffed Barbara, deciding that she wasn't going to be the victor in this row. It was unusual for Cassie to lose her cool and there was no point in tempting fate.

"With pleasure," snarled Cassie. "Just keep your maulers off my clothes or I'll make you sorry." She was so angry that her voice shook.

"Huh! You and whose army?" Barbara scoffed derisively, her bad nature triumphing over caution as she sashayed through the bedroom door. She didn't get far! Cassie was pushed beyond the limit. Catching her sister by her ponytail, she yanked hard and followed up with a swift, hard slap to the younger girl's cheek.

"Ooooww! Ouch! You fucking bitch, Cassie Jordan!" Barbara shrieked, as Martin, John and Irene came rushing out of the sitting-room to see what all the fuss was about.

"Hey! Hey! break it up!" John exclaimed, doing his big-brother act. He was as tall as fifteen-year-old Barbara.

"Sock her one back," yelled Martin weaving in and out waving his fists like Muhammad Ali. Irene burst into tears. None of them heard the front door opening.

"What's going on here!" Nora demanded, marching down the hall to stand between her two daughters.

"It was hhh...her. *She* started it," sobbed Barbara pitifully.

"Cassie Jordan! I'm ashamed of you! I can't leave the house for five minutes and the place is in uproar. And you the eldest. A fine help to me you are, with your Aunt Elsie coming. Your father persuaded me to let you out to that party, but after this carry-on you can just forget it. Barbara, you're not dead yet. Is that room of yours tidy? John and Martin, get out and clean the yard," Nora commanded in such a tone that no one dared argue further. "Irene, honey, stop crying. I brought you home a barley-sugar stick. Come on into the kitchen. I have it wrapped up for you."

In utter frustration at the whole affair, Cassie burst into tears and fled to the bathroom, leaving her siblings open-mouthed in shock. Cassie never cried. It was a glum family that went to bed that night in a spick-and-span bungalow.

CHAPTER FIVE

Nora lay in bed, going over in her mind every place that had been cleaned, every job that had been done. The place was like a new pin. Not even Elsie could find fault with it. It was funny—with any of her other sisters, she didn't mind a bit. She'd tidy the house, of course, and have things nice, but she'd never go as overboard as when Elsie was coming. It was a bit ridiculous at her age to be intimidated by her eldest sister. But that had always been the way between her and Elsie, ever since they were children.

Sometimes she could see a little of herself and Elsie in Barbara and Cassie. Barbara, for all her impudence, was impressed and often in awe of Cassie, something that Cassie was just not aware of. Barbara covered it up well with her sharp tongue. But behind it, the younger girl longed to be accepted by Cassie and Laura and Aileen and the gang. Being Barbara, she just couldn't be happy with her own group of friends. She had always had that streak of "I see and I want," no matter how hard Nora had tried to erase it.

It was so hard raising children! Nora sighed. Tomorrow she'd ask Cassie to make a bit more of an effort with Barbara. After all they were sisters and they'd need each other some day. But knowing her two daughters, Nora had to admit that it was Cassie who would end up making the effort.

She *had* been a bit hard on Cassie today. A twinge of guilt niggled and would not go away. She had really wanted to go to that party. There was probably some fellow she fancied at it. And then, of course, the rest of the gang would be there. In spite of herself, Nora smiled in the dark. That Aileen O'Shaughnessy! She was terribly fond of her, and indeed of Laura Quinn. They were good friends to Cassie and Nora knew you'd always need good friends more than anything in this life. Aileen had been at the wake. Dressed in a trenchcoat, with a beret perched sideways on her titian curls, she had looked like a member of the French Resistance. Nora was surprised to see her there. But her widowed mother was with her so she had obviously gone to keep her company. It was so strange to see Aileen murmuring the Rosary and looking as if butter wouldn't melt in her mouth. No doubt she would go on to the party later.

Nora tossed restlessly. She should have let Cassie go, she supposed. Her eldest daughter was rarely troublesome; in fact, Nora depended on her a great deal. Maybe too much. That was always the way with the eldest, though, wasn't it? Maybe she was a bit too strict with her. Jack maintained that she was. But of course Jack was as soft as marshmallow. Children needed a firm hand. They had to learn that they couldn't have everything they wanted. Not that Cassie was in the habit of asking for much. She had her job in the shop and contributed towards her own clothes and was very generous to her brothers and sisters. She had even bought herself a new outfit for the party. These things were so important to teenagers. John was wanting to go to discos now, and was beginning to take a welcome interest in his appearance. His latest thing was to beg her to let him get a leather jacket. Nora had put her foot down very firmly.

Both he and Martin were saving hard for a pair of Doc Martens, whatever they might be.

Tomorrow, she'd make it up to Cassie. She'd give her a couple of quid and tell her to take the girls to Kentucky Fried Chicken on Main Street for a treat. Nora's last conscious thought was to remind herself to refill the holy water font at the front door. Elsie had caught her out once before with an empty font.

❧

Jack Jordan lay beside his wife, willing sleep to come. He was dead tired. He had been working like a slave painting the outside of the bungalow, cutting lawns and weeding flower-beds because of *the visit*. Of course it was always the same when his sister-in-law was coming. Nora got herself into such a tizzy. And the strange thing was, usually she was such a capable woman and things did not get to her. But then Elsie was such a domineering woman. Every time she came she'd have something to criticise. Once, at the christening of one of the children, they had served a little buffet and Elsie had announced to all and sundry, at the top of her voice, "Your crisps are stale." Poor Nora had been mortified and he had felt like planting his boot up his sister-in-law's backside. As far as Jack was concerned, Elsie was downright rude. But of course he couldn't say such a thing to his wife. Oh deary me, no! It was all right for Nora to criticise Elsie or the rest of her siblings, but it did not go down well if he or anyone else criticised *them*. They were a tight clan, the Freyns. That was the way it was with families, he supposed. Poor old Cassie had been mighty upset this evening. And to think he had managed to get Nora to change her mind about letting her go to the party. No easy feat in the mood she was in. And then they had to walk in and find Cassie and Barbara swinging out of each other. That had been the end of that! Cassie was like him in that respect, rarely losing the cool, but when she did lose her temper, watch out!

Jack yawned. Maybe Elsie could do with a bit of temper heading her way. If she said one thing out of place, one thing mind, then he'd really let her have it this time. For years he had been restraining himself out of consideration for Nora. But he'd had enough. His whole family was out of sorts because of Elsie's visit. Nora was like a devil; Cassie had missed her party; Martin and John hadn't even been allowed to go to the scouts tonight. Poor Barbara had had to clean out her wardrobe. A terrible torture, given Barbara's wardrobe. Jack put his arm around Nora, who had finally fallen asleep. One word out of you tomorrow, Elsie, and you're for it, he promised himself, his humour brightening up immensely at the thought of giving the dreaded Elsie what for!

❦

Don't fall asleep! John warned himself, as he cast a faintly envious eye on his snoring younger brother, Martin. Cassie was depending on him tonight and he just couldn't let her down. It wasn't often she asked for his help. He sat himself up against his pillows and stared determinedly into the semi-darkness. Just as well there was a good moon, they'd need all the help they could get. Not that he couldn't handle the assignment, he assured himself. James Bond 007, licensed to kill. That was him! Special agent on Her Majesty's secret service. Ready to defend the world against the evil SPECTRE. He had got the message from HQ that one of their agents, code-name Elsie, was heading into town tomorrow. He'd be waiting! In the meantime he hoped that Assignment

Cassie would hurry up and begin, as he was finding it terribly hard to keep his eyes open. He blinked and yawned, allowing himself to slide a little under the blankets. His eyelids drooped but then he thought of Cassie asking for his help. Stay awake, he ordered himself sternly, sitting up once more. With a sigh of resignation, 007 began to try and recite the alphabet backwards. He had found this an excellent method of staying awake when on assignment in the past.

❦

Barbara lay feeling thoroughly sorry for herself as she cast her mind back on the events of the evening. To think that Cassie had actually pulled her hair and slapped her across the face and had got away with it. Life was so unfair. Her sister had incurred no extra punishment for her outrageous behaviour and that really annoyed Barbara.

Mind, she had got a terrible fright when Cassie lost her temper. It was most unusual for Cassie to lose the cool like that. It was obvious she was very upset about not going to this party. But still! To attack her own sister so viciously. It just wasn't on. And then not even to apologise. Only Irene, her younger sister, had shown any concern for Barbara. As she was cleaning out her wardrobe, while Cassie sat in stony silence on her bed opposite, doing her homework, Irene came in, put her arms around Barbara's neck, gave her a hug and offered her some of her barley-sugar stick. Barbara had been quite touched. Irene was such a little softie, bless her. Well, Cassie could go and jump from now on. She was going to be *so* cool to her. Cassie could never keep up a fight, no matter how hard she tried. But this time Barbara had no intention of accepting any apology. She wasn't

going to pretend that they *were* talking, even for Aunt
Elsie's benefit. If Aunt Elsie wanted to know the reason
for the coolness, Barbara would be the first to tell her.
Just to prove that Miss Cassie wasn't the saint everyone
thought her to be! Huh! Some saint, with a temper like
that. She could have had Cassie up for assault and battery
if she had a mind to. Highly indignant, Barbara drifted
off to sleep, too upset by the emotional trauma she had
experienced to be able to read even a page of that great
literary masterpiece *Jane Eyre*, the story of another put-
upon soul!

❦

Listening to her younger sister's rhythmic breathing,
Cassie gave a relieved sigh. She thought Barbara was
never going to go to sleep tonight. Of course she was
acting the martyr now and, knowing *her*, Cassie suspected
it could last for weeks. A myriad emotions surged through
Cassie as she lay in the dark waiting to be sure that her
sister was well and truly asleep. Although her anger had
sustained her through the evening, now, typically, she
was beginning to feel guilty about hitting Barbara. She
really had made a show of herself, losing her temper like
that. Why couldn't she be like Laura, who was excellent
at asserting herself and expressing her anger rationally,
instead of losing control and becoming inarticulate and
resorting to violence. Pitiful behaviour and not very adult,
she chastised herself. She had really demeaned herself
and Barbara would rub it in for weeks.

Resentment overcame guilt. To think that Nora had
intended to let her go to the party after all. If Jack had
been able to persuade her to let Cassie go *before* they had
gone to the wake, there wouldn't have been any row.
Nora could be dead unreasonable at times. Well, there

was nothing for it! She was going to that party, come hell or high water. She couldn't be in much worse trouble than she was in already. John was going to help her getting out and getting in. They had made their plans earlier in the evening. He was a real pet. It had been his suggestion that she go to the party, despite the fact that her mother had forbidden her to go.

"It's only because Ma's in a tizzy over blooming Aunt Elsie. She's not herself. Otherwise she'd have let you go." So John rationalised as they sat feeling sorry for themselves over mugs of hot chocolate at bedtime. "Martin and me weren't even allowed to go to the scouts."

"Martin and I," corrected Cassie glumly, wishing that Aunt Elsie could be transported to another planet.

"Why don't you go anyway? You can climb out my bedroom window and no one will know. And I'll let you in whenever you get back."

Cassie's eyes widened. The thought had never crossed her mind. It all seemed so simple. Slip into John's room when everybody was asleep, climb out his bedroom window and climb back in when she got home. No one would be any the wiser.

"What if Martin wakes up?"

"He won't!" John assured her. "He sleeps through thunderstorms and everything. Anyway, he's not a snitch. He wouldn't tell!"

"What if Barbara wakes up to go to the loo and sees I'm gone?"

"Hmm..." John pondered this trickier one. "We'll just have to put a dummy in the bed. You know your big old teddy?" Cassie nodded. When she was a child the teddy had been bigger than her. "Put a nightdress on it and put it curled up in the middle of the bed, with the head under the pillow. No one will ever know the difference."

"Thanks!" grinned Cassie, beginning to accept the feasibility of the plan. More than anything she wanted to go to that party, even if she spent only a couple of hours at it. She really would love to see Donie Kiely, with his gorgeous brown eyes that always seemed to be looking at her lately. Even Aileen had commented on it.

"He fancies you, I'm telling you, girl. You'd better do something about it at this party." She was currently having a hot and heavy romance with a soldier she had met at a barbecue on the beach. In fact, she had told the girls earnestly, this was "it." Her soldier was fast becoming the love of her life and she was seriously contemplating going the whole way with him. Cassie and Laura envied Aileen her courage. They would never have the nerve to do it, they decided after long and serious discussion; Laura because of her elder sister Jill, who was an unmarried mother, banned from the family home by her father, and finding the going tough. She had belatedly discovered that her pilot boyfriend, the father of her child, was married and already the father of two. He just didn't want to know about Jill and her baby.

Cassie knew that she'd feel so guilty it wouldn't be worth it. She'd never be able to look Nora in the face again. Nora was terribly strict about matters like that. Religion, mothers—nothing like that would put a halt to Aileen's gallop once she made up her mind about something. Aileen always had the courage of her convictions and Cassie and Laura admired her greatly. Unfortunately, Aileen's soldier wouldn't be at the party tonight but Donie Kiely would, and Cassie was determined that for once she was going to do exactly what she wanted to do. And that was go to that party. Nora, Barbara and Aunt Elsie could just take a back seat for once. Cassie had only one life to lead and if she didn't take her chances, she had only herself to blame.

As unobtrusively as possible she took her new jumper and trousers from the cupboard while Barbara was tidying out her wardrobe, giving deep dramatic sighs in the process. Casually, Cassie gathered up her make-up and brought it into the bathroom for when she would need it later. She had a quick five-minute shower and got into her dressing-gown, making a great show about creaming her face. She hoped to God that Barbara would go to sleep early. After all, it was Friday night and she might decide to read all night. One of their rules about sharing the bedroom concerned what time the lights were switched out. After years of listening to their arguing, Nora had decreed that on weekdays the bedside lights were to be switched off at midnight, but on Friday and Saturday nights they could leave their individual lights on as long as they wished. Sometimes Barbara could be real mean about it. Knowing that Cassie had to get up to work in the shop on Saturday, she might read until three in the morning, leaving Cassie silently cursing under the bedclothes, waiting for the blessed darkness.

If Barbara decided to have one of her marathon read-ins, Cassie could forget about going to the party. She decided to do her homework to take her mind off her problem. Sitting on her bed, she tried to engross herself in the joys of Orwell's *Animal Farm*, one of the books on her exam course, and one which she loathed. She was sorely tempted to take out a romantic novel she had just started, called *Sullivan's Reef*, where the heroine had just been kissed by a devastatingly handsome older man, a deep bruising kiss that left her breathless. Her first French kiss! It was so romantic. Cassie couldn't wait to get back to it. She had had a lucky escape up in the library earlier on when Mother Perpetua had nearly caught her reading it instead of conjugating her French verbs. That would have been a disaster: Perpetua was forever confiscating romantic novels from the class and they never got them back, and Cassie *had* to find out what happened next in *Sullivan's Reef*. It was a treat she would look forward to tomorrow night, she decided, getting stuck into an appraisal of Napoleon's character. At least if she had some of her homework done, she'd enjoy the party even better and it would take her mind off the waiting.

For once, the gods were with her. Barbara, still giving heartfelt sighs, decided to put out her light and have an early night, worn out by the traumas of the evening. Cassie waited a little while, finished her Irish poetry question and then slid into bed and put out her light. Shortly afterwards she could hear Nora and Jack going to bed themselves. Across the room, Barbara breathed deeply and evenly. As quietly as she could, Cassie slipped her nightdress over Big Teddy's head, arranged him in the middle of the bed, placed the pillow over his head and softly padded out the door with her clothes under her arm. Looking back she could see that he made a nice satisfying mound. Swiftly she dressed, applied her make-up and, carrying her shoes in her hand, slipped into John's room. Her brother, heavy-eyed but still awake, was waiting for her. "I thought you were never coming! Come on," he whispered dramatically, "the coast is clear. Have you got your coat? It's getting a bit windy outside."

"Yeah, I've got everything," Cassie whispered back.

"I've put my bike just under the windowsill. You can go on that if you like. It will save you having to walk in those high-heeled things." He opened the window and she climbed up on the sill.

"Thanks, John, you're a brick," Cassie said, planting

a kiss on the side of his cheek, much to his disgust.

"Aw, Cassie, I bet I'm covered in lipstick. Now listen carefully. The plan is: I'll leave the window open a little bit and when you get back, stick your head in and wake me up and I'll help to haul you in. OK?"

"OK," agreed Cassie as she swung her legs over the window-ledge and slid to the ground. "See you later."

"Have a good time," John whispered, giving a mighty yawn. Cassie carried the bike over the grass, although she wasn't too worried about her parents hearing, as their room was at the other side of the house. A bark that came from behind her made her nearly jump out of her skin. Drat! Mr Spock, the family collie, so named because of his rather pointed ears, came galloping out of his kennel to investigate. Recognising Cassie, he gave a howl of excitement. Adventure beckoned. His nose quivered, his tail wagged and he barked excitedly. "Shut up, Spock!" Cassie hissed. "Back inside." She pointed a stern finger. Spock's ears drooped. Big brown eyes gazed at her appealingly. A dog and a bike! What kind of a way was that to go to a party? Still, it was better than not going. "Come on," she said, laughing in the breeze. Mounting the bike she sallied forth along the coast road with the moon shining silver on the waves that crashed against the shore and Spock loping along beside her.

CHAPTER SIX

"Where were you?" shrieked Aileen, catching sight of Cassie. The new arrival was being ushered into the packed sitting-room by the hostess, Kate Rooney.

"It's about time!" Laura exclaimed, appearing through

the throng.

"I nearly didn't get here." Cassie divested herself of her coat, ran her fingers through her hair and grinned at her friends. Aileen, dressed to thrill in shocking-pink bell-bottoms, surveyed her admiringly. "Wait till Donie Kiely sees you," she teased. "He'll probably ask you to marry him on the spot!"

Cassie blushed. "Sshhh! People will hear you. Is he here?"

Aileen affected an American drawl. "He sure as hell is, honey."

Kate arrived with a glass. "Here, Cassie, relax, have some punch. I'll be serving supper soon," she smiled, gliding off to talk to Margy Kane and her boyfriend.

"Wow! Punch! How sophisticated," murmured Cassie, who couldn't in a million years imagine Nora allowing her to have an unsupervised party, complete with punch. She took a sip. It was delicious.

"Why were you so late?" Laura asked. Cassie gave them the details.

"Tough times ahead, girl!" laughed Aileen, who knew Aunt Elsie of old. Aunt Elsie did not approve of Aileen O'Shaughnessy, ever since the time she had swanned into Jordans' in a pair of purple hot-pants during one of Elsie's visits. Definitely not a fit person for her niece to be associating with. The more disapproving Aunt Elsie got, the more outrageously Aileen behaved.

The last time she had visited, shortly after the famous retreat, Aunt Elsie had been eager to know how the girls had got on, and enquired if it had been of great spiritual benefit to them. "Wouldn't it be a great blessing if Cassie or Barbara or Irene became a nun or one of the boys became a priest?" Elsie had said piously. Cassie nearly choked at this, and Aileen and Laura, unable to contain themselves, guffawed at the idea. Aunt Elsie was furious. "What is so funny, pray?" she asked icily. "In my day it was a great honour to get the call from God. But, then, in my day we were properly brought up," she declared, sweeping regally out of the sitting-room to tell Nora of their impudence. They had been made to apologise and Aunt Elsie told Cassie later that evening that Laura and Aileen were not suitable companions for her as she had seen a terrible deterioration in her niece's behaviour since she had started consorting with the pair of them. For ages after, the girls teased Cassie unmercifully, calling her "Sister Cassie."

"You'll need something a bit stronger than punch to cope with Saint Elsie," Aileen smirked, leading Cassie to a corner of the room. "I fecked a few bottles of stout and a few fags from the wake. My contribution to the party."

"You did not!" Cassie was half-shocked, half-amused.

"Sure, there was loads of stuff there, and nobody was taking any notice of me, so I slipped a few into the pockets of my trenchcoat. I mean, I did say the Rosary and things while I was there," she added plaintively.

"Of course you did," said Laura soothingly. "Hurry on and open the bottles!"

It was a wonderful party. They sang and danced and devoured the lovely salad buffet that was spread out for them in the big dining-room, passing around plates of crispy cocktail sausages and melt-in-the-mouth sausage rolls. Kate Rooney certainly knew how to give a party, the girls agreed between mouthfuls of food. Cassie filled a paper plate with goodies and brought it out to Mr Spock, who was patiently guarding her bike. He wagged his tail so hard with delight that it was a wonder it didn't fall off. When someone put on Roy Orbison singing "Pretty Woman" and Donie Kiely asked Cassie to dance, she felt as if she had died and gone to heaven. Tall, dark and handsome Donie Kiely, who could have had his pick of any of the girls of Port Mahon, was dancing with her and asking for the next dance. All the worries about climbing back in the window later on, and guilt about deceiving her parents, slipped away and she danced a slow set in Donie's arms and wished the night would never end.

At around one-fifteen, Kate's parents arrived back from Dublin and everybody prepared to leave. Donie had already asked Cassie if he could walk her home and she said she had her bike and her dog and asked if that mattered. He laughed his good-humoured laugh and said it was no problem whatsoever. She really liked him, she decided, as they walked along the sea road, with Donie wheeling the bike for her and Mr Spock trotting demurely alongside, full to the gills with all the food he had eaten and ready for a nice cosy snooze in his kennel. It had got much colder and wilder and gusts of wind swirled around them. The sea was white-capped and foamy but Cassie didn't care; she was as happy as a lark.

Donie was studying English and history at UCD, he told her, and was planning to teach when he had his degree and H Dip. He lived in digs near the university during the week but came back home to Port Mahon at the weekends to help his father, who was a market-gardener like Jack. They had so much in common, really, she thought happily, wishing that the walk home would never end. He was so easy to talk to and when he smiled at her with those gorgeous brown eyes it was magic. He had the most beautiful manners too, walking on the outside of the footpath, wheeling the bike for her. Andy, her previous boyfriend, had never been so considerate. It gave her a nice glow. A thought struck her. He was so mannerly he would probably want her key to open the front door for her. How would she explain about it being locked. How on earth could she climb in the window in front of him. Hell! What a dilemma!

Her bubble of happiness burst with a bang. They were almost at the entrance to the farm. Spock, anxious to get to sleep, galloped on ahead.

"Is this it?" Donie smiled.

"This is it," Cassie murmured, coming to a halt. "Donie...mmm...I won't ask you in for coffee." She continued hastily, "It's a bit late and...um...well, my mother's a little bit old-fashioned." Oh this was awful, she could feel her cheeks burning in the dark. She had never felt so flustered in her life.

Donie smiled down at her. "She sounds just like mine," he reassured her. "Don't worry about it. I'll see you to the door, anyway."

"No, no, honestly, this is fine, it's just a minute up the drive." She was practically babbling now.

"Are you sure? It's a bit dark."

"It's not at all, I'm well used to it." They smiled at each other.

"Can I see you again?"

Cassie couldn't believe he was saying the words she had been longing to hear all evening. "I'd like that," she answered shyly.

"Tomorrow night?"

Cassie laughed. "My Aunt Elsie is coming tomorrow so I'd say I'll be expected to entertain her. Sunday?" she asked hopefully.

"Will I come and collect you?"

"Could I meet you in town instead? It would suit me better, with my aunt and all," she added lamely. It would be too hard to think up explanations if Donie came calling to the door. "How about Kentucky Fried Chicken on Main Street? We could have coffee?"

"That would be great," Donie agreed enthusiastically. "We could go to the pictures if you like. I usually go back to Dublin on Sunday night but I could leave it until Monday morning this time." Mentally, Cassie heaved a sigh of relief. All she had to do now was climb in through John's window and she was made up.

Bending his head, Donie kissed her lightly on the lips. "Goodnight, Cassie. Thanks for a lovely evening. I'll see you on Sunday at seven."

"I'll be looking forward to it." She smiled up at him, her heart dancing with happiness. It was nice to have a boyfriend again like her friends. Although Laura and Aileen were great about including her in everything, sometimes she felt a bit of a gooseberry. They would be delighted for her; they knew she had fancied Donie for ages. She watched Donie striding back the way they had come. He turned and waved and she waved back and watched until he was enveloped by the night.

She sped across the lawn up to the house and over to John's window. She left her brother's bike where Donie had leant it against the gate-post. It would be fine there until the morning.

Cassie looked and looked again and her heart sank. Someone had closed the window. It must have been rattling because of the wind and Jack had probably come in and closed it. Damn! Gently she tapped against the window-pane. "John! John! Let me in!" she said as loudly as she dared. Thank heavens Jack and Nora slept at the other side of the house. She knocked again, louder this time. Not a budge out of John. What in God's name was she going to do? It was getting really stormy and it wouldn't be long until it rained. She hoped Donie got home before it started. She knocked again, feeling quite desperate, and froze as she saw the light go on in the adjoining bedroom.

Oh goodnight, this is it, she thought forlornly as Barbara's face appeared at the bedroom window. She caught sight of Cassie and her mouth dropped. The sisters stared at each other and Cassie waited for Barbara to rush into Nora's and Jack's room. Instead, the younger girl opened the side window. "If Mam found out about this, you'd be killed," Barbara lectured tartly as Cassie began to haul herself in. It was more awkward than she had anticipated and Barbara had to grab her under the arms and pull. Finally she was in and Barbara closed the window. Cassie waited for her younger sister to say, "I'm telling in the morning," but Barbara said gruffly, "I won't tell, if that's what you're afraid of."

Cassie couldn't believe her ears. "Thanks, Barbara," she muttered uncomfortably. "And...umm...I'm sorry I slapped your face and pulled your hair. I lost my temper." She added magnanimously, "If you want to wear any of my clothes, you can," remembering the remark Barbara had passed about how Aileen was a better sister than she was.

"Oh!" Barbara was taken aback by the generosity of the peace-offering, but, being Barbara, she didn't waste a minute capitalising on it. "That jumper you're wearing is nice. It's new, isn't it? Could I wear it to the disco on Sunday night?"

Typical, thought Cassie to herself. But tonight she didn't care, Barbara could have whatever she wanted. "You can have it, but just be careful of it. It cost me a fortune."

"I will. Goodnight, Cassie."

"Goodnight, Barbara," Cassie echoed, slipping out of

her clothes and removing Big Teddy from the bed. Sliding down between the smooth sheets, she pulled the patchwork quilt up around her and yawned in the darkness. It had been an extraordinary day. So much had happened, she thought sleepily. Who would have thought it would all have turned out so well.

❧

Aunt Elsie arrived on the twelve-thirty train on Saturday and Jack collected her. Her first comment as she walked through the door of the sitting-room where Nora and the family were waiting to greet her was that the picture of the Sacred Heart was crooked, and would Jack kindly straighten it, as it was a sign of disrespect to the Almighty. She had started as she meant to go on!

The following morning, the Sunday of the planned date, Aunt Elsie awoke feeling extremely poorly. Her tummy was at her and she declared she would stay in bed for the day and drink only hot milk with pepper. Aunt Elsie was such a demanding patient. "Cassie, would you get me my Rosary beads; they've fallen off the bed." Then, "Would you get me a cold flannel and hold it to my forehead. I think I'm getting a migraine." And later, when the migraine had passed but a cold seemed to be developing, "Would you make me a hot drink with cloves and lemons and bring me a spoonful of honey. My throat is ticklish." By five-thirty, Cassie was like a cat on hot coals. She hadn't even had a chance to wash her hair, which had gone all flat after the wind on the night of the party. They *couldn't* expect her to stay in tonight. Hadn't she stayed in all last night to play cards with Aunt Elsie? Well, tonight she was going out with Donie, come what may! Fortunately, exhaustion overcame Aunt Elsie and Cassie was delighted when rumbling snores were heard from Irene's bedroom, which Aunt Elsie had taken over for the duration of her visit. Irene was sleeping on a camp-bed in her sisters' bedroom, much to her dismay. She missed all her cuddly toys and posters.

With her hair washed and her make-up on, Cassie began to feel much better and her spirits lightened as she prepared to depart. "Just meeting the girls," she said airily, poking her head around the sitting-room door where Nora and Jack were endeavouring to relax for a while. She wasn't exactly telling fibs, Cassie reassured herself; she undoubtedly would bump into Laura and Aileen at some stage in the evening.

"Don't be too late," Nora warned.

"I won't, Mam. See you later."

"Enjoy yourself," her father smiled.

"I will, Pops," Cassie promised. He was the best in the world, she thought fondly as she headed for the front door.

"Cassie!" A faint voice came from the direction of Irene's bedroom. Drat! thought Cassie. Please God, don't let her be awake. Let her sleep for another five minutes.

"Cassie!" The autocratic voice definitely sounded stronger. Cassie was rooted to the spot. Why do you do things like this to *me*? she argued silently with the Almighty. She couldn't waste any more time. If she didn't go now, she'd be late. Donie might think she had stood him up!

She was just about to slip out the front door when Aunt Elsie appeared at the bedroom door. With her long silver hair braided and her high-necked red flannelette night-gown falling in folds to her bony feet, she looked like someone from another century.

"Did you not hear me calling you?" she demanded. "I'm feeling much better. I'd like some tea and toast and a soft-boiled egg before you go off out gallivanting. It's a fine thing to think that you make the effort to come and see your relations and they couldn't be bothered to stay in and spend an hour or two with you."

Cassie almost burst with frustration. She didn't want to draw attention to herself by saying to Nora that she was in a hurry. Nora would only say, "The girls will wait for you; you're often much later going out." Cassie didn't want her mother becoming suspicious. She couldn't say she was meeting a fellow as Nora would want to know where she had met him, and she'd be getting into deep waters and big fibs after her unlawful attendance at the party. Maybe now that she and Barbara were sort of reconciled, her younger sister might oblige in preparing Aunt Elsie's tea. "I'll ask Barbara to do it," Cassie said placatingly. "I'm in a bit of a hurry."

"That's lovely," Elsie snapped. "In too much of a hurry to get a bite to eat for a poor sick woman! Barbara will burn the toast; she always does. It will take only five minutes of your precious time and after that I won't impose on you again." The tone was mega-martyr, as Elsie shuffled back into her room.

By the time Cassie had prepared her aunt's tea, she was frantic. She was dead late. She had planned to make a calm, cool, collected entrance into the restaurant, having taken her time getting there. Now there was nothing for it but to borrow John's bike. The chain on her own was broken and it was being repaired. So much for dignity—she'd have to go on her first date on a bike! Not a bit sophisticated, but what could she do? But then she discovered that John was out on his bike! All that lay in the shed was Jack's old crock and Nora's High Nellie.

Taking her life in her hands, Cassie mounted her mother's antique and wobbled precariously down the drive with Spock barking encouragement. The saddle was so high that her feet barely reached the pedals and she knew one false move could do her a lot of damage. Grimly concentrating on avoiding the potholes, she headed in the direction of Port Mahon. Less than three-quarters of a mile along the road, High Nellie got a puncture and with a malevolent hiss the tyre went flat, the bike wobbled and Cassie landed in the ditch.

Almost in tears she picked herself up, dusted herself down as best she could and started to walk the rest of the way.

Donie was waiting patiently, despite the fact that she was over an hour late. "I knew you weren't the kind of girl to stand a fellow up," he said calmly, as she, hot and flustered, tried to explain. They were too late to go to the pictures so they had coffee and cream cakes. Donie mended the puncture and they went walking along the beach in the moonlight before he took her home.

After that they started to date regularly and once Aunt Elsie had left and equilibrium was restored in the Jordan household, she took Donie home and introduced him to her parents. They liked him immensely. For her seventeenth birthday he took her to dinner in The Windmill in Skerries, a gorgeous, intimate restaurant, where he presented her with a gold chain, the first real piece of jewellery she had ever owned. Cassie was sure that she could never in her life be so happy again.

CHAPTER SEVEN

"Look, Barbara, make things easy for yourself. Pops taught me this trick once and I never forgot the names of the

Great Lakes," Cassie instructed her younger sister, who was frantically swotting for a geography exam the next day and could not for the life of her memorise the difficult and unfamiliar names.

"I just hate geography," moaned Barbara, sucking the end of her pen furiously.

"Yes, well, if you learn this you'll never have any trouble with the Great Lakes at least. Just think of the word 'homes.'"

"Homes?" Barbara echoed in confusion.

"Yes," explained Cassie patiently. "'Homes' gives you the initials of each of the lakes. Huron, Ontario, Michigan, Erie, Superior. Simple!"

"Gosh, that's good. If we get that question tomorrow, I'm away on a hack!" exclaimed Barbara. "Thanks, Cassie."

"No problem," her elder sister assured her. She smiled to herself. For all Barbara's sophisticated airs and graces, she could be quite the child sometimes, when she was being herself and not projecting an image.

Cassie was making a huge effort to get on better with her sister. And so far, touch wood, it was paying off. After the dreadful row they had had six months before, things had changed between them, and for the better. It had really cleared the air, that row. Cassie had never realised just how much Barbara had felt ignored by her. It wasn't a deliberate thing. Cassie, busy with her own concerns, had her own set of friends. They went places and did things together and, quite honestly, she never gave her younger sister a thought. As far as she was concerned, Barbara was a nuisance who was always wanting to wear her clothes and make-up, and who never kept her half of the room tidy.

The night of the row had marked something of a turning-point in their relationship, Cassie mused, as she watched her sister studying her geography. She had made the effort to get on with Barbara, lending her her clothes, asking her and Judy, Aileen's sister, to go out with the gang occasionally, much to the delight of the two younger girls. It was great to be part of the "in" crowd and nobody was more "in" in Port Mahon than Cassie, Laura, Aileen and their gang, Barbara and Judy happily agreed. It made them feel so grown-up to be part of the scene, and Barbara, in particular, revelled in it.

It was now almost the end of May. Very soon Cassie would be sitting the Leaving Certificate, her final exams before leaving school to embark on a whole new adventurous life. Although they hadn't broached the subject at home, Cassie, Laura and Aileen had agreed that as soon as they possibly could they were going to get a flat together in Dublin. Once they were working, there'd be no stopping them! Of course, a lot depended on how they did in their exams. If the results were good, the world was their oyster. Cassie had her heart set on studying architecture. Laura wanted to study law, and Aileen, who was a leading light in the Port Mahon Dramatic Society, was going to be an actress! It was all so exciting, they just couldn't wait. In the meantime, the intrepid trio were engrossed in their studies, much to the relief of Mother Perpetua and the teaching staff of Saint Imelda's.

Nearly finished, Cassie told herself as she completed the question on Yeats.

Think where man's glory most begins and ends,
And say my glory was I had such friends. Discuss.

It had been the easiest question in the world to answer. All she had to do was think of Laura and Aileen and Donie and she knew exactly what Yeats was talking about. She was so lucky to have friends like them. She smiled as she thought of Donie. They were still going out together and she was crazy about him. Thank God tomorrow was Friday and he'd be home from college for the weekend. Their reunions were lovely, something to look forward to when he was coming home and something to look back on when he was gone.

Packing away her school books, Cassie felt incredibly lighthearted. Soon her exams would be over and she'd be up in Dublin and she'd be able to see Donie several times a week instead of just at weekends. It would be just wonderful. She couldn't wait!

She'd miss school a lot though, she reflected, as she slipped out of her uniform. She had thoroughly enjoyed her years there, especially her last year as a sixth year. It was nice having the juniors regard you with respect and awe. It was nice having a kitchen to yourselves where you could cook lunch and sit gossiping with the others after years of dining in the noisy hurly-burly of the refectory. Sixth years were allowed to go down the town at lunchtime and often the girls from 6S treated themselves to a take-away from Macari's, which made the best chips in the country and which had a special offer that suited 6S down to the ground: buy twelve singles and get one free! They would return to the sixth years' kitchen, laden down with fish and chips, and make tons of hot buttered toast and pots of milky coffee and gossip and giggle to their hearts' content for the duration of their lunch-hour.

The teachers, too, now treated them as adults. Class discussions were lively and challenging, particularly those in the religion class with Sister Eileen, where they discussed social justice and social inequalities and Vatican Two. And, of course, love and sex and contraception and divorce, as they prepared to step out into the world to make their own choices and decisions.

Of course, some things never changed. Iron-willed Mother Perpetua had never forgiven them for their vulgar ditty and treated 6S as her sworn enemies in life. They were the devils' daughters as far as she was concerned. And what of the incorrigible Aileen O'Shaughnessy, possibly, in Mother Perpetua's view, the devil himself? Not even the mantle of dignified sixth year could quench her irrepressible spirit. Aileen was as wild as ever!

Her salvo at the beginning of sixth year had been a masterpiece. She discovered that Miss Marshall, who taught English to the first years, was out sick and that the group of timid newcomers were patiently awaiting a replacement. She appropriated a black gown, pulled her auburn tresses back in a severe bun and streaked her hair with chalk-dust, borrowed Una Hickey's thick-lensed glasses and strode into the classroom of the unfortunate first years. There she terrorised them for ten minutes before ordering them to present an essay to Mother Perpetua, their form nun and religious tutor, the following morning. The essay was entitled "The apostles' wives were the first deserted wives. Discuss."

Perpetua was spitting with fury as she tried in vain to discover the identity of the mysterious, white-haired bespectacled teacher. Of course, she had her suspicions but she could prove nothing. Much of her wrath fell on the hapless first years, who practically to a girl had agreed with the premise concerning the deserted wives and who were soundly berated as heathens by Mother Perpetua for doing so!

No, indeed, Aileen had not changed and Cassie hoped she never would. She slipped a sweater on and walked down to the kitchen to tell her mother she was going over to Five-acre-field to see her dad. She had been so busy lately, stuck in her books morning, noon and night. Well, tonight she felt like a break. She wanted some fresh air to clear the cobwebs from her brain. A good brisk walk was just what she needed. She hadn't gone walking with Jack for a while and she was looking forward to a nice long chat with him.

It was a lovely early summer's evening. The birds were singing uproariously. The sun, now beginning to sink low in the sky, was reflected in the hundreds of panes of glass in Jack's glasshouses. He wasn't in the glasshouses tonight, though. His farm manager, Pat, and several of the seasonal workers were looking after the ripening tomatoes while Jack was spreading seaweed on his early potatoes. He had gone down to the beach on his tractor after the last storm and got a load of rich pungent seaweed to nurture his crop. It was, in his opinion, the best of fertiliser. Cassie had heard him tell Nora at lunch that that's what he'd be doing tonight. Her father was such a hard worker, Cassie reflected. But he loved what he did. He was a real son of the outdoors.

She had a nice cool bottle of beer for him and a couple of thick corned-beef-and-mustard sandwiches. He'd be delighted with them; they were his favourite. Whistling gaily, Cassie climbed the gate to the field that ran parallel to the road she was walking on. Behind it lay the big field every one called Five-acre-field. Strange that she couldn't hear the tractor. He'd said he'd be here! She breathed deeply, inhaling the tangy sea air, enjoying her walk. Port Mahon was a great place to live. A nice seaside town, and not too far from the bright lights of the capital.

The grass was a really luscious green, she thought in admiration as she strode briskly on her way. Her father hadn't planted this field; he was leaving it fallow this year so it would produce a better crop next year. The big dark-green hedgerow ahead of her was obstructing her view of the adjoining field but she could see the gate was open, so Jack must be in there. Maybe he was having a problem with the tractor, as it definitely wasn't running. All she could hear was the birds singing and the raucous scream of the seagulls as they circled overhead.

Entering Five-acre-field her heart almost leapt out of her body and a soundless scream rose to her lips at the sight that met her eyes.

"Pops! Oh Poppa, I'm coming!" Cassie cried, as she dropped the basket with Jack's supper in it and ran faster than she had ever run in her life.

CHAPTER EIGHT

"I'm coming, Poppa. Oh God! God! Please let him be all right," she beseeched the Almighty with terror in her heart. Nothing could happen her big strong father, the one they all looked up to, the one they all ran to when they were in trouble. Fathers were supposed to be invincible, weren't they?

Maybe he had walked away from it. Maybe he had gone to get help. Please let that be what had happened.

She found her father lying beside the tractor. He was unconscious, a trickle of blood flowing down the side of his face where he had hit a sharp-edged stone on impact with the ground. At least he was breathing, she thought frantically, trying to rouse him.

"Wake up, Pops, it's OK. I'm here, Cassie's here. Someone will be here in a minute. Come on now, Poppa, wake up!" God! What should she do? She couldn't bear to leave him there all by himself but she'd have to go and get help. Sobbing with fright, she kissed him softly on the cheek. "I'm going to get help, Pops, I'll be back in a minute. Please wake up and tell me you're all right," she pleaded as she loosened the shirt buttons at his neck and turned his head sideways. "I love you, you're the best father in the world. Please wake up. Please!" Jack remained unconscious. After saying an act of contrition in his ear, Cassie kissed him again and ran as fast as she could towards the road. Five-acre-field had never seemed so huge and her legs felt as though they were full of lead. Although it seemed like an age, Cassie was very fit and it took her only a couple of minutes. She was running back the way she had come, towards the glasshouses, when Brendan Doyle, the postmaster, drove past. Cassie waved wildly and Brendan stopped.

"Quick! Quick, get help! Poppa's fallen off the tractor and he's unconscious."

Brendan blanched. "I'm on my way to the telephone. You go back to him," he instructed.

Again she had to make the run across two fields and again it seemed to take for ever. Jack looked ashen, and Cassie had never felt more scared as she knelt beside him, afraid to take him in her arms in case he had spinal injuries. "I love you. I love you. I love you," she told him over and over, rubbing his hands between hers to keep them warm. It seemed like an eternity but in reality it was only about twenty minutes before Brendan came to help with Pat and the lads from the glasshouses. In the distance, the urgent wail of an ambulance siren broke the stillness of the balmy evening.

Nora arrived in the station-wagon, white-faced with shock, just as the ambulance men were lifting Jack into the ambulance. John was with her, trying to be brave, his lower lip trembling as he struggled to compose himself and act the way he thought a man should. After all, he was thirteen and the eldest son.

"You go in the ambulance with Jack. I'll follow with Cassie and John," Brendan offered kindly. And Nora, dazed, did as he suggested. A neighbour was taking care of Irene and Martin, and Barbara was over at Judy's. Cassie asked Brendan to pick her up; Barbara would be wondering where everybody was if she came home to an empty house. Her younger sister nearly died when Cassie, in a trembling voice, told her what had happened.

They arrived at the hospital to find Nora standing anxiously in the casualty waiting-room. She was shaking and Cassie immediately went and put her arms around her. "Come on, Mam, sit down. We'll get you a cup of tea. It will be all right now. Don't worry, the doctors and nurses will take care of Poppa." Her mother's eyes brimmed with tears, her shoulders slumped. Cassie was dismayed at the effect the last few hours were having on Nora. The only time her mother was ever fazed was when Aunt Elsie was coming. Apart from that, Cassie had never seen her other than in total control of any situation, even an emergency.

Looking at her now, quite distraught with worry, Cassie faced for the first time the fact that her mother was not the omnipotent being her daughter had always imagined her. Nora was experiencing exactly the same fears and anxieties as her children. It grieved Cassie to know that she could never again look on her mother the way a child does. From that moment, it was Cassie who would do the protecting and Nora who would be the protected one. It was the moment Cassie left childhood and carefree days behind her and assumed the mantle of responsibility of the eldest child.

Eventually they were allowed into the intensive care department, where Jack lay in a small room which could be monitored from the nurses' station. It seemed to Cassie that her great bear of a father had shrunk, as he lay motionless and grey under the starched hospital sheets. He was in a coma, the doctor informed Nora gently, after a brain haemorrhage. He said the medical term was aneurysm. Jack's condition was critical.

Watching her mother gently stroking Jack's hand, talking softly to him, Cassie realised for the first time that Jack and Nora had a relationship that was quite apart from being parents to the five of them. She had never thought of her mother and father as a couple who had once dated as she and Donie dated. It was strange to see them in this light and her heart went out to Nora. She was really devoted to Jack. It showed in so many little ways: the way she had his slippers warming at the fire in the winter; the way she always gave him the crispest piece of crackling of the roast pork; the way she fussed, making him change his clothes if he got a drenching; the way she got up every morning to make him a mug of tea. All the years of doing these little things. And all the years Cassie had assumed that was what mothers did. It had never crossed her mind to think that was what love was all about. With her head stuck in romantic novels, love to her had been great passion, flowers and chocolates and romantic walks, such as she enjoyed with Donie. All the time her mother and father were deeply loving each other and she had never even noticed.

"Come on, now, Jack love. Wake up for me, now. You've slept long enough. Oh Jack! Jack!" Cassie felt a huge lump in her throat as Nora's voice faltered. At the other side of the bed, John, his cowslick sticking up even more than normal, his face white and tense, was holding Jack's other hand.

"Come on, Pops, you've got to get well. I helped the lads with the side-shooting of the tomato plants, in number one glasshouse, so we're all ready to go into number two!" The doctor had told them to talk to Jack and John was doing his best.

Barbara was sobbing into her handkerchief and Cassie put her arm around her. "Stop crying, Barbara, it's upsetting for Mam!" she whispered, longing to break down and howl herself.

"I'm frightened, Cassie," Barbara gulped.

So am I, Cassie screamed silently as fear made her insides icy-cold. But she said nothing, just gave Barbara a reassuring hug and went to stand at Nora's shoulder. Periodically the nurses came in and asked them to leave as they performed tests on Jack to see if he were responding at all. They were terribly kind, bringing them tea to the little room where they waited, and, as Cassie realised, looking back, preparing them for the worst with great sensitivity. "It's not looking too good," one of the sisters gently told Nora and her, and Cassie realised with a numbing sense of shock that her father was going to die. Jack couldn't die! she wanted to scream. He was her father! He was invincible. It was all a terrible nightmare. Soon she would wake up and see his smiling ruddy face at the bedroom door saying in his cheerful way, "Rise and shine. The weather's fine," as he always did in the morning, calling her to get up.

In disbelief, she watched the hospital chaplain anoint her father. The family knelt beside the bed and said a Rosary, praying fervently that God might change his mind about taking Jack from them. There were millions of other people out there, Cassie thought angrily, murderers, rapists; why not pick on them? Jack was a good man. A great husband and father, a fine friend and neighbour. No one was ever turned away empty-handed from Jack Jordan's door.

Please God, don't let my daddy die. Cassie buried her head in her hands and tried to stop the tears that were streaming down her face. She heard her father give what sounded like a deep sigh. Her eyes met her mother's and she saw frantic fear reflected in them. "Jack! Jack!" Her mother was on her feet. The nurse felt for a pulse she knew was not there.

"I'm sorry, Mrs Jordan," she said gently, as Nora sobbed "No! No!"

Just as she thought she was going to scream, Cassie caught sight of John's face. He looked as if he were about to faint. Gripping his father's hand tightly, he was saying, "Don't worry, Pops, I'll take care of Mam and the girls. Don't you worry about anything,"

Cassie thought her heart was going to break. "Why?" she asked the priest, in utter bewilderment. "Why?"

"Your father has gone to his eternal rest. To a wonderful new life. It is God's will," the priest said consolingly.

"If that's God's way of showing his love for us I hate him," Cassie replied bitterly as she took her sobbing mother in her arms.

How she got through the next few days she never knew. Everybody turned to her. Nora seemed unable to make even the simplest decision and it was left to Cassie to organise everything. The funeral had to be arranged, death notices put in the paper, relatives informed. Strangely enough, it was Aunt Elsie who was her greatest support. It was Elsie who helped Nora pick out the suit that Jack was to be laid out in, and Elsie who baked tea-bracks and scones for when the neighbours called to pay their respects. It was Elsie who forced a glass of brandy down Nora's throat when her younger sister started to shake just before they went to the mortuary to say their last goodbyes to Jack.

Jack looked so peaceful in his coffin. He didn't even look fifty-six. He had been cut down in his prime. Cassie stood looking at him, unable to grasp the fact that he was dead and that she would never see him again. It was so unbelievable to think that this time yesterday he was alive and teasing her about her great romance and now he was cold, so cold and lifeless, with not a breath in his body. After kissing him for the last time, Cassie watched as they lowered the lid on her father's coffin and the physical pain of her grief was so intense that she cried out. Beside her, Aunt Elsie, stony-faced, squeezed her hand. Cassie sat through the prayers in the church, holding John's and Martin's hands, the boys trembling beside her. It was so hard to concentrate, so hard to believe that it was Jack who was lying in the coffin at the foot of the altar. Afterwards, a stream of friends and neighbours queued to shake hands with the family. Donie was among them, and squeezed her hand in support. When Laura and Aileen stood in front of her, tears streaming down their faces, she broke down. They held her close, sobbing as though their hearts would break.

Eventually they got back home. The house was so empty. Every minute Cassie expected her father to walk through the door, to hear his laughing voice saying as he always did, "Any chance of a cuppa?" Dozens of neighbours and friends called, as was the custom in the country, and she and Elsie were kept busy making tea and sandwiches. "The joys of being the eldest," Elsie said drily, as she made yet another pot of tea. Cassie smiled at her aunt and at that moment felt very close to her.

Later that night, when Nora had finally fallen into a sedated sleep and the others were in bed, Cassie sat with her aunt having a last cup of tea, reluctant to go to bed, knowing that they still had the ordeal of the funeral to go through.

Cassie spoke her thoughts aloud. "I just don't understand it."

Elsie looked up from one of the socks that she was darning. "You're not supposed to understand it, my girl, and if you get that into your head, believe me, it will be a great help to you in life." She bit off the thread and laid the sock neatly aside. "I know precisely what you are feeling, Cassie. I remember the terror I felt when my mother died. My mother was my greatest friend. I depended on her for everything. I was engaged, you know..."

Elsie's blue eyes glistened and a faraway look came into them. Cassie was amazed. She never knew that Aunt Elsie had been engaged. Had never thought of Aunt Elsie as having boyfriends, or romances. "I was young too, you know," Elsie sniffed, reading her thoughts. Cassie smiled. These last few days, she had come to realise that her aunt's bark was much worse than her bite.

"My beau was killed on D-Day during the last world war and I grieved so much I wanted to die myself. Why? I kept asking my mother. Why?" Elsie took Cassie's hand in hers. "My mother stood me in front of the picture of the Sacred Heart and said, 'I have no answer for you. He's the one who knows all things. You must put your trust in God because no one can carry their burdens alone. Thy will, not mine, be done, you must say to yourself when there is no understanding.'" Elsie smiled at her niece. "It took me a long, long time to learn the wisdom of her words, Cassie. I stopped fighting God and let him have his way and found my peace of mind. I'll pray that you and your mother and the family do the same. Now go to bed, it's late. You have to be brave for one more day and then you have to set your shoulders and get on with living."

Her aunt's words churned around Cassie's brain as she sat in the funeral car on the way to the church the following morning. She had not slept and felt utterly exhausted. It was a horrible dismal morning, misting rain. Beside her, Nora sat immobile, eyes staring unseeingly ahead. Cassie took her mother's hand in hers. It was damp and sweaty. "Are you all right?" she asked anxiously.

"I wish it were over."

"It will be soon," Cassie soothed.

What was Jack doing now, she wondered as she heard the priest tell the packed church what a loss her father would be to the community. Could he see what was going on? Had he met his mother and father? Were they waiting for him? Was there a life after death? Or was there nothing at all? If only she knew. If only he would give her some sign to say that he was all right. With a start she realised that the Mass was almost over. The priest was standing over the coffin. "May the angels lead you to the gates of paradise," he intoned. How beautiful, Cassie thought. May the angels lead you to the gates of paradise. What a comforting prayer. A sunbeam shone brightly through the stained-glass window above the altar and Cassie knew that it was a sign from Jack. When they left the church the sun continued to shine gloriously and she knew it was a sign from her Poppa. She just knew it.

Cassie held her mother tightly as they watched Jack's coffin slide into the grave. Ashes to ashes; dust to dust. No one ever escaped death. Laura and Aileen came over to her to sympathise, tears pouring down their cheeks. "Thanks for coming," Cassie said gratefully.

"Of course we'd come!" said Laura, who was deeply shocked by Jack's death. If her own father had died she wouldn't have been as upset.

"It's a pleasure!" exclaimed Aileen earnestly, unchar- acteristically at a loss for words. She realised what she had said and began to babble. "I didn't mean it's a pleasure. I meant...I mean of course I'd come—you're my best friend. Where else would I be?"

Cassie and Laura caught each other's eye and stared at the red-faced Aileen, whose sang-froid had totally deserted her. "Oh God! I've just put my size elevens in it," she said sheepishly. In spite of her trauma, Cassie couldn't help herself and gave a little giggle. Who else but Aileen would say "it's a pleasure" to come to a funeral?

"Idiot!" grinned Laura.

"I know! I know! Cassie, you know what I mean. I'm really so sorry."

"Of course I know what you mean. And I'm glad you're with me. It really helps. Please come back to the house."

Laura demurred. "Oh Cassie, we wouldn't like to impose."

"You wouldn't be imposing. You could help make the tea. Please come back with me. Donie'll be there as well. All the ould wans will be coming and I just can't face them again. If anyone else tells me God is merciful, I'll scream."

"Is Perpetua coming back?" enquired Aileen. A large contingent of the nuns had come to the funeral and no doubt one or two of them would come back to the house to pay their respects.

"You know Perpetua! As nosy as they come. Don't you know she'll be back."

"What an opportunity to put Brooklax in her tea!" murmured the incorrigible Aileen.

❦

Nora was devastated by her husband's death and all the family seemed to be turning to Cassie for consolation. Irene had taken it very badly and got a terrible asthma attack and didn't want to go to school at all, even after the doctor had said she was sufficiently recovered. Cassie tried to persuade the child that she should go back. She knew that because her father had died so suddenly, Irene was afraid that something might happen to her mother and she had always been a clingy child where Nora was concerned. This was understandable. But Cassie felt Nora should make her go to school and get on with it. Irene couldn't expect to go through her entire life being sheltered from its hard knocks.

Barbara, although still terribly upset and prone to bursting into tears, seemed to be coping quite well. Cassie thanked God for her younger sister's resilient nature. Although Barbara was grieving as much as the rest of them, Cassie knew that a little part of her enjoyed the attention of classmates and neighbours who were deeply shocked by the tragedy that had struck the Jordan family. Barbara insisted on wearing black, even to school, and acted the part of the tragic heroine superbly.

John seemed to grow up overnight. He did his chores and much more, and Cassie depended on him greatly.

Nora had decided to accept the offer of one of her neighbours to lease the farm from her. Now that Jack was gone, her heart wasn't in farming and, besides, the rent would be a good steady income. And she wouldn't have to be worrying about all the thousand and one things that are involved in running a big market-garden and farm combined. The neighbour assured John and Martin that they would be given summer work in the glasshouses if they wanted it, when he saw that the boys were upset at the thought of losing the farm.

"We're not losing it!" Cassie had assured them. "Mam's only leasing it for the time being because she doesn't feel up to running it herself at the moment. She can always decide not to renew the lease when the time comes and run it herself when the two of you are older and able to take over for her." This was a great comfort to John, who had always been extremely interested in working with his father. Martin, who was more interested in the methods of heating the glasshouses than the agricultural side, was relieved that he wouldn't have to go side-shooting tomatoes after school, although he knew he'd be stuck working on the farm during his summer holidays.

Over and over again, her mother would ask Cassie, "Did I make the right decision? Did I let Jack down by leasing the farm? Should I have tried to run it myself? Pat Kearns is a good foreman. He would have kept me on the right track."

Over and over again, Cassie would reassure her mother, "Mam, it was the right thing to do. The fruit-farm is still ours and you always have the option of not renewing the lease but for the time being you know it will be well looked after until you do decide to run it yourself. And this way you've got a steady income and you don't have to be worrying on that score. Pops would be very proud of the way you're handling things."

"I hope so!" Nora would weep and Cassie's heart ached for her distraught mother.

There had been so much to do in the weeks following Jack's death. His will had to be taken care of. Cassie had had to help her mother with a lot of business concerning his insurance policies and bank accounts. Fortunately Jack was an organised man and everything was fairly straightforward. Eventually all that remained to be done was for her father's clothes to be disposed of.

"Cassie, I can't do that," Nora sobbed. "Will you decide what to do with them and take care of them for me?" Cassie's heart sank. It was the one thing she dreaded. Getting rid of Jack's clothes was so final. Like banishing him from the home. At least with his clothes hanging in the wardrobe you could pretend that all was well and he was just out in the fields. Don't ask me to do it, she wanted to beg her mother. She was so weary. So tired of having to make decisions for everybody. But it was something that had to be done, this final thing that would really confirm that Jack was gone for ever.

In the end, Aunt Elsie came to her rescue. "I'll help you," she told her beleaguered niece over the telephone. "The sooner you do it the better for yourself and Nora. Meet me off the train. I'll stay for the weekend." They spent an afternoon sorting out Jack's belongings. The clothes that were good enough to give to the St Vincent de Paul they washed and ironed. The rest Elsie put in a refuse sack which Martin and John burned. Cassie cried her eyes out. She kept a plaid shirt, one of Jack's favourites, for herself. She could still get the scent of her father on it and she hugged it close, rubbing her cheek against its worn softness, whispering his name over and over. Nora kept her husband's dressing-gown.

CHAPTER NINE

Cassie sat her Leaving Certificate less than a month after Jack died. It was almost impossible to study but it was a relief in a way to go back to school and try and get some revision done for her exams. All the teachers and nuns were very sympathetic to her—even Mother Perpetua did her best—and encouraged her to put her heart into her studies. The thought of the exams took her mind off her great loss and the disruption at home, and when the time came to sit them she managed to blot out her grief and concentrate on the papers. On the day of her maths exam, Cassie had felt her heart sink as she read the paper. Maths had never been her strongest subject. At the desk in front, Laura, head down, was busily writing. Maths was no problem to Laura. To her left, Aileen was looking extremely perplexed. They caught each other's gaze. Aileen threw her eyes heavenwards and grimaced dramatically. Cassie grinned.

Cassie managed to answer a few questions and was sitting chewing her pen, pondering the relationship between a, b and c on a linear equation. She was flummoxed. She sat in the silent exam hall, staring into space. Then a very strange thing happened. For a brief moment she had the strongest sense of her father; then her mind seemed to clear and the answer to the problem just came into her head. "Thank you, Pops," she whispered. Laura had given her a prayer when Jack died and it gave Cassie great comfort. She learnt it off by heart and said it to herself each night. It was called "Togetherness." Now she said it to herself, knowing that somehow Jack had been with her in her difficulties.

*Death is nothing at all. I have only slipped away
    into the next room.*

*I am I and you are you. Whatever we were to each
    other that we still are.*

*Call me by my old familiar name, speak to me in
    the easy way you always used.*

*Put no difference into your tone, wear no forced air
    of solemnity or sorrow.*

*Laugh as we always laughed at the little jokes we
    enjoyed together.*

Play, smile, think of me. Pray for me.

*Let my name be the household name it always
    was. Let it be spoken without the shadow of a
    ghost in it.*

*Life means all that it ever meant. It is the same as
    it ever was.*

*What is death but a negligible accident? Why
    should I be out of your mind because I am out
    of your sight?*

*All is well, nothing is lost. One brief moment and
    all will be as it was before.*

They were exactly the words that Pops would have said to her. He of all people would not want her to be mournful. He would always be with her—hadn't he just proved it by helping her with her maths paper in her hour of need? He hadn't left her at all!

With a lighter heart, Cassie turned her attention back to her maths paper, and when the exam was over, she was cautiously optimistic that she had passed. As usual, the whole gang gathered afterwards in Kentucky Fried Chicken, to discuss their answers over snack boxes and coffee.

"I know I've failed," wailed Aileen, running inky fingers through her coppery curls. "It was a woeful paper, an absolute disaster! I've a good mind to complain to the Department of Education. It's put me off my lunch!"

"Calm down," instructed Laura, the mathematical expert of the gang. She had taken the honours paper. She glanced through the paper. "Hmm, tricky enough. What answer did you get for this one?"

The rest of them compared their answers and most of them seemed to have achieved similar results.

"See this one about naming the triangle? That wasn't too difficult," Laura remarked, smiling comfortingly at the downcast Aileen, who brightened up immediately.

"That was dead easy. I thought it was a bit of a trick question actually," Aileen replied, forgetting that she had lost, her appetite and cheerfully taking a bite out of her chicken leg.

Laura's face fell. "What made you think that? You had to name the triangle, A, B or C, whichever was the appropriate one. It's quite a straightforward question."

Aileen's jaw dropped. "Oh dear!" she murmured. "I couldn't think what they meant. So in the end I thought they just wanted us to name the triangle and I couldn't think what to do."

"What did you call it?" Laura said sternly.

Aileen grimaced.

"Come on! Tell us!" Cassie grinned. Knowing Aileen, it was bound to be good.

"Well," said the mathematical genius to her captivated audience, "I named it Fred!"

The girls nearly fell off their chairs laughing.

Several months later when the exam results came out, it was no surprise that Aileen had failed maths! Cassie had done much better than she had hoped for. All her studying had paid off and, despite the trauma of her father's death, she had coped well with her exams and had earned the coveted place in the School of Architecture in Bolton Street. Nora did not greet the news enthusiastically. She pointed out to her daughter that if she were to continue studying for another four years Cassie would be twenty-one before she was in a position to get a job. With four other children to educate she had finances to think about. And besides, Nora remarked, a lovely-looking girl like Cassie would certainly get married and have children and what use would her qualification in architecture be to her then? Nora firmly believed that women should stay at home and look after their children and allow men to be the breadwinners.

Women can have children *and* a career, Cassie wanted badly to retort. She wanted to argue with her mother about her attitudes and she desperately wanted to study architecture. Laura was going to UCD to study law and they had planned to share digs. Nora nearly had a fit when her daughter presented her with this scenario.

"But Cassie, I need you here. I'd be worried sick about you up there in Dublin on your own and I've enough to be worrying about without that. I'm very surprised at Mrs Quinn allowing Laura to live in Dublin. Why can't she go in and out on the train? Anyway, that's the Quinns' business. Laura is getting a grant. You wouldn't be eligible for one and I just couldn't afford to support you for the next four years, Cassie."

"I'd support myself!" Cassie said earnestly. "I'll get a part-time job in a pub or supermarket. They stay open late in Dublin, I'm sure I'd have no trouble finding a job."

Nora bristled. "Indeed and you will not get a job working late in a pub or a supermarket. I'm not having you out at all hours in a strange city. The streets aren't safe to walk on up there. Mrs Atkins had her bag snatched at Amiens Street station in broad daylight! Imagine what it's like at night! No, Cassie, I'm sorry, I can't allow it. I'd never forgive myself if anything happened to you. Jack wouldn't have allowed it," she declared.

He would! He would! Cassie wanted to yell. Jack would have talked her mother round, calming her fears, making a joke about her and Laura living together in the big smoke. What did her mother want her to do? Live in Port Mahon for the rest of her life? If only Donie hadn't decided to go and become a priest, maybe he might have persuaded her mother to allow her to come and live in Dublin by promising Nora he'd take care of Cassie. But no! He had to let her down as well by going and shutting himself up in the seminary in Maynooth, where he was no use to her at all.

It had been an awful shock for Cassie when Donie told her right out of the blue after her father died that he had decided to enter the religious life. Cassie had been devastated. They had been dating for months and she was really happy being with him. There was something so kind and nice about Donie. He treated her so well and with such respect. Too much respect, she had often thought ruefully. It was always he who stopped their lovemaking and drew back when things were getting hot and heavy.

At the beginning Cassie had been very impressed by his restraint. Obviously Donie respected her and that was good. He never mauled her or groped her and he always made her feel special. But as their relationship progressed and her feelings for him grew stronger, Cassie, unable to ignore the natural desires of her young body, wished that he would occasionally forget his restraint and experiment a bit more. There were lots of things you could do without actually doing "it." She couldn't bring herself to discuss the problem with the girls. After all, Aileen was now a woman of the world, having been deflowered in the Skylon Hotel in Drumcondra, where she had spent a weekend of glorious abandon with her soldier lover before he was posted off to a tour of duty in the Middle East. Mrs O'Shaughnessy was under the impression that her daughter was staying at a house run by a religious order that was holding an open weekend for young girls who felt they might have a vocation!

Laura and Cassie had been vastly impressed by Aileen's daring and deeply envious of the fact that she was no longer a virgin. And to have stayed the weekend in a hotel with a man! How thrillingly sophisticated! And the amazing thing was that their friend felt not the slightest bit of guilt. Not even the teeniest bit. She had thoroughly enjoyed herself, she had told the girls. Now that she was getting the hang of it. It had been a bit disappointing the first time. Aileen was nothing if not honest.

"Did you bleed when your hymen broke?" Laura asked, fascinated.

Aileen made a face. "Don't talk to me. Believe me, girls, the first time is not the slightest bit romantic. We've been led up the garden path there, I can tell you, but things do improve. It's rather nice doing it in the shower."

Laura and Cassie nearly choked with envy. Cassie knew, no matter how hard she tried to assure herself that she was a woman of the Seventies, that if she made love to Donie, she'd be riddled with guilt! Riddled with it! This angered her deeply. Why should she feel guilty about something that was obviously so nice and pleasurable? Why was sex invented if people were made to feel guilty about it? Not that Cassie wasn't aware of the dangers relating to sex. Hadn't she seen with Laura's elder sister exactly what could happen as a result of having sex without taking precautions? Jill was now living on her unmarried mother's allowance trying to raise a child by herself. Aileen had assured the girls that she had used a contraceptive and they expected nothing less of her. They would act the same when their time came. If their time *ever* came, thought Cassie mournfully. Laura would do it when the time was right for her. But Cassie and her guilts—would she ever do it? Or would she die wondering, that is, unless she got married? What a woeful thought!

"You're always feeling guilty about something or other, Cassie Jordan," she snapped at herself in irritation. "I wish you'd cop on to yourself. You're a real pain in the neck."

Donie was no help whatsoever. "It's not right, Cassie," he'd say miserably when she tried to tell him that she was quite willing to be a bit more adventurous. She wondered unhappily if it were because she was not desirable enough. Maybe it was her fault. Maybe she was sex-mad or even a bit of a nymphomaniac and that was scaring Donie off! Romance had its problems, that was for sure.

When Donie told her one evening that he was thinking of becoming a priest, she was utterly shocked. She felt even more of a failure. If she had been desirable enough, surely he would never have even contemplated such a course of action. If Donie had told her there was another woman in his life, she could not have been more dismayed.

The girls were speechless when she finally told them. "Bloody idiot!" Aileen snorted. "What a waste!"

"Imagine going to confession to Donie Kiely!" Laura muttered glumly, giving Cassie a comforting hug.

"Don't hate me," Donie begged Cassie, the weekend before he left for Maynooth.

"Don't be daft," Cassie had said miserably. "Of course I don't hate you."

"Cassie, you're the only one I've ever loved. But at least I've got to see if I can get this out of my system. Maybe it won't work out. But I think it will. It's something I've been putting off for years and I can't ignore it any longer. Try to understand. Try to be my friend at least."

"We'll always be friends," Cassie comforted the troubled young man at her side. She cared too deeply for him to end their relationship on a note of reproach. He looked terribly relieved and held her close and she knew deep in her heart that Donie Kiely would come out of Maynooth a priest.

He *did* become a priest but for the rest of her life, he was one of her staunchest friends, a pillar of strength in her life.

If only he had waited at least until she was settled in Dublin, life would have been much simpler. But with Donie in Maynooth, and Nora in the frame of mind she was in, Cassie's dream of a career in architecture was shattered. Unwilling to upset her mother, she stayed in Port Mahon and began a secretarial course that left her screaming with boredom and frustration.

Chapter Ten

"You'll have to practise, I'm afraid, Miss O'Shaughnessy," Cassie heard Sister Madeline tell Aileen. She too had been told to practise closing a door while keeping her eyes firmly on the interviewers. They were now going to practise seating themselves gracefully in their chairs while still facing their interviewers. This was all a result of the visit to Saint Imelda's by a deportment and etiquette teacher, Miss Vera Wrigley, who went to schools all around the country giving advice to girls. They learnt how to "start from the outside in" when faced with a bewildering array of cutlery at a formal luncheon or dinner. They learnt how to press their peas against their forks rather than spearing them and having them pop into their partner's lap and cause embarrassment all round. They were advised on grooming and warned not to have too heavy a hand with their make-up.

"You don't want to look as if you've put it on with a trowel," Miss Wrigley recommended, "and, besides, young men prefer a more natural look." She showed them how to walk properly. "Shoulders up. Head straight. Abdominal muscles tucked in with arms swinging loosely by the side and fingers loosely bent." They spent an hour and a half marching around the yard in single file, practising their deportment and feeling like prats. And all the time Cassie and Aileen were stuck in Saint Imelda's Commercial College for Young Ladies, Laura was up in Dublin as free as a bird, leading a wonderful life on campus. Cassie and Aileen were going mad with envy.

They might as well be still at school, Cassie reflected dolefully as the bell went for the end of class and they prepared to go to the typing-room. True, they were called "Miss" and they had a common-room where they could smoke if they wished. But bells still went, homework had to be done, and life was altogether unexciting. Even having a smoke didn't give the same satisfaction as the illicit smoking parties in the boarders' bathroom used to give. The thrill was gone out of it when you were allowed to do it.

The interviews for the banks were coming up, hence the practice and preparation for interviews. Cassie and Aileen had already sent in application forms for the position of clerical officer in both Dublin Corporation and Dublin County Council. In the meantime they were learning to type and do shorthand and book-keeping and accounts. Aileen and book-keeping did not see eye to eye. She could not get the hang of debit the receiver and credit the giver, much to Sister James's exasperation.

Sister James was almost six foot tall. Skinny and angular, with a beaky nose and a sharp tongue, she was one of the most self-righteous, self-important, puffed-up busybodies it had ever been their misfortune to meet. The entire class loathed Sister James. Mother Perpetua was a darling in comparison. In particular, Aileen and Sister James could not stand each other. From their first encounter, when Aileen's début accounting exercise did not balance, it had been all-out war. Aileen was at a disadvantage because she was not mathematically inclined, a disadvantage that the gawky nun exploited to the full. Still, Aileen was well able for her and the rest of the class eagerly looked forward to their spats. Today they would have Sister James for last class after their typing and then they were free for the weekend.

Clacking away on her manual typewriter, Cassie tried to concentrate. It was almost the middle of October but they were having an Indian summer and there was still great heat in the sun, which was blazing in through the windows and making her feel extremely lethargic. It reminded her of the Fridays when she was still at school and longing for the weekend to start. She stifled a sigh. That was the problem—this college was like school, not a real college. If things had gone according to plan, she should have been up in Bolton Street, studying architecture.

Instead she was stuck at a typewriter in Saint Imelda's with the likelihood of being stuck in Port Mahon for the rest of her life. This was a thought that filled her with dismay. It was quite obvious that even if she *did* get a job in Dublin, Nora would expect her to commute daily. To do otherwise would be seen as a betrayal of the family.

It was a problem that taxed Cassie's brain many a night. Was she being selfish in wanting to go and share a flat with the girls in Dublin? Was Nora right to expect her to stay at home? Was that where her duty lay? For all Nora would see of her, she might as well be living in Dublin anyway. After all, it would be almost seven by the time the train rolled into Port Mahon station. If she decided to go out for a few hours, she wouldn't be home before twelve, and then she'd be going to bed. The next morning she'd leave the house before eight to get to work on time. She might as well not be there.

Aileen was in the same boat. Her mother had been widowed some years before and there were just the two girls, Aileen and Judy. Mrs O'Shaughnessy was not happy about her elder daughter's future plans. For years, Aileen had had to tell her mother the most outrageous fibs in order to be able to lead any kind of a life. It wasn't that she wanted to be telling fibs, she moaned to the girls, and she genuinely meant it. But if she didn't, she would never have been allowed to do anything, and would have had no life at all. It was a matter of self-preservation!

Laura had observed her mother's life as a skivvy to her father and decided years before that she was having none of it. She had hardened herself so that when the time came, she had been able to leave home with not an ounce of guilt or regret. As she said to Cassie and Aileen, her mother had made her bed and was lying on it, unwilling to make any changes in her life. No woman had to put up with what Anne Quinn put up with unless she wanted to.

"Don't be emotionally blackmailed!" Laura had advised her two friends. "It's not fair. You're not children any longer. You're adults and you've got to take responsibility for your own lives, just as your mothers have got to take responsibility for theirs. It doesn't mean you're going to be any less supportive or that you won't be there when they need you. And don't ever think it. Don't dare feel one bit guilty!" Laura was very firm about it and Cassie envied her for the way she could reason things out and make decisions that were not clouded by feelings of guilt or responsibility.

She knew Laura was right and she could see that it wasn't she who was being selfish, but her mother. And yet...and yet...Nora *was* her mother and how could she leave her in the lurch so soon after Jack's death? But she'd have to do it some time and so would Aileen, and the longer they left it, the harder it would be. Sighing, she continued typing for the umpteenth time, "The quick brown fox jumps over the lazy dog."

"I'm really looking forward to going up to see Laura tomorrow. Aren't you?" Aileen said cheerfully as they sat waiting for Sister James to arrive for their last class. "I'm dying to see UCD."

"Me too," said Cassie. "It sounds so exciting. All the blokes she's meeting and all the parties she's going to. She's having a ball. I don't know how she gets any studying done. What with her part-time jobs and all."

"There's one thing about Laura. She knows what she wants and she goes for it. She'll get her degree without any problem." The arrival of Sister James cut short any further conversation and they began to study the intricacies of the petty-cash book. All went well for a while and then Aileen was asked a question. Aileen, who had been mentally rehearsing the part of Mrs Pearse, which she was playing in the Port Mahon Dramatic Society's production of *My Fair Lady*, was taken completely by surprise.

"You haven't a notion, have you? You're wasting your time here. And you've a nerve even to consider applying for the bank, Miss O'Shaughnessy!" Sister James was working herself up into a very satisfying rage. She had a loose lower lip and prominent teeth and when she lost her temper or spoke quickly the person opposite her was quite liable to be sprayed.

Aileen had just about enough of Sister James. Glaring at the nun and wiping her cheek, she retorted coldly, "Kindly say it...don't spray it." Just then the bell went. Gathering her books, she marched from the classroom, leaving Sister James red-faced and speechless. The rest of the class hid their grins, delighted that the unpopular nun had finally got her comeuppance. Only Aileen would have the nerve to do it! Sister James was so flustered she completely forgot to give the girls any homework.

"I feel much better after that, I can tell you," Aileen confided, as she and Cassie walked along the main street on their way home. Cassie laughed.

"You really got her where it hurts. She was flabbergasted."

"Well, I wouldn't normally pass remarks like that but she was just so smart, she was asking for it. For someone with her posh accent who is always telling us how well-bred she is, she's mighty rude," Aileen sniffed.

"Don't know where she got that accent from. My Aunt Elsie knows her family and they came from Kerry. They moved up to Dublin years ago. But she's from Kerry all the same." Cassie was feeling slightly peckish. "Come on, let's go into Tum Tums for a bite to eat," she said to Aileen, who needed no second urging. Tum Tums had recently opened in Port Mahon and did a roaring trade. The home-made soups were the talk of the town. Although it was only four-thirty in the afternoon the place was almost full. Friday was market-day in Port Mahon and the main street was a hive of activity.

Aileen and Cassie managed to secure a window-seat and sat back in their pine chairs, perusing the menu.

"I think I'll have the Chicken Kiev," Cassie decided.

"And I'll have the lasagne, please," Aileen told the waitress. "And a pot of tea for two."

"It's nice to treat ourselves now and again, isn't it?" Cassie declared, knowing that Nora would go mad if she saw them. Her mother had a dinner prepared at home. Well, she just wasn't in the mood for smoked cod today and that was that.

"It's the perfect way to start off the weekend," Aileen agreed. "Tomorrow is going to be a great day. And we deserve it." She pointed to the up-market boutique across the street. "I see Vogue has a sale on. I wonder if there is anything nice there."

"Nothing you or I could afford, so forget it," Cassie said firmly. Aileen could get carried away quite easily where clothes were concerned. Vogue was way out of their league. All the rich farmers' wives and the wealthy women of Skerries and Balbriggan and the rest of north County Dublin came to Vogue to shop. They watched a trio of glamorous women emerge from the boutique, carrying the distinctive black-and-gold bags with Vogue blazoned on them. "We'll be like them some day," she said to her friend.

"That's if we ever get out of Port Mahon," Aileen replied glumly. "Well, Mother will just have to get used to the idea that I'm not going to be tied to her apron-strings for ever. Really, Cassie, she's very demanding. My dad died years ago and Mother still hasn't learnt to stand on her own two feet. For God's sake, don't let your mother get too dependent. For her own good as well as yours." Aileen was uncharacteristically serious. Cassie knew she and her sister, Judy, had a hard enough time with Angela O'Shaughnessy, who tended towards the neurotic.

"Don't worry, Aileen, Mam will get back to herself and you and I will get up to Dublin one of these fine days. Our time will come," Cassie said with more confidence than she felt. It wasn't that she hated home or Port Mahon. In fact there were times when she loved where she lived, particularly in the summer and autumn. Port Mahon was a thriving little town and there was plenty to do there, but Cassie knew it was time to spread her wings. She felt terribly restless. A whole new world beckoned, if only she could make the break.

"Oh look!" Aileen pointed. "Hit-and-Run strikes again! Isn't he obnoxious?" Looking out the bay window, Cassie could see the town's traffic warden poised for action. Nicknamed Hit-and-Run by one of the town wits, his *modus operandi* was perfectly described by his nickname. A timid little man, fearful of confrontation, he would stand in the shelter of a shop doorway while taking details of his intended target. Once the ticket was written he nipped out, placed it behind the wiper and was gone. As there were double yellow lines on both sides of the main street he had a busy time. Market-day was a particularly nerve-wracking day for him and right now he looked totally harassed.

Cassie and Aileen sat enjoying their meal, watching the to-ing and fro-ing along the street, commenting on this one and that one and quite enjoying themselves. Before they left Tum Tums, they had discussed almost all the inhabitants of Port Mahon.

❦

An hour later, full to the gills, Cassie sat at the dining-table at home gazing unenthusiastically at the steaming plate in front of her.

"I hope that's not dried up, Cassie, love," Nora fussed. "I didn't know you'd be late."

"It's fine, Mam. It looks delicious," her daughter fibbed. Barbara was over at Judy's house. John was out the back chopping wood, and Martin and Irene were watching TV.

"Cassie, I was just wondering," Nora began diffidently. "Well, I was thinking of going to an ICA meeting tonight. You don't think it's too soon, do you?" The question was music to Cassie's ears. Her mother hadn't been to her ladies' club meeting since Jack died. It was a good sign that she was thinking of going. It meant that she was starting to get back to her old self.

"I think that's a great idea, Mam. Of course it's not too soon. It's what Poppa would want. He'd go mad if he thought you were going to turn into a recluse."

"Well, maybe I'll go and get ready so," Nora replied, kissing her daughter on the top of her head. "You're a great comfort to me, Cassie. I don't know how I would have managed without you."

"You'd have managed fine," Cassie smiled at her mother, though her heart sank. Having her mother say things like that made it much more difficult for her to think about going to live in Dublin. Why couldn't she be just like Laura and go! Cassie knew there were times she was much too soft. It was something she was going

to have to work on. She couldn't go through her life
carrying on like this or she'd end up a basket-case!

CHAPTER ELEVEN

Two months later, having done a very successful job
interview, Cassie was offered a position with Allied Isles
Banks. Nora was ecstatic. To get the bank was a great
thing, more prestigious, indeed, than getting the
Corporation or County Council. It would be wonderful
to be able to go to her ladies' club and tell them all that
Cassie had got the bank!

Cassie wasn't sure how she felt. She had just applied
for the position, as she had applied for several others,
did the interview along with thousands of others and
got the job. At least it would get her out of the secretarial
course. It would mean she would be on a training course
in Dublin initially, although she was told she could be
sent anywhere the bank had a branch, and that included
all around the country, Northern Ireland, England and
Scotland and the Channel Islands. This would make
things much easier when the time came for her to leave
home. Nora couldn't argue about it, whatever she might
feel. Cassie was to start her training course as a junior
bank official in the new year. She would do a two-week
course at the training centre in Ranelagh before being
assigned to a branch.

It was a good way to start a new year, Cassie reflected,
as she sat on the train heading into Dublin on the first
morning of her course. She hoped 1973 would be the
start of a new life for her. At least it couldn't be much
worse than the year that had just passed. Christmas had

been terrible for them. Of course, the first Christmas was always the worst for a bereaved family.

Jack Jordan had loved Christmas. He threw himself into the decorating with gusto, taking great pride in his Christmas tree. Not just any old tree for Jack. It had to be the right one, usually a magnificent bushy specimen that dominated the sitting-room. Festooned with twinkling lights and decorations and tinsel, it was always a sight to behold. He would scour the countryside looking for the most perfect pieces of holly, out of which he would fashion beautiful wreaths to decorate the front door and windows. On Christmas Eve, he and Nora would place a lighted candle in the sitting-room window, as was the custom in the country, to welcome the arrival of the Infant Jesus.

On Christmas Day, after Mass, the house would fill up with family and relatives, and an air of infectious gaiety prevailed. Succulent smells emanating from the kitchen would waft around the house, proving too much for the guests. They would invariably end up wending their way out to Nora, who would allow them to taste her mouth-watering turkey and stuffing. Jack loved it. He would go around urging people to "drink up, there's plenty more." Later, people would start to leave in dribs and drabs to go and get their own dinners, and the family would be alone, ready to enjoy the feast that Nora had prepared. As Jack said grace, he would always add, "Thank God we're all here together to share another Christmas. I'm the luckiest man in the world, with a wonderful wife and five great children."

Cassie tried to swallow the lump that rose in her throat at the memories that had come flooding back. Tears slid down her cheeks and hastily she brushed them away. Fortunately no one was looking at her as the early commuter train sped towards the city. Everyone was too engrossed in books and papers or staring at the turbulent grey sea that lashed the big rocks along the coast.

The Jordan family had decided not to decorate the house this past Christmas and they had gone to Nora's younger sister, Betty, and her family for Christmas lunch. Betty and her husband, Dermot, had gone to a lot of trouble and Nora and the rest of them were very appreciative but it was hard to keep up the façade of jollity even while they were with their relatives, and the nearer they got to home that evening the more heavy-hearted they got. The rest of the night had been spent looking at TV, which at least kept the younger ones occupied. It had been utterly dismal and Cassie was relieved it was all over. Maybe next year wouldn't be so bad.

What would it be like on the training course, she wondered? What kind of people would be doing it? Laura was going to meet her at lunchtime and that was something to look forward to. Although her college holidays weren't over yet, she was back in Dublin for her part-time jobs. Poor old Aileen was facing another term at Saint Imelda's. She had got a job as clerical officer in Dublin Corporation and was on a panel waiting to be called. Everyone knew that Sister James had been triumphant when Aileen didn't get the bank, but she never made the mistake of tangling with Aileen again. Aileen had been delighted for Cassie when her friend did get the bank but Cassie knew that Aileen really dreaded going back to Saint Imelda's without her. At least, when they were together, they were able to cope with the boredom and restrictions by having a laugh. Cassie didn't envy Aileen having to put up with Sister James for another term. The sooner her friend got her job with the Corporation, the better for her sanity. Would the time ever come when they could get their flat together? Cassie just hoped so, and the sooner the better.

The train was slowing down now as they started to travel through the outer suburbs of Dublin. It wouldn't be long before she was starting on her career as a junior bank official.

❦

Aileen sat by herself in Tum Tums, sipping a cup of strong coffee and eating a thick slice of buttered cherry log. She was thoroughly pissed off, so pissed off that she had decided not to go to classes today. She really missed Cassie. She envied her too. Not a nasty envy, mind, never that. Just envied her the fact that she was finally on her way. She would be earning her own money and she'd be in a position to make the break from Port Mahon. That is, if she could make the decision to go. Aileen sighed. No one knew better than she what it was like to have a clinging mother.

Angela O'Shaughnessy was the most clinging person in the country. Probably in the world! She was one of these people who always wanted someone dancing attendance. "I'm only a poor widow!" she'd say and Aileen would be ready to strangle her. Angela was not poor. Her husband had left her quite comfortable, with a nice semi-detached house of which the mortgage was paid off on his death. At least she hadn't been left with five children to rear like Mrs Jordan. As far as Aileen could see, she and Judy had practically reared themselves. All Angela ever did was go to Mass in the morning, do a bit of shopping and prepare a meal for the three of them. Then she spent the rest of the day doing the *Irish Times* crossword and watching quiz shows and soaps on

TV. Her mother actually led a charmed existence and in her own way she was quite contented, if she would only admit it to herself. She was not one for ladies' clubs and committees like Nora Jordan, more's the pity. At least Cassie's mother had interests in the outside world. If Angela went to the ladies' club it might have given her something to occupy her mind and she would have less time to dwell on her aches and pains and imaginary problems. Unfortunately for Aileen and Judy, Angela liked hibernating in her little nest, letting the rest of the world go by. But she didn't want to hibernate by herself. She wanted her daughters to hibernate with her. Well, too bad, Aileen thought. No more hibernation for her, thank you very much. She was getting out as soon as she could.

If only this job with the Corporation would come up. She had no idea how long she would be on the panel before she was called. To be honest, she would have loved to get the bank. The social life was terrific and they had a great amateur dramatic society where her acting talents could have flourished. Unfortunately she hadn't been able to make head or tail of some of the aptitude tests. The ones with circles and triangles were totally confusing. After her performance at the tests she had known that she wouldn't get the job. It had been a disappointment for her but she didn't let on to Cassie. She didn't want Cassie to feel bad about her success. If there was one person who deserved something nice to happen to her, it was her best friend.

Aileen toyed with the idea of ordering another slice of cherry log. She might as well, she decided. It would help to pass the time and it was lovely and warm here in Tum Tum's. She couldn't spend the whole day here, more's the pity. She didn't feel like ambling around the town, it was too cold and miserable. If she went home and pretended she was sick, Angela would start fussing like nobody's business and probably call out the doctor. What was a girl on the mitch to do? Aileen had a brainwave. The Port Mahon Dramatic Society intended to present *Calamity Jane* with herself in the lead role. There was lots of scenery that needed painting. She would take herself off to the club and spend the day there. If she had had her wits about her, she could have gone into Dublin and met Laura and Cassie for lunch! Now that would have been nice! Laura was really looking well these days. She had taken to life in Dublin like a duck to water. The lucky thing. One thing about Laura was that she knew what she wanted and nothing stood in her way. Well, Aileen was going to take a leaf out of her friend's book, she decided, as she took a satisfying bite out of her second piece of cherry log.

❦

Laura sat with her coat on, huddled over a one-bar electric fire in her room. She was studying hard. Her hands were numb and her feet were like two ice-blocks. Really this room was the pits, damp and cold. It was furnished with a lumpy single divan, a wooden wardrobe, an old-fashioned chest of drawers whose drawers stuck whenever she tried to open them, and a small desk to study at. It was depressingly decorated: faded pink wallpaper with huge cabbage roses, a brown carpet and yellowing lace curtains that were pretty tattered. There was no comfort whatsoever. Still, the room was cheap and would do for the time being. And she was able to walk to college. It was a brisk forty-minute walk from the dilapidated redbrick house in Ranelagh out to Belfield, but Laura was used to walking and didn't mind. Besides she saved a fortune on bus-fares. The only thing was that she was starving when she got in in the evening and the food was downright bad. Anyway, she thought, now that Cassie had finally got a job, the time would surely come when she would be living in Dublin instead of commuting and they could get a flat together. She hoped fervently that this would happen soon, though if Cassie were sent down the country that would be the end of that idea. Laura's heart sank at the thought. For so long the three of them had been planning on sharing a flat in Dublin. It would be great fun, Laura just knew it. If only Cassie could leave home. It was unreasonable of Nora to expect her to commute daily to the city. But Cassie was so soft where her family were concerned. Then of course she had a happy family life, something Laura had never experienced.

Her eyes darkened as unhappy memories crowded in: the rows at home; her father acting the tyrant; her brother coming home drunk; and her mother passively accepting the way her husband treated her. Laura's hands clenched. Just thinking about her father could make her furious. Who was he to think they should all be at his beck and call? Why did Peter Quinn think he had the right to be treated like a god? Throwing a tantrum if his dinner wasn't on the table at one on the dot. Expecting Laura to clean the bath after him. Expecting Anne to agree with everything that he said. Oh she was well out of it! If she had to stay in cheap digs for the rest of her life, it was better than putting up with the abuse she got at home from her father. Why her mother put up with it, Laura could not understand.

"Why don't you leave?" she asked Anne several times after there had been a row at home. "Why don't you just tell him to feck off and get his own dinner for a change? Why do you put up with it?"

"Where would I go? What would I do?" her mother responded tiredly.

"You could get a job, get a little place of your own," Laura urged. But she could see that the thought of being alone and standing on her own two feet was far more terrifying to her mother than having to put up with her husband's abuse. Well, that was her mother's choice and, try as she might, she could not make her change her mind. Laura knew that as soon as she could, she was getting out.

Getting the grant for college had been a godsend. She didn't have to ask her father for a penny. At last she was free of him. From now on she would make her own way in the world. Leaving home to come to Dublin had been the happiest day of her life. Not even these grotty digs could get her down. This was only temporary. Things would improve. She had stayed at home only for Christmas Day and St Stephen's Day—that had been more than enough. Anyway, she had had the excuse that she had to get back to her part-time jobs.

Some of the people in college had felt sorry for her having to come back to Dublin so soon, with term not even started. But Laura didn't mind a bit and it was a great opportunity to get some studying done. It was most important that she keep up with her studies. She didn't want to have to cram in the weeks before the exams. One thing she could say about herself was that she was disciplined. But then she had reason to be. She had a goal to reach, the goal of independence. When she saw some of her classmates going to parties morning, noon and night, missing lectures and treating the whole thing as a great lark, she thought they were crazy. Of course they were the ones with rich daddies who didn't have to worry about where the rent for the digs was coming from. A nice life if you could have it.

Not that she was becoming a recluse or anything like it. Laura fitted in well at UCD. She liked being part of campus life. It was great crack and some of the parties she went to were brilliant. She had joined the debating society and enjoyed nothing more than a good rousing debate. No one could get the better of Laura in a debate. She had proven her mettle as a speaker. But she knew she had to get all her exams first time. She wouldn't have the luxury of taking repeats if she failed. If she wanted to make her way in the world she had to get her degree and find a job quickly. After that she could have the most hectic social life in the world!

Laura gave a huge yawn. Mind, it was hard going making your way in the world. She worked three nights a week until 12.30 a.m. in a restaurant in Wicklow Street. *And* she did part-time work in a newsagents on Sundays. It was difficult enough working, studying and trying to have a bit of a social life as well but she was coping, and she was happier than she had ever been in her life. She was as free as a bird, answerable to nobody except herself. What more could a woman ask for? If only Cassie and Aileen could be with her and they could get a nice little flat together, everything would be perfect.

❧

Nora stood at the sink, washing up after breakfast. The house was so quiet this morning. All the children had gone back to school and Cassie was gone to Dublin to take up her new job. Jack would have been so proud of Cassie getting the bank. Nora's eyes smarted and an aching loneliness overwhelmed her. She started to cry. Oh Jack! Jack! I miss you, she wept silently, tears streaming down her cheeks and plopping into the sudsy water. Why did you leave me all alone? She tried to keep up a brave face for the children but sometimes it was impossible.

Today she felt really alone for some reason. Probably because Cassie was gone up to Dublin. Well, she'd have to get used to not having her coming in from school, helping to dish up the dinner and sharing a gossip with her over a cup of tea. From this on it would be late in the evenings when Cassie got home. It was a long old trek into and out of the city. Nora sighed. She knew Cassie had her heart set on getting a flat with Laura. But she was so young to be out in the world alone. Cassie kept saying she was eighteen. But eighteen wasn't old enough to be living on your own in a strange city. You had only to open the papers and read about attacks on women and muggings and robberies to know that Dublin was not a safe place to live in. At least in Port Mahon there was very little crime and you could walk the streets in safety. What the Quinns were thinking of allowing Laura to live up there in digs was beyond Nora. But then, of course, Laura was headstrong. And if all she heard was true, Peter Quinn was a difficult man to live with. But Cassie had no family problems. Why on earth would she want to be going up to Dublin, to live in God knows what kind of a flat, having to cook her own dinner and do her own washing, when she had a fine, warm, comfortable home to come to, with her mother having her meals cooked for her when she came in and all her washing done for her as well? Nora shook her head in mystification as she washed the marmalade dish.

And then to have Elsie of all people telling her that she should allow Cassie to go and live in Dublin and make her own way in life. Nora had been stunned!

"You don't want her to end up like me," Elsie had challenged her, much to her younger sister's surprise.

"An old maid who did nothing with her life. I should have left home and got a job when Anthony died during the war. But I stayed at home with Mother and never went anywhere and never did anything, and many is the time I regret it. Don't bind Cassie to you, Nora. You depend on her too much as it is." Nora had felt like telling her to shut up and mind her own business and not be interfering.

Deep down she knew there was some truth in what her eldest sister was saying. But, God above, she didn't want Cassie to leave home. Not yet, at any rate. Maybe in a couple of years. Maybe when she was twenty-one. Nora's eyes brightened. That wouldn't be for another three years. Tonight when Cassie got home she would tell her that she would let her go to Dublin and live in a flat when she was twenty-one. That would solve all the problems and cheer Cassie up. A thought struck her. Wouldn't it be terrible if the bank sent her to Cork or Galway or some such place? Then she'd *really* be gone.

"Jack, make sure Cassie isn't sent away from home," she implored her deceased spouse, raising her eyes heavenwards as she dried her hands and picked up the tea-towel to dry the dishes.

CHAPTER TWELVE

The train was trundling into Amiens Street station. Cassie stood up and joined the rest of the early-morning passengers as they pushed and shoved their way out the doors. Walking along the cold tiled platform, Cassie wished the butterflies in her stomach would fly elsewhere. She was feeling a bit nervous. But she comforted herself with the thought that everyone else on the course would probably feel the same.

She emerged onto the steps of the station to cross the street towards Talbot Street and gazed around her. There were people and cars and buses everywhere. So this was the famous rush-hour! And at last she was part of it. This thought cheered her up immensely. She strode briskly down Talbot Street in the direction of O'Connell Street, where she would get the number 11 or number 13 bus which would take her to Ranelagh. She had already done a trial run with Laura so she knew exactly where to go for her bus and exactly where to get off. At least she wouldn't be panicking looking for the training centre when she got to Ranelagh. She crossed Marlborough Street into North Earl Street. There were sales on everywhere. Soon, she'd have money to spend in them. Crossing the street she peered into Clerys side window. She'd love to go in and have a browse, but time did not permit it. After all, she didn't want to be late on her first day. But she'd get in one of these days.

Next Friday would be her first pay-day and she was going to have a ball. She had promised to bring John, Martin and Irene into town to go to the pictures and then to Fortes Café afterwards for burgers and chips. They were greatly looking forward to the treat. She was going to buy her mother a briefcase. Nora had recently been elected to the position of secretary in her ladies' club and consequently had a lot of paperwork to do. A briefcase was just what she needed to carry all her papers. She intended buying Barbara the poster of Steve McQueen astride his motorbike. She was always raving about it so that would be her treat. For herself she was going to buy a copy of Gone With the Wind and read it from cover to cover. With her first week's wages well spent she rounded the corner into O'Connell Street and saw a number 13 bus heading in her direction. Running to the bus-stop she joined the queue and boarded the bus and began the final leg of her journey to her destination in Ranelagh.

🍂

There were twelve new recruits in the class, including herself, and they were welcomed by the chief executive of the company before being introduced to their course tutor. They were given a brief history of the organisation and then a run-down on its structure before stopping for tea, mid-morning. Cassie exchanged brief life-stories with the others and because it was a small group it was easy to get to know the rest of her classmates. Then they were measured up for their uniforms before breaking for lunch. Laura was waiting in the foyer and they went to a pub in Ranelagh and had soup and a sandwich while Cassie told her friend of all the things that had happened so far.

"It sounds really interesting. Do you think you're going to like it?" Laura bit into a tuna salad sandwich and took a gulp of tea. She was starving.

"If ever I get the hang of it," laughed Cassie. "To-morrow they're going to show us how to count notes. Seemingly there's a knack to it."

"Where do you think you'll be sent?"

Cassie shook her head. "I don't know yet. We'll be given an envelope on the last day of the course telling us what branch we're assigned to. It could be anywhere."

"God, I hope they don't send you down the country. That would ruin our plans altogether," Laura said glumly.

"I won't be able to leave home right away even if I stay in Dublin," Cassie warned. "It's too soon after Pops. Mam would go spare!"

Laura nodded encouragingly. "I know that. But keep working on it."

"Don't worry, I will," Cassie said.

The rest of the day passed in a blur as the raw recruits were taught about the philosophy of banking, with particular reference to Allied Isles' operation and aims for future expansion. They were sent home with a folder full of information which they were told to have read for the following morning.

It was a tired girl who returned home to Port Mahon that night. It had been a very long day. Cassie thought her brain was going to burst, it had so much to assimilate. When she got home, she sat in front of a blazing fire, the centre of attention, wriggling her toes to try and get some heat into them. There had been no heat on the train and she was frozen. As soon as she thawed out and got some food inside her she was able to start answering the dozens of questions asked by her mother and her curious brothers and sisters. When Nora informed Cassie that she would allow her to move to a flat in Dublin when she was twenty-one, Cassie was too tired to argue.

❧

The two weeks were fascinating but hectic. The trainees learnt about the basic structure of the Allied Isles' organisation. They were shown the correct way to count cash by wetting the thumbs and counting away from you. Nancy, the girl who was showing them, did it fast and effortlessly while the rest of them were all fingers and thumbs. But by the end of the session Cassie was quite pleased with her progress. One of the blokes, Gary Hooper, was totally defeated by the method and his wad of notes landed on the floor several times, much to his dismay. Nancy was very patient and eventually they all felt they had mastered the rudiments of counting cash. They learnt how to cash cheques and balance cash and how to take lodgements. They spent a couple of days learning about customer service. They were shown how to greet and deal with customers. And then they did role-playing, pretending to be nasty customers or customers with unusual queries while their partner, who was playing the part of cashier, tried to deal with them. They had sessions on grooming and self-presentation and by the time they were finished they were all dying to get into a branch and show off their newly acquired skills.

The last day of the course found them all having a final lunch together in the staff canteen. They were nervously awaiting the fateful white envelope which would tell them which branch they were to be assigned to.

"I hope to God I don't get Dame Street!" Gary moaned. Dame Street was the bank's main branch, their busiest operation in the country and totally intimidating to a novice.

"Me too," murmured Stella, a quiet girl from Galway.

"I wouldn't mind Dame Street at all!" Lou Musgrove said confidently. "It's the place to be if you want to get on quickly. You're right under the noses of the powers that be if you want to make a good impression and get noticed. I know. My father's a bank manager!"

There was silence at the table. If they had heard it once, they had heard a thousand times that Lou Musgrove's father was a bank manager. They were heartily sick of it—and him. The bank manager's son excused himself to go up and get a second helping.

"That little fat baldy bollox. I hope he gets sent to the Outer Hebrides," Gary muttered, half to himself. He had had enough of the other bloke's boasting and blowing. A guffaw went around the table and Gary reddened, a bit embarrassed in front of the girls. "Oh excuse me, ladies, I forgot where I was."

"Don't worry," Cassie said cheerfully. "We all feel the same about the little gobshite. And I can tell you one thing, I'm damn well going to make sure I get to be a manager before he does. Can you imagine having to take orders from him!"

"Wash your mouth out with soap," laughed Raymond Burton, a good-looking Corkman.

"Shhh! here he comes," warned Stella, as the boastful one arrived back to their table with his plate piled high. "Food's good here. Might as well make the most of it, especially when it's subsidised. My father maintains that if you feed staff properly you'll get twice as much work out of them."

It was on the tip of Cassie's tongue to say, "It obviously hasn't worked with you!" but she restrained herself. She had partnered Lou on two sessions in the training course. She had done all the work and he had tried to take over the presentation and pretend he was the brains behind it. No doubt Lou Musgrove would get places. He certainly had the gift of the gab but he wasn't going to climb on *her* back to further his career.

She wondered where she would be sent. Nora would have a heart attack if she were appointed to anywhere else but Dublin. In her heart of hearts she would prefer to be left in Dublin for a year or two at least and not only for her mother's sake. She didn't want to be miles away from Laura and Aileen. That kip Laura was living in was a disaster but there was no possibility yet that she could afford a flat on her own. At least if Aileen and she were sharing the rent, she'd be able to manage OK. More than anything, the three of them wanted to realise their teenage dream of sharing a flat. All three of them got on like a house on fire and sharing a flat would be terrific.

Apart from all that, Cassie liked what she had seen of Dublin. There was so much to do and see and explore. All the art galleries and museums, all the bookshops. The other day when they were let off early she went into Eason's Bookshop in O'Connell Street, the biggest bookshop in the country. She got so immersed in browsing, dipping into this book and that, going upstairs to the art section and downstairs to the music and gift section and then back up to the books and magazines, that she completely forgot about the time and had to run all the way to Amiens Street. She made the train with seconds to spare. If she were assigned to work in a branch in Dublin and managed finally to make the break from home, Cassie would be as happy as Larry!

An hour later the personnel manager stood in front of the class with twelve white envelopes in his hand. "Ladies and gentlemen, I'd like to congratulate you on completing a very successful training course. All of you have the ability to do well and advance in your careers in Allied Isles Banks. I'd like to give you your assignments and wish you all the very best of luck in the future. If you have any problems at any stage of your careers please don't hesitate to get in touch with me. Good luck!"

He came around from his desk and handed each of them the envelope that would mark the beginning of their banking career and change their lives completely.

"Hell!" she heard Lou Musgrove mutter when he saw where he was being sent.

Heart thumping, Cassie opened her envelope and gave a little gasp when she saw the name of the branch to which she had been assigned.

*Report to the manager in headquarters on Dame
Street on Monday next at 9 a.m.*

Cassie nearly died. The very place they had all, with the
exception of Lou Musgrove, dreaded being sent to. And
she had got it. She didn't know whether to laugh or cry.
At least I'm staying in Dublin, she kept telling herself as
she stood swaying on the packed train as it slowly left
Amiens Street for the journey home. Some of them had
been sent to branches in the suburbs, others had been
sent to branches in the country. Lou Musgrove had been
sent to a small midlands bank and he was raging. A
country bank did not suit the image he was planning for
himself.

"What have you got that they sent you to Dame
Street?" he asked Cassie sarcastically. She glared at him.

"Obviously something that *you* haven't got!" she said
coldly. *She* would have been much happier to have gone
to one of the suburban branches. They were much less
intimidating than Dame Street.

The following Monday morning found her in her
new navy-and-white uniform, standing outside the huge
wooden doors of the Dame Street branch. Hesitantly she
knocked on the door. No answer! She knocked again,
feeling a bit of a fool as people passing by gave her
sideways glances. The bank didn't actually open its doors
for trading until ten o'clock but she had been told to
report for work at nine. Cassie felt herself beginning to
get a bit flustered.

"Hi!" said a pleasant voice at her side, and Cassie
turned around to see a red-haired girl in navy uniform
smiling at her.

"Is this your first day?" she smiled. "Honestly, they
never tell new staff about the side entrance. I don't know

how many lost souls I've rescued from this door. My name is Jeanne. Come on, this way." Cassie heaved a sigh of relief. Thank God for the attractive good Samaritan at her side or she could have been stuck there like an idiot until ten.

"I'm Cassie," she introduced herself.

Jeanne smiled reassuringly. "It's awful starting off on your first day. And here of all places. I was petrified at first but you'll get used to it very quickly and there's a great staff here." She rang the doorbell at the small side entrance and a porter let them in.

"Morning, girls. How's the crack?" he greeted them cheerfully.

"Tommy, this is Cassie. She's just starting so be nice to her—for a day or two at least. If you can manage that!" Jeanne said, with mock severity.

"Nice! I'll treat her like a queen," Tommy laughed. "Red carpet and all!"

"Tommy's a great character," Jeanne laughed, as they walked along a carpeted corridor with doors on each side.

"I was told to report to the manager," Cassie said.

"You poor thing!" teased Jeanne. "Mr Hurley is nice enough. He expects you to work. Doesn't mind if you make a mistake once but won't stand for the same mistake being made twice. He's strict, but if you've got a problem he's very kind." They turned right and went up a grey-carpeted stairs. They stopped outside a door with the manager's name on it. "Here you are, Cassie. Good luck on your first day. I'll see you around."

"Thanks very much, Jeanne." Feeling lonely, Cassie watched the other girl head back down the stairs. Her palms began to sweat and she was really nervous. This was it! This was where it all began. Taking a deep breath,

Cassie knocked on the door and was called to enter.

"Good morning. Miss Jordan, isn't it? We've been told to expect you." The tall grey-haired man came from behind his desk, hand outstretched. He was kind-looking and quietly spoken.

"Good morning, Mr Hurley," Cassie responded, giving him a firm handshake. He had a nice airy office with a window looking out on Trinity College. She observed this as her new boss motioned her to sit down. He spoke to her for about ten minutes, telling her that Dame Street was an excellent branch to work in from the point of view of gaining experience. If she worked hard she could expect promotion. Allied Isles firmly believed in equality for women and promoted people because of their ability and not because of their gender. In this respect they were streets ahead of their competitors, most of whom expected women to retire on marriage and take the lump sum that they were entitled to. Allied Isles was a thriving go-ahead organisation and Cassie could, if she wished, go far.

Cassie knew he was not exaggerating. Allied Isles were the *crème de la crème* of the banking companies in Ireland and she was extremely lucky to have secured a position with them.

"I'll just get a staff officer to have a chat with you now, Miss Jordan. She will show you the attendance book that you sign every day," Mr Hurley said pleasantly as he pressed a buzzer on his intercom. A middle-aged woman entered the room and Mr Hurley introduced her as Mrs O'Brien.

"This is our new trainee, Miss Jordan," the manager smiled. "I'll leave her in your capable hands."

By five o'clock, when it was time to leave work, Cassie didn't know whether she was coming or going. Mrs

O'Brien had shown her where to sign on, then brought her to the locker-room, where she was given a key to one of the stainless-steel lockers. It would be hers for as long as she worked in Dame Street. Then she had been shown the ladies' and then she had been taken on a guided tour of the bank. It was really rather awesome. The public area was huge. Massive wooden counters ran around the walls behind which, at numerous grilles, dozens of cashiers worked busily, dealing with the queues. Huge pillars stretched from marble floor to intricately carved ceilings, making the place look even more impressive.

In the ledger-room staff worked on twenty-five huge ledgers, painstakingly entering every transaction. Mrs O'Brien told her that Allied Isles were planning a huge computerisation programme and that the ledgers would be obsolete within the following eighteen months. "You've come in at a very good time," the staff officer remarked. "They're going to spend millions on modernising and you'll be here right from the start. If you want to get on, my advice to you is perhaps to start doing some computer courses in the autumn when the evening classes start."

Good advice, thought Cassie to herself, and perhaps a way out of her dilemma about leaving home. If she were doing classes to further her career, Nora would have no option but to agree to her leaving. Stay at home until she was twenty-one indeed! Already she was heartily sick of commuting. It was tiring and such a waste of time.

She spent the rest of the day down in the bowels of the bank, filing cheques. It seemed to her that there were millions of them! And they all had to be filed numerically in hundreds of grey filing cabinets. She was given a metal tray on castors and told to file the contents.

A number of other staff were filing away, some of them quite middle-aged. Jeanne, who had met her in the canteen at the afternoon tea-break, told Cassie that these were people who for one reason or another had never made management or got promoted.

"There's some great characters there, though. You'll have a lot of laughs," the other girl assured her. "I spent my first six months there."

"Six months!" exclaimed Cassie in horror.

"That was good going," laughed Jeanne. "Some people have been left there for a year!"

As Cassie sat on the train going home, grateful for having been able to get a seat, she ached with tiredness. She had a pain in her back from bending, three of her carefully manicured nails were broken and she was absolutely mesmerised by numbers. She didn't think she was going to stick it! And this was only her first day!

🦃

After six months of filing, Cassie was brought upstairs to the typing pool, where she spent her time typing correspondence. She got to know a huge number of people at work and, being outgoing and gregarious, fitted in very well. The social life in the bank was very good and there was an excellent social club that she had joined. The only problem was traipsing in and out of Port Mahon and making sure to leave early enough to get the last train home. It made things very awkward.

After eight months of commuting, she finally told her mother that she was getting a flat! "I've got to start a computer course in the evenings next October and there's no way I can go to college at night in Dublin if I'm living in Port Mahon," she explained patiently to her mother.

"Couldn't you do a computer course here in the technical school?" Nora demanded. "I don't want you living up there, Cassie. Aren't you fine here?"

"Mam, I've got to do the course in Dublin. It's one that's been recommended by the bank and if I want to get ahead and eventually become a manager I'll have to study. When I become a senior bank official I'll have to do banking exams to be promoted!" She said this hoping to appeal to her mother's proud ambition for her. The way Nora went on in Port Mahon, you'd think Cassie ran the Dame Street branch of Allied Isles!

It wasn't that she *had* to do the computer course, but of course she didn't say that to Nora. But Cassie reasoned if she did the course, she'd have some idea about computers when they were introduced and it would look good on her record that she had done some extra-mural study with a view to promotion.

More importantly it would finally mean that the girls could get their long-desired flat together. Laura, having completed her first year at UCD, was in America making as much money as she could. She had acquired a J-1 visa and had gone at the beginning of summer after sitting her exams. Cassie had assured her that at the end of September when she came back they would definitely go looking for a flat together.

Aileen had finally been called by the Corporation and was, as she described it, "rotting away" in a dingy office in the inner city, filing little pink and green slips, invoices and receipts. She hated it! However, once a fortnight she got a cheque into her hand and that made up for a lot. Sick to the teeth of getting the train into Dublin, she had bought herself a little Mini a couple of months after starting work and now she and Cassie commuted in style! She too was determined to join the flat-hunting expedition when Laura came back. If Angela were going to have a nervous breakdown about it, she'd just have to get on with it.

By the time September came, Nora had more or less resigned herself to Cassie's going.

"Lucky you!" Barbara muttered sulkily. "I'll be left to do everything."

And about time too, thought Cassie unsympathetically. What Barbara would do around the place wouldn't be noticed.

"You'll come home Friday nights for the weekends, won't you?" This was a statement rather than a question from Nora.

"We'll see, Mam. I could have classes on Friday nights," Cassie explained gently. She and Aileen had decided not to get into the trap of coming home every weekend unless they wanted to. Start as you mean to go on was their motto.

In spite of herself Cassie felt a bit guilty. She knew it wasn't reasonable, it was just that she realised how much her mother looked forward to her coming home in the evenings and hearing about all the goings on at work. Still, when she had the flat maybe Nora would come up and stay a night or two and they could go shopping. When she put this proposition to her mother, she stared at her as if she were mad.

"And leave the children here on their own. You must be joking, Cassie!"

"Some children," scoffed Cassie. "Barbara's nearly eighteen. John's fifteen. They're not children any more, Mam; they're well capable of looking after themselves for one night."

"Well, we'll see," Nora agreed, slightly mollified.

CHAPTER THIRTEEN

Laura arrived home from America towards the end of September and serious flat-hunting got under way. The three girls agreed to live either in Rathmines or Ranelagh. Ranelagh if possible. This would be perfect for Cassie when she was studying for her banking exams. It suited Laura fine for UCD and Aileen didn't care where she lived as long as she got out of Port Mahon. Besides she had the Mini so she was mobile.

Aileen and Cassie both took a Friday afternoon off to look at the flats Laura had ringed in the paper. Laura had gone to a few places because she was not back at college yet, but she hadn't seen anything she liked. "The greatest kips, I can tell you. Some landlords have an awful neck!" she moaned in disgust as they met up in Conways Pub in Parnell Street. They were going to have lunch before heading off on the trail. Aileen had been waxing eloquent about the heavenly mushroom vol-au-vents they served for lunch so Cassie and Laura agreed it was time they sampled them.

The place was crammed, the fog of smoke making it hard to see. It was an old-fashioned pub of great charm and always did a roaring trade at lunchtime. It took a while for them to be served but they finally got a table and were soon tucking into a hearty lunch. Aileen hadn't lied—the vol-au-vents were superb!

"Mother's not talking to me!" Aileen informed Cassie and Laura as she popped a forkful of tasty pastry and mushroom into her mouth.

"She won't be able to keep it up," Cassie responded. "Don't worry. Mam was like that at the beginning but she's getting used to it now."

"You don't know Mother!" Aileen retorted gloomily. "Martyr of martyrs."

"Ah don't worry about it, Aileen!" Laura advised. "Your mother's being totally unreasonable. It's not as if you were cutting her out of your life, for God's sake!"

"I know! I know!" sighed Aileen. "It's just the way she goes on, it's enough to wilt you."

"She'll come round, you'll see!" Cassie comforted her. "Tell her you'll have her to stay for the weekend and she can go shopping. That will cheer her up!"

Aileen brightened up immediately. "Oh I never thought of that!"

They finished lunch, Aileen fed her meter and they went down Henrty Street to look for a pair of jeans for her. She was thrilled with the lovely pair of Wranglers she got, but her good spirits disappeared when she arrived out to her car to find that she had been given a ticket for illegal parking. "For crying out loud," she shrieked. "What the hell did he give me a ticket for? There's still ten minutes on the meter. Someone's going to suffer for this." She glared around her, looking for the offending traffic warden.

"The car in front has one as well and he's got half an hour on his meter," Cassie said, puzzled.

"As a matter of fact," Laura said calmly, "no one is allowed to park here at all right now. It happens to be a clearway."

"Who said that?" demanded Aileen pugnaciously.

Laura pointed to the sign further down. "That says it!"

"Why didn't you tell me when we were parking?" snapped the furious Aileen.

"Because I didn't notice it," retorted Laura, angry herself. "And besides, I didn't think we'd be so long."

"Huh! Some lawyer you'll make if you can't notice what's staring you straight in the face," Aileen scowled, totally unreasonable.

"Well, if *you're* so perfect, and after all you *were* the driver, why didn't *you* notice it? You shouldn't be allowed behind the wheel of a car!" The friends glared at each other.

"Oh for God's sake!" interjected Cassie. "I'll pay the fine if it's going to be such a big deal! Are you going to stand here and fight for the rest of the afternoon?"

"Don't *you* start!" snapped Laura.

Cassie began to get angry. "Listen here, Laura, it's OK for you. You're a lady of leisure swanning around the place. I had to take a half-day off work and I don't intend to spend it standing arguing outside Conways Pub!"

"I am not a lady of leisure either, Cassie Jordan," Laura exclaimed indignantly. "And you have a nerve to say so!"

"Well, you get much longer holidays than I do. You're on holidays now!" Cassie declared huffily.

"I might get long holidays, Cassie, but I'll have you know I worked my butt off in America doing waitressing jobs. Surely it's not too much to have a fortnight off before facing back to the slog in college?" Laura was starting to feel very sorry for herself.

Aileen started to giggle. "And we were going to live happily ever after together in a flat. A flat, I might point out, we haven't even got yet."

"Listen to her!" Laura said to Cassie.

"You started it," Cassie said crossly to the instigator of the row.

"I humbly apologise," Aileen murmured demurely, looking as though butter wouldn't melt in her mouth.

Laura threw her eyes up to heaven. "It's a wonder to

me, Aileen O'Shaughnessy, how you've survived on this planet for so long without somebody succumbing to the urge to murder you."

"Sorry!" Aileen excused herself. "It was the shock of the ticket, especially after being so careful to feed the blasted meter. They should have a big notice on them! "I think you'll make a fantastic lawyer. Even better than Perry Mason!"

"Liar!" laughed Laura. "I didn't intend to demean your prowess as a driver. You know I'm totally in awe of your skill behind the wheel."

"No need to be sarcastic," grinned Aileen. "Cassie, are you coming or are you staying?"

"I must be mad wanting to share a flat with you pair," said Cassie, good humour restored. That was the nice thing about the girls, she reflected, as they drove around by the Rotunda. Any tiff they ever had was speedily resolved, grudges weren't held and if you had anything to say you could get it off your chest, secure in the knowledge that the friendship wouldn't suffer. That was the mark of real friends and Cassie knew she would find no truer friends than Laura and Aileen if she were to search for the rest of her life.

The first flat they looked at in Rathmines was a disaster. The landlord, a scruffy little man, showed them upstairs. The three of them looked at each other in dismay. The wallpaper, of a dirty grey pattern, was peeling in parts. The bedrooms had a terrible smell and the bathroom was grotty.

"Thanks very much," Laura said politely, "but it's not exactly what we're looking for."

"Crikey, did you see those curtains?" Cassie said in disgust. "They must never have been washed and I'd say they're there since the year dot!"

"And he had the cheek to call it an apartment! Some people are terrible chancers!" Laura sniffed. "Drive on, Macduff," she ordered their chauffeur, who had been rendered speechless by the landlord's nerve.

They viewed eight flats in various conditions, most of them not much better than the first, and were beginning to get disheartened as they drove along Beechwood Avenue in Ranelagh to see the last one on their list.

"Large modernised ground-floor flat, suit three/four. Girls only," Cassie read out as Aileen drew to a halt outside a two-storey redbrick terraced house. "It looks well kept from the outside anyway. That's usually a good indication," she observed, as they climbed out of the Mini.

"Windows and curtains are clean. I wonder is it too big for us. It said to suit four," Laura said glumly. She was beginning to lose hope at this stage.

"Look, if it's anyway decent and we can manage the rent, I think we should take it. And it said three *or* four; it just means we'll have more room," Cassie said firmly. It was obvious that unless they were prepared to pay a king's ransom they weren't going to get anything spectacular.

"Quick!" hissed Aileen. "Here's another car-load of women. Ring the doorbell so we get first refusal."

It was the best they had seen. And most importantly, it was clean. There were two double bedrooms with plenty of wardrobe space, a small but functional bathroom, a kitchen which had a table and four chairs, cooker, fridge and an old twin-tub washing-machine, which was an unexpected bonus. The sitting-room had a comfortable sofa, two armchairs and a bookcase. A big bowl of roses stood in the open fireplace. With the afternoon sun streaming in through the window, it looked very nice.

"We could do a lot with it," Cassie whispered as they inspected all the rooms once more.

"And the ground-floor flat gets the back garden so we'd be able to lie out in the summer," Laura pointed out.

"I think it's beautiful!" Aileen whispered excitedly, as the opposition came into the room they were standing in.

"It's not bad. I think we should take it," a tanned slim girl from the other group said to her two companions. Cassie, Laura and Aileen slipped discreetly out of the room.

"It's make your mind up time, girls. I think we should go for it!" Laura said.

"Me too. Definitely!" agreed Cassie happily.

"Yippee!" laughed Aileen, as they went in search of the landlord.

❦

They moved in that weekend! Such excitement! Aileen's Mini, laden from top to bottom, made three journeys from Port Mahon on Saturday. Nora, utterly taken aback by the speed of events, could only "tut-tut" her way around the house, saying she hoped Cassie wasn't making a big mistake.

Angela O'Shaughnessy developed a migraine and took to the bed.

"If we don't go now, we'll never go," Aileen said grimly as she helped Cassie carry out some of her books and tapes under Nora's disapproving eye. They were almost ready to leave.

"Have you even got a saucepan?" Nora growled.

"Oh!" exclaimed Cassie. "I never thought of that."

Her mother disappeared back into the house. "Wait

there!" she ordered. Twenty minutes later she arrived out to the car with John and Martin carrying a cardboard box between them. "There's a few pots and pans and plates and cups there and I've three blankets and a few old sheets inside if you want them."

"Oh Mam!" Cassie flung her arms around her mother's neck. "Thanks a million. You're the best in the world!"

"Go on with you. You might ring me to let me know you've arrived safely. I've never seen anything like that in my life!" She indicated Aileen's Mini, which had more bulging black sacks in it than a refuse truck.

"I will, Mam, and I'll come home on Tuesday night to stay and tell you all about it," Cassie promised.

John reappeared, carrying his old hurley. "Here, take this in case you ever need it at night," he said gruffly. Her brother was taller than she was. John had turned into a fine young man.

"Thanks, Johnny," Cassie smiled at him. "You'll be coming up to stay with me now and again, won't you?"

"Sure thing," he agreed.

"And you too, Martin," Cassie did not forget her younger brother, who was trying to fit the cardboard box in on top of the black sacks.

"Yep!" he said.

Barbara stood in the doorway with a cross face. She utterly resented Cassie's leaving home. She was *so* envious of her older sister. How she longed to be taking off to Dublin to live in a flat and lead a sophisticated life, instead of being stuck at home, studying for the Leaving Cert and being left to do all the housework. Barbara felt truly sorry for herself.

"See you on Tuesday, Barbara," Cassie said.

"Yeah," responded her sister sulkily.

"I wish you weren't going, Cassie. I'll be very lonely

for you," Irene confided. Cassie hugged her young sister.

"I'll be home on Tuesday night, Irene, and I'll come home some weekends and you and Mam will be able to come and visit me now and again. Won't that be lovely? We'll be able to go into Dublin and look around all the shops and have a meal together and we'll have a great time."

"That will be brill!" Her younger sister cheered up immediately.

Cassie looked at her mother standing forlornly in the middle of the drive. She felt a sharp twinge of guilt. Maybe she was being terribly selfish. "I'll see you Tuesday, Mam."

"All right, then." Nora met her daughter's eyes and took two steps towards her. "Mind yourself, pet," she said, giving her a fierce hug.

Cassie struggled to keep the wobble out of her voice. "I will. I love you. Thanks for everything!"

"Right! Off we go!" Aileen exclaimed cheerfully, seeing what was happening. Ushering her friend into the car, she scorched down the drive before Cassie knew where she was.

"Best way to do it," she said gently. "No point in getting maudlin."

"I feel a real bitch," Cassie said, the tears coming into her eyes. All she could think of was the lonely look on her mother's face when she hugged her goodbye.

"I know!" sighed Aileen. "I do too and it isn't fair! For Chrissakes it's not as if we're going to Australia and we'll never see them again. We're only going to Ranelagh, for crying out loud."

"I know," Cassie sniffed, "but we're leaving home all the same. I suppose it's bound to upset them."

"I swear to God," vowed Aileen grimly as she swerved

to avoid a pothole and ended up driving into a bigger one that caused the car to rattle loudly, "if I ever have a daughter I'll never say one word to her if she wants to go and get a flat. In fact I'll help her look for one."

"Me too," agreed Cassie.

"What the hell's the matter with you two?" Laura enquired when she saw the two long faces that presented themselves to her an hour and a half later. She had brought her stuff over on the first trip and had been left behind to make room and more importantly to start unpacking.

"Just a touch of the guilts!" Aileen confessed.

"Shag the guilts," Laura swore succinctly. "Come on, let's have a cup of tea to cheer ourselves up. I've the kettle on for the last twenty minutes. I bought us a packet of chocolate biscuits to keep us going and then we'll start doing your unpacking. I've done loads already!"

It was quite late by the time they were finished unpacking all their bits and pieces. Although the place was already clean, they scrubbed and washed the kitchen and bathroom. Cassie and Aileen decided that because Laura was studying and would need some peace and quiet, she should have a bedroom to herself.

"I wonder would the landlord allow us paint the rooms ourselves," Cassie mused as she hung up the last of her clothes in her half of the wardrobe. The oatmeal walls of the bedroom were very drab and just crying out for a lick of new paint. Already Cassie was planning colour schemes.

"It's a real adventure, isn't it?" Aileen said enthusiastically as she arranged her collection of black cats on her half of the dressing-table. "Imagine being able to do exactly what we want when we want. Oh bliss! I'm going to lie in tomorrow until noon."

"Me too," said Cassie.

CHAPTER FOURTEEN

Cassie had forgotten it was Sunday. When she woke up in a strange bed, with Aileen across the room from her, she didn't know where she was for a minute. Then comprehension dawned. This was her new flat. This was the first day of the beginning of her new life. It was a beautiful September morning. The sun would be shining on a sparkling turquoise sea in Port Mahon, she thought, with the tiniest hint of nostalgia. The thought was quickly banished as she hopped out of bed, taking care not to wake the sleeping beauty in the other bed. Aileen snored gently in a little symphony that Cassie was going to have to learn to live with. Quietly she slipped into the bathroom. There was no sound from Laura's room; she too was obviously fast asleep. Cassie had found it hard to get to sleep the night before. Her thoughts kept returning to Nora and the look on her face as Cassie had said goodbye to her. How could some people cut their ties so easily? Cassie envied them. But she was too entangled in her bonds of guilt.

How did one get rid of one's guilt? Why did she have these feelings? Barbara would never be troubled by such things, nor Irene; she was so used to worrying about herself exclusively. John would be like her. He too would feel a responsibility towards their mother. Maybe it was because she was the eldest. Aileen was like her, but then look at Laura. She managed very well to make her choices about her life and not feel badly about it. Well, Cassie was going to do the same. Today was a beautiful day and she was going to enjoy it.

They had gone shopping the previous night and spent a fortune, setting themselves up with the basics. They had decided to put ten pounds a week each into the kitty. Laura was taking charge of it. So much would be saved up for the ESB and heating; the rest would be used to buy communal requirements like milk and bread and sugar and toothpaste and toilet-rolls. Last night in the supermarket they had had a communal trolley into which they had put everything for which they would be sharing the bill. Then the total was divided by three. They also had their own baskets for personal purchases. It was the fairest way and they were all quite happy with it.

Then, at supper, they had worked out a rota system for their housekeeping. Each of them would have a week during which they would be responsible for keeping the bathroom clean and doing the vacuuming and dusting. Of course it was expected of them all that they would leave the bathroom and kitchen tidy after use. It was only fair and they wanted to live harmoniously together and not end up bickering about who was doing what or who wasn't. As regards cooking meals, they would be flexible. If they were all there together, they would eat together; if not they would look after themselves. In theory it all seemed very sensible but only time would tell if things were working out and going to plan. As Aileen said seriously, sharing a flat was like getting married and it could be the end of a beautiful relationship unless they got their act together.

Cassie made herself some tea, and poured cornflakes into a dish. Opening the back door she sat on the step and raised her face to the sun. It was going to be a scorcher for sure. A day for serious sunbathing, despite the lateness of the season. It was a real bonus that they had the back garden. It was a nice mature little garden with a good square lawn and trees and shrubs in abundance. Along the back wall, banks of nasturtiums made a riot of colour. Up beside her, an urn of tumbling night-scented stock perfumed the early morning air. Cassie sniffed appreciatively. The smell of night-scented stock was so beautiful. Jack had loved it and it reminded her of him. Tonight as dusk fell it would smell really wonderful. It was unusual, she felt, especially after some of the flats she had seen, to get such a nice, well-tended garden. But the landlord had told them that until last year a widow had lived in this house and the garden had been her pride and joy. One night her house had been broken into and vandalised. Forty years of happy memories had disappeared forever, as fear invaded her life and every corner of the home she had once loved. Unable to sleep at night, afraid to go out for fear of what she might find when she returned home, she had suffered a breakdown. In the end she had given up her home and her lovely garden and her independence and gone to live with her married daughter. Just another crime statistic, but in reality a woman whose life had been utterly changed by a criminal.

There were new aluminium windows in the house now, with safety locks. But the landlord had told them to be conscious of their security, making sure to lock up when they went out and to leave a light on at night. These were simple little precautions that seemed strange after living in Port Mahon, where some people never locked their doors and a burglary was a rarity and the talk of the town for ages.

Ranelagh was a very nice area to live in, the landlord had said reassuringly when he saw their worried faces, but in this day and age it was better to be safe than sorry. Cassie hoped the woman was happy living with her daughter wherever she was, but it was a pity all the same to have had to leave such a beautiful home and garden.

There wasn't a sound but the birds singing and the occasional dog barking. Cassie sat enjoying her sunny solitude. She made herself another cup of tea and had another bowl of cornflakes. Of course it was only eight-thirty on a Sunday morning when most normal people were enjoying a lie-in. But she knew she couldn't go back to bed. She would get her *Gone With the Wind* that she had finally treated herself to and read a bit of it, and then go to ten o'clock Mass in Ranelagh church. Neither Laura nor Aileen went to Mass any longer as they felt it had no bearing on their lives. But it wasn't a chore to Cassie.

In Port Mahon she had quite liked going to Mass. There was always a great air about the town on Sunday morning. People dressed in their best. They had time to stop and greet each other as they came in all directions to the church. At eleven-thirty Mass, Cassie's favourite, the choir always sang and the rafters would be raised as the congregation accompanied them in the old familiar traditional hymns. Cassie liked singing in church. She liked feeling part of the community. It gave her, in some strange way, a sense of security. This was her time and her place; her forbears had been here before her and her descendants, if she had any, would be here after. Laura and Aileen thought she was crazy to enjoy going to Mass. They could think of far better things to do with that hour on Sundays, but Cassie didn't mind. She liked it and so she went and if she *were* mad, who cared? To each his own! Besides, somehow, at Mass she always felt closer to Jack.

She spent a very relaxed hour sitting on the step reading her treasured novel. She was nearing the end of it and Scarlett was just about to face Melanie, having been caught embracing Ashley by India Wilkes.

Reluctantly Cassie got up and put the book aside. She'd finish it later on. She couldn't wait to see what was going to happen. Cassie thought Scarlett was magnificent, a woman who did what she wanted and to hell with convention. She would love to be like Scarlett O'Hara, but somehow or another she knew she was more of a Melanie!

Dressed in a cotton summer dress, Cassie slipped silently out of the house and turned towards Ranelagh church. Other people were walking in the same direction and Cassie smiled to herself. Port Mahon, Ranelagh, it didn't matter; all over the country, all over the world, on Sunday mornings, people went to church.

Walking along at a brisk pace, Cassie gazed around her new environment. It was really very attractive. In the distance, the church tower was framed by the Dublin mountains. She hadn't realised they were so near to the mountains. Today, it was so crisp and clear, they seemed very near, their patchwork of greens and golds and purples so close it was as if they were just down the road. Redbrick houses similar to her own lined both sides of the street; most of them were well kept and cared for. Unkempt gardens and unpainted doors were the exceptions. Passing a window with the blinds raised, she could see children playing inside in the sitting-room. From what she had seen since her arrival in the area, there seemed a good mixture of young and old and in-betweens. Many houses were in flats but just as many were owned by families. There was a very nice atmosphere about the place and Cassie knew instinctively that she was going to like living here.

The church, which seemed huge and imposing from the outside, was a pleasant surprise to Cassie. In ways it reminded her of Our Lady, Star of the Sea in Port Mahon.

They even had the same stations of the cross. And the sun shone through the stained-glass windows just like at home! After Mass, she bought the Sunday papers. All she was going to do today was laze out the back eating and reading. It was so pleasant. At home Nora would be fussing about having the roast in the oven before going to church and there'd be a queue for the bathroom and general mayhem and any poor unfortunate who was trying to have a lie-in could forget it. Here there was just peace and quiet and the freedom to do as you please was a joy. She stopped at the newsagents to buy some chocolate as a treat. After all, it was their second day in the flat and that was as good an excuse to buy chocolate as any!

❦

The girls were up when she got back. They were having breakfast and Laura was already in her bikini.

"Let's not waste a minute of it," she beamed. "Isn't it a dream of a day?"

"I think I'm having a dream," Aileen said as she dipped a finger of toast into the runny egg in front of her. "Here I am, sitting in my nightdress at the breakfast-table, with my two best buddies, preparing to spend a blissful day sunbathing, with nothing more to do than to decide what paper to read and when to have dinner. And then to decide which pub I will bring you to for a drink tonight. After years of getting up to bring Mother her breakfast in bed and listening to her trying to decide whether to have carrots and broccoli or peas and turnips for lunch, which is always served at one-thirty promptly. Then the washing-up has to be done and afternoon tea and biscuits prepared for her. By which time it's well into the afternoon and a whole day is wasted. I can't believe I'm going to be lying out in the sun by eleven-thirty!"

"Believe it!" laughed Laura.

Before long they were stretched out on towels, oiling Ambre Solaire onto their skins. "I love the smell of this," Cassie confessed as she rubbed it onto her midriff.

"Mmmm! Me too!" said Aileen, who, in spite of her copper curls and fair skin, tanned beautifully. "It's so foreign. You know, I think we should go abroad next year. We could start saving now. And we could wait until Laura comes home from the States with a bit of money. We could go mid-September."

"Oooh, yesss!" squealed the other two when they heard this brainwave. In a state of euphoria they began planning for their first holiday abroad as they lay stretched out, munching the chocolate Cassie had brought home.

It was really the most perfect day. They lay listening to Solid Gold MacNamara on Cassie's transistor as all the greatest hits were played, often singing aloud in accompaniment. After a rousing rendition of Neil Diamond's "Cracklin' Rosie," they decided they were parched and Aileen was dispatched to the nearest off-licence with a contribution from the kitty while Cassie and Laura went inside to prepare lunch. They had bought a cooked chicken and various salads and some soft rolls. It didn't take a minute to prepare. Cassie quickly washed the crispy lettuce and put it on the three plates. Carving the chicken expertly, she added the meat to the lettuce while Laura arranged slices of tomato, radish and cucumber artistically around the edge. They made a pot of tea and carried the lot out to the garden.

Aileen arrived, brandishing a bottle of Dubonnet in one hand and a bottle of white lemonade in the other. "The man in the off-licence said this was just the thing for a hot summer's day!" she grinned. The picnic was scrumptious. They had coleslaw and Waldorf salad and egg and onion to add to their meal and they sat in a circle and tucked in, washing it down with sips of ice-cold Dubonnet and white.

"What is it about eating out that makes food so much tastier?" Laura mused as she spread some egg and onion on a bread roll, added a slice of chicken and a spoonful of coleslaw and took a huge bite.

"Don't ask me!" Cassie murmured happily, cheeks bulging.

"All I know is that I'm starving for no reason at all," Aileen reflected. "We'd better be careful or we're going to end up as huge as hogs."

They decided their friend spoke wisely. So from now on, they would pig out on Sundays and maybe Saturdays but during the week they would eat prudently.

The rest of the day passed in a lazy haze. They read the papers and their books and Aileen's musical snores rent the air as she dozed off. Cassie was in that lovely state of lethargy, neither awake nor asleep, just totally relaxed. More relaxed than at any other time since her father's death. She had made the right move, she knew it, and things could only get better.

"We got a great colour, didn't we?" Aileen preened as she pranced around the bedroom after having her shower, dressed in only a pair of white briefs. They were getting ready to go out on the town.

"Can I wear your white cotton top if you're not wearing it?" Cassie asked. "Mine's in the linen-basket at home. I'll have to collect it on Tuesday."

"Of course you can," Aileen replied cheerfully. "Could I have some of that gorgeous pink nail varnish you're wearing?"

"Be my guest," Cassie handed her the bottle.

"Are you ready yet?" Laura queried, poking her head around the door. Of course she looked sensational in a pair of black tailored pants and a loose white knitted top, with her jet-black hair hanging like a shiny curtain around her face. Aileen, in an eau-de-Nile batwing top and white jeans, looked as fresh as a daisy, while Cassie in the white cotton top with a short beige pencil skirt looked tanned and vibrantly healthy, her chestnut locks glinting after a day in the sun. There was nothing like a day's sunbathing to give a healthy glow and they looked a very attractive trio as they entered the Burlington Hotel. They had decided to go for a drink before heading off to Annabels nightclub.

The hotel was abuzz as a group of Japanese tourists checked out and a coach-load of Americans checked in. It was just as well they had walked, Aileen reflected; otherwise they would never have got parking. Besides, she wouldn't have been able to drink. In spite of her zany ways, Aileen had a core of sense to her and she never drove after drinking. They sat perched on bar stools, enjoying Bacardi and Coke, watching the activities around them. They were laughing and chatting and thoroughly enjoying themselves when two rather drunk middle-aged men joined them at the bar. The first introduced himself as Will Paxwell and offered to buy them a drink, urged on by his companion, who, he told them, was called Mick Browne. They were in PR, they informed the girls with an air of great self-importance. Cassie glanced at Laura, whose expression unmistakably said, So what?

"Come on now, girls, what are you drinking?" Will said expansively as he breathed whiskey fumes all over them.

"We're fine, thank you," Cassie said politely, wishing they'd scram. They'd been enjoying themselves until this pair offered their unwelcome attentions.

"Oh come on, doll! You're a nice-looking bird. I'd like to buy you a drink!" leered Mick, putting an arm around Cassie's shoulder. Cassie froze. She didn't want to cause a scene, but she was damned if a drunk man, a complete stranger, thought he could put his arm around her just like that. What was it with some men that made them think women were there purely to stroke their egos and make them feel good? Well, times had changed and so had women and she wasn't going to sit and be mauled by an ignoramus. Giving Mick an elbow in the ribs that made him gasp and wheeze in shock, Cassie stood up and glared at the puffy-faced man. "I do not want a drink from you. I am not a 'bird' or a 'doll' and please leave us to have our drinks in peace."

"What the fuck are you? Some kind of fucking feminist or something? All I'm offering is to buy you a fucking drink!" Mick blustered angrily. "What you need is a good six-inch prick inside you and I'm just the man to give it to you." There was real venom in his voice.

Cassie turned her back on him. She was shaking inside. She felt sick and somehow violated by his crudeness.

"Listen, buster!" Laura hissed icily. "Get lost or you're going to be had up for harassment. Believe me, I'm a lawyer."

Aileen turned to Will, who was staring blearily at them. "Take your obnoxious little friend and clear off before I call the manager."

"The manager's a personal friend of mine," muttered Will, as he took the furious Mick by the arm. "Come on, Mick, don't waste your time on these lezzers."

"Yeah, fucking lezzers, that's what they are. Wouldn't know what to do with a real man," Mick wheezed as he and his friend reeled off, leaving the girls shaken.

"Are you all right, Cassie? You've gone a bit pale?" Laura asked anxiously.

"Can you believe that?" Cassie demanded. "Can you not even go and have a drink with a few friends in this day and age without having to put up with that crap?" She felt so angry and helpless. At that moment she hated every man in the universe.

"And the awful thing is that he is the one who feels hard-done by? He's the one who thinks he's got a God-given right to treat women like dirt. *And* he expects them to like it," Laura fumed.

"They've ruined our night and our perfect day!" Aileen raged, glowering at the barman, who had just passed by and given her an innocent smile.

"Well, if they do that, they've won, and I'm not letting two creeps like that ruin *my* day," Cassie retorted, trying to regain her composure. "Come on, let's have another drink and forget about the bastards!"

"Right on! That's my girl!" Laura assented.

"Three more Bacardi and Cokes, please," Aileen ordered the bemused bartender. "Did you see the ears on that Will creep? Dumbo had nothing on him. His mother should have pinned them back when he was a baby. I'm sorry I didn't call him Big Ears," she muttered regretfully.

"Did you see the other old yoke with the head dyed off him? He must have been sixty if he was a day," Laura scoffed.

"Probably a eunuch to boot!" Aileen was still highly indignant.

Cassie laughed. "Ah forget them. They're pathetic and not worth a minute of our time. Come on, let's drink up and go down to Annabels. I'm dying for a bop. I haven't been dancing in ages."

"Me neither!" said Aileen "Come on, let's hit the road!"

They didn't have far to go. Annabels was the hotel's night club and was one of the most popular nightspots in the city. It was packed with glamorous young people intent on having a good time, and before long the girls were out on the floor dancing, the incident in the bar completely forgotten. Cassie met Jim Walsh, one of the guys who had done the training course with her, and they started comparing notes about their respective branches. He was with two friends and they all joined Aileen and Laura at the bar and spent the rest of the evening together. They came back to the flat for coffee after the disco.

It was lovely to have the freedom to bring back friends to the flat, even though it was the early hours. It was not something that could be done on a regular basis in Port Mahon, Cassie reflected. Although her mother had never objected to her bringing Donie in for a quick cup of coffee after he left her home, Nora didn't like Cassie to keep very late hours. Aileen was not allowed to bring men home under any circumstances and Laura wouldn't bother because there was no way she would introduce anybody to her father. It was just so liberating to be able to invite people home for coffee and laughs and a chat, knowing there would be no disapproving faces in the morning.

"It was a day of days," Aileen said happily as she snuggled down in her bed. She was snoring in seconds.

The first of many, Cassie promised herself, as she switched out her bedside light and fell asleep.

❧

It was the kind of day that was to be repeated many times over the months that followed as the three of them adapted to living together, thoroughly enjoying the freedom of doing as they pleased and living the life they wanted to.

When Cassie went to stay on her weekly overnight visit home, Nora frequently moaned about the fact that she missed her daughter's company but Cassie eventually began to be able to let it in one ear and out the other. All of the family had come to stay in the flat at one stage or another and Barbara in particular had been most impressed. This was exactly the way she wanted to live, she confided in her elder sister. As soon as she left school, she too was going to come up to Dublin and live a life of glamour and sophistication just like Cassie. When the girls took Barbara and Judy to Annabels, they were ecstatic.

Angela O'Shaughnessy had not spoken to Aileen for a month after her departure from the family home in Port Mahon but Aileen had weathered the storm well. She had pretended that things were normal, and when she went home on her weekly visit she acted as though nothing untoward had happened. Eventually Angela could put up with it no longer as it almost killed her not being able to moan, and she made it up with her. Besides, it was very handy having Aileen in the city. She could get her daughter to do all kinds of messages for her, like getting her crochet cotton from Trimmings on the quays. Aileen used to come back from Port Mahon practically foaming at the mouth because of the list of messages her mother had given her to do.

Angela so enjoyed her first shopping weekend staying at the flat that she began to make plans to come up once a fortnight. Aileen had to put her foot down. Staying at the flat, having her daughter and the girls cooking for her, with not a thing to do except act the lady, suited Angela down to the ground. And she would have been a very regular guest if Aileen hadn't said no. She pointed out to her mother that Laura and Cassie might want to bring *their* mothers up and besides they couldn't be expected to have visitors all the time. Of course Angela had got huffy but fortunately this time it didn't last too long as she wanted to come up to Dublin to do her Christmas shopping and she had to be talking to Aileen for that!

CHAPTER FIFTEEN

It was the girls' first Christmas in the flat and the excitement was mighty. Although the three of them were busy socialising with boyfriends and workmates, they had decided ages ago that they would keep this particular Saturday free to decorate the flat and celebrate their first Christmas as independent women.

"Let's bunker in, light a huge fire and I'll cook one of my gourmet dinners," Aileen suggested. Cassie and Laura guffawed. Aileen was not the world's greatest cook.

They started off the morning with a big fry-up, a rare treat as they were usually too poor to afford the luxury of rashers and sausages. Cassie had volunteered to cook breakfast. Humming to herself, she got the pan out of the cupboard and switched on the grill. The kitchen was cold, it always was in winter, but once the cooker was going there'd be a bit of warmth in the place. It was hard to believe she had been living here only since the end of September. And what a difference it made not having to commute in and out of Port Mahon to work.

Aileen appeared at the kitchen door, shivering. "Brass monkey weather, isn't it? I'll stick on the Super-Ser." She wheeled the gas heater in from the sitting-room and lit it. Cassie smiled at the sight of her friend huddling over the heater. Aileen was a very cold creature and winter was a trial to her. At the moment she was dressed in a pink flannelette nightdress, quilted dressing-gown and pink bedsocks. As well as having an electric blanket, she brought a hot-water bottle to bed. The only time Aileen ever longed to be married, she had confided in Cassie and Laura one night as they sat talking over supper, was on a bitterly cold winter's night. Then a husband would come in very useful.

"That smells gorgeous!" Laura arrived, already dressed and raring to go. She had been up studying since six. She wanted to have her assignments finished so she could go into town with the girls and enjoy herself with out feeling guilty. Cassie had great admiration for her friend. She was really slogging her guts out to get a good law degree and holding down two part-time jobs as well

"This will keep us going," Cassie said to the girls as she dished up rashers, sausages, eggs and pudding, adding two slices of crispy fried bread to each plate.

"Yum yum!" Laura dived on her breakfast, giving the impression that she hadn't eaten in weeks, whereas she had in fact scoffed a pizza with her college friends for supper the night before. Laura never put on a pound, much to the envy of the other pair; they were constantly watching their weight, with varying degrees of success.

Cassie had been out with Jim Walsh for a Chinese meal. She saw him occasionally but it was just social dating, really. They enjoyed each other's company but it wasn't the romance of the year.

Aileen had broken it off with POD, as she used to call Peter O'Donoghue, her soldier boyfriend. He spent months abroad on tours of duty and their relationship had suffered badly because of it. The best thing was a clean break, she told the girls. There was now a man called Liam Flynn in her life. He was an architect, Aileen informed them. The girls had never met him and Aileen didn't talk a lot about him, which was totally unlike her, so they respected her privacy and didn't pry. They knew Aileen would discuss him when she was ready.

"What's for dinner?" Cassie asked as she dipped her fried bread in tomato ketchup and took a satisfying bite.

Aileen smirked. "Chicken à la Aileen. Remind me to get cashew nuts in the village."

"Cashew nuts! How posh!" grinned Cassie. "Can we afford a bottle of wine?"

"I'll check the kitty," Aileen said, responding with alacrity to the mention of wine. "Yikes, I think we've been robbed!" she exclaimed in dismay a minute later, appearing in the doorway with the kitty jar in her hand. "There's only thirty pence left!"

"Calm down," Laura interjected, coolly leaning over to pinch one of Aileen's crunchy rasher rinds, which she proceeded to eat with relish. "The coalman called and said he wouldn't be around again before Christmas so I got a couple of bags. And we were out of toothpaste and loo-rolls so I got some."

"Never mind, we can make provision for a bottle out of the Christmas fund," Cassie said cheerfully. They had been putting a couple of quid aside over the previous few weeks especially for Christmas. Today it was going to be spent.

"Speaking of the Christmas fund..." Aileen sat down again to finish her breakfast. "I saw a dote of a Christmas tree down the village. It will be perfect in front of the window but we'd better get a move on in case someone nabs it!"

Half an hour later they were ensconced in Aileen's Mini on their way into the city. Zooming through Mornington Road, as was her wont, Aileen passed within inches of a terrified cyclist and narrowly avoided sending a startled cat to its eternal rest. Her driving skills were on a par with her cookery ones!

"Go easy!" murmured Laura. "We want to be alive to eat this 'gourmet' dinner."

"You're perfectly safe!" retorted their flatmate as she swung left into Ranelagh village and came to a screeching halt on double yellow lines outside the greengrocer's. "I'll just tell them to keep the tree for us," she said airily, hopping out of the car and forgetting to put the hand-brake on.

The traffic was brutal as the world and his mother headed into town to do their Christmas shopping and they were bumper to bumper the whole way in. Cassie and Laura were pleading for valium as Aileen lane-hopped with abandon to the sound of horns hooting in their wake.

When they finally got to Henry Street, it was buzzing with carol-singers and street-traders and throngs of people doing their Christmas shopping. "Let's get to it!" said Cassie, pulling out the list. Tinsel, decorations, balloons, fairy lights for the Christmas tree, snow for the windows—they didn't know where to start. They decided to have a cup of coffee and a cream slice in the Kylemore to plan their strategy. "I think we should go to Hector Greys for the lights," Cassie mused. The others nodded in agreement as they sipped the hot milky coffee and made short shrift of cream slices.

The stalls on Henry Street were a delight. They rooted and rummaged through decorations, deciding what would suit and what wouldn't. Laura held up a beaming cherub with gold-and-silver wings. "Ah look at this little angel. Isn't she adorable? We could put her on top of the tree."

"And look at these!" Aileen exclaimed, holding up six little robins, "we could put these on the branches."

"I like these Santa Claus lights. Could we get one set here and the others in Hector Greys?" Cassie asked, holding up a set for their inspection. They all agreed that they were perfect. They bought coloured balls and tinsel and completed their purchases in Hector Greys as planned. Then they went on the trail of their Christmas outfits.

"I hate these communal changing-rooms," muttered Cassie as she struggled into a slinky black dress. Beside her a blonde was undressing, with a perfect figure—and a tan to add insult to injury. She wore beautiful silk lingerie and Cassie felt totally inadequate in her white cotton briefs and bra.

Aileen caught her eye. "I'm going to treat myself to some new underwear! Silk too!" she whispered.

"So am I," vowed Cassie. "And I'm going on a diet!" She bought the dress in a bigger size.

Laura bought a beautiful red silk shirt and a pair of black matador pants. Aileen could find nothing that she liked and was beginning to feel very down in the dumps.

"Let's try Girls Only," suggested Laura.

Aileen made a face. "I don't like their stuff. Some of it is real cheap and tarty-looking."

"Yeah, I suppose so. Come on, let's try that little Indian boutique down Liffey Street. They've lovely stuff there!" Laura said encouragingly.

"Maybe we'll just go home." Aileen was becoming despondent.

"Come on!" ordered Cassie. "We're not going home until you've got your outfit."

Ten minutes later Aileen was twirling around in a beautiful fringed Indian skirt with a matching shawl, over a white blouse. The rich autumnal colours of the skirt and shawl suited her auburn hair beautifully and she looked lovely. It was an unusual outfit, but pure Aileen.

"Thanks a million for putting up with me," Aileen bubbled as they left the shop, clutching her purchases to her bosom. "I was really starting to get desperate."

"So were we!" Laura said drily, and laughed at the expression on Aileen's face. "Only joking, honey!" she teased.

"I think we should have a quick cuppa and then go solo for half an hour," Cassie suggested, leading the way upstairs into Woolworth's café.

"They do real fat sausages in here. I think I'll have some," Laura mused. It was a long time since breakfast and the cream slices earlier on had been only a snack.

"More sausages!" Aileen exclaimed. "OK, we'll have a plate of sausage and chips between us," she said firmly. "I want you to be able to eat my fantastic dinner!"

By four thirty, weary but triumphant, they headed for the car-park. As well as getting all their decorations, they had managed quite a bit of Christmas shopping. The air had turned very chilly and they could see the carol-singers' breath as they lustily sang "Silent Night" to an appreciative crowd outside Arnotts. The Christmas lights twinkled against the dusky-pink sky and people pushed their way along the crowded street. Henry Street at Christmastime had an atmosphere all of its own and

Cassie loved the hustle and bustle of it, and the women of Moore Street singing, "Five for twenty the Christmas wrapping paper!" and "Get your Cheeky Charlies!"

Their chanting brought back childhood memories to Cassie as she followed Aileen and Laura. When the children were small, her parents had always brought them into Dublin for a treat just before Christmas, and even now, years later, she could still remember the great sense of awe and excitement she had felt as a child. In those days when crime was not rampant, none of the shops had shutters on the windows. Jack and Nora would walk the length of O'Connell Street and Henry Street with five open-mouthed children in their wake, gazing through shop windows at the wondrous displays of toys and fancy goods. The illuminated Christmas trees along O'Connell Street and the lights strung across Henry Street gave a fairytale illusion of another world. Trying to make up one's mind about what to ask Santa for when there was such an array of goodies to choose from was part of the excitement. John and Martin, in particular, changed their minds every shop window they came to.

Then, on their return home, having stopped for the treat of treats, fish and chips out of Macari's chipper, the Jordans would all sit down at the big dining-table and Nora would hand out pens and paper. The next hour would be spent writing and re-writing the precious letters to Santa Claus. All five epistles would be ceremoniously placed in the chimney, which was especially cleaned for the occasion. The excitement when all the letters were found to have disappeared the following morning was indescribable. If she had one wish, Cassie thought, as she gazed at the good-humoured pandemonium around her, it was to be a child just once more and to be in Henry Street with Jack and Nora and the others on a crisp frosty night before Christmas.

"Come on! Stop dawdling! We've to collect the tree," Aileen reminded her, pushing forward through the crowds like Queen Boadicea heading to battle.

They arrived back at the flat with the tree sticking out through both rear windows of the Mini and Laura and Cassie perched precariously on the front seat, trying to avoid the pine-needled branches. Aileen's dote of a tree had turned out to be a fat little bush.

An hour later, Aileen, fortifying herself with cooking sherry, serenaded them with "Hark the Herald Angels Sing" as she prepared their repast. Cassie and Laura were struggling with the unruly little tree. Try as they might, they could not get it to stand straight in the bucket of soil. Like a dipso, it kept toppling sideways. "I'll fix you!" muttered Laura grimly, marching out past the singing Aileen to the back yard. Locating a sturdy piece of wood, she went back in and rammed it up against the base of the tree. That did the trick.

"That deserves a drink!" Cassie approved, busy putting a plug on the lights.

"Hear! Hear!" cheered Aileen, appearing with the sherry bottle in one hand and the wine bottle in the other and a holly wreath on her head. "Take your pick!"

"Aileen O'Shaughnessy, you are the limit!" laughed Laura. The smells wafting from the kitchen were mouth-watering but Aileen just smirked as they begged to know what was for dinner. "Wait and see!" She disappeared to her domain and the girls got down to the serious business of decorating. Everything was going to plan and Laura and Cassie were thrilled with their artistic endeavours.

Twenty minutes later a horrified shriek emanated from the kitchen and Cassie and Laura rushed in to find the frying-pan simmering under a froth of bubbles as

Aileen rent the air with every curse in her wide and varied vocabulary.

"What did you do?" the girls shrieked in unison.

"I thought it was the drum of salt!" wailed Aileen, "and it was the washing-up liquid! My beautiful dinner is ruined!"

Cassie caught Laura's gaze. They stared at each other and then they were laughing, laughing until the tears ran down their cheeks, clutching their sides as they howled with mirth at the sight of Aileen aghast in front of her bubbling frying-pan.

"It's not funny!" Aileen shrieked in outrage. "The chicken is ruined!" This only made the other pair laugh louder. "Well, you can starve then!" she retorted, beginning to laugh in spite of herself.

"That's the best laugh I've ever had," gasped Cassie, wiping her eyes five minutes later. "This is one of your star turns, O'Shaughnessy."

"Glad you enjoyed it," giggled the now-recovered Aileen. "We'll have to use the rent money to buy dinner!"

By ten-thirty, the flat was decorated to their satisfaction, the windows with snow and red tape— Cassie's idea—the tree a masterpiece of twinkling lights, sparkling balls and glittering tinsel. Holly adorned the pictures and a huge spray of mistletoe hung from the lightshade. They had wrapped the Christmas presents they had bought and these lay under the tree, artistically arranged by Cassie, who was good at such things. She had wrapped the bucket holding the tree in silver foil and it caught the reflection of the lights in a shimmer. A small crib was placed on top of the television.

Sitting in the firelight, with just the glow of the fairy lights to illuminate the room, the girls tucked into the fish and chips that Aileen had fetched for them. Another bottle of wine helped to ease the trauma of the ruined dinner and they were thoroughly enjoying their evening at home together.

Lifting her glass, Cassie smiled at her two best friends. "To our first Christmas in the flat and to many more to come!"

"Happy Christmas," smiled Laura, lifting her glass.

"And many happy returns," grinned Aileen, as she clinked her glass with theirs.

CHAPTER SIXTEEN

Cassie and Aileen had gone to bed but Laura was busy writing her Christmas cards. Sitting on the floor in front of the still-red fire, she gazed around the decorated room with pleasure. She hadn't wanted to go to bed; it was too nice sitting in the gentle glow of the Christmas tree lights. The difference the decorations made to the room! It had been a real treat for her to decorate the room today. In fact the whole day had been a treat. Laura wasn't used to such a fuss being made about Christmas.

At home they didn't bother much about decorating. Oh they got a turkey and pudding, but most of the day was spent in front of the TV and the only decorations were a few bits of holly and whatever cards the family received. Peter didn't believe in decorating Christmas trees.

At home as the days got nearer Christmas, things would get tenser and tenser. Her elder brother would be arriving home drunk every evening. Her maternal grandmother would be coming to stay for Christmas as usual, and Peter would be making nasty remarks about being lumped with his mother-in-law yet again, and Laura's mother would become pale and pinched-looking as the tension mounted and she longed for the whole awful carry-on to be over as quickly as possible.

For as long as she could remember, Laura had hated Christmas. There had always been rows. Rows between her mother and father, rows between her grandmother and father, and then, when her brother had started drinking, rows with him. This year she was spending only Christmas Day at home and then she was coming back to the peace of this little flat on St Stephen's Day. Cassie and Aileen were both spending Christmas and St Stephen's Day in Port Mahon, so she would be the only one here. But she didn't care. She just couldn't cope with home any longer. It was so wearying and soul-destroying hearing the same old arguments and then listening to her mother moaning bitterly about it all.

How many times had Laura told her to put her foot down and demand to be treated with respect? How many times had she told her to tell one of her sisters to take her grandmother for a change? How many times had she told her to kick her brother out of the house and make him stand on his own two feet? He might think twice about coming home paralytic with drink and puking all over the place if he had to clean up after himself and take responsibility for his actions.

Every year Anne Quinn gave out about her husband, mother and son making Christmas a misery for her and every year Laura told her to do something about it. This year, she had even suggested that her mother spend Christmas in the flat with her and to hell with the other three. Laura thought it was the perfect solution. It would really give the others something to think about and perhaps finally make them realise that Anne was no longer prepared to be a doormat. But her mother had refused the offer.

"I couldn't do that," Anne responded limply. "It wouldn't be fair—and besides, what would people say?"

"Who cares what they say? And why wouldn't it be fair?" Laura retorted vehemently, feeling so angry with her mother she wanted to shake her. "Is it fair the way you're treated year after year? For God's sake, Ma, stand up for yourself and make them respect you."

Anne just shrugged her shoulders listlessly. "Sure, they take no notice anyway of anything I say or do or want," was invariably the defeatist response.

If her mother would only make some small move in the right direction Laura would give her every encouragement but that whiny, resigned acceptance of her lot infuriated her so much she frequently had to bite her tongue when listening to her mother's complaints.

Well, she'd go home on Christmas Day and that would be her duty done and then she'd get to hell out of that pathetic household and come back to Dublin and the lovely new life she was carving out for herself.

Laura stared into the glowing embers. She *was* creating a new life for herself, and very nice it was too. She thoroughly enjoyed university life, being part of the student body, participating in debates, joining the different societies, drinking gallons of coffee in the huge cafeteria while arguing points of law with her classmates, studying in the huge library with hundreds of others, all bonded by the common desire to get their exams and make their mark on the world. Campus life was a joy to Laura, unlike some of her peers who found the place vast, soulless and lonely. Life at UCD was what you made of it and Laura Quinn was making the very best of it.

As well as her academic life, she had her working life.

In order to make ends meet with her grant she always had to have part-time jobs. Still, it was all going to plan. If only she could secure a really good degree! That was all she cared about at the moment. A good degree would mean a good job, and a good job would mean security and independence. They were her top priorities.

Setting her alarm for the crack of dawn, Laura snuggled down in her cosy bed and fell asleep.

❧

Aileen tossed and turned, unable to go to sleep. In spite of her bedsocks her feet were freezing and she was very loath to get up and reheat her hot-water bottle. Cassie slept like a baby in the other bed. And so she might, thought Aileen enviously. Cassie deserved to sleep soundly. She wasn't making a bags of her life like her best friend was.

Aileen sighed deeply. Today had been a good day, a great day actually, apart from the ruined dinner. But that had only added to the fun. The other pair had roared laughing although Aileen was raging with herself. She had really wanted to cook them a nice dinner. She didn't do much cooking, not even when it was her turn on the rota. She would far prefer to hoover or polish and it often ended up that she did Laura's chores for her while Laura did her cooking.

Living in the flat with the girls was a joy, all she had ever thought it would be. It was such a relief to get away from Port Mahon and her clinging, demanding mother. Her poor sister, Judy, was really feeling the brunt of it now and Aileen had warned her to make the break when her time came. Honestly, mothers could be such a problem sometimes. It wasn't that she didn't love Angela; of course she did. And she had a lot for which to be grateful to her. But Angela overdid the poor helpless widow and Aileen had got weary of it. Even if Cassie and Laura hadn't come to live in Dublin, Aileen would have come on her own. Her mother had tried so much to smother her when she was growing up that she had felt utterly trapped. At least now she could live some sort of a life of her own.

Come the New Year she was going to have to do something about that life, she decided restlessly. She was going to have to do something about her job, number one.

Aileen found her job stultifyingly boring. Every morning she signed in at nine, went to her dingy little cubbyhole and began to arrange the invoices and receipts that were brought across from the main office. There were hundreds...thousands of them—pink forms, green forms, white forms, duplicates, triplicates. These were filed downstairs in the huge brown-and-cream window-less room where she spent half her time. At eleven she had a fifteen-minute tea-break with the cleaner, Mrs Hardy. If it weren't for Mrs Hardy she would have gone completely mad.

"Himself has a hangover and it serves the miserable old git right. He's the crankiest old bastard I've ever met," she informed Aileen the previous day. She was referring to their esteemed staff officer and immediate superior. Mrs Hardy always referred to Mr Alden as "himself."

"I know I shouldn't be talking about him behind his back when he isn't here to offend himself, but I think he's a bit too fond of his drop, if you know what I mean."

Aileen had to struggle to keep her face straight when she heard Mrs Hardy coming out with "offend himself." She had been working in the office only two days when

Mrs Hardy told her that the girl who had worked there previously had gone to work in Zomby Araby. Mystified, Aileen had later learnt that the girl had gone to work for an oil company in Saudi Arabia. Mrs Hardy and her malapropisms were the only light in Aileen's otherwise dull as ditchwater day. At eleven-fifteen precisely the boss would come down for his tea and Aileen would return to her filing until one o'clock, when she would sign the attendance book and go for lunch until two-fifteen. Then it was back to the grindstone. The afternoons were spent typing, a routine broken only by a fifteen-minute tea-break at three-fifteen. At 5 p.m. she signed herself out and knew that the next day and the day after that would be exactly the same. It was the most soul-destroying thought, and she knew for a fact that her promotional prospects were pretty hopeless. There were scores more like her in the Corporation and getting promoted was something that took years. You could work hard for your pay or, like her boss, you could do feck all, it didn't matter. You still got paid your cheque every fortnight. It was desperately hard to motivate yourself, and Aileen was beginning to lose the battle. She knew of people who had done the same job for years and years. Well, she wasn't going to be one of them. She wanted out.

Then there was her love-life! Aileen's brow furrowed in the dark. Trust her to go and complicate her life by falling for someone like Liam Flynn. If only she could bring herself to talk to the girls about him. It would be such a relief to confide in them about this man who had come into her life and turned it upside-down, bringing her to the highest of highs and the lowest of lows. Many times she had almost blurted out the whole story but, afraid of what they might think of her, she had bitten her tongue. She had never kept anything from Cassie and Laura before and it troubled her deeply. After all, they were her best friends and always there, come hell or high water. She would tell them in the New Year, seek their advice perhaps, although she knew before asking what their advice would be.

She wasn't looking forward much to Christmas. No woman in her position would be, she thought glumly pulling the sheets up under her ears. She wished she were lying in Liam's arms. She'd be warm all over then, she reflected drowsily, as her eyes began to close.

❦

Cassie had gone to bed tired out after their long eventful day. She had thoroughly enjoyed every minute of it and the flat looked really nice and festive. It had been lovely to spend an evening with the girls as their evenings together were few and far between, what with Laura and her part-time jobs and study and Aileen with her amateur dramatics and the mysterious Liam Flynn.

She was kept busy with her extra-mural computer course and her participation in Allied Isles' social club. She had joined the basketball club, basketball having been her favourite sport at school, and tomorrow she was due to play a match in Killester against a team from one of their banking rivals. She was looking forward to it immensely. If there was one thing she enjoyed, it was a good vigorous game of basketball.

She couldn't say she was exactly looking forward to Christmas. It would be nice to spend time with the family and she was looking forward to giving them all the presents she had bought them, but home still felt very lonely without Jack and it was twice as hard at Christmas. All she could do was think of the good times ahead.

Once Christmas was over, the three of them were going to get dozens of holiday brochures and pore over them to decide where they were going to spend that much-desired first holiday abroad together. She was also going to start an evening course in interior design. It was something she had always wanted to do and there were quite a few courses on offer in the city. So that would be something to look forward to. She was also going to paint and decorate the flat, with the landlord's permission. He had told the girls they could have two weeks rent-free and that he would supply the materials if they wanted to decorate. He wasn't a bad old stick really. He owned about six houses around the city that he had let in flats, and drove a big BMW, but behind it all he was decent enough and they knew if they were in a fix as regards locking themselves out, he would always help.

So really, between her decorating and studying and planning the holiday, Cassie had a lot to look forward to in the next year and if she got down in the dumps over Christmas, she would just focus on those positive things. Letting images of the day's events drift through her mind, she fell asleep almost instantly

CHAPTER SEVENTEEN

Cassie stood in Port Mahon cemetery on a blustery May morning the following year. She gave a guilty start as she realised that the memorial service was over and she had been daydreaming for most of it. Yes, it was hard to believe Jack was dead two years and that her life had changed so completely.

She waved at Aileen, who waved back. She'd have to

ask her for a lift back to Dublin. That hadn't been the plan at all. Robbie MacDonald, her boyfriend since New Year's Eve, was supposed to have come for lunch and the service today and then they were going to drive back to the city together and maybe go for a meal or to the pictures. But of Robbie there was no sign. There had been no phone call to say he wasn't coming and she just didn't know what had happened. It wasn't as if he didn't know where Port Mahon was. She had brought him home soon after they met and introduced him to Nora and the family, and he had been out to visit them several times since.

Maybe he'd got a puncture or something and had been delayed. Maybe he'd be at the house when they got home. Taking Nora's arm, Cassie walked slowly down the pathway to the gates of the cemetery, her mind only half-concentrating on the greetings that were coming her way from friends and neighbours. Where on earth was Robbie? She'd kill him when she got her hands on him!

❦

Robbie MacDonald sat in a chair in his apartment. He was in the horrors. He had woken up with the most excruciating hangover after his night on the town the night before and decided to have a drink to cure it. Several drinks later, he was totally pissed. He knew he was supposed to be doing something with Cassie that day, but for the life of him he just couldn't remember what it was. His head drooped to his chest. He'd just have a little nap and then he'd be fine and he'd give Cassie a ring and find out what it was they had planned to do. He'd have a shower and freshen up, as he had slept in his clothes. God, he couldn't remember a thing

about getting home last night. It must have been one
hell of a party!

He took another slug of whiskey. Cassie was always
at him about drinking. Women! They were the greatest
fussers. What harm was a little scoop now and again?
Robbie MacDonald's eyes closed and he fell into a
drunken stupor. Not even the insistent ringing of the
phone could rouse him.

❦

Cassie reached Robbie's apartment block. His car was
outside. This was really weird. Maybe he was sick or
something. Concerned, Cassie rang the doorbell. In the
car-park, Aileen was waiting for her. It was tea-time.
They had driven up from Port Mahon and her friend
had offered to drive her over to Robbie's apartment. She
knocked again, waiting anxiously for a response.

She was turning to go when Robbie came to the door.
He looked a sight and it was quite obvious that he had
slept in his clothes. Cassie felt her heart lurch with
dismay. When he opened the door she could smell the
whiskey fumes off him.

"Hi, Cassie," he slurred.

Anger ripped through her. "That's it! We're finished.
I don't want to see you again! Nobody is going to treat
me like dirt and especially not you, Robbie MacDonald!
You should be ashamed of yourself." Running down the
steps she threw herself into the car. "Get me out of here,
Aileen, before I commit murder. Men! Why do we
bother?"

Tell me about it! said Aileen glumly to herself as she
turned the car in the direction of their flat.

CHAPTER EIGHTEEN

"I can't find my passport!" Aileen muttered frantically, delving into her leather bag, which at time sresembled a miniature sack. Robbie's car was speeding towards Dublin airport.

Laura was not impressed. "Oh for Chrissakes, Aileen, didn't we tell you to put it with your tickets?"

"Do you want to turn back?" Cassie asked irritably. This was supposed to be the beginning of their holiday, not an endurance test. Honestly, there were times when she could kill Aileen.

Her flatmate's auburn head had all but disappeared into the cavernous bag and Cassie did not hear the garbled response. Laura threw her eyes up to heaven. Being thoroughly organised and practical, she just could not understand how Aileen managed to get herself in such tizzies.

"Where did you have it last? Is it with your tickets?" Laura demanded, in her best prosecuting attorney tone.

"I can't find *them* either!" wailed Aileen, surfacing for air.

"Are they in your case, do you think?" Cassie said as calmly as she could.

Laura was not quite as patient as Cassie. She had been looking forward to this holiday for months. "How could you mislay your passport and tickets? What kind of an idiot are you? If we miss this flight, Aileen, so help me, you are in trouble."

"Oh shut up, Miss perfect. We're not all seasoned travellers like you," Aileen retorted angrily as a hot sweat suffused her. Where the hell had she put her tickets and passport? She remembered saying she must put them in a safe place when she was packing. Somewhere that she could put her hand on them when she needed them. She was pretty sure she hadn't put them in her bag; that was filled with suntan lotions and paperbacks, and sweets for the journey. Aileen definitely remembered saying she wouldn't put them in her bag so she wouldn't have to root. They were crossing the Liffey now into the northside. Maybe she'd better ask Robbie to turn back. The girls would kill her and she didn't know where to start looking back at the flat. Aileen felt like bursting into tears. Her heart was starting to pound. She ran her fingers inside her shirt collar, feeling the pulse beating at her throat.

"Stay calm," Robbie said kindly. "We'll turn back if we have to. We've loads of time."

"Thanks Robbie," Aileen said to her only ally in the car. Her little finger touched something hard, and she almost stopped breathing with relief. Of course! She had put her passport and tickets in the inside pocket of the cotton shirt she had bought especially because it had an inside pocket!

"I've found them," she said brightly. Icy silence from her flatmates greeted her discovery as they sped along a dusk-dimmed Dorset Street.

It was only when they were on the airport road with the lights of the control tower and complex shining brightly in the distance that the other two recovered their equilibrium.

"I'll take your tickets and passport," Laura ordered. "I'm not going to have a heart attack every time you go looking for them."

"OK," Aileen agreed meekly, handing over the offending articles. Laura could be so bossy sometimes, but at least the passport and tickets would be in safe hands and she wouldn't have to be worrying about them.

Laura, having been through it all before on her trips to the USA, took charge of their check-in and had them in the queue for the star flight to Rhodes before they knew it. Cassie gazed around her at the milling crowds queuing at the check-in desks and felt excitement shoot through her. Their first longed-for foreign holiday, for which they had made so many plans, was finally happening, and she intended to enjoy every minute of it. Here they were finally in Dublin airport waiting to board their flight to the sun-kissed Greek island.

The gods of Olympus had given the island as a bride to the sun god; that's what it had said in the brochures and that's what had made them choose Rhodes. They had checked out the brochures in the travel agents, all of which promised the loveliest of holidays at the cheapest price. Never having been on a package holiday before, none of them knew where to begin.

"We're not going to Spain," Aileen said firmly. "I want to go somewhere exotic. Like Egypt!" She was always the intrepid one of the trio.

"What can we afford?" Laura, the practical one, enquired. After all, she was working only part-time and the other two weren't loaded either. Greece was perfect for them. It was exotic and it was cheap. They were seduced by the pictures and descriptions in the brochure of sunny blue skies, temperatures in the eighties, unspoilt landscapes with no high-rise buildings, turquoise swimming-pools surrounded by roses, hibiscus, bougainvillaea, jasmine and honeysuckle growing in profusion. It looked like paradise. They booked for the last two weeks in September. Laura would have earned money from her summer work in America and she wouldn't be due in college until the beginning of October. It would also give Aileen and Cassie a chance to save.

It was wonderful plotting and planning. The organised one had lists to cover every contingency. Suntan oil from factor ten to two, after-care and moisturising lotions, plasters, travel-sickness pills, mosquito-repellent. It was a wonder they didn't have to pay for excess luggage!

Once they got got rid of their cases, they wandered over to the big glass windows that overlooked the tarmac. In the distance, a jet, its red-and-green lights flashing, roared off down the runway and disappeared into the velvet darkness.

"I wonder is that ours?" Cassie pointed out an Aer Lingus 737 that was being refuelled and loaded with baggage.

"It's exciting, isn't it?" Aileen's eyes sparkled. As was the case for Cassie, it was her first flight. Laura was already a veteran, having twice flown transatlantic return.

"Let's go and have a drink before we hit the duty-free!" ordered the seasoned traveller, leading the way to the bar on the next floor.

"There's a woman talking a bit of sense," Robbie laughed as he put his arm around Cassie and gave her a squeeze. She'd really miss him on the holidays but they had been suggested before she started going out with him and it wouldn't be fair to let the girls down. Besides, she and Robbie were going to go away for the October week-end and she was really looking forward to it. They had had a wonderful few days down at the Rose of Tralee in August and they had gone to Cork for the weekend a fortnight before. Just even thinking about it gave her a warm glow. Robbie was special.

"Would you two love-birds stop gazing into each other's eyes and re-enter the planet?" Aileen teased. "I was asking would you like another drink." Robbie had bought the first round.

Cassie laughed. She didn't mind being called a love-bird, as it was the first time in her life that she really felt she was one. Sipping their Bacardis in the dimly lit lounge high in the airport building, watching charter flights taking off and landing, the girls felt like jet-setters. They had given themselves plenty of time so that they could enjoy a drink with Robbie without having to rush to board the plane.

Robbie shook his head. "Not for me, thanks, I'm driving." Cassie gave his hand a squeeze. Robbie had promised her he would no longer drink over the limit when he was driving.

"We'd need to get a move on if we want to have time for the duty-free," Laura reminded them, glancing at her watch. They followed her to the boarding gates and Robbie kissed Cassie hard.

"See you in two weeks. Have fun."

"I'll miss you," Cassie told him softly.

"I'll miss you too. You'd better go," Robbie said, reluctantly, drawing away from her. "The girls are gone through." Giving her boarding pass to the official, Cassie passed through the gates and Robbie waved at her until she was out of sight. All of a sudden two weeks seemed like an eternity. Stop your nonsense, she told herself crisply, and walked over to join her friends, who were admiring some duty-free jewellery. Cassie wanted to buy a camera, Aileen wanted perfume and Laura wanted sunglasses. They also wanted to buy some duty-free fags and drink.

Forgetting the time, they browsed happily and had to be paged to board the plane. The mortification of it! Everybody else was sitting waiting for them as a hostess ushered them to their seats. Cassie and Aileen gasped as the plane thundered down the runway and lifted its huge bulk into the air. It was a beautiful night and the lights of Dublin sparkled like diamonds beneath them. Ooohing and aaahing, they tried to make out landmarks and were instantly able to recognise the high towers of Ballymun and, as the plane banked and headed out over the Irish Sea, the twin ESB towers. Settling back, they prepared to enjoy the long flight.

Everything on the flight was such a novelty to Cassie and Aileen, and Laura regarded them with benign amusement as they tucked into the meal that was served about an hour after take-off, both of them enjoying every mouthful of the pre-packaged food.

They weren't the only ones. There was an air of gaiety and anticipation in the plane that was utterly infectious. A singsong started after the meal had been cleared away and the girls joined in lustily. Gradually people began to doze off. The lights on the plane were dimmed as it flew on its long journey across Europe. They had picked a night flight because it was the cheapest but Cassie, who was sitting by the window, would have dearly loved for it to have been daylight so she could see the sights below her. Eventually her eyes closed and she fell into a half-doze. Aileen was snoring beside her and Laura was reading *Valley of the Dolls*, which was apparently brilliant, and which Cassie was going to borrow during the holidays.

A couple of hours later, the hostesses announced that they were making their descent towards Rhodes and advised them to change their watches to Central European time. A hum of excitement scorched through the aisles as the plane circled the airport and people craned to look out the windows to get their first sight of the island. The oven-blast of heat, the chirping of the crickets, the overpowering scents of the flowering shrubs hit them as they descended the steps of the plane. Cassie would never forget it. For ever after it was one of the best things about a holiday for her—that moment when you get the smell of a new country. They couldn't see much in the velvet darkness as they drove along to their accommodation, but what they saw looked promising, although it had been a bit of a shock to notice policemen with guns on their hips at the airport. The courier gave her talk on the bus, warning her clients to be careful in the sun, to stay away from mopeds and not to over-indulge in ouzo.

"Spoilsport!" whispered Aileen, and the others grinned. The courier told the three of them that their accommodation would be basic but comfortable. Most of the others on the flight were staying in hotels but the girls couldn't afford such a luxury and had taken rooms in a guest-house. The coach pulled up outside a white-washed two-storey building smothered in luscious blooms and the girls smiled happily. It looked perfect. They were shown to a big white-painted room that had three beds, a wardrobe, a sink and, to their delight, a balcony. The curtains were a lovely blue, edged with a symmetrical Greek pattern that matched the covers on the beds, and blue woven rugs covered the polished wooden floors. The three of them thought the room was gorgeous and assured their courier that they were perfectly happy. Tumbling into bed, they fell asleep, dying for the morning in order to have a good look at Rhodes.

CHAPTER NINETEEN

"Get up! Get up! The sun is splitting the stones!" Laura urged her two slumbering flatmates. She had said the magic words. Instantly awake, Cassie and Aileen flew to the balcony and gazed out in ecstasy. Skies bluer than they had ever seen before greeted them. The sparkling Aegean caressed the golden beach just below them. Palm trees swayed, birds sang, little white-washed villas lay smothered in pink and red and purple flowers. It surely was paradise. In a frenzy of excitement they rushed to put on shorts and T-shirts. The sun was shining and they wanted to get out.

They had been told by their courier that the little taverna just down the road served delicious food, including breakfasts, so they repaired there with all haste. Sitting in the shade of an olive tree at a small table covered by a fresh green gingham cloth, they ate their first Greek meal of fresh crusty rolls that melted in the mouth and honey and yoghurt and juicy peaches that had the juice dribbling over their chins. This first morning they didn't linger over their food despite the urgings of the friendly taverna-owner to have more hot strong coffee. Getting a really good tan was their overriding desire and first priority.

"I wonder is it raining at home," Cassie said, as they stretched their already lightly tanned bodies on loungers under straw shades on the golden beach of Trianda Bay. It had been a nice summer at home and Aileen and Cassie had made the most of it, but Laura, who had been working in the posh seaside resort of Nantucket on the east coast of the US, was the brownest of the three, much to the chagrin of the others. They lay, protected by factor ten, caressed by a warm breeze and watching the world go by as they began the delightful process of unwinding. When they bathed in the Aegean, it was clear and warm, and they swam lazily, enjoying themselves immensely.

Later in the afternoon when the scorching sun got too hot, they ate more rolls and delicious cheese at their table on the balcony and sipped cool beer to wash it down. Too impatient to have a siesta, they decided to explore a bit and headed for the town of Rhodes, ten minutes along the coast. It was Sunday and siesta-time and there were very few people about, just a few foreign tourists like themselves.

There were two towns, the old and the new, and they decided to explore the historical old town. Cassie, who had done her research in Rathmines Library and who also had her guidebook, was able to tell them that the Old Town was divided into various quarters, the Knights' Quarter, the Turkish Quarter and the Jewish Quarter. Their first point of exploration, they decided, as they pored over the street maps, would be the ancient Knights' Quarter. They spent a fascinating couple of hours wandering through the narrow streets and squares of an area that had changed little since the fourteenth century, when the Knights of St John had made it their stronghold during the great crusades. Little passageways and courtyards were occupied by merchants selling their wares and led to vantage points with magnificent views of the harbour below. The three girls were busy taking photos that would have put Lord Snowdon to shame.

Odós Ippotón, the Street of the Knights, the most famous mediaeval thoroughfare in Europe, was very impressive. It was a narrow cobbled street with archways at each end, and the palaces and inns where the Knights lived were magnificent. The Knights' hospital, built on

Roman ruins, now housed the Archaeological Museum of Rhodes and had free admission on Sundays. It was just opening after the lunch-break. As they explored the museum with its priceless artifacts, Aileen observed, "This sure as hell beats filing pink and green forms."

They headed back to Trianda Bay about an hour later and did another spot of sunbathing, went for a swim and then got dressed up for a night on the town.

That night they sat at a quayside taverna overlooking Mandraki Harbour, admiring the yachts of the jet-set of Europe as they waited for their meal to be served. Three more contented young ladies could not have been found. The dream holiday was everything they imagined it could be. Mandraki Harbour was beautiful, guarded by the famous Rhodian landmarks, the statues of a stag and a doe. Its three stone windmills stood solidly on the opposite quay as they had done since the Middle Ages. Behind them, all lit up, was the Nea Agora, the market-place, which they intended to explore the following day. Around them at the many crowded tavernas along the quayside people sat and ate their meals, charmed by the music of the bouzouki and the chirping of crickets.

After their delicious meal of *fagri*, baked sea-bream and a Greek salad, Cassie produced her little guidebook. A colleague of hers had already been to Rhodes and had given her a list of recommended nightclubs and discos.

"Well, where do you want to go? Number One, 2001, Zorba's and Copacabana are the nightclubs. The discos are Aquarius, Mi Lord, Step-by-Step, Stones."

"I'd like to go somewhere there's Greek dancing," Laura proposed. "We can go to discos at home."

"Good thinking," agreed Cassie. "Isn't the bouzouki lovely? It makes you want to get up and dance."

"Mmmm," Aileen smiled. "I love watching Greek men

dance. It's so...earthy and masculine...Did you see *Zorba the Greek*?"

"Yeah," Cassie nodded. "It was a brilliant film."

"I'll ask the waiter where there's Greek dancing," Laura decided. Costas was the waiter's name and he was absolutely gorgeous. He told them that if they waited about twenty minutes there would be Greek dancing in the open air down by the harbour. "*Efcharisto*," Laura thanked him. She had gone to the trouble of learning a few words of Greek and loved making use of them.

"*Típota*." Costas gave Laura a lingering smile as he assured her she was welcome before striding off to get them more coffee.

"He fancies you," teased Cassie.

Laura was actually blushing. "Oh, don't be daft!"

"Oooh, she's gone scarlet," giggled Aileen, who had indulged in several glasses of the house wine and was feeling on top of the world.

"That's sunburn," protested Laura.

"My eye," smirked Aileen, holding out her glass for a refill.

They danced until the early hours and were escorted home by three Adonises who begged to see them again.

"We're going home tomorrow," Aileen informed them merrily. "Let's not limit ourselves," she advised the other two as they applied lashings of moisturiser before falling into bed, exhausted but completely satisfied with the first day of their holiday.

❦

It was a week later. Cassie was stretched luxuriously on her lounger on the beach, reading *Valley of the Dolls* and thoroughly enjoying it, as Laura had promised she would. Reaching down she picked up her glass of ice-cold beer and took a long draught. This really was the life. Home and all its attendant worries seemed so far away. What a pity the first week was over, the time was just flying by. Here on Rhodes it was like another world. She'd like to come back here with Robbie some day. Now *that* would be special!

It was funny; this time last year she hadn't known him and now he was one of the most important people in her world. She met him at a New Year's Eve party organised by the social club at work. She noticed him smiling at her as she stood helping herself at the buffet. Mmm, she thought to herself, he's nice! He was tall, about six foot, and bearded. A silky black beard and black curly hair were the first impressions she had of him, but on a second inspection, what had most struck her were his kind, smiling eyes. He was terribly popular and everybody seemed to know him. Later, when a sing-song started, he took out a guitar and led the singing, his deep baritone voice filling the room.

"Who is that?" Cassie asked one of her colleagues.

"Oh don't you know him? That's Robbie MacDonald. He's PA to the chief executive. He works in Branch Network Development in Head Office. He's a really nice guy!" Sandra informed her. Mind you, Sandra, who was in her late thirties, unmarried and getting desperate, thought every bloke was a really nice guy. She had had a few drinks too many that night and confessed to Cassie that she had even answered an ad in the personal columns of a social magazine. That was how she had met her escort to the party. Derek, who was at least twenty years her senior was a portly, bald, slick-talking businessman. Cassie didn't like him at all. He held her hand too long when Sandra introduced him and he kept making smutty jokes which were not amusing.

Cassie had read an article somewhere that single women should be wary of men over forty who had never married and looking at Derek she could understand why. What she could not understand was Sandra's desperation. Being married was not the be-all and end-all, she reflected, as she watched Sara O'Reilly and Ken Taylor grope each other on the dance-floor while their respective spouses sat stony-faced at their tables. Who'd want to be married and miserable?

Mind, it was easy for her to say something like that with the reassurance of her youth. She might feel completely different if she were almost forty and without prospects. Somebody like Derek might seem like an answer to a prayer if she were in Sandra's position, though somehow Cassie felt she would never be *that* desperate.

Just then a scuffle broke out on the dance-floor as Sara O'Reilly's husband, unable to take any more of his wife's blatant flirtation with Ken Taylor, made a lunge for the other man. In a second, Robbie was between them, holding them apart, calming things down. Diplomatically, he advised both couples to call it a night and organised taxis for them, making sure they were kept separated until the taxis arrived. He managed what was potentially a very nasty scene in a most skilful manner and Cassie was very impressed. At the time for "Auld Lang Syne," she a little thrill of delight when she realised that he was next to her in the ring and knew he had manoeuvred it deliberately. "I've a feeling this is going to be a great year," he grinned, his hazel eyes twinkling as he introduced himself and wished her a Happy New Year. The spent the rest of the night together dancing and chatting and she felt as though she had known him all her life. He was so easy to talk to and he had a terrific sense of humour. When he asked to see her home, she happily agreed, although she was a bit surprised to see that he was driving himself. He had had a few drinks; too many, she thought. "Do you want to get a taxi instead?" she suggested.

"Not at all, I'm fine," he assured her, and it was quite obvious that he was well able to handle his drink as he didn't seem a bit affected. When he asked to see her again the following weekend, Cassie agreed with pleasure.

They began dating and a whole new life opened up for Cassie. Robbie was a very sociable man with lots of friends and Cassie was soon having a hectic social life. With his great voice and guitar-playing skills, he was much in demand for parties and ballad-sessions and was in his element drinking pints of Guinness and singing rousing ballads with an enthusiastic crowd of friends. Cassie enjoyed that type of thing to a degree, but there were times she wished Robbie and she were alone, especially late at night when everybody had had too much to drink and she was bored listening to loosened tongues talking rubbish. Cassie really loved her times alone with Robbie. Whether they were out tramping the countryside on the quest for the perfect picnic-spot or sitting in his apartment doing the crossword together or playing Scrabble, she just loved their companionship. She had not had a serious boyfriend since her time with Donie and, being older now and more mature, she was enjoying having an adult relationship. And she had to admit it was nice having a man's arms around her again. There was nothing she enjoyed more than a good cuddling session and Robbie MacDonald was one of the world's greatest cuddlers.

Cassie met Robbie's parents and thought his mother a very nice woman who obviously worshipped the ground her son walked on. She spoilt him outrageously and fussed over him as though he were a child. His father was more taciturn, surprisingly for someone who had a son as extrovert as Robbie. His sister, Lillian, was pleasant but a little distant and Cassie felt the faintest hint of an atmosphere in the household that she could not explain. She chided herself for imagining things but on subsequent visits the impression intensified.

Robbie and she had their first row on the Sunday he was supposed to come out to Port Mahon for the memorial service and he got absolutely smashed the night before, a state that lasted until late the following afternoon. Cassie was hurt and angry and they had a ferocious row when he told her to stop nagging him and acting like a shrew. She hadn't spoken to him for a week. If Robbie had one fault it was his inability to say no to his mates when they decided they wanted a few jars. He was OK when he stuck to beer but once he started drinking spirits he never knew when to stop. It worried Cassie but when she tried to talk to him about it he just pooh-poohed her concerns and wouldn't discuss the matter.

Two months later he was supposed to collect her on a Friday evening after work but didn't turn up. She rang his apartment and got no answer. By Sunday when she had had no word from him and hadn't been able to get in touch with him, she rang his parents' home. Lillian answered and when Cassie explained that she had been trying to contact Robbie since Friday and was wondering if anything was wrong, Lillian said a little brusquely that she hadn't a clue where her brother was, but knowing him, he was on a bender somewhere and adding that if Cassie had any sense she wouldn't waste time worrying about him but would do herself a favour and finish her relationship with him. Cassie had been really shocked by the younger girl's words and the bitterness in her voice. Frantic with worry, she rang his office the next day, only to be told that he wasn't in and they hadn't heard from him. It was Wednesday before he got in touch with her and it was quite obvious from his lined face and rheumy eyes that he had been on a hell of a drinking bout.

Deeply upset, Cassie told Robbie to get lost, that she didn't want to see him again. If Robbie MacDonald was going to start standing her up to go on drinking batters with his mates, he could go to hell. Apologetic and ashamed of himself, he had inundated her with flowers and laid siege to her with phone calls begging her to see him. In the end, Cassie was so miserable to be fighting with him that she agreed to meet him. They went back to his apartment to talk and Robbie apologised repeatedly, tears in his eyes as he swore never to behave like that again. When she started to cry, Robbie was even more horrified by her tears.

"Cassie, Cassie, please don't cry. I'm such a swine, I'm sorry! I'm sorry! I love you, Cassie; I wouldn't hurt you for the world!"

Flinging her arms around him Cassie sobbed, "I love you too, Robbie. I was just so worried about you. If you've a problem with drink, can't you go and see the welfare officer at work? He'll help. I know a few people who've been helped like that."

"Don't worry, Cassie, I can give it up any time and that time is now. From now on it's pints only!" He took her hands in his and gazed into her eyes. "Did you mean what you said about loving me?"

She nodded mutely. How could she help but love him? Despite his faults, Robbie MacDonald was the most lovable man.

"Oh Cassie, I never met a girl like you. I love you

too," he said, pulling her to him and kissing her passionately. She stayed with him that night and Robbie very lovingly and gently made love to her for the first time. His tenderness and sensitivity touched her deeply as he helped to ease her shyness. Unlike Aileen, who hadn't an inhibition in the world, and Laura, who was the epitome of self-confidence, Cassie was a bit shy about her body and had dreaded the moment of losing her virginity as much as she looked forward to it. Would it hurt like they said it would? Would she bleed and make a mess? Would she know what to do and how to please Robbie? Were her breasts big enough? Were her thighs too fat? Would she snore when she fell asleep and what would happen when they woke up in the morning if Robbie wanted to kiss her and she had a taste in her mouth? All these little problems had caused Cassie a lot of anxiety. It had never dawned on her to wonder if Robbie would please her or if he would be too small or too fat or have BO. Her conditioning had led her to think that with sex it was all-important to please your man. Cassie had not given much thought to her *own* pleasure and satisfaction.

In the end it had all been so natural and Robbie made her laugh the whole time, especially when he was showing her how he put a condom on, modelling it for her benefit and giving a running commentary. She was tense the first time in spite of herself but gradually Robbie helped her to relax and she began to enjoy herself, loving the feel of his silky beard against her breasts as he took each of her nipples in turn in his mouth and ran his tongue over them, making them harden with desire. When they finally went to sleep in the early hours she curled herself in against him, savouring the protective feeling of his arms around her. The next morning she sneaked into the bathroom to brush her teeth and laughed when Robbie came in to do the same thing. Later, sitting in one of his shirts at his kitchen table as he prepared scrambled eggs on toast, Cassie knew she had crossed a threshold in her life and was glad that she had done so.

However, her strict Catholic upbringing robbed her of complete fulfilment and happiness. A little stab of guilt assailed her now and again as she thought of how shocked Nora would be to see her at this moment and she reflected a little unhappily that according to the laws of the church she was now in a state of mortal sin because she had given her love to a man she loved very much. Why should that be so wrong? It wasn't as if it were a one-night stand or anything like that. She had thought long and hard about whether or not to make love to Robbie and had ended up taking her decision because she loved him and sex was an expression of the love she felt. Wouldn't it be much worse if she was out robbing old people or dipping into the till at work? Fine to call *that* type of thing a mortal sin but what she had shared with Robbie had been something loving and tender and how people could call that a sin was beyond her...

Lying on the beach in Rhodes, she smiled to herself. She had spent many happy loving hours with Robbie since that night and for the most part, she could keep the guilt at bay. She hadn't told the girls yet; the moment hadn't ever been quite right. Besides they didn't seem to be together that often lately; they were busy with their individual lives. That's why this holiday was so nice. It was good to share fun times together again. Maybe she'd tell them about Robbie before the holidays were over.

Cassie smiled, remembering how Aileen had proudly

told them about her first time with her soldier in the Skylon Hotel. Aileen wouldn't know the meaning of the word guilt, Cassie thought a little enviously. Aileen quite often stayed out all night and it was obvious that she was sleeping with her boyfriend, Liam Flynn. Cassie hadn't met him yet as Aileen had never brought him home but she had spoken to him on the phone and he sounded terribly dishy. He was obviously a bit older than Aileen, so maybe that was why she hadn't brought him home. Whatever the situation, Cassie knew one thing: Aileen would thoroughly enjoy her sex life and not feel one bit guilty about it, the lucky girl!

CHAPTER TWENTY

I wonder if he misses me, Aileen thought, as she lay on her stomach, cheek resting on her arms, gazing out at the sparkling blue sea. Beside her, her two friends were enjoying a good read but Aileen couldn't settle down to her book. She had just finished a Mary Stewart and enjoyed it immensely but somehow or other she just could not get into the Georgette Heyer she had brought with her.

Her thoughts kept straying back home to Liam. She really had it bad about him, she thought glumly, and the awful thing was she didn't really know exactly what he felt for her. If the girls knew that she was having an affair with a married man they would call her all kinds of an idiot. And yet she wanted them to know. It was terrible keeping something so important to herself. Nobody knew, not one other person, just herself and Liam, and Aileen, who was not naturally secretive, was beginning to find it all a terrible strain.

At the beginning she had thoroughly enjoyed the intrigue and the drama of her relationship, but now, after more than a year, she was beginning to find it tiresome and even a little bit seedy. How she envied Cassie her relationship with Robbie. They seemed so happy together and they sure as hell didn't have to sneak around making love in the back of a car or waiting until the flat was free.

She wasn't stupid, she knew what she was letting herself in for when she had started her affair with Liam, but way back then it didn't seem to matter. All that had mattered was that this gorgeous handsome man was terribly interested in her and all she could think about was making love to him. Aileen sighed deeply. It was a bit of a nuisance sometimes being such a sensual person. How Laura managed without ever having had sex, Aileen could not fathom. It wasn't that she was a nympho-maniac or anything like it. She would never have casual sex but she enjoyed sex very much and this was one of the reasons she was continuing to have an affair with Liam. The sex was sensational, really earth-shattering. Liam Flynn was a tremendous lover. Just thinking about it was making her weak at the knees.

Some of these Greek men were pretty sexy too. Aileen could not understand how Laura could resist the advances of the delicious Costas. Costas actually reminded her a little of her lover. Mind, he was much younger than Liam, who was forty-five, more than double her age. That was part of the attraction too, she admitted to herself. That this suave, attractive sophisticated man could be interested in her really bolstered Aileen's already very positive image of herself.

She met Liam Flynn in the office when he came to

check out some data. He was an architect for the Corporation and architects were the people she had most dealings with, them and the planners. She had looked up one day to find this well-dressed man standing at her desk with a list of enquiries for which she had to supply data. He was the fifth architect she had dealt with that afternoon and all of them had given her the impression that theirs was the most urgent and important business and she wasn't to dream of keeping them waiting for their information. What was it about some of them that made them so arrogant? Well, Aileen had had enough of them. She was in a foul humour anyway. The boss had the nerve to reprimand her for being late back after lunch—even though he never put in a full day's work! She wouldn't have been late except that some bastard had double-parked her. Fortunately, after she had fumed for twenty minutes, the driver in front of her returned and she was able to get her car out, but not before she had surreptitiously let the air out of the two nearside tyres of the car that was blocking her. Sitting at the traffic lights, she observed the owner of the double-parked car stroll unconcernedly towards it. He'd soon stop whistling, she thought smugly, as the lights went green and she left him looking down at his tyres, utterly dumbfounded.

"If you could get me this information urgently, I'd be much obliged," the man in the expensive-looking camel-hair coat was saying pleasantly.

"I'm sorry, you won't have it until tomorrow," Aileen informed him ungraciously. "There were several other queries made ahead of you and I haven't even started on them yet." Honestly, they were all the same, standing there puffed-up with their own self-importance. She wouldn't mind but she had a suspicion that half the work some of them did was for their own thriving little sidelines. They might in theory work for the Corporation but there was a hell of a lot of private work done on company time, if office gossip was anything to go by. Aileen didn't see why she should have to kill herself on their behalf while they got paid handsome fees as well as their salaries and she was paid a pittance.

"It is terribly important," the man urged, smiling at her. He was good-looking in a mature sort of a way, Aileen conceded. Of average height, he was well built and had a handsome face with a nice straight nose. Aileen liked a good masculine nose and a well-shaped mouth. He passed the test on the mouth too. His eyes, which were a sort of bluey-grey, were long-lashed and were now crinkled up in a smile at her.

"Couldn't you put me at the top of the list just this once? Rita always looked after me very well," he added, referring to her predecessor.

Did she indeed! Aileen gave a mental sniff. Whatever chance he had of securing her cooperation he had just blown it by his reference to the perfect Rita.

"I'm afraid, Mr—?" She arched an eyebrow.

"Flynn, Liam Flynn." The man lowered his gleaming leather briefcase to the floor and reached out and shook her hand.

"I'm afraid that would be unfair to the others, who also have urgent work, or so they tell me. I'll have the data delivered to you before lunch tomorrow," she told him firmly.

The architect raised an eyebrow at her tone. "Dear me," he said drily, "it must be terrible to be so busy. I won't detain you from your work a minute longer."

Aileen glowered at him. Sarcastic creep. Let him go and piss off. If he wasn't careful he wouldn't get his data until the following week!

Liam Flynn strode out of the office and banged the door behind him.

"And good riddance to you too," she muttered, banging her typewriter keys with a vengeance. Just to annoy him, she didn't send Kevin—the boy messenger, to give him his correct official title—to deliver the information required by the arrogant Mr Flynn until late the following afternoon.

Kevin informed Aileen with a smug smile that Liam Flynn had commiserated with him for having to work with someone who was not only grumpy but inefficient as well. Aileen was furious. How dare that man have the nerve to discuss her with a junior member of staff. How absolutely unprofessional!

"Do you want a pair of boxing gloves?" Kevin enquired cheekily. He liked Aileen, she was great gas, not like that dry old stick Rita, whose face would crack were she ever to risk a smile. He was currently teaching Aileen how to bet on the horses, one of his favourite occupations, although she hadn't had much luck so far. Still, that would change—he had a great tip for a winner that very day.

"Kevin, I am not in the humour for your juvenile wit," Aileen snapped. "There's a manila envelope in the post-basket to be delivered to City Hall, some stuff to go to Housing and some to Dangerous Buildings. So get on your bike!"

"Crosspatch! Just for that, I'm not giving you the name of a sure-fire winner," Kevin retorted as he gathered up the post.

"Ha! That's one favour you'll be doing me," grimaced Aileen.

"Should I call into His Nibs and see if he's got anything

more to go? Maybe I won't," he reflected. "He's probably making *the* phone call."

Aileen's eyes lit up. It was a well-known fact that Mr James Alden, her superior officer, rang his daughter in America once a week. Mrs Hardy, the cleaner, told Aileen he'd been doing it for the last five years, courtesy of the Corporation, but because the bills weren't itemised he was never caught. Every Friday afternoon at three-fifteen precisely, Mr Alden phoned his daughter. It was now three-eighteen.

"Go in! Go in and see if he hops!" Aileen urged, her bad humour disappearing at the prospect of a bit of devilment.

"You go!" Kevin challenged her. "Go on. I dare you!"

Straightening her skirt and smoothing her hair, Aileen knocked lightly on the door and waltzed in without waiting for an answer.

"He hopped about five feet and got all red in the face and practically bit the head off me when I asked him was there any more internal mail to go with you," Aileen chuckled heartily.

"I'm going to bug that office one of these days," Kevin snorted. "Just think of what we'd get on tape."

"Excuse me." A voice intruded on their mirth. It was Liam Flynn. "I think there's an error in your data." He handed Aileen a sheaf of papers.

"What?" Aileen snapped. "There couldn't be."

"If you don't mind, I'd like these facts re-checked. There *is* an error."

"Certainly. But if you don't mind coming with me you will be able to see for yourself that the information is correct," Aileen said icily. How dare that superior being question her work! She was always meticulous at her job. She led the way downstairs to the room where the files were kept and pulled out the relevant drawer.

"See for yourself!" she said, thrusting the papers back at him.

"Very well," he said shortly. Comparing the notes with those in the file he informed her calmly, "There's an error here all right but it's in the original file."

"Well, that's not my fault. They were here long before I came. Maybe you should ask the obliging Rita about it some time." She was still smarting from his remarks to Kevin and couldn't resist this jibe.

He smiled sardonically. "That might be a little difficult, considering she's in Saudi Arabia."

Smart-ass, thought Aileen angrily. "Excuse me, I've got to get back to work," she snapped.

"Oh yes! I interrupted you and your young colleague," the architect drawled sarcastically.

Aileen had had just about enough. "Listen here, you!" she exploded. "I'll thank you to keep your smart remarks to yourself. And furthermore kindly do not discuss me with another member of the staff. I think your comments to Kevin were totally unprofessional! And unjustified," she added indignantly.

They glared at each other, and then Liam smiled and held out his hand.

"You're absolutely right," he said disarmingly. "I'm sorry."

"Oh!" Aileen was completely wrong-footed.

"You're not inefficient and..." he paused, his eyes twinkling, "you're not grumpy."

He had a very attractive smile and she liked the way his eyes crinkled up at the corners. She decided that he definitely was rather dishy.

"Apology accepted?" he smiled.

Never one to hold a grudge and not usually so prickly,

Aileen found herself smiling back. "You caught me on a bad day!" she admitted. "I don't usually go on like this."

"This place would put anyone in a bad humour," Liam smiled, indicating the dingy filing-room. "Don't worry about it."

"At least it's Friday and there's only another hour to go," Aileen observed cheerfully, her good humour beginning to reassert itself.

"Ah yes. Friday evenings! The perfect antidote to Corporation blues." Liam stood back to allow her to precede him upstairs. He was very mannerly, she noticed. He had gone down the stairs in front of her, as a gentleman always should. Good manners always impressed Aileen.

"I don't know your name," he smiled as they paused in the hallway.

She smiled back at him. "Aileen O'Shaughnessy."

"Well, until the next time, Aileen." He shook hands again. "Enjoy your weekend."

"You too," she replied, smiling again as she watched him leave. She had to admit he was a bit of all right, compared to some of the drips she had to deal with.

She looked forward to Liam's visits from then on and when he casually suggested taking her to lunch one day she agreed. She really enjoyed it. Liam was a witty, entertaining man and his comments about some of his colleagues for whom she also worked for made her laugh heartily.

He told her that he was married with two teenage children and that he lived in Bray in a house he had designed and built himself.

She had lunch with him several times and soon it became clear to both of them that a physical attraction was developing between them. At first it was just an accidental touch of a hand or a shared laugh that turned into a long smiling gaze. Both of them were ready for an affair. If it had not been Liam for Aileen and Aileen for Liam, it would have been someone else. Liam told Aileen that he felt his wife had lost interest in her marriage. She had put on weight, didn't take much of an interest in her appearance any longer and was going through a difficult early menopause. He was trying to be supportive, he explained, but there were times he felt he was just a nuisance to his wife, and that all she wanted was to be left in peace to watch her soaps on TV and smoke herself to death.

"Maybe she needs hormone treatment or something," Aileen suggested. Her mother had been going through the change for as long as Aileen could remember and she was making sure Judy and she knew all about it. She certainly empathised with poor Liam.

"She's been to doctors and they've all told her more or less to put up with it. Do you know something, Aileen? In a way I think she's enjoying it. I think she's glad of an excuse not to make an effort and just slide into middle age. Well, I don't want to be middle-aged yet. I've worked hard to achieve what I've got, I want to enjoy it, not sit beside a fire every night with my slippers on, dozing in front of the TV."

Aileen looked at his hard angry eyes and thought, Mrs Flynn, you're not the only one going through a mid-life crisis!

Liam wanted to know about her life, about her boyfriends. "Tell me everything," he commanded. "I envy you your youth, I envy you with your life ahead of you. I feel I'm in such a rut. In twenty years' time I'll be collecting my pension and you won't even be the age I am now."

"You're much too young to think about pensions, you daft man!" she smiled. "Forty-five is a sexy age. Look at Sean Connery, look at Kirk Douglas. I wouldn't say no to them," she teased.

"Would you say no to me?" Liam stared at her and it was as if everybody else in the restaurant had frozen in time, all sound, all motion, suspended. There were only she and Liam staring at each other across the table. Aileen's insides went a bit wobbly. This was the first time he had voiced what was in both their minds.

"Well?" he asked softly.

"I don't know." It was the only answer she could give him. All her flippant chat seemed to have disappeared and the effect those bluey-grey eyes were having on her was like something out of a romantic novel.

Liam smiled. "And I thought you knew everything," he chided good-humouredly, breaking the tension.

He had taken her to a small restaurant on the sea-front in Sandycove. It was her pay-day and she had an extra hour at lunchtime for cashing her cheque. But she never used that hour to cash her cheque—Cassie always did that for her, so she wouldn't have to queue. Because she was in no rush back to work, they went strolling along the sea-front.

"We're going to have an affair, you know? You and I," Liam said seriously as they stood staring out at the waves surging into Scotsman's Bay.

Aileen said nothing. She knew he was right.

In silence they walked back to the car. Polite as always, Liam opened her door for her before getting in himself.

He turned to her. "Are you angry with me?"

She stared at him, committing every line of his hand-some face to memory. Reaching out in a spontaneous gesture, she touched the side of his jaw gently with her forefinger. "Of course I'm not angry." In fact she was deeply flattered that he was so attracted to her. Aileen had heard some of the typists from the other offices refer to Liam Flynn as "a fine thing" and she heartily endorsed the recommendation. Turning his face, he pressed his mouth against the palm of her hand and she was almost electrified at the contact.

"You're beautiful," he muttered, and then he was kissing her, his tongue tasting hers as it explored the softness of her mouth, his hands entwined in the silkiness of her titian hair.

Breathless, she drew away from him. "Someone might see!" she murmured.

"Let them. I don't care." His voice was not quite steady. "All I know is I want to make love to you. Take the afternoon off and we'll go somewhere."

She was so tempted to say yes, to let everyone go to hell and spend the afternoon making passionate love to this gorgeous sexy man who wanted her as much as she wanted him. Mundane little matters made their presence felt. First of all he was married! That should be a no-no. But she knew now it wasn't going to make a difference. Doing a swift mental calculation she knew that she was still a day or two on the dangerous side of her cycle. The first thing she was going to do was go to the Family Planning Clinic and go on the pill. As well as which, if she took the afternoon off, her car would be locked in the car park for the week-end. Besides, she was not exactly dressed for seduction. Today's lunch had not been planned. She knew that she had a hole in the crotch of her tights. Those one-size things were a disaster! And her bra, which had once been snow-white, had turned a pale shade of pink as a result of a clash with a red sweatshirt in the washing-machine. She hadn't shaved her legs either. Not that it would make any difference with the state Liam was in—she could be as hairy as a mountain gorilla and he wouldn't notice, so anxious was he to make love to her. But nevertheless...she would prefer for the first time to have all her little jobs done and be wearing something a little sexier than holed tights and a pale pink bra! It would make her feel better and more desirable.

"I can't, Liam. Take me back to work," she said firmly. He reluctantly did as he was bid.

She spent the entire weekend fantasising about him, so the following Wednesday when he arrived downstairs to where she was filing her loathed pink forms, she practically fell into his arms. They kissed hungrily in the dusty dim room, touching and caressing each other in a frenzy of desire.

"I want you now," he muttered hoarsely. "I want to make love to you standing, sitting, kneeling, lying. I thought about it the whole weekend. It's all I can think about. Aileen, you're driving me crazy. If I don't get rid of this," he pressed hard against her, "I'm going to explode." Leaning against a filing cabinet with his body thrusting against her, Aileen thought she was going to explode herself. Unbuckling his trouser-belt she arched her leg around his hip and drew him to her. Today she was wearing ivory French knickers and a matching camisole top and silk stockings and suspenders. Like the boy scouts, she had come prepared!

It was the most satisfying lovemaking of Aileen's entire life. Hungry for each other, they writhed wildly between the filing cabinets in the windowless basement that was the filing-room. Moaning and groaning, panting with desire, Aileen couldn't have cared less if the City Manager himself had stood in the doorway watching them. Not that there was much likelihood of that. No one ever ventured into the filing-room of their own free will. Aileen was the only person who had to work there. She doubted if her boss even knew how to find the place.

"That was something else!" Liam gave her a great bearhug as their breathing returned to normal and they stood clinging to each other. "Come on. We're getting out of here. You go and say you're taking the day off sick or something and follow me out to the Killiney Court Hotel."

Aileen stared at him. "Now?"

"Now!" he ordered, laughing.

He could have told her to follow him to the moon and she would have gone. She had just sampled paradise and she wanted more.

They parted at the top of the stairs, he to get his car in the car-park, she to visit the ladies' room. Down the hall in the kitchen she could hear Mrs Hardy and Kevin arguing the toss about how much he was behind in his kitty payments. Mr Alden would be down for his elevenses soon and she wanted to be gone by then. She caught sight of herself in the mirror. Her hair was tumbling over her shoulders in glorious disarray; Liam had buried his face in it to stifle his groans. Her eyes were sparkling with pleasure, cheeks flushed with passion. The healthiest-looking specimen she had ever seen! Tidying herself up and composing herself as best she could, she marched down the hall to Mr Alden's office and knocked on the door. Her boss was sitting shuffling papers around the desk, listening to Gay Byrne on his little transistor. Of course, *she* wasn't allowed to have a radio in her office!

"I'm going home sick. I don't feel well," Aileen announced.

"Aah!" said Mr Alden, who didn't like to be bothered with such things. "Do you think you'll be able to resume duty tomorrow?"

"I don't know," Aileen said truthfully. If Liam did half the things he planned to do, she mightn't be able to walk tomorrow. The thought of it sent a hot spurt of pleasure coursing through her veins. "I'll ring in," she said hastily, anxious to be gone.

"Well, leave a sick note and send in a doctor's certificate if you're out longer than two days!"

Typical, thought Aileen, closing the door none too gently after her. You could be dying on the spot and all they'd care about would be their blooming sick notes and certs. She had a good mind to take a week off. God knows she deserved it. Mr Alden sat on his arse from Monday to Friday doing next to nothing while she was swamped with work. Well, today she was going to forget such an entity as Mr James Alden existed. Not stopping to chat, she told Mrs Hardy she was going home sick. "You know yourself," she whispered.

"You should take a glass of brandy for them period pains. It could be your Ethiopian tubes. That's what was wrong with me!"

Not wishing to get into a discussion about Mrs Hardy's Fallopian tubes, Aileen just nodded and flew out the door. She drove to Killiney where Liam was waiting in the foyer of the Killiney Court Hotel.

They spent the rest of the day in bed!

Restlessly Aileen got up from her lounger. "I'm going for a swim," she told Cassie and Laura, who seemed engrossed in their books. If Liam were here now, she knew they'd be making love. But it wasn't enough any longer. She was fed up waiting for the phone to ring, fed up with plans being suddenly broken because Monica, his menopausal wife, wanted to visit her parents, or go shopping, or was having friends over and he just couldn't get out of it. She was fed up going to hotels or making the most of the occasional night when Laura and Cassie were not be staying in the flat. She was fed up being accommodating and having to make sacrifices. She had even given up her drama nights on many occasions when Liam was free to see her. Most of all she was fed up waking up alone. Not once in their relationship had Liam been able to spend a whole night with her. Surely if he loved her as much as he said he did he would want to leave his wife and live with her, especially if Monica were the pain he made her out to be. His children were practically grown up. They'd be doing their own thing soon enough and Monica would be free to watch *Dallas* and *Dynasty* and *Knot's Landing* and *Coronation Street* to her heart's content.

They couldn't go on like this. He *must* want to change things. The thing that frightened Aileen was that she wasn't sure if he wanted to change things or not. From his point of view he had the best of both worlds: her to make him feel young and good about himself and a wife to look after him. Diving into the surging surf, Aileen promised herself that things were going to change when she got back from her holidays. Liam was going to have to make a choice!

CHAPTER TWENTY-ONE

Reluctantly Laura closed the covers of her book. She hated coming to the end of a novel that she was really enjoying and Brian Cleeve's *Cry of Morning* was an

engrossing read. It was a real page-turner about life in
Dublin in the boom times of the Sixties and she was
sorry to finish it. Beside her, Cassie was up to her ears in
Valley of the Dolls, while Aileen had gone for a swim.
Maybe she'd go for one herself in a minute.

The warm breeze rippled across her tanned body.
Even though it was very hot, there was always a lovely
island breeze to help cool you down. Laura was really
glad they had come to Greece. She had been a bit worried
when Aileen was talking about going to Egypt. She'd
never have been able to afford that. This holiday was her
treat to herself for the last two years of slogging and,
God, she had slogged her guts out. But it had paid off.
Laura smiled broadly. She had done really well in her
exams, second class honours, grade one. Only Ted Nolan
had done better than her. Maybe if she didn't have to
work part-time and could have spent more time studying,
she would have done better. But it couldn't be helped.
She had to work to supplement her grant, unlike Ted,
whose father was a gynaecologist and who was absolutely
rolling in money. Well, her finals were coming up next
year and she was aiming for a first.

It would be tough going from now on. Financially as
well as academically. She wouldn't be able to go and
work in the States next summer. That time would be
spent studying for her autumn finals. That was why she
had worked from dawn until dusk this year in America.
It had been one hell of a summer and she had come back
home worn out but happy with the amount she had
earned. With careful budgeting she'd manage fine. This
holiday was a godsend though. It was great to forget
about studying and working. And it was such a treat to
eat out and for her to be waited on for a change. Waiting
on tables was no easy job, especially in America. People

there wanted service—and fast. She had been run off her feet. Fortunately she was used to waiting tables in her waitressing job at Capri, the Italian restaurant she worked in at home, although the pace wasn't as hectic as it had been at Jacques, the seafood restaurant where she worked on Nantucket Island. That had been an experience and a half! Exhausting wasn't the word for it. Nantucket was a lovely place, though. She was glad not to have spent another season in New York. The humidity in August in New York had almost killed her the first year. At least there was a sea breeze in Nantucket. She had been lucky to get the job.

She was waitressing in Boston when a girl she knew from college had bumped into her one day and told her that her brother-in-law had opened a new restaurant in Nantucket and was looking for waitressing staff. Laura jumped at the opportunity. She had heard so much about the beauty of Nantucket Island, situated twenty miles south of the southeast tip of Cape Cod. Shaped like a pork chop, it was only fifteen miles long and two and a half miles wide. All she'd need was a bike to explore it.

She had taken the bus from Boston and the steamship from Hyannis Port and found herself in a whole new world.

Jacques was divided into two sections, a very exclusive restaurant where gourmet food was the order of the day and the clients wore only designer label clothes, and downstairs where Laura worked, which was less expensive, more informal and more family-orientated. The food was fabulous and Philip, the owner, made sure his staff ate well, because they sure as hell had to work hard. Laura had never tasted anything to equal the chowder and the succulent Nantucket Bay scallops.

Despite working from early morning until after

midnight, Laura managed to explore the whole island during her time off. There were no buses and everybody cycled around on those cute old bikes with the baskets on the front. For some reason, they always reminded Laura of Katharine Hepburn. The island was a cyclist's dream with special bike paths and she particularly liked the Cliff Road and Hummock Pond Road. The names fascinated her, especially the street-names in the town: Easy Street, India Street, New Whale Street. Quince Street with its quaint old houses was her favourite. Exploring the town itself had been a pleasure.

Nantucket was once a great whaling port and thriving commercial centre. Retired whalers had built fine mansions that retained their elegance. She had visited the Whaling Museum, the Jethro Coffin house, the oldest house on the island, built in 1686, and the old mill dating from 1746. It was all fascinating and Laura promised herself that some day when she had money she was going to come back as a tourist, with nothing else to do but explore this lush, beautiful island with its long sandy beaches and low undulating hills, carpeted with heather and blueberry bushes and flowering plants.

All in all it had been a pretty good summer, she decided, sitting up and looking at Aileen swimming up and down. She had worked damn hard and saved a lot of money, but she had really enjoyed Nantucket and was relishing her holidays. It was just like old times with the girls, before they had started their romances. Laura sometimes envied Aileen and Cassie their carefree existence. They had their jobs and secure salaries while she had a further year of study and she wasn't even sure of getting a job then. It would be nice to to have a boyfriend, too. Sometimes she felt a little lonely when she heard them making plans dates, but although she had been asked out many times by guys at college and clients from the restaurant where she worked, Laura knew that nothing must stop her from achieving a first. She had done well in her exams this year; she must do better at her finals. After that she could have all the romances she wanted.

Standing up, she smiled at Cassie, "Come on, let's dunk Aileen for the crack."

"You're on!" grinned her friend, laying aside her book. Laughing, they ran down the beach and dived into the sea after their shrieking flatmate.

❧

"Where will we go tonight?" Cassie asked as she concentrated on trying to get the varnish on her toe-nails and not on her toes. She was sitting on the balcony with Laura and Aileen, wrapped in a fluffy white bath-towel. They had all had showers and were beautifying themselves for their night on the town. It had become a ritual they enjoyed, relaxing after their showers rubbing lashings of moisturiser on their tanned bodies as they chatted and laughed about the day's events. Then when they were dressed, they would sip a cool drink and watch the sun sinking into the Aegean, a spectacular sight that never failed to delight them.

"I think we should go to Vasileo's," Aileen said, as she twirled around in front of the mirror to inspect her tan.

"Fine," agreed Laura, who was, as usual, the first to be dressed. "Is that OK with you, Cassie?"

"Sure, the food there is scrumptious."

"So are the waiters," giggled Aileen, remembering the flirtation she had carried on with a gorgeous brown-eyed hunk a few evenings previously.

"Aileen O'Shaughnessy, you behave yourself tonight,"

warned Cassie with mock severity.

"Huh! Do you hear who's talking?" Aileen sniffed indignantly as she covered herself from head to toe in Johnson's Baby Lotion. "You and Stavros weren't doing too badly. Wait until I get home and tell Robbie all about it."

"Don't you dare!" Cassie exclaimed in horror. Robbie wouldn't like it to think she had been flirting with another man.

"That's changed your tune, miss," laughed Aileen. "Don't worry, your secret is safe with me."

Cassie gave a sheepish grin. "It's just that Robbie's special."

"Do you hear that, Laura?" Aileen arched an eyebrow. "Robbie's special. We'd never have guessed, would we?"

"Oh never!" grinned Laura, pouring out their drinks. "You'd never think that for a minute."

"Funeee!" Cassie waved her fingers in the air to dry her nails.

Aileen flopped into the chair beside Cassie, eyes glinting mischievously. "Are we talking about walking-up-the-aisle special?"

In spite of herself, Cassie blushed scarlet.

Aileen sat bolt upright. "Laura, did you see that? Look at her! Cassie Jordan, what's going on here? There's more to this than meets the eye, or I'll eat my hat."

Cassie met Laura's gaze. "Well! What *is* the story here?" Laura asked softly. "Is Robbie the one?"

"I think so," Cassie admitted, smiling.

"Have you taken the big step?" Aileen enquired discreetly.

Cassie laughed at her euphemism. "Yep."

"And you never told us!" chorused the other two indignantly.

"Well, I kept meaning to, I just never seemed to find the right time."

Laura raised her glass. "Two down, one to go."

"Laura, you're the last of the three vestal virgins unless you've been doing something we haven't heard about in Nantucket."

Laura shook her head. "Sorry to disappoint you, Aileen. You'll be the first to know. And speaking of things we don't know about, what's the story about this Liam guy. You're playing him very close to your chest."

"You can say that again," Cassie agreed. Mind, she would never have had the neck to approach Aileen about Liam in such a direct manner as Laura had.

It was Aileen's turn to blush in a most uncharacteristic manner.

"Come on, spill the beans!" demanded Laura, laughing.

Aileen took a gulp of her drink. "Well, he's an architect...and...um...he's older than me. He's forty-five, although that's not...that old," she added a little defensively, noting their surprise. "And, well...he's married." It all came out in a stammering rush and she was so glad that at last she had told them. Now she stared anxiously at her friends.

"Oh, Ahh..." Cassie was momentarily stuck for words. She and Laura had discussed the mysterious Liam and come up with a few scenarios but, surprisingly enough, the idea that he might be married had never crossed their minds.

"You're not serious, Aileen!" Laura exclaimed in disgust.

Aileen felt the blood drain from her face at the sight of Laura's accusing face. Her heart sank. She might have expected Cassie to be a bit shocked, but she thought

Laura would have taken the news in her stride. Laura was so...well...hard wasn't exactly the word, tough maybe. Of them all, she had seen much more of life, what with her travels and her studies. Aileen was very taken aback by her reaction.

"Oh I know, I'll probably be consigned to hell's fires," she said airily, her tone a little brittle to hide her hurt and dismay.

"Oh for God's sake, Aileen! That's typical of you. Can't you be serious about anything?" Laura seemed to be keeping her temper with difficulty.

"Look, forget I said anything," snapped Aileen, getting up from her chair. "It's really none of your business anyway and I'm not in the humour for one of your bossy lectures."

"Oh grow up, Aileen!"

Aileen spun on her heel and faced her friend.

"No! You grow up, Laura. What the hell do you know about it? You've never had a relationship in your life. All you care about is getting a first-class honours—"

"Oh come on, let's not have an argument," interjected Cassie hastily as she saw tempers rising.

Aileen exploded. "She's not going to stand in judgement on me, Cassie! The trouble with Miss high-and-mighty holier-than-thou virgin here is jealousy. We've done it and she hasn't, because she's afraid of her life of getting involved with anyone. There's a free space where sex is concerned on her precious timetable!"

Laura's face reddened with fury. "You fuck off, Aileen O'Shaughnessy! At least I don't have to resort to stealing another woman's husband. That's the lowest of the low. And I don't sleep with every Tom, Dick, and Harry just because I can't control my hormones."

"You bitch!" Aileen's eyes widened. "I'm not stealing

anyone's husband," she fumed. "She doesn't give a damn about her marriage. All she wants to do is sit and vegetate in front of the TV. If the marriage were working Liam wouldn't be looking for companionship elsewhere and—"

"Huh!" snorted Laura. "What a convenient answer. Is that how you justify it to yourself? Is that how he justifies it to you? What about all the years that woman supported him when he was making it to the top? What about the sacrifices she's had to make? And what's he going to do now? Trade her in for a new model because the old one is a bit worn from having performed her wifely duties? It makes me sick!"

"Laura, calm down!" ordered Cassie. This was getting out of hand.

The other girl turned on her, shaking with emotion. "Don't you tell me what to do, either. I suppose we should be honoured that you were actually able to make the supreme sacrifice and come on holidays with us. We've seen precious little of *you* lately, now that you have your precious Robbie! Except when you have your fights with him and then you come running back to us."

"*Laura!*" exclaimed Cassie in disbelief, hurt and stunned by what her friend had just said.

"Oh, leave me alone!" Grabbing her bag, Laura rushed across the room.

"Where are you going?" Cassie asked sharply, trying to keep the hurt out of her voice. She felt sick. One minute they had been laughing and teasing—and now this. In all their years of friendship they had never had a scene like this. Oh yes, they'd had their tiffs and got over them. But this was different. There was a lot of resentment and bad feeling surfacing here.

"I'm going out. I want to be by myself!" Laura snarled, slamming the door behind her.

Aileen burst into tears. "Bitch!" she sobbed. "Who does she think she is? Do you think I'm a slut? I've only had two relationships. That's not excessive for someone of my age!"

"Of course I don't think you're a slut," Cassie said wearily.

"At least you don't judge people," Aileen sniffed.

"Who am I to judge anybody?" Cassie gave a watery smile. "Do *you* think I've been...neglecting you and Laura because of Robbie?"

"Well, you've been spending lot of time with him," Aileen conceded. "But that's understandable," she amended, seeing Cassie's stricken face. "Laura just doesn't understand what it's like to want to be with someone but she could try and make some effort to understand, instead of mouthing off like that."

Cassie sighed. "She really lost the cool tonight."

"Yeah, and she's lost a friend too," Aileen said grimly.

"Don't be hasty. She might come back and apologise," Cassie said, trying to understand what had caused Laura to fly off the handle.

"She can go to hell!" swore Aileen, pulling a sundress over her head. "Will we just go to the taverna? I don't feel like going into Mandraki."

"Me neither," Cassie said unhappily, wishing she was at home with Robbie.

They sat chasing their food around their plates with their forks, not eating much, and saying very little.

"If Liam's marriage were working, I wouldn't be involved with him. It was on the rocks long before he met me," Aileen said earnestly.

"Look, Aileen, I wouldn't dream of telling you how to run your life. You're a big girl now, you know what you want. The only thing I'd say to you is, be careful you don't get hurt."

Aileen gave a deep sigh. "I know you're right, Cassie. I know I'm an idiot but I'm just crazy about him. He's great company, we have such fun together, he's very romantic and kind and he's...I'm...I love making love with him. You know yourself," she added miserably. "I just can't believe that Laura said the things she said, and to you as well."

"Well, you know Laura. She's very black-and-white and that's why she's so good at her legal stuff. But she'd want to cop on to herself about the way she treats her friends. There was no excuse for blowing up like that," Cassie observed crossly. She was really annoyed with Laura, now that the shock of the row had worn off. She might not approve of Aileen having an affair with a married man but there was no need for Laura to talk to her the way she did. It just wasn't on. A little bit of tact and the whole thing could have been avoided. Despite Aileen's bubbly zaniness, she could be quite sensitive. Laura had been her friend for too long not to realise that.

"Do you want to go into Mandraki, or would you like to stay here and have a drink?"

"If you don't mind, Cassie, I think I'd just like to go to bed, I've got a splitting headache," Aileen confessed.

"Well, I think I'll go for a walk then," Cassie decided. "I'll see you later." They set off in different directions, Aileen to cry herself to sleep, Cassie to walk along the curving beach of Trianda Bay.

It was as usual a beautiful balmy night. The moon hung like a huge melon-slice just above the horizon, its reflection dappling the silvery waters of the Aegean. Across the bay Cassie could see the lights of Turkey twinkling in the distance. They had wanted to take a day-trip to Turkey but because of hostilities between

Turkey and Greece, this was now impossible. It made no difference anyway now. It looked as though the holiday of a lifetime was going to end in disaster.

God, she couldn't get over Laura, and the way she had turned on her as well as the unfortunate Aileen. A stab of guilt pricked her. Laura was right about her spending so much time with Robbie lately and as a result she supposed she had neglected the girls. Although Aileen had Liam to keep her busy, Laura must have been feeling a bit out of things. Cassie had to admit she had been thoughtless and she could see why Laura was annoyed. But still, she could have mentioned it in a calm and rational manner. There was no need to carry on like a raging lunatic. Depressed, she turned around and began to walk back to the guest-house.

The room was in darkness and Aileen was asleep when she got in, so she took her book and poured herself a nice cool beer and sat outside under the little wall-light. She was going to wait up until Laura came home and she was going to talk to her best friend calmly and coolly about their differences and Laura's accusations.

She rehearsed a hundred times what she would say to Laura. "You were perfectly right, Laura. I have been neglecting our friendship and for that I am sorry, but you had no business yelling at me the way you did and I think you went too far with Aileen. I've apologised to you, you should apologise to Aileen and we should forget the whole business and enjoy the rest of our holiday."

Laura didn't arrive home that night.

❧

"I wonder if we should go to the police." It was the following morning and Aileen was frantic.

"Calm down, will you. Getting excited isn't going to help!"

"Oh God, I said some pretty horrible things to her myself," Aileen muttered, taking a deep drag on her cigarette. "You don't think she did anything foolish, do you?"

Cassie was trying to remain calm. "For heaven's sake, Aileen, will you stop that kind of talk. She probably booked into another guest-house for the night. She'll be back when she cools down."

"We were supposed to be going to Lindos today," Aileen reminded her.

"I think you can forget that for the moment."

They were lying sunbathing on the balcony when Laura finally waltzed through the door. Ignoring the girls, she gathered together some toiletries, a change of clothing and some beachwear. She stuffed the lot into a large beach-bag. "I'm going to Faliraki for the day. Bye," she said shortly before marching through the door with her head held high. Aileen and Cassie watched her go, mouths agape.

"Creepers!" Aileen exclaimed. "She's something else! Going to Faliraki for the day indeed."

"She sure is," agreed Cassie grimly. Faliraki Beach was on the other side of the island and it was the most popular beach on Rhodes. So Madam Laura was going to Faliraki without a word of apology or explanation as to where she was last night. Cool wasn't the word for it! Cassie scowled. "Come on, let's hire bicycles and cycle to Kremasti and Paradision. I'm damned if we're going to sit here moping all day."

Laura didn't come home that night. The other two girls were furious.

"Well, fuck her!" Aileen swore angrily over breakfast the following morning. "I never thought Laura would be so petty."

"I just can't make it out," sighed Cassie, sinking her teeth into a juicy plum. "I've never seen her behave like this before and we've been friends since we were children."

"It's really ruined the holiday," Aileen said sadly.

"Yeah!" nodded Cassie. "She'll probably move out when we get home."

"God. I should never have opened my big mouth about Liam!" Aileen berated herself.

"Listen, Aileen, nothing short of murder could justify her behaviour yesterday, and by golly, is Laura Quinn going to get an earful from me when I get a chance to talk to her again." Cassie had never felt as mad in her life.

"It is a bit much all the—"

"I'm sorry!" A familiar voice interrupted their conversation and they looked up to find Laura standing behind them. They had been so engrossed in giving out about her that they had not seen her get off a passing bus at the stop just opposite the taverna.

"So you should be!" Cassie said shortly.

Laura's eyes brimmed with tears at her tone. "Cassie, Aileen, I'm really sorry and ashamed of myself. Please don't freeze me."

In the face of her tears, their anger evaporated. Laura never cried.

"Oh come on, sit down. Have you had breakfast?" Aileen asked solicitously, pulling out the chair beside her. Laura shook her head, unable to speak.

"Have some with us then." Cassie put a comforting arm around her best friend's shoulder and gave her a hug. "We've just ordered another pot of coffee and I'll tell Nichos to bring some more rolls and honey."

Laura turned to Aileen. "Aileen, I'm so sorry. Those

things I said to you, I really didn't mean them. It's just…"
She swallowed hard and looked at her two friends. "Well,
my father has been having an affair with Jennifer Casey
for the past six years and I just thought of the pain it's
caused my mother and I guess I flipped," she explained
unhappily.

"Jennifer Casey, Sergeant Casey's wife?" Cassie was
stunned. This was all news to her. Jennifer Casey was a
blowsy middle-aged woman who thought she was a
femme fatale.

Laura nodded. "I actually caught them having sex
one day while my mother was in hospital having a
hysterectomy. It was awful. I suppose I've been holding
it in until now. I've never told anybody. Aileen, I'm
sorry; that was no reason to take it out on you."

"It's OK, Laura, it's nothing I'm proud of anyway,"
Aileen murmured. To tell the truth, Laura's angry words
had given her a lot of food for thought. Maybe Liam
Flynn *was* being unfair to his wife. Maybe she was causing
that woman a great deal of pain and grief. She felt so
confused.

"Well, I'm really sorry, anyway. Are we still friends?"
Laura asked anxiously.

"Of course we're friends. My God, if we can't have a
row and get over it, it wouldn't be much of a friendship,
would it?" Aileen leant over and gave Laura a hug.

Laura turned to Cassie. "I'm sorry for what I said
about you and Robbie."

Cassie smiled. "Laura, you were perfectly right. I'm
the one who has to apologise. I *have* been neglecting my
friends, I promise it won't ever happen again."

Cassie was relieved the row was ended. She should
have known better than to be worrying. It took a big
person to say sorry. And Laura was that. It wouldn't be

in her character to hold a grudge. Pettiness was not part of her friend's nature.

Laura smiled with relief. "Boy, I've been so miserable, I couldn't even eat. Now I'm starving." She bit into a crusty roll. "This is scrumptious."

"Where did you go?" Aileen asked curiously.

Laura put her coffee cup down and made a face. "Well, I've a confession to make now, Aileen. It's something I'm not that proud of either." She took a deep breath. "I spent the last two nights and yesterday with Costas."

"Lucky you!" Aileen grinned.

"Close your mouth, Cassie," Laura said, half-laughing.

"Sorry!" smiled Cassie. Laura was full of surprises these days!

"I was really mad when I left the other night, as you know, and I went into Mandraki." Laura ran tanned fingers through her silky black hair and sighed. "I suppose as well as everything else I was feeling a bit jealous. You and Aileen were in relationships and, as Aileen pointed out, I'd never had one. That stung." She smiled at Aileen. "You're a tough cookie in a fight."

Aileen laughed. "You're no slouch yourself!"

"Anyway, I went into our taverna on the harbour and Costas was there and he could see I was on my own and upset and he was really nice to me and…and I can't believe that I actually went to bed with him. I just wanted to get the first time over and done with, I suppose. I just wanted to see what all the fuss was about. Isn't that pathetic?" she sighed ruefully. "I guess what's even more pathetic is that I still don't know!"

"Oh Laura!" Cassie exclaimed sympathetically. "When it's the right time for you it will happen, honestly. How can you expect yourself to have time to work and study and have a relationship? It would be impossible.

You always expect far too much of yourself!"

"Well, I made a complete idiot of myself this time. Didn't I?"

"Don't be daft!" Aileen said stoutly. "And besides, Costas is too much in love with himself to have time to make sure you were enjoying yourself, so forget about it. All you need is the right man and, girl, he's out there somewhere."

"Maybe, maybe not. Who cares anyway, I've got you pair," Laura declared as she buttered another roll. "What's on the agenda today, then?"

❦

The rest of the holiday passed very pleasurably. It seemed as though their brief bust-up had brought the three girls even closer together. It had strengthened their friendship, made them more aware of one another's needs. When, tanned and glowing, they boarded the plane to go home, it was with a great sense of reluctance and regret. Rhodes had been a paradise to them, a haven from their cares and responsibilities. The night before they left, they sat sipping ice-cold beer and watching the red-gold sun turn the Aegean Sea and the Greek sky a dusky red as it dipped below the horizon and extinguished itself.

"Let's make a pact that the three of us come will back here in ten or twenty years' time," Aileen proposed. "Just the three of us, OK? No husbands or boyfriends.

"You're on!" laughed Laura.

"It's a deal," smiled Cassie as they raised their glasses to toast their promise.

❦

"It's hard to believe it's over, isn't it?" Laura murmured as they stood waiting for Aileen, who had had the misfortune to be stopped by the customs. They were now informing her that she was well over the duty-free limit and she could either pay the duty or have her excess drink and cigarettes confiscated.

"Trust Aileen to get into a fix!" Cassie remarked, trying to hide her grins at the faces the redhead was making.

"She's not the only one who might be in a fix," Laura said forlornly. Cassie turned to look at her. "I was working out my dates on the plane home. I didn't take precautions when I slept with Costas. I hope to God I'm not pregnant!"

Jesus, thought Cassie to herself, that would really ruin everything for Laura. "You'll be fine, don't worry," she said reassuringly, wishing she could believe it. Robbie and she were always so careful. He was very good like that, Cassie thought gratefully, and it wouldn't be long until his arms were around her. She was dying to see him. Hurry up, Aileen, she silently urged her friend.

Just a few yards away on the other side of the smoked-glass partition door, Robbie was waiting for them. At last, Aileen was ready and they pushed their luggage trolleys through the doors, Cassie craning her head to get a look at him. There he was, head and shoulders above the rest! She waved vigorously. "Robbie! Robbie! Oh Robbie!" She flung herself into his arms and then felt as though she had been walloped by a truncheon, as a familiar whiff caught her nostrils.

"Hi, Cassie," he slurred, his eyes focusing on her only with difficulty. "I'm glad you're home."

Cassie drew away from her drunken boyfriend, hating him.

🐛🐛🐛

Book II

1978–1985

CHAPTER TWENTY-TWO

Cassie, Aileen and Laura could never have foreseen just how much their lives would change in the next few years as their careers took shape and their romances had many ups and downs.

Cassie worked hard in the bank. Her superiors saw from the start that she was interested in her work and was not afraid to show initiative. She had performed her secretarial duties very efficiently, but her aim was to get a job on the counter, where she would finally be dealing with the public. One day while she was typing a letter for the manager, she noticed that he had made an error that could have been embarrassing for the bank. She had brought it discreetly to his notice and he had complimented her on her attention to detail and also on the excellent quality of her work. "I think it's time, Cassie, that you got some experience as a cashier," he said, smiling at her, and she was thrilled with herself. At last! The counter. Some people had to wait *years and years* to get a counter position.

Cassie took to the job like a duck to water. With her open, friendly nature she soon developed a great rapport with her customers and she thoroughly enjoyed the bustle of the cash desk. It was great experience and her understanding of the customer side of things deepened as she became familiar with yet another aspect of banking.

By the time she was eligible to do the interview for the position of senior bank official, after five years in the job, she felt confident that she had got enough working experience to gain the promotion. It was going to be a tough interview but Robbie tutored her for weeks beforehand and that was a great help.

"You'll walk it!" Robbie assured her. But Cassie wasn't over-confident. There were a lot of talented people going for the interview and not everyone would succeed. The night before, Robbie sat her down in his apartment and went over in detail some of the questions that she would be expected to answer. After that, he took her notes and books away from her, spread a sheet on the rug in front of the fire, told her to take off her clothes and covered her in soft fluffy towels as he warmed some massage oils. As his hands firmly but gently kneaded the tension out of her bunched-up shoulder muscles, Cassie felt herself start to relax. A soothing Glenn Miller cassette played in the background. Robbie stroked her expertly. He could really give a good massage. There were times, she had to admit, he was a tower of strength for her.

If Robbie MacDonald could stop his bouts with the bottle he would be absolutely perfect. It wasn't that he drank every day or anything like it. Months would go by and Robbie wouldn't touch spirits, but then something would snap, particularly if he were under pressure, and he would go on a bender that might last four or five days. No one at work knew of his problem because he disguised it well. But it had caused rows in his family for years and Cassie came to understand that was why there was often tension in his home when she visited. His mother was blind to his faults, wouldn't hear a word against him and took his side always, alienating her husband, who felt very resentful about the way his wife protected Robbie instead of making him face up to his problems. His sister, Lillian, who had lived with the hassle since Robbie had started drinking in his late teens, barely spoke to him and several times told Cassie that she was letting herself in for trouble if she stayed with him. Cassie hated to see the friction and she knew it really upset

Robbie, who behind it all had a heart as soft as butter. But she knew herself, from the pain, anger and despair she suffered whenever he went off on his binges, that she couldn't blame her boyfriend's father and sister.

Every time Robbie went on a bender and let Cassie down, she broke it off with him, but then he would come back to her and say he was sorry and that he'd never do it again and she'd relent because she loved him.

At the interview she kept her cool and didn't let the interviewers rattle her. The computer courses she had taken impressed the interview board. When, as Robbie predicted, she walked the interview and was promoted to the position of senior bank official, he took her out to dinner to celebrate. They went to the Mirabeau in Sandycove, the poshest restaurant in Dublin, and over a candle-lit dinner, Robbie proposed to her. Delighted with her promotion, happier than she had ever been, Cassie joyfully accepted. The following day they went into Weir's of Grafton Street to pick the ring. Cassie chose an elegant solitaire and then as she and Robbie kissed on a bench in Stephen's Green he slipped the ring on her finger and held her tightly to him as he told her he loved her. Nora was delighted at the news.

Two weeks later he went on the batter and she flung the ring back at him and told him she never wanted to see him again. She was devastated. "How can he keep doing this to me, especially now that we're engaged?" she sobbed to Laura, who had been through this particular scene several times.

Concerned for her friend, Laura said, gently but firmly, "Cassie, I think Robbie's an alcoholic and he needs to accept that and go for help. If he doesn't, you've got to face up to the fact that this is going to be the pattern of your life from now on."

For a moment Cassie almost hated Laura. Who was she to stand there and say things like that? Things would always work out well for Laura! Filled with resentment, anger, confusion, she rushed out of the flat and started to walk. How could someone bring you from the heights of happiness to the depths of despair, as Robbie repeatedly did with her? Was Laura right? Was this the way it was always going to be?

Not if you end it and take control for yourself, a voice inside Cassie seemed to murmur. But she couldn't imagine life without Robbie. He was so much part of her life now that she had forgotten what it was like to be on her own. She stood on Portobello Bridge, looking down at the murky waters of the canal. She couldn't even remember having walked through Ranelagh. The sun was starting to set. It was a crisp cold winter's evening as she walked along the canal, hands stuffed into her jacket pockets, her face creased into lines of worry. Smoke swirled from the chimneys of the redbrick houses and the air had that faint acrid smell of sulphur. No longer adorned with their summer foliage, the trees that lined the canal bank were naked and bare, making the canal seem bleak and lonely, and matching her mood perfectly.

She walked as far as Harold's Cross Bridge and then on impulse took a bus into town. It was a Saturday evening and all around her as she walked along O'Connell Street there were bustling crowds. People walked with a purposefulness that depressed her as they did Christmas shopping or met dates for a meal before spending a night on the town. They all had places to go, unlike her. The Christmas lights, which would normally delight her, made her feel even more heavy-hearted. Listening to a group of carol-singers sing, "O, tidings of comfort and joy," brought a lump to her throat so big that it almost

seemed to choke her and to her horror she felt tears roll
down her cheeks. Was this what Robbie MacDonald had
reduced her to? Bawling her eyes out in the middle of
O'Connell Street? Passing the GPO, Cassie turned left
into Henry Street and with a great effort managed to
compose herself. She was cold. It had been freezing along
the canal. A cup of coffee in the Kylemore would warm
her up. There was a queue and she was tempted to turn
away but she couldn't face the thought of queuing for
a bus to go home. Neither could she see herself going to
a movie on her own. She hadn't brought enough money
to do any shopping, even if she wanted to.

Unhappily Cassie moved along the queue and selected
a creamy chocolate éclair to eat with her coffee. She
found an unoccupied table in a quiet little corner, sat
down and cupped her cold hands around her steaming
coffee cup. She wondered what Robbie was doing. An
ache of worry gripped her, a cold trembly sort of fear
that made her intestines spasm and her throat constrict.
It was always the same, this horribly familiar nauseating
feeling over which she had no control. Was he on the
tear with his mates? How she despised some of those so-
called friends of her boyfriend. Leeches, who let Robbie
buy drinks all night for them when he was on a bender.
She hated too the barmen who gave him credit, knowing
that he would always be back to pay his debts, not caring
that he was too drunk to drive or that he was causing
grief and great worry to those who loved him. How long
could she live with these feelings of futile rage and misery
and helplessness? Could she go on like this for the rest
of her life? Would it really mean that if she stayed
engaged to Robbie? Worn out and heavy-hearted, Cassie
drank her coffee, ate a bit of her cake, which tasted like
sawdust and which she could scarcely swallow, and then

went to queue for a bus outside Clery's. If this was the best she could do at entertaining herself, it was a pretty pathetic effort, she thought miserably.

Unwilling to let her mother know that anything was wrong, Cassie didn't go home for two weeks and when she finally did go home and her mother asked where her ring was, she fibbed that she was getting it tightened.

She was so shattered that she found herself making silly mistakes at the bank, and in desperation she took a couple of days off work. Laura's words kept coming back to her, chasing around her brain until she felt as if she were going to go crazy. "The pattern of your life from now on." Was her best friend right? Would it always be like this? She'd have to tell them at home. That would be Christmas ruined for Nora, who was delighted that at last her eldest daughter was going to marry and settle down. Imagine breaking off your engagement after only a couple of weeks! What would they say at work? She couldn't hide it forever. People were expecting her and Robbie to go to all the functions organised by the social club for Christmas.

Cassie got home from work one evening to see Robbie's car parked outside the flat. He was sitting waiting for her.

"Let me alone, Robbie, I don't want to talk to you. It's over between us. I just want to get on with my life," Cassie said wearily as Robbie walked up the path beside her.

"I joined AA," Robbie said quietly.

Cassie stopped in her tracks. "You did what!"

"I joined Alcoholics Anonymous. I love you, Cassie. I can't bear to lose you and if this is what it takes I'm willing to give it a try. Please, Cassie, just give me one more chance and I promise I'll try to stay off the booze."

Cassie flung herself into his arms. "Oh Robbie, Robbie, I'm so glad. I love you. I'll help you beat this thing. Oh this is the happiest day of my life. I've been so lonely without you."

"Me too," whispered Robbie, hugging her close, blinking away the tears from his eyes.

Incredibly relieved that he had at last taken this big step, Cassie felt her old sense of optimism resurface. This time it was going to work out, she just knew it.

❦

Eight months later, with Robbie still on the wagon, she was asked whether she would be interested in transferring to London. She would be working in a most up-to-date computerised services department that had just been established, a job for which her superiors thought she was well suited. Cassie was flattered and excited by the offer but she was reluctant to accept the transfer. If she weren't there with Robbie to encourage him to attend his meetings, would he fall off the wagon? If she weren't there to go out with him would he fall back on his old drinking buddies for companionship?

"You can't use that as a reason not to take the job," an Al-Anon counsellor told her. "Robbie has to stay on the programme because he wants to. Because he acknowledges that he's an alcoholic. Whether you are here or not should make no difference. You cannot allow yourself to be used as a crutch, Cassie. You will do your relationship with Robbie a great deal of harm if you do not let him take responsibility for his own drinking. By refusing the job in London you would be denying him that responsibility."

Cassie knew her counsellor spoke the truth but she spent a few troubled days wondering whether to go or stay. In the end it was Robbie who persuaded her to accept the transfer, telling her that it was a great opportunity and that he could always look for a transfer himself in the future. "The money's good, Cassie, and you'll get a lump sum for disturbance money that we could put towards the wedding. Besides, it's an opportunity of a lifetime. They don't offer jobs like this to everyone. Believe me, Cassie, they're grooming you for a managership. You know Allied Isles' position on equality, it's second to none. You'll be able to continue studying for your banking exams over in London. You'll have a year done here by then." Cassie was at that time taking night classes run by the bank for employees who wanted to take exams. What her fiancé said made good sense, and Cassie told her employers she'd be very happy to transfer to London in January of the following year.

CHAPTER TWENTY-THREE

"You're being transferred to London!" Nora repeated, shocked by the news her daughter had just imparted. Cassie nodded, smiling.

"It's a great opportunity, Mam. It's very good experience and they must think I'm capable of it. London's a much sought-after transfer."

"When will you be going?"

"I'll be starting in January. It's a nice time to start. Not only is it the beginning of a new year, it's the beginning of a new decade. Roll on the Eighties."

"Oh dear!" Nora sat down wearily in the armchair that Jack used to sit in to read his paper.

"Aren't you a little bit glad for me?" Cassie asked

lightly, although she had been dreading telling her mother the news.

Nora sighed. "I'll miss you, Cassie. It was bad enough when you went to stay in the flat in Dublin. But going over there! When will I ever get to see you?"

"I'll come home for my holidays," Cassie assured her.

"I've heard that before, and then you go off gadding about with that other pair," Nora sniffed.

Cassie felt her good humour evaporate. Honest to God, Nora was never satisfied. She came home at least once a week to stay overnight and for the past couple of years since she had got her own car she often came back to Port Mahon twice during the week. She always spent part of her holidays at home, helping to decorate or whatever else her mother wanted, and still Nora begrudged her the foreign holidays she had taken with the girls. She sighed deeply. She was twenty-four years old, a senior bank official now, she'd been living away from home and fending for herself for the past six years, and *still* her mother could make her feel like a sixteen-year-old and guilty as hell.

"We won't be going on holidays this year, and anyway, now that Laura is getting married, she won't be coming with us any more." It was hard to believe that Laura of all people was getting married. She was the first of the trio to go and in the process she had amazed everybody, not least herself.

"Very sudden, this marriage," Nora remarked tartly. "There's no urgent reason for it, is there?"

"Mam!" Cassie exclaimed in annoyance. No doubt half the parish were thinking the same thing.

"Well, you have to admit it was very sudden," Nora retorted. "And besides, look at that sister of hers who's an unmarried mother! Sure, Laura was hardly engaged at all! I mean, after all, you've been going with Robbie for years, you're engaged this past ten months and you still haven't set a date for your wedding."

Cassie smiled to herself. So that was it! Of course, she should have known that Nora was very miffed at the thought of Laura getting married before Cassie. To Nora, as to many of her generation, marriage was the be-all and end-all of a girl's life. To be an unwed woman was a disaster of gigantic proportions. Wanting to be a career woman was totally incomprehensible.

"Mam, Robbie and I won't be getting married for at least another year," Cassie retorted firmly. "I told you that before."

"Well, what does he think about this London thing?"

Cassie grimaced. "Well, naturally, we're going to miss each other and he's not too pleased about that, but from a career point of view he thinks it's terrific. He might look for a transfer, too."

"You're not going to live there *permanently*?" Nora exclaimed in horror.

"Mother, I don't know what we're going to do yet. If Robbie gets a transfer, we might get married sooner than we thought. It all depends. He's not going to apply until the project he's working on is finished." Cassie tried to keep the edge of irritation out of her voice.

"Don't do a rushed job on me, Cassie, I'll want plenty of time to prepare for your wedding. The cake will have to be made and I'll have to paper the sitting-room and do a job on the bathroom, and I still have to put the finishing touches to the front porch."

Cassie shook her head ruefully. First her mother was moaning because Laura was getting married before her; now she was telling her to give her plenty of notice. You just couldn't win! What she still had to do in the front porch, Cassie could not fathom; it looked perfectly fine to her. But she wouldn't be Nora if she weren't putting the finishing touches to something or other.

"Why didn't Barbara come home with you?" her mother enquired, poking the fire and sending a shower of sparks up the chimney as she threw on another log.

"Because she was working on a story," Cassie fibbed. She didn't want to hurt her mother's feelings by saying that Barbara preferred to stay in the flat in Dublin rather than visit her mother in Port Mahon. There were times when Cassie could murder Barbara for her thoughtlessness. Now that they were living together again there were times that she could just murder Barbara anyway.

"Switch on the TV, Cassie, it's time for the news. Thank God the *Late Late* will be back soon. Saturday night isn't the same without it."

Cassie did as she was bid. The news was full of the Pope's forthcoming visit to Ireland and Nora watched it eagerly. Cassie had promised to accompany her to the big Mass in the Phoenix Park and her mother was greatly looking forward to the event. Both Irene and Barbara had made excuses not to bring Nora to the Mass. Irene had told Cassie that there was no way she could cope with a crowd of a million people, she just wasn't good in crowds. Barbara, who was now working as a journalist, was "on duty," as she called it, writing a report for the *North County Dublin Chronicle,* the newspaper where she had made her début as a junior reporter after leaving school. Although she no longer worked on the paper, having graduated to a third-rate daily called *The Irish Mail*, the *Chronicle* often published her articles when they were stuck. She wouldn't possibly be able to go with her mother, Barbara assured Cassie. She would be with the press corps doing in-depth reporting.

Cassie knew full well that she would be quaffing champagne at the latest "in" spot with Noreen Varling, her ex-editor from the *Chronicle*. Noreen liked to think that she was a force to be reckoned with in journalism. She liked to see and be seen and champagne was all she drank. Barbara had always been mightily impressed by her, from the first moment she had gone to work as her secretary after leaving school. On one occasion, when a reporter who was supposed to be covering a big ploughing championship had called in sick, Noreen was so stuck that she had to send Barbara instead. Her efforts had pleased the editor and thus began Barbara's journalistic career. Now, Barbara was also drinking champagne, thrilled to be part of the very exciting and glamorous Dublin scene that Noreen was introducing her to.

Cassie thought how typical it was that once again it was left to her to make the arrangements and look after their mother. It wasn't that she minded that much, but she just thought the other pair could make more of an effort. After all, Nora was now getting on in years and she deserved a little bit of consideration.

Cassie got up and went out to the kitchen to make a cup of tea for her mother before the film started. She didn't normally come home on Saturday nights. They were usually spent with Robbie, but he had been in Belfast for the last two weeks on an assignment in one of their Northern branches and so she had come home, much to Nora's delight. She filled the kettle and took some of her mother's home-made scones out of the pantry, and liberally spread them with butter and jam. She was just as glad to be away from the flat anyway, she mused, licking the knife. No doubt Barbara and Ian, her sister's latest boyfriend, would be getting ready to go out on the town. Cassie could feel her blood-pressure rising. Ian got on her nerves. You would think he owned the flat the way he carried on in it. There had been more rows about that. In a way, her transfer to London couldn't have come at a more opportune time because she couldn't live with Barbara for much longer. It certainly wasn't like the old days of living with the girls.

Cassie sighed. It had been such fun living with Laura and Aileen but it couldn't last for ever. Laura had been awarded a first-class honours degree, got the apprenticeship she longed for and met her future husband, all within the space of one year. After six months, Laura had gone to live with Doug Donnelly, her hunky boyfriend, and Aileen's sister, Judy, had come up to Dublin to work as a car hire rep in Dublin airport. Laura's sister, Jill, who used to work there before she had the baby, had put in a good word for her. Judy had moved into the flat and it was an arrangement that worked out fine. Cassie liked Judy. She was as bubbly as Aileen but much less self-confident, due no doubt to having spent so much time under the influence of a mother as domineering as Angela O'Shaughnessy.

Then Aileen, utterly fed up with the Corporation and depressed because of the hopelessness of her love affair with Liam, decided that she was going to be a beautician and chucked in her good, permanent and pensionable job to do a beauty therapy course, much to her mother's fury. It had taken her a year to qualify and when she received her diplomas, she went to London because there were more openings there than in Dublin. Aileen was now doing very well. She had secured a post as beautician in a plush Mayfair salon and she was delighted to hear of Cassie's transfer to London. "We'll have a ball when you come over. London's great!" she told Cassie. It was nice to hear the old enthusiasm in her voice again. Aileen had gone through a very rough patch as a result of her affair with Liam. She planned to come home for Laura's wedding the following month and the three of them were going to get together and have a fine old time catching up on the news.

It was great for Cassie to see her two best friends doing as well in their careers as she was doing herself, but she missed their company in the flat.

Telling Nora that she was going to work in London was the difficult part. Cassie knew her mother wouldn't like the idea but between now and the New Year she'd have time to get used to it. Watching her, engrossed in the Saturday movie, she could see that her mother was ageing. Her thick, wavy chestnut hair was liberally sprinkled with grey and the lines around her eyes and mouth had deepened considerably. However, her skin, with its faint rosy hue, was still as soft as a baby's. Nora still went to her ladies' club, was still active in the community and looked after Martin and Irene, the only two of her offspring still living at home. These interests would always sustain her, Cassie comforted herself, as she stretched lazily in front of the fire. It was nice being at home all the same. It was true what they said—there was no place like it. She decided she'd have a nice walk along the beach the next day.

Her mother interrupted her reverie. "Cassie, would you ever switch on Irene's blanket for me?" she asked as the commercial break began. "She likes to have it on for a while to heat up her bed." Cassie had to smile. The way her mother still babied her youngest daughter, who was all of seventeen years old! And the things she got away with! Irene never had to lift a finger in the house and she was allowed to stay out until all hours—a far cry from when Cassie was growing up. That was always the way, wasn't it: the youngest always had it much easier. Barbara was for ever giving out about Irene. But then Barbara always had a chip on her shoulder about something. Right now she was in a huff because Nora had given John a loan to buy a few acres of land to start off his own business. John told his mother he would prefer to run his own farm rather than take over the management of hers and Nora had agreed that it was better for him in the long run to have his own place. Then there'd be no arguments. Barbara felt John was getting special treatment. She could do with a loan to buy a car but there was no offer of financial assistance forthcoming from her mother.

Barbara could still be so petty, Cassie reflected, as she switched on her sister's electric blanket. She and that great lump of a detective she was currently dating were a great match. A cute hoor, Laura had called Ian Murray, and Cassie had had to agree with her friend's assessment of Barbara's boyfriend. What her sister saw in the Donegal detective, Cassie could not imagine.

CHAPTER TWENTY-FOUR

Barbara sashayed into the bedroom with a couple of cans of beer and a plate of chicken sandwiches and watched with pleasure as her boyfriend's face lit up. Whether it was the sight of *her*, in her black see-through negligee, or the sight of the beer and sandwiches that caused his pleasure, she was not sure. Ian was a man of few words. But of course, that was part and parcel of being a detective. They never gave much away; they were trained to keep their own counsel. His mates were all the same, watchful and silent. Barbara loved it. It turned her on. She always enjoyed being with them for an evening, all these strong, manly, silent types. She felt so dainty and feminine when she was in their company. Being a feminist and a journalist could be tough going at the best of times but with the crowd of male chauvinists that Ian hung around with one had to be rapier-sharp. Barbara never let them away with a thing and she knew she impressed the hell out of them. She impressed the hell out of *herself*, if the truth were known.

She had come a long way from her small-town roots in Port Mahon. Now she was a cosmopolitan career woman on the way up. How she loved that word cosmopolitan. She even bought *Cosmopolitan* religiously every month and devoured its articles on sex and the single girl and how to please yourself as well as your man. She could really identify with the articles about career women. That was what she was, a career woman, and she intended going as high up the ladder as she could. Cassie and Laura weren't the only ones who could get ahead in their careers. Barbara was hot on their tails. The set she mixed with was sophisticated and smart. Of course, Noreen, her mentor, would settle for nothing less.

It impressed Barbara no end the way Noreen went to the Horseshoe Bar at the Shelbourne every Friday and drank champagne as she mixed with all the movers and shakers. For the life of her, Barbara could not understand all the fuss about champagne; it tasted like bubbly apple juice to her and gave her heartburn. But that was neither here nor there. It was what Noreen Varling drank and therefore it would be what Barbara drank from now on.

She missed working with Noreen, missed their long gossipy lunch-hours. Noreen knew every bit of gossip going: who was having an affair with whom, politicians,

actors, actresses, socialites and ladies who lunch—Noreen
knew them all, and all the seedy little secrets that
circulated faster than Concorde around the hot spots of
the capital. Noreen liked being a big fish in a little pond
and had never hankered after a post on one of the dailies
but she had encouraged Barbara to take the position of
junior reporter in *The Irish Mail*, when the job came up.
"You'll be right in the thick of things and you'll go far!"
she assured her protégée and proceeded to give Barbara
a glowing reference. Lots of champers had been quaffed
when Barbara got the job.

There were times, of course, when Barbara got fed up
with her job. Like today, for example, when she was
instructed by the features editor to do one of those silly
vox pop things and interview celebrities on what they
thought of the Pope's forthcoming visit. Most of the
responses were pretty boring crap, but Arlene Ford, the
flamboyant award-winning actress, had drawled in that
unmistakable husky voice that quite frankly she wasn't
the slightest bit impressed by the Pope or his visit but
that box-office takings would be down and, as she was
on a percentage, would His Holiness care to reimburse
her for her lower earnings, seeing as it was his fault in
the first place.

Barbara was delighted with the quote but the lily-
livered features editor wouldn't run it for fear of
controversy. It was enough to make a saint curse—and
she was no saint! If she were the features editor there'd
be a lot of that sort of thing—and much more. She'd
really have the pages of *The Irish Mail* humming. Still, in
time she'd get there. Even Ian was impressed with how
ambitious she was.

It was through doing an article on the courts that she
had met Detective Ian Murray. He was giving evidence

in the case of some criminal gang involved in drug trafficking and Barbara was covering the case for the *Mail*. They had got talking, rather Barbara had got talking, Ian giving monosyllabic answers to her questions. The following day he rang the *Mail* and asked her to go out for a drink. Barbara accepted with delight—his silent demeanour had made a big impression on her. He was about five-eleven in height and stocky of build with a black moustache and black hair. His eyes were a cold slate-grey. With Ian it was hard to know what he was thinking. For some reason this excited her. Barbara had always loved a challenge. They arranged to meet in McGrath's pub in Drumcondra as she was doing a piece on the Archbishop's Palace just up the road.

Sitting waiting for him, Barbara observed small groups of prison officers, guards and detectives drinking in the smoky bar. With its proximity to Mountjoy Prison, it wasn't surprising to see so many law enforcers there. You just couldn't miss them with their short-back-and-sides regulation hair-cuts and their wary way of observing everything that was happening. Obviously this was one of Ian's haunts as his station on Griffith Avenue wasn't too far away. She wished he would hurry up. Despite her role as a modern Irish feminist, she didn't like sitting in a pub on her own for long. He was twenty minutes late, during which time she got up and went to the loo twice, re-touching her make-up and brushing her hair. She looked well, she felt, with her newly-cropped hairstyle.

Barbara had decided she needed a new image and went to Peter Mark and had her long mousy hair chopped. Highlights and a short layered look had made all the difference and she had been delighted. Now she really looked the part. The only thing was that her short hair caused more of her ears to be displayed than she cared for. Barbara was rather sensitive about her ears; they were *big*, unfortunately. The next time she got her hair done she would ask the hairdresser to layer her hair down over them. Nevertheless, in her black polo with just a silver chain for decoration and her grey pencil-slim skirt, she felt elegant, a real cosmopolitan woman.

After several drinks, beer for him, vodka and orange for her, he took her to Captain America for a meal. Barbara was impressed. She had never been there before. Her salary just about covered the occasional sortie to the Royal Dublin Hotel for lunch in the bar. Barbara did most of the talking as Ian listened and asked her the odd question. Getting information out of him was like drawing blood from a stone, but she found out that he was from Letterkenny in Donegal and came from a family of six. He was thirty, he owned a house in Santry which was let in flats and he lived in a flat in Drumcondra.

They went for a drive to Sandymount strand and he tried it on, his hands roaming over her like an octopus. Barbara told him in no uncertain terms to mind his manners. It wasn't that she was a prude but she was damned if he thought he could get away with anything on the first date. In keeping with her woman-of-the-world image, Barbara had lost her virginity several years back to Dentist Burke's son. It had happened one night after a dance her secretarial college had organised. It had been a rushed messy affair and she had not been impressed, nor had subsequent couplings done much to improve her opinion. But avid readings of the glossy monthly mags had sent her on the trail of the orgasm that had so far eluded her. She was on the pill; she knew what she wanted. Maybe Ian was the man to give it to her, but not on the first date. *Never* on the first date. Barbara was a woman of principle!

After the third date when she saw him eyeing up a tarty-looking blonde in McGrath's she went to bed with him, although she was still on the quest of the fabled orgasm. Not that she let on to Ian. She moaned and groaned and puffed and panted and she knew by him that he thought Casanova was only trotting after him! That night she found out that he was a Special Branch detective and entitled to carry a gun, which almost made up for the disappointment in bed. Just wait until she told the girls she was seeing a Special Branch detective! They'd *have* to be impressed by that.

They weren't, and Barbara was furious. The first time she brought him back to the flat and introduced him to Aileen, Cassie and Judy, Ian plonked himself in front of the TV after the introductions and switched over to the Leeds–Everton match.

"Yeh don't mind, do yeh?" he mumbled. "Any chance of a cup of tea?"

Aileen had been watching *Coronation Street* and her eyebrows nearly shot off her forehead as she caught Cassie's wide-eyed gaze. Judy babbled something about making tea and went scuttling off to the kitchen. It had been a strained visit.

"Listen, Barbara, the next time Sherlock Holmes comes visiting I won't be so polite about letting him watch his football match, OK?" Aileen informed her coolly over breakfast the next morning. Thank God she was going to England after her exams were over. Barbara couldn't stand Aileen and the feeling was mutual. They were always rowing. A few weeks before, when Barbara had left the grill dirty and Aileen had come home from work to cook her dinner there had been a screaming match as Aileen had called Barbara a slovenly bitch and Barbara had countered by calling Aileen a pathetic old maid. At least Laura was living with someone and Cassie was engaged to Robbie. If Aileen, who was manless, were feeling frustrated, she was not to be taking it out on her flatmates.

Aileen was so furious that she had issued Cassie with an ultimatum. "Either she goes or I go."

"For God's sake, I've had enough, Barbara!" Cassie yelled. "If you can't make an effort, go and get your own place!"

"Typical!" screeched Barbara. "You take her side against me every time." Slamming the door behind her she got the train to Port Mahon and went home to pour out her woes to Nora. Her mother lifted the phone and gave Cassie a piece of her mind.

Cassie was sizzling with anger and told Barbara in no uncertain terms that she should cop on to herself and grow up, instead of running home to her mother with every little upset. The coolness in the flat lasted for ages. Even Judy was annoyed with her and that really bugged Barbara. She had been so looking forward to coming to live in Dublin and to sharing the flat; Cassie Aileen and Laura had a ball living together. When Laura went to live with Doug Donnelly, conveniently leaving the way open for Judy and then Barbara to take up residence, the two younger girls had been delighted. After all, it was a flat for four and with Aileen going to the UK, there was no reason why Judy, Cassie and she should have any less fun and good times.

When Aileen sarcastically called Ian Sherlock Holmes, Barbara had to bite her tongue. She didn't want there to be another row, because she'd really have to go and get a place of her own if she upset them all again and moving was such a load of hassle.

Mostly they went back to Ian's flat at night from

then on. If Aileen thought Barbara was slovenly, she should see Ian's pad! Dirty shirts strewn all over the place, a mountain of dishes in the sink, the bed unmade. Barbara was a bit disgusted. Some men, if they hadn't a woman to look after them, just hadn't got a clue. When she knew there was going to be nobody in the Ranelagh flat, Ian stayed the night and she really enjoyed those evenings, sitting in front of the fire with him, and then going up to her and Judy's shared bedroom, where at least the sheets on the bed were clean.

When Aileen left and went to England Barbara was delighted. No more nagging from that quarter. Cassie was lucky, she had a room to herself and Robbie could stay over if he wished. Barbara was almost sure that Cassie and her fiancé were sleeping together. If Nora knew she would be horrified. It was a pity Barbara hadn't got her own room; then she wouldn't have to wait for the times she had the flat to herself to bring Ian over for the night. Since Aileen left, she'd had the flat to herself only three times in the space of six months.

To have a Saturday night in the flat on her own was a precious treat, Barbara reflected, sitting on the bed beside Ian as he tucked into the chicken sandwiches. It wasn't her chicken either, it was Judy's. She'd have to get a cooked chicken somewhere tomorrow before her flatmate came back. That chicken was supposed to be Judy's dinner. It really was a stroke of luck that Robbie had gone to Belfast and Cassie had decided to go home. Judy was in London visiting Aileen and wasn't due back until tomorrow afternoon so Barbara and Ian could relax and have a lie-in and linger over breakfast. Sighing contentedly, she nestled close against her boyfriend. Ian belched as he finished his second can of beer. "That was nice grub. Any more chicken left?" he asked.

Barbara was just about to get out of bed to go to the kitchen when she heard the key in the door.

"Shit!" she cursed aloud. Cassie must have come back from Port Mahon. Her lovely peaceful weekend was up the creek!

❧

Judy O'Shaughnessy was in an awful rush as she slipped her key into the lock of the flat. Her heart sank when she drove up in the taxi to see that Detective Murray's car was parked outside the door. She found him terribly hard going and what Barbara saw in him she could not make out. Anyway, she didn't have time to be worrying about Barbara and Sherlock Murray, as Aileen had unkindly christened him. Judy grinned as she thought of Aileen. She had thoroughly enjoyed her few days in London, and had come back with her eyebrows and eyelashes tinted, legs waxed and nails manicured. It was handy having a beautician for a sister. Still, she needed to be looking her best this weekend of all weekends.

Tonight, Andrew Lawson was picking her up at ten-thirty to take her to dinner at Capri, the plush restaurant Laura had once worked in. She knew Andrew Lawson in a business capacity. His firm often rented cars for his clients at the airport and she had to deal with them. She had met him several times in Sachs nightclub and had even danced with him but it wasn't until she had found herself unexpectedly sitting beside him on the plane to London that she had ever got into a conversation with him. He was gorgeous, drop dead gorgeous and she had really enjoyed the flight. When he asked her what she was doing on the following Saturday night she hadn't let on that she was going to be in London, just in case he asked her out.

"Nothing planned," she murmured lightly, telling a little fib.

"Would you care to have dinner with me, then?" he enquired, his eyes smiling into hers in a way that had left her quite bemused. He had the most striking green eyes.

"I'd love to," Judy responded, hoping against hope that she'd be able to get a flight on the Saturday afternoon instead of Sunday afternoon. She gave him her address before they touched down. Watching him stride off the plane, his trenchcoat flapping behind him, she thought, wow!

"Huh!" teased Aileen when she heard of this development after they met at Heathrow. "So I'm being dropped for a dish in a trenchcoat." She had just managed to get a glimpse of Andrew in the arrivals hall.

"Oh he's something else," bubbled Judy. "All the girls on the desk are mad about him. He's always got women raving over him."

"Well, play it cool," warned her sister.

"As a cucumber," Judy assured her.

"What's the news from home? How are Ma and Cassie and Laura and Barbara?" Aileen was chuffed to see her sister and they settled down on the taxi-ride to exchange all the gossip. Judy had been looking forward to the few days with Aileen, although her mother had nearly had a fit when she said she was flying over to London.

"And leaving me here all alone with not a sinner to call on if I'm in trouble? That's lovely! The pair of you haven't a thought for your poor old mother. That other one"—thus did Angela O'Shaughnessy refer to her elder daughter—"doesn't give a rap about me. Taking off to London to put make-up on other people's faces when she had a perfectly good permanent and pensionable job in the Corporation. I hope you're not getting any such ideas, my lady!"

"No, Mother, I'm not," Judy said patiently. "I just have a few days' holidays and I thought I'd pop over and see Aileen." That remark was a mistake.

"Oh! And you couldn't be bothered to spend a few days with your poor mother. This house needs to be papered and painted. I don't see you helping me the way Cassie Jordan helps her mother. You could have asked me if I'd like to go with you," Angela sniffed. "I wouldn't mind a trip to London myself."

"Oh that would be impossible, Mother. I've booked on an Apex flight and you have to book them weeks in advance!" Judy fibbed hastily, with visions of her lovely few days being ruined completely.

Judy's mother was so put out that it was only talking to Cassie that made Judy stick to her plan.

"You'll get on that plane, Judy O'Shaughnessy, if I have to put you on it myself," the older girl threatened. "It's only for a few days and your mother will be fine, believe me. She can always ring Mam if she has to."

It was such a relief to get on the plane, away from the tensions of the flat and away from her mother. It really wasn't working out, sharing with Barbara. Even though they had been friends for years, Barbara was not an easy person to live with on a day-to-day basis. Come live with me to know me, or words to that effect, someone had once said. Well, it was true of Barbara. When there had been just Aileen and Cassie and herself in the flat, it had been fun, but then Barbara had arrived and the whole atmosphere of the place had changed. It was amazing how one person could effect such a trans-formation. Barbara was so totally self-centred and blithely unaware of the fact that when you were living with other people you had to make an effort and make allowances. She was incredible, actually, and Judy didn't know what she was going to do when Cassie left to go to London to live. Judy didn't think she could cope with Barbara on her own.

It had been so relaxing in London with Aileen...well, not relaxing, exactly! Her sister had whizzed her around showing her the sights, but it had been a terrifically exciting few days and Judy had enjoyed it immensely, particularly the shopping for clothes. The icing on the cake had been Andrew Lawson's dinner invitation, in honour of which she had bought a little black number in Richard's Shop. Judy glanced at her watch as she struggled into the hall with her duty-free bags and case. She'd have to get a move on, as the only flight she could get had left her very stuck for time.

Rushing into the bedroom, she came to a halt at the sight of Ian Murray sitting bare-chested in Barbara's bed, surrounded by beer-cans and empty plates, and Barbara glaring at her, quite shameless in a black negligee that hid nothing at all.

"What are you doing home?" Barbara demanded. "You weren't supposed to be home until tomorrow!"

Judy was speechless. Barbara was making *her* feel like a culprit.

A rare anger ripped through Judy. After all, it was *her* bedroom as well as Barbara's and she was paying exactly the same rent.

"I want to get changed, Barbara! If you don't mind...Detective Murray," she said coldly.

"Uh, oh right," muttered the embarrassed detective. "If you could just excuse me until I get dressed."

"Certainly," Judy snapped icily. The cheek of that Barbara one trying to make her feel bad about coming into her own bedroom! By golly, when she got her on her own there was going to be the mother and father of a row. Judy marched into the kitchen to put the kettle on for a badly needed cup of tea. On the table, the bare carcase of a cold chicken sat in lonely splendour. Judy picked at it absentmindedly as she waited for the kettle to boil. Her eyes widened as a thought struck her. When she flung open the fridge door her suspicions were confirmed. Her chicken had been devoured. She had cooked it specially so she would have something to eat on her arrival home from London, not realising that she was going to be wined and dined by Andrew Lawson, and now Barbara and beady-eyes had gone and scoffed it. It really was the last straw! Judy decided. The straw that broke the camel's back. Some things were going to change—and how!

CHAPTER TWENTY-FIVE

"Cripes, would you look at the radiant bride! What the hell is the matter with you?" Aileen flung her arms around Laura, who was standing with Cassie in the arrivals hall in Dublin airport.

"It's good to see you. You look great," Laura grinned, hugging her friend back.

"Can't say the same about you, dear. You need the services of a fairy godmother...or a beautician! Hi, Cassie! How's the girl?"

"All the better for seeing you, you rip!" Cassie laughed, as she too was enveloped in a great bearhug.

"Lead the way to the bar, women. I could murder a Bloody Mary," Aileen said, her eyes dancing with pleasure at the sight of the girls. "I think the pilot was suffering from Parkinson's disease. It was a hell of a jumpy flight." Aileen rolled her eyes dramatically and Cassie thought to herself that, really, her friend should have pursued an acting career. She would have won an Oscar by now.

Ten minutes later, seated at a quiet table in a corner of the bar, they sat sipping their drinks, glad to be in one another's company.

"Well, what's the news? Has anyone disembowelled Barbara yet?" Aileen asked cheerfully as she took a slug of her Bloody Mary. The other two guffawed. Judy had told her sister about the unmerciful row that had ensued on her unexpected arrival from London. As a result of this, Judy was now sharing a bedroom with Cassie, and Barbara was still in a huff almost a month later.

"Except for the fact that Judy is going to a dinner-dance and staying over at Andrew Lawson's, you'd be sharing Barbara's room tonight," Cassie informed her.

"A lucky escape, then. I must remember to thank the suave Mr Lawson when I see him," Aileen smiled. "I'm looking forward to tonight."

"So am I," Laura said emphatically. "I might as well warn you, girls, I'm going to get pissed as a newt."

"That's a fine attitude for the bride-to-be to have, I must say," Aileen remarked. "What's wrong with you, anyway? I thought you'd be on cloud nine. You don't seem very happy about getting married, if I may say so."

"I'm not!" Laura retorted glumly as she dolefully popped a couple of peanuts into her mouth. Aileen arched an incredulous eyebrow at her friend and caught Cassie's eye. Cassie shrugged her shoulders and threw her eyes up to heaven.

"Why not, for heaven's sake? If I were marrying

someone like Doug Donnelly I'd be ecstatic. He doesn't by any chance have a twin brother, does he?" Aileen demanded.

"It's not Doug, it's the marrying of him. if you know what I mean," Laura sighed. "Do you know what the parish priest had the nerve to say to me?" Laura sat up straight. "He told me that I was to give myself totally to Doug. Mind, soul and body!"

"So! What's so awful about that? Sounds rather delicious to me. And getting the priest's blessing to do it too. What more could you ask?" Aileen was mystified and Cassie stifled a giggle. She had heard all this a hundred times before.

"The point is, Aileen, he didn't tell *Doug* to give himself totally to me, mind, soul and body!" Laura was almost spluttering with indignation. "And then he had the nerve to tell me not to trouble Doug with trivial little problems like if I'd burnt my fingers getting his dinner, until he'd had time to relax after his hard day at work. He told me I could mention it casually in conversation later on. Did you ever hear anything like it? What about *my* hard day at work? He didn't tell Doug not to tell me about *his* burnt fingers when he's getting *my* dinner! That old fart is living in cloud-cuckoo-land."

"Yes, well, that *is* a bit much, I agree," Aileen murmured soothingly, trying to keep her face straight and avoid Cassie's eyes.

"I should have got married in a registry office. It's what I wanted to do all along. Isn't that what I said to you, Cassie?" Laura turned to Cassie for confirmation.

Cassie answered her friend patiently. "Yes, Laura, but your mother would never have coped with that. You know how she's setting such store by this wedding. And doing everything properly."

"Oh Lord! Don't talk about my mother and doing the right thing. She's driving me round the twist: Da won't sit beside the priest at the top table as etiquette says he should and she's going bananas," moaned Laura.

"Have another drink!" urged Aileen.

"I have to go to the loo first. I'll get another round on the way back." Laura sighed deeply, excusing herself from the table.

"Boy, am I glad you're home!" Cassie grinned ruefully. "I just can't do a thing with her. I've never seen her so uptight."

"Sounds like a terminal case of pre-wedding nerves to me," Aileen grinned. "How's Doug coping?"

"Just wishing to get the whole palaver over so Laura can get back to normal. At least he's got a nice family. That father of hers is an out-and-out bastard, Aileen. I know she's dreading going up the aisle on his arm. She resents it because she really hates his guts. She's just going through this charade for her mother," Cassie sighed.

"Ah, poor old Laura, that's tough going. Imagine your wedding being so awful that you just want to get it over and done with? It's kind of sad, isn't it?" Aileen's eyes clouded with concern for her friend. "We'll make a real fuss of her. I'll get at her tomorrow and give her a massage and a facial and by the time I'm finished with her she'll be a new woman." Aileen smiled at Cassie and took her left hand in hers to examine the sparkling solitaire. "How's Robbie? Have you set a date yet?" She studied her friend intently. She had never seen Cassie looking so well and happy. Her eyes sparkled, her skin glowed, her chestnut hair with its glints of gold was a shining, luxuriant mane. "Love suits you, Cassie," Aileen said quietly. "I wish I could meet someone..."

"You will, Aileen. One of these days when you least

expect it, he'll be there," Cassie assured her earnestly.

"I know I'm supposed to be a liberated career woman and all that and I'd never say it to anyone else but you but there are times I'd give anything to be married," Aileen confessed. "I'd like to be married to a nice strong manly man who'd put his arms around me and take care of me and tell the world to go to hell! But the trouble is, I just can't find a nice manly man. They're all married! I wonder if I'm looking for a father figure?"

"Probably," smiled Cassie, who had never met anyone like Aileen for analysing herself and others.

Aileen ran her fingers through her titian curls and sighed. "Frankly, I wish I'd grown up in the Fifties. There were real men around then, Cassie. I was watching a film with Rod Taylor in it the other day and, girl, he was in his prime. What a jaw-line! What a body! And those eyes! And what have we got today? David Bloody Cassidy and John Travolta. I ask you? Tragic, isn't it?" Aileen laughed. "Don't mind me, Cassie, it's just when I see the pair of you all settled I get a bit panicky. Daft, isn't it?"

"No, it's not a bit daft. There's no shame in wanting to get married, for heaven's sake, no matter what the feminists say," Cassie retorted.

"You're right! Rod Taylor, I'm heading your way," chuckled the redhead as she made room for Laura, who had arrived back with another round of drinks.

"Or Richard Burton, or Peter Finch, or Burt Lancaster," Cassie mused, thinking of manly men of the Fifties.

"What are you on about?" inquired Laura curiously.

"We're selecting a manly man for Aileen," Cassie giggled lightheartedly.

"Oooh! How about Sean Connery?" Laura suggested.

Aileen rolled her eyes and crossed her long shapely legs. "Stop it, you're making me randy," she breathed.

"Well, I don't know about you pair but I'm starving, so drink up and let's hit the Sunflower," Laura instructed crisply. She'd been looking forward to their Chinese meal since Cassie had suggested it a couple of weeks back.

A few hours later they were seated at a window table in the Sunflower Chinese restaurant on O'Connell Street. The lights of the capital's main thoroughfare below them were reflected in the polished curved glass of the window. It was early evening and there were only a few other diners besides themselves. In the background soft music played as the waiters murmured in Chinese among themselves. Cassie was secretly pleased to see that Laura was much more relaxed as she tucked into her pork chow mein.

They had planned how they would spend this last evening together, and both girls were going to stay the night in their old flat in Ranelagh with Cassie. They lingered over their meal, catching up on all their affairs, and then they drove back to the flat to change for a night out on the town.

They were dancing on a crowded dance-floor in Sachs nightclub a couple of hours later, thoroughly enjoying themselves. They couldn't remember the last time the three of them had been out together with no boyfriends or fiancés to cramp their style.

"*He* looks quite manly," Cassie giggled, nudging Aileen and indicating a suave man standing at the bar.

"Hmmmm," approved Aileen. "Excuse me while I go flirt."

Ten minutes later she was back, wide-eyed. "You'll never guess who that was!" she exclaimed.

"Who?" Laura and Cassie were agog.

"That was Father Paul!"

The girls stared at her blankly.

"Remember! Father Paul whom we all fell in love with at the retreat years ago at school. And guess what?"

"What!" The other pair was astounded.

"He wants to see me home! He's left the priesthood!"

"Oh Aileen!" they shrieked with laughter. Trust her!

"He's gone to the loo. Come on, let's get the hell out of here. I don't think I could cope! I'm getting too old for this!"

Snorting with laughter they made their way out of the nightclub in double-quick time and hailed a taxi. They piled in and laughed the whole way home.

❧

Cassie and Aileen had gone to bed but Laura, who was sharing her old room with Barbara, found herself unable to sleep. She had really enjoyed the day with the girls and she still had tomorrow morning, the eve of the wedding, with them, while they waited for Robbie to arrive with the wedding cake. Then she would head home to Port Mahon for the wedding that was costing a fortune. It really galled Laura to have to spend her hard-earned money on things like the organist's fee and flowers for the church, when she hadn't wanted this church wedding or all the palaver. Thank God for Robbie's friend who was a chef and was making the wedding-cake for half-nothing.

She slipped out of bed and went down to the kitchen to make herself a cup of tea. It was strange being back in the flat with the girls. She had got used to living in the apartment in Donnybrook with Doug. She wished he were here with her now to tell her to stop worrying about this blasted wedding. Doug never let trivialities like weddings bother him. He was too busy plotting and planning his next deal. Laura smiled. Doug was consumed by his business deals. He was the hardest grafter she had ever met. He had been making a deal the first time they had met. She threw a piece of cardboard box into the still-red fire and watched it blaze with a little smile on her face.

Doug Donnelly! He was something else. He walked into her life while she was waiting tables in Capri. He was so intent on his conversation with his companion as they were leaving their table, that he bumped right into Laura and caused her to spill half the scaling contents of a coffee-pot all over her left hand and arm. It had been so painful that she cried aloud as blisters formed on her skin. Doug was horrified. She sustained quite a bad burn and he insisted on taking her to a hospital casualty department. They were there for hours. It being late on a Friday night, the place was packed with brawlers and boozers and accident victims and, although Laura was in pain, she had to wait until the worst cases were treated before she was finally taken care of.

Her escort introduced himself to her as Doug Donnelly and, in spite of her discomfort, she took note of the concerned eyes ringed by a sweep of long black lashes. She had seen him wining and dining various people in the restaurant. He was obviously a businessman, she decided, after she had seen him in a few times. Tall and well-built, he had a strong handsome face, and Laura found herself giving him several covert admiring glances. But that was all she was ever able to do because she was kept so busy.

Sitting beside him in the casualty department, her arm and hand throbbing painfully, her black-and-white uniform stained with coffee, Laura had felt pretty miserable. She had urged him to go away, saying that she would get a taxi home, but he wouldn't hear of it.

They didn't get out of the hospital until after 3 a.m. and when she asked him in for coffee, to her surprise he agreed.

Oh lordy, I hope the place is tidy, she thought in panic as she struggled to get her key in the door. Her left hand was bandaged and useless.

"Let me," Doug offered kindly, taking the key from her and inserting it in the lock. The first thing Laura saw as she entered the sitting-room was Aileen's supper dishes. She'd kill Aileen in the morning. She was always leaving dirty dishes about, despite Cassie's and Laura's protestations. "Sit down," she invited the man at her side, while she discreetly edged the dishes under the armchair with her foot.

"Don't you think *I* should make the coffee?" Doug suggested, indicating her bandaged hand.

"Oh sure!" Laura had forgotten her infirmity. While he made the coffee, she slipped into the bathroom for a quick check. Just as well she did, she decided, as she observed the wooden clothes-horse in the bath, festooned with a variety of bras, pants and tights. It was hard to get clothes dry these days and the girls had to resort to the clothes-horse. Laura pulled the shower curtain. Some things were best kept unseen when a girl was trying to make an impression.

The dawn was breaking and the milkman had left his milk bottles on the doorstep before Doug finally left. He and Laura had started to talk and completely forgotten about the time. Exchanging life stories, they had found they had a lot in common. Doug had as much ambition as Laura and was currently in the process of setting up his own video production and facilities company. Hence all the business meetings in Capri. These meetings he was having would decide whether or not he was going to have his own company and it was an incredibly important time for him. Laura was fascinated by the complexity of his plans, particularly the legal aspects. Having done a little company law, she was able to ask some very pertinent questions. It was a stimulating, lively conversation and when he asked her out for a meal she accepted with pleasure. "As long as it isn't Capri," she said jokingly.

They started seeing each other and before long Laura knew without the shadow of a doubt that Doug Donnelly was the man she wanted to spend the rest of her life with. This had come as rather a shock to her. It certainly wasn't what she had planned. Falling in love had not figured in her plans at all but until then she had never met a man like Doug. For the first few months of their relationship, she told him she could meet him just once a week. Her finals were coming up and she was working like a Trojan at her revision. Doug accepted her decision with no argument. He quite understood how important it was for her to get a first in her exams. He knew what it was like to want to be the best at something even though it might cause blood, sweat and tears. He could understand Laura's ambition; it wasn't so different from his own. It was this empathy that really drew her to him and the night her results came out and her dream of a first-class honours law degree came true, he bought a bottle of champagne and later in his apartment they made love for the first time.

Doug was a tender, passionate lover but Laura's deep-seated desire to be in control, as a result of her hostility towards her father, caused her immense problems with her sexuality. She could never let herself go completely and enjoy their lovemaking. That would be giving too much control to Doug.

After meeting her father and seeing at first hand the destructive anger of their relationship, Doug understood what the problem was. He knew that he had a very difficult task ahead, one that required a lot of tact, sensitivity and patience. All he could do was his best.

It had been a revelation to Laura that a man could show such tenderness to a woman. It was the first time she had ever experienced it in her own life. She had watched the way her father treated her mother and until she started growing up had thought it was the norm. Her relationship with her father had made her cynical about men, apart from Cassie's father, Jack, whom she had adored. She associated men with power and by not getting involved with them she felt she was keeping control of her own life. Watching Cassie and Aileen enjoying the company of their lovers had sometimes left Laura feeling empty and unfulfilled but she had buried these feelings and concentrated on achieving her ambitions. Only once, the time they had been on holidays in Rhodes and Aileen had touched a sensitive nerve during their row, had those feelings erupted and got the better of her. Those awful unbearable feelings of inadequacy, those feelings that somehow she was different to other women. Was she, Laura Quinn, held in high esteem by her peers, afraid of sex?

To prove that she wasn't, she had slept with Costas, the Greek waiter. But really it hadn't proved anything. It was just a two-night fling, something that *she* initiated, and then she had never seen him again. She remembered now that she had even risked getting pregnant. She must have been crazy!

When Doug asked to see her again, she was scared, really scared. Not only was she afraid of sex, she was afraid of getting involved in a relationship with a man in case it threatened her most prized possession, her control. But being the gutsy pragmatist that she was, Laura sat herself down and gave herself a good talking-to. Was she content to lead half a life? Miss out on all the joys a good relationship could bring? She had seen how happy Robbie and Cassie were. She had also seen how unhappy Cassie was when Robbie went on his benders. But that was part of it all, the swings and roundabouts. After her first meeting with Doug, Laura had known instinctively that he could end up playing a major role in her life if she were prepared to take the risk. Never one to back down on a challenge, Laura had taken a deep breath and got on with it.

Not for a minute had she regretted getting involved with Doug. He had encouraged her as she set out on the trail of a job, had listened as she moaned how hard it was to be taken on as an apprentice by a good firm. She suspected also, although nothing was ever said directly, that her being a woman was no advantage to her. Doug just nodded and agreed and then made her type out a brand-new CV, got twenty photocopies made and instructed her to get going to deliver them to all the major practices in the city. Laura had got a copy of the Law Directory, which contained the names and addresses of the practices, from the Incorporated Law Society in Blackhall Place.

She secured an apprenticeship in William Bennett Solicitors, one of the most prestigious offices in the country, and Doug told her firmly, "It's no less than you deserve."

When Doug asked her to move into his Donnybrook apartment Laura had at first refused. Leave the girls, give up her independence? No! It was unthinkable. But as their relationship deepened and as she gradually began to enjoy the physical side of it, Doug dominated her thoughts more and more. Sitting in Blackhall Place where she was attending lectures towards the end of her apprenticeship, her mind would drift away from the droning of her lecturer to think of Doug. She would wonder how he was getting on with the search for the new premises for the video production company, which he had finally set up. He was operating from rented premises that had already proved too small, as new business was generated by word of mouth from more than satisfied customers. Being with Doug was so stimulating. They were always bouncing ideas off one another and she had to admit he was terribly sexy and the more he made love to her the more she was liking it. He asked her again to move in with him and this time Laura agreed.

Needless to say, she hadn't announced the news at home and as far as the family were concerned she was still living in the flat with the girls. It had worked out well, living with Doug. He was quite content to share the household chores. He didn't expect her to look after him and often, if he were home first, he would have the dinner ready and a fire lighting. To him, her career was just as important as his and she knew she was exceptionally lucky to have found a man who felt like that. When he asked her to marry him Laura said yes, without a qualm. Doug was her soulmate, her first and only love.

A registry office wedding would have suited her fine as Doug wasn't pushed one way or another, but Anne Quinn had been devastated when she heard of her daughter's plans and begged Laura not to make a disgrace of her.

Laura was really torn. She knew that Jill, her elder

sister, who was a single parent, would never go through a church wedding if *she* got married, and to have her other daughter married in a registry office was almost as much a scandal for her mother as Jill's situation.

Laura's wedding would be a chance for Anne Quinn to be seated by her husband in the front of the church, giving an appearance of family harmony, and to thumb her nose at Jennifer Casey, Peter's mistress. With deep misgivings, Laura asked Doug if he would mind a church wedding and he assured her that it didn't bother him one whit, if that was what she wanted. To think of walking up the aisle with her father, to have him give her away and then to have to listen to him pontificating in his father-of-the-bride speech was enough to make her physically sick. Peter had been furious at the idea of a registry office wedding with just a few close friends to celebrate at a restaurant after it.

"I wouldn't give it to them in this town to say I couldn't have a reception for my daughter. I'm going to pay for your reception, miss, and let that be an end to it. Book the Port Mahon Arms Hotel," Peter ordered. "We're not going slumming it in the Harbour Way Hotel like some of them in this town who think they are my betters."

Laura was tempted to tell him to go to hell. Only the surprised and pleased expression on her mother's face made her hold her tongue. This one thing she would do for her mother but after that, Peter Quinn would never ever again tell her what to do.

Then the arguments about the guest list and the menu started, until in the end Laura had just thrown up her hands at the whole affair. Let them do what they wanted, argue as much as they liked; *they* wanted to host the wedding, let them. She had given them Doug's guest list and her guest list and left them at it. If they wanted to argue about inviting Aunt Nellie and Uncle Billy, let them.

The stress of it all made her break out in a rash. Three days before the wedding she got a plethora of spots on her chin, and her eyes watered from an infection. It was no wonder Aileen had shrieked when she saw her at the airport. Rinsing her cup out, Laura sighed ruefully. Radiant bride indeed! A banshee would look more radiant than she was, right this minute. Still, Aileen was going to give her a facial and massage in the morning and do wonders with her make-up on the day of the wedding, so all was not lost. Doug wouldn't recoil in horror at the sight of her. Yawning hugely, Laura went to bed and dreamt that in the middle of the ceremony she turned around to find her father and his mistress making love at the back of the church as Anne stared at them, a silent scream issuing from her mouth.

Laura woke up crying.

Chapter Twenty-Six

Aileen was in that delicious state between waking and sleeping. She stretched luxuriously in her old bed, which was now Judy's, and thought how nice it was to be at home with the girls. Although she loved London with its fast, urgent pace of life, she really missed her pals. But she had done the right thing going over there to work. There were far more opportunities for beauticians because of the bigger market, and she was glad she had given up her job as a permanent and pensionable officer of the Corporation. Aileen was just not permanent and pensionable material.

Ending her affair with Liam had been the hardest thing she had ever done. Even now after all this time, just thinking about him could make her want him. In his arms, her restlessness would cease and she would become contented, almost serene. And then he would go home to his wife, and she would wonder was their marriage really on the rocks. Did they really not make love any more, as Liam assured her? And if that were the case, why then didn't he just end it once and for all and come and live with Aileen.

She had been tormented and besotted with him, craving his company and their wonderful sessions of sensual lovemaking that made her want more and more. The loneliness she felt when he left her to go home to his unloved wife was indescribable. Desperate to assure herself that Liam Flynn's marriage was really on the rocks, she had rung his wife, just to hear the voice of the grouchy, tetchy woman that she imagined Monica Flynn to be. The pleasant, cultured voice that answered her call made Aileen's insides go cold and she had hung up, palms sweating.

That woman sounded nothing like the woman Liam had described to her. She even sounded quite young. Maybe they had visitors! Somehow, the next weekend, she had managed to edge the conversation around to the family and Liam had confirmed her worst fears by telling her that because they had the house to themselves at the moment his wife had decided to redecorate, and if there was one thing he hated, it was decorating. He dreaded having workmen in the house because it interfered with his creative processes when he was designing buildings and drawing up plans.

"Thank God I have you to come to," he murmured

in her ear as his hand slid up under her jumper, the feel of his long caressing fingers against her breast making her ache with desire. They had just had a meal and were cuddling in his car out at the back of the airport. It was dark and private, with only the occasional roar of a jet taking off or landing to disturb them. They often made love there. Banishing her fears Aileen kissed him with a passion that aroused him frantically, and tearing the clothes off each other they made urgent, mind-blowing love. When he left her home, Aileen cried her eyes out in the privacy of her bedroom.

The following Friday she took a half-day and drove to his house in Bray. She knew the address. It was on his business cards and she had found one of them once on the floor of his car and kept it.

She knew she was being paranoid but she couldn't really help it. She wanted to see if the workmen really were there and maybe she would get a glimpse of Liam's wife, this menopausal woman who was letting herself go. "You're a fool; you're crazy, nuts, pathetic, pitiful; you haven't an ounce of pride!" she cursed herself aloud as she pulled up at the traffic lights at the church in Shankill. Just up the road was Bray, where he lived, and her heart started to beat a bit faster. "It's not too late to turn around and go home!" she argued with herself, and caught sight of the driver in the car in the opposite lane staring at her. Aileen glared at him. Couldn't a girl argue with herself if she wanted to?

Liam lived on a quiet tree-lined road outside the town. Luxurious houses, all architect-designed, stood in their own grounds. Midway along, she found Valhalla, his house. Aileen slowed to a halt and cast an eye around to see if anyone were watching her suspicious behaviour. Like most of the houses she had passed, it was well back off the road for privacy. Mature pine trees surrounded the grounds and hid her from view. She could see a Spanish-style bungalow gleaming in the bright sunlight. An arched veranda encircled the house. Aileen gave a great sigh of relief as she spotted a painter white-washing the outside. At least he hadn't told her lies about decorating. She edged a bit nearer and her eyes widened as she caught sight of her lover's car up the drive. He had told her he was going to a conference of architects for the day and wouldn't be able to meet her as usual for lunch. What the hell was he doing at home, then? It was only three-thirty? He must be sick or something. A woman in shorts came around from the back of the house pushing a wheelbarrow, a tall, shapely woman, her ash-blonde hair tied back from her face with a scarf. She smiled at the painter and Aileen heard the man say, "You've a lovely garden here, Mrs Flynn."

"It takes a lot of hard work," the woman laughed as she began dead-heading with a secateurs. It was the voice of the woman who had answered the phone, and looking at her as she worked energetically at her shrubs Aileen knew with a sinking feeling that this was not a woman who was letting herself go and sinking into menopausal middle age, as Liam had claimed at the beginning of their affair. Monica Flynn seemed pretty vibrant from where Aileen was sitting. Just then, Liam walked out the front door and Aileen almost jumped, so unexpected was the sight of him.

"Monica, I'm off, darling," she heard him call to his wife. "You want some garlic and olives. Is there anything else?"

"Don't forget the After Eights," the woman called cheerfully. "Get a big box. You know JJ. He can't stop once he starts eating them."

Aileen didn't wait to hear any more. Oh God, Liam must *not* see her here! She got into the Mini and scorched up the road as though the devil himself were on her heels.

"Bastard! Bastard! Bastard!" she swore, as she turned on to the winding coast road in the opposite direction to which she had come. Obviously Liam was going into the town to shop; he wouldn't be coming this way. Aileen had heard songs about heartache but she never realised that your heart could actually physically pain you. It was a searing pain that seemed to envelop her, as images of what she had seen danced around her head.

Darling! He had called his wife darling! How could he? They must be having guests for dinner. Aileen knew JJ Doyle. He was also a Corporation architect and a friend of Liam's. She pulled the car on to the hard shoulder, crossed her arms over the steering-wheel, rested her head on them and bawled her eyes out. She felt so stupid and so, so used. "Liam, Liam, Liam!" Over and over she cried his name aloud. If only he hadn't lied to her. If! If only she hadn't come today. If only Monica Flynn had been a dumpy, dowdy woman. If only...Life was full of if onlys. They were the two most futile words in the English language.

Her head was throbbing to match the dull, heavy ache in her heart and she knew she couldn't sit there for ever. The thought of driving into the rush-hour traffic oppressed her and how could she go home and assume a façade of normality when she just wanted to lie down and die? Switching on the engine, she wiped her eyes and drove further along the coast. It was such a lovely evening and the beauty of the blue, sparkling sea and green cliffs seemed to mock her misery. It was her own fault, of course. Getting involved with a married man led to nothing but unhappiness and torment. And she had thought she could cope. "Ha! You idiot, Aileen O'Shaughnessy!" she cursed herself bitterly. Driving past a sprawling bungalow she noticed a Bed & Breakfast sign. She could always book in. It would save her the harassing drive into the city and she could be alone. She'd got paid today and because she hadn't met Liam for lunch for once she had cashed her cheque so she wasn't stuck for funds.

Aileen prepared to reverse and caught sight of herself in the mirror, eyes swollen and red from crying, hair a mess. No one would let her past the door looking the way she did. She wiped her eyes, slapped on some foundation and eye-shadow and mascara, added a touch of lipstick, ran a comb through her hair and reversed back to the house.

It would look odd, she supposed, that she had no luggage. Then she remembered that she had a sports bag with some swimming gear in the boot. That would do fine.

A smiling, middle-aged woman answered the door and Aileen told her that she'd like bed and breakfast for the night.

"Certainly, if you'd like to come this way, I have some single rooms free," the woman replied.

Aileen was shown to a pretty green-and-white bedroom with a shower and toilet *en suite*. It was lovely, very clean and just what she needed. And the price was reasonable.

"Do you have a phone I could use?" Aileen marvelled at how normal her voice sounded. It must be her theatrical training, she thought wryly. The woman led her down the hall and told her that tea would be served at five-thirty if she wished to have some.

Aileen dropped the coins into the callbox and dialled Cassie's work number. She hadn't said she wouldn't be home and it was only fair to ring and tell the girls so they could lock up properly.

"I won't be home tonight, Cassie. I'll see you some time tomorrow," she said in her most cheerful voice.

"OK, Aileen, have a good time." Cassie obviously thought she was going out on the town with friends. Or else that she was spending the night with Liam.

"Thanks. Bye, Cassie," Aileen said forlornly, her lower lip wobbling. By the time she got back to her room she was in tears again. Locking her door, she curled herself up in a ball on the bed and sobbed like a child.

She lay on the bed for almost an hour weeping intermittently and then she got up and sat in front of the mirror at the dressing-table and stared at herself. She was not a pretty sight!

"You'll get over this, O'Shaughnessy, because it's your own fault that you got into it. Now cut the crap. Stop being melodramatic and tidy yourself up and go down and have some tea!"

She tied her hair up, undressed and took a shower. Wrapped in a soft fluffy bath-towel she sat once more in front of the mirror and applied fresh make-up. No one, not even Liam Flynn, was going to make her look anything but her best. Aileen had always loved making up for a role and often spent hours experimenting with cosmetics. She was proud of the way she could change her appearance just by styling her hair a different way and changing the shades of her facial make-up. She'd leave her hair up, she decided, as she lightly stroked on some blusher. Having dressed once more, she unlocked her door and walked in the direction of the dining-room, which was right beside the phone. Several people were already seated eating and the lady of the house smiled at her from behind the buffet-table which was laden with salads and cold meats and home-made breads and tarts and scones.

"Help yourself, dear," she told her. "There's a nice little window table vacant over there. I'll send Mary over with the tea when you're ready."

Aileen didn't know if she was hungry or not. It was ages since she had eaten but even though her stomach was empty, she didn't know if the hollowness was from hunger or from the shock of what she had seen earlier. Starving yourself isn't going to help, she thought glumly, as she forked some cold meat and salads onto her plate and took a couple of slices of fresh home-made brown bread. Sitting at her window table overlooking the road and the sea, she could hear a mixture of German, English and Scottish accents at the other tables in the room. There were still quite a few tourists about, despite the fact that it was early autumn. The rest of the guests were tucking in and enjoying themselves hugely. Aileen felt terribly lonely.

Eat your tea, she ordered herself fiercely. It was a very tasty meal and she felt the better for it. Afterwards she decided to go for a stroll to get some fresh air. She hoped that massive doses of sea air would help her to sleep.

It was a forlorn hope, she realised, as she tossed and turned several hours later. Her mind kept replaying scenes of her relationship with Liam.

That first prickly encounter. The first time he had looked deeply into her eyes and she had known that he was attracted to her. That first utterly satisfying afternoon so long ago when they had made love together over and over. The time he had bought her a Russian wedding ring and told her that he loved her more than he had ever loved anybody. She had been walking on air for weeks after that. Cloud nine? She'd been on cloud ninety-nine! And then...this afternoon. Well, it had happened and no amount of wishing could turn the clock back.

❦

Aileen drove back to the flat the following morning with her mind made up. First thing on Monday morning she was resigning her job. She just couldn't face the thought of working in that office, seeing Liam every week, realising what a fool she had made of herself and knowing that despite his lies she was still in love with him. She *could* ask for a transfer but that could take forever, and besides, she was vegetating, doing a job she hated and with not much more to look forward to if she stayed doing clerical work in the Corporation. A drastic change was called for and a drastic change was going to be made. At her mother's insistence she had opened a savings account when she started to work. A regular amount was deducted from source and now she had quite a tidy little sum. It would do her fine for what she had in mind. The only person who could do anything about the disaster that was currently her life was herself. She had to pick up the pieces and get on with it and get herself out of the mess she was in.

The first thing she had to do was to tell Liam their affair was over.

He couldn't believe his ears. "Why?" he demanded, mystified.

"Liam, it doesn't matter. Let's not get into whys and wherefores. It's bringing me no happiness. You're doing your wife an injustice. After all, you married her for better or for worse," Aileen said quietly, trying to keep the bitterness out of her voice.

"But you know my situation. It's never bothered you before. Why now, all of a sudden?" There was an angry edge to his voice and for a moment Aileen was tempted to tell him of her trip to Bray the previous Friday. Pride made her hold her tongue.

"Surely I'm entitled to an explanation?" he said softly, taking her hand in his.

"You're entitled to nothing," Aileen said sharply, afraid her resolve would weaken. Before he could say anything else, she walked out of the restaurant where they were having lunch and drove off too quickly for him to follow her.

No doubt he would go back to the office thinking that she was returning to work. Well, let him go. There he'd be told that she had resigned from her job and was using her remaining leave in lieu of notice. On her instructions, Cassie and Laura always told him she was unavailable when he phoned, as he did frequently. Once, he had even come knocking at the door but she hadn't been in and Laura had told him in no uncertain terms to let her alone.

Cassie and Laura had been incredibly supportive when she told them that she had ended her affair. They knew she was suffering and they did their best to keep her heart up and were full of encouragement for the step she was going to take.

It was too late in the year to enrol in the Beauty Academy for the course she had selected, so Aileen did temporary secretarial work until the following September. The ups and downs of temping suited her restless mood, and going from one job to another kept her on her toes. She had been toying for ages with the idea of doing a one-year full-time course in a beauty school; one of her friends in the theatrical group had done it and was now gainfully employed in her own beauty salon. It was an expensive course but the fees covered uniform, books and her kit, which included electrolysis equipment, beauty accessories and make-up. She could have done a basic beautician course which would have qualified her to do facial treatments, manicure, pedicures and waxing but the course she had chosen would entitle her to become a beauty therapist, qualified to give body treatment and massage as well.

The Beauty Academy was off Wicklow Street and at her selection interview, Aileen was told that there was no point in doing the course unless she was prepared for a year of extremely hard work, as it was a very intensive programme. After successfully completing the course and passing her British Confederation exams, which involved a practical and written test, she could do the CIDESCO exam leading to an internationally recognised diploma. This would assure her of employment in any country. Aileen was determined. This was her chance to get off her butt and make a go of things for herself.

On the first day of term she and thirty-nine other raw recruits assembled to hear Madame Junot, the head of the school, tell them that henceforth she expected them to arrive punctually, in uniform and impeccably groomed. Half of the classes would be practical and half theory. The class was divided in two so that twenty of them would do practical work in the morning while the other half would do theory and then they would do a turnaround in the afternoon.

After coffee and a get-to-know-you chat with the other girls, Aileen's class were sent to the practical room for their first session. Ten of them had to strip to bra and pants and there were a lot of shy fumblings as the girls prepared nervously for action. The ten were then placed at the tender mercies of their ten equally nervous colleagues as they began to learn the rudiments of body and facial massage. After half an hour the roles were reversed.

After lunch the class began the study of the skin. Soon Aileen was quite addled. There were so many layers and so many terms—the epidermis, the dermis, nerve endings and hair follicles and twenty-one different muscles in the face. Aileen staggered home, exhausted but determined.

As the course progressed, the girls in the class got to know one another and enjoy their studies, particularly the practicals. Eyebrow and eyelash tinting was a firm favourite but in the beginning, until they got more experienced, there were a lot of purple eyes. The lip, chin, underarm and leg waxings always caused shrieks of pain but never as loud as when the bikini-line was being done. Electrolysis was a different kettle of fish. They had all spent many hours of practice probing the hair follicles in the leg without current but Aileen would never forget the first time she did electrolysis with current. Her hands shook, but soon she was quite practised, and Laura and Cassie, who were her guinea-pigs on many occasions, were rewarded later on when Aileen beautified them for nothing.

The theory was more of a problem. Aileen found anatomy and physiology terribly boring but she per-severed. They had to learn the details of five muscles every night and her flatmates often heard her muttering weird names like biceps, the radials, the rectus abdominis, the gastrocnemius. The spellings nearly drove her nutty, let alone the pronunciations.

Sitting her first end-of-term exam, she scanned the

paper anxiously:

> *Describe the functions of the liver and spleen.*
> *Describe the digestive system in detail with diagrams.*
> *Describe the functions of the blood.*
> *Name the bones of the skeletal system.*

Aileen heaved a sigh. Even doing those first four questions, she was quietly confident that she would pass. She had studied very hard and by chance these particular questions suited her. She passed her first term-exam comfortably and that gave her a great boost. Thus encouraged, she kept her nose to the grindstone.

Quite a few of the girls in her class were what she privately termed "rich kids," whose fathers paid for the courses, and whose future livelihood would not depend on their success. Discipline in the academy was strict and a few of them were unable for the pace of study and the hard work. There were quite a few girls like Aileen who intended to make beauty their career and there was a great comradeship among this group which pleased Madame Junot very much. She enjoyed teaching eager, interested pupils. Before their final exams she took several of them aside, including Aileen, and told them that they would pass their exams with no trouble. When people came to her looking for ex-students she could recommend she would be delighted to give them references. Aileen was thrilled with herself. Nevertheless, on the day of her final exams the following April, she was more than apprehensive as she began written and practical exams in face, body and electrolysis. But she passed these exams with honours, and two months later she had to face four external examiners for her practical and oral exams to obtain her CIDESCO diploma. Sitting in front of the four strangers, knowing she had to answer four sets of eight questions, Aileen's palms were damp with sweat.

"Describe the vertebra, please," the first questioner began. Aileen couldn't believe her luck. She had actually been reading it up outside as she awaited her turn.

Aileen passed her exams with flying colours and the celebrations that took place the night after the results came out would live long in her memory, as would the hangover she had suffered as a consequence. The following August, she went to London to take up an appointment in the plush Mayfair Beauty Salon, having been highly recommended by Madame Junot, whose friend owned the salon.

It was the start of a whole new life and though she really missed the girls, and her heart still ached over Liam (and her mother wasn't talking to her), Aileen knew without doubt that she had definitely taken a very positive step in her choice of career and that her life could only improve. All the hard work she had put in was starting to pay off and she was quite proud of herself. She had picked herself up, dusted herself down and got on with it. Now she was finally doing something with her life and even if she wasn't in a relationship, with luck that would change. Although this time she would be very wary and married men were strictly off limits. Once bitten, twice shy and all that.

Listening to Cassie's regular breathing in the bed opposite her, Aileen smiled. It was lovely to be home for Laura's wedding. She'd thoroughly enjoyed her day with the girls, and Cassie coming to London to work in the New Year was something she was really looking forward to. Turning onto her stomach and resting her face on her hand Aileen fell asleep and had the most satisfying erotic dream involving Rod Taylor. Or was it Richard Burton? It didn't matter...

CHAPTER TWENTY-SEVEN

The niggle of disquiet wouldn't go away and for the umpteenth time that day, Cassie found herself casting an anxious look at the clock. It didn't help that she had a hangover from the night before. From the sitting-room she could hear appreciative "mmms" from Laura as she submitted herself to Aileen's ministrations and had a facial. Robbie had told her he'd be at the flat with the wedding cake around eleven. It was now ten to twelve and there was no sign of him. She had rung his apartment in case he stopped there first but there was no answer.

He could have got a puncture on the way down from Drogheda; he could have slept it out; he could have called on his parents. Why did she always have to think the worst, Cassie scolded herself, as she tidied up the kitchen after the long, gossipy breakfast they had enjoyed. Barbara flounced in with a face on her. "Not much chance of getting a lie-in with the racket you lot are making," she growled.

"Oh Barbara, don't be such a grouch. It's Laura's last day as a single woman. You should have gone home for the weekend if you wanted peace and quiet," Cassie retorted.

Her sister raised an indignant eyebrow. "Well, I ask you! That's really cool."

"I'm going to Mass, Barbara. I left a cooked breakfast keeping warm over the saucepan for you if you want it."

Barbara was slightly mollified.

Actually Cassie hadn't intended going to Mass this Sunday morning but she wasn't in the humour for Barbara and, besides, a few extra prayers for Robbie wouldn't go amiss.

She popped her head around the sitting-room door. "Girls, I'm just off to Mass. Won't be long."

Laura, swathed in towels, grunted. Aileen waved an oily hand. "Don't rush. This one here is a disaster area, believe me. I've got my work cut out for me."

It was a crisp, bright morning, and despite the fact that it was the end of October it was quite mild, Cassie walked briskly along Beechwood Avenue towards the church. That old familiar anxiety chilled the pit of her stomach and she felt terribly heavyhearted, all the old fears resurfacing because of Robbie's non-appearance.

Stop worrying, she told herself; there's an explanation. I'm sure he hasn't gone back on the booze. Why would he, after all this time? She tried to reassure herself as the priest gave the blessing and the Mass began. She murmured the responses automatically, her mind miles away, going over and over the details of the arrangements she had made with Robbie.

Robbie had gone up to Drogheda to a friend of his who was a hotel chef. His friend had made Laura's wedding cake and Robbie was to deliver it to the flat in Ranelagh. That had been the plan. He had gone up on Friday night, phoned her on his arrival, and phoned again on Saturday morning. He had sounded fine on both occasions, his usual cheerful self. He hadn't phoned on Saturday night because he knew Cassie and the girls were going out. She was terrible for not trusting him. She was daft to be worrying, she told herself, as the priest began his sermon. It was always the same, though, if he were a bit late meeting her or phoning her. She always assumed the worst, because so often in the past the worst had been the reality.

He's in AA; he's stopped drinking, she told herself fiercely.

It's the October weekend and he's with an old drinking buddy, shot back her devil's advocate. O Sacred Heart of Jesus, I place all my trust in thee. O Jesus, please don't let him be drinking, she implored the Almighty in a silent, heartfelt plea.

Think positive, she ordered herself as she left the church, sprinkling herself with holy water for an extra blessing. She almost ran home, so desperate was she to feel the blessed sense of relief that would wash over her when she saw the familiar old metallic Escort parked outside the flat. Anxiously she scanned both sides of the road and her heart lurched in disappointment when she failed to see any sign of her fiancé's car.

"Hi! Did Robbie ring by any chance?" Cassie tried to keep her tone light and airy.

"No," Aileen replied, "but your mother phoned and said would you bring her home a carton of fresh cream and she wants to know if you want her to keep a bit of dinner for you and Robbie. And Barbara's gone out with the dashing detective," she added, grinning.

Laura saw the expression on Cassie's face.

"Ring his friend at work and see what time Robbie left Drogheda," she suggested quietly. She had noticed Cassie's anxious glances at the clock earlier on and she knew Robbie long enough to know the score. *And* she was just a little bit concerned about her wedding cake.

"He's a bit late, isn't he? Tell him if he doesn't hurry, he'll be late for tea, let alone dinner," Aileen remarked, unaware of Cassie's *angst*.

Once again she tried his apartment and once again she got no answer. She'd phone the hotel in Drogheda as Laura had suggested. Her stomach tightened in anticipation.

"Chef O'Halloran didn't arrive in for work today,"

she was informed by a bored receptionist. Cassie felt sick as her heart plummeted to her toes. Where was Robbie and where was the cake? What was she going to say to Laura? Cassie didn't have to say anything. Laura knew by the look on her friend's pale face that she had not succeeded in contacting Robbie.

"Come on," she ordered. "We'll drive to Port Mahon and leave a note for Robbie to follow us if he arrives." There was little chance of it and Laura knew it. If she had been able to put her hands around Robbie MacDonald's neck, she would have strangled him for what he was doing to Cassie. To hell with the cake; it was Cassie she was worried about.

Cassie sat down heavily on the sofa. "What will we do if he doesn't come home with the cake?"

Aileen's jaw dropped. She hadn't really cottoned on to what was happening until now. "He'll be here," she assured Cassie comfortingly. "He's not going to let Laura down on her big day." Laura had no such delusions and even Cassie could only imagine the worst scenario.

"We'll get an old cake somewhere. Don't worry about it," Laura said gently, sitting down on the sofa and putting her arm around her friend's shoulders.

Cassie started to cry. "Where will we get one? Today is Sunday. You're getting married tomorrow and it's a bank holiday. We won't be able to get one anywhere. Oh Laura, I'm sorry, I'm really sorry. Your wedding's going to be ruined."

Laura caught her by the shoulder. "Now, you listen to me, Cassie Jordan. I'll buy a couple of Oxford Lunches and we'll get your mother to slap a bit of white icing on them and no one will know the difference. *You* have absolutely nothing to be sorry for. You are not responsible for Robbie's actions and get that into your thick skull.

I'm going to say something to you that you won't like, but I'm one of your best friends, and that gives me the right. I'm telling you now, Cassie, if you marry Robbie, you are going to have a repeat of this scene over and over and over again. You've got to realise that Robbie loves drink far more than he loves you because he's addicted to it and I just don't think he's got it in him to give it up. Robbie doesn't like responsibilities and you're going to have to face that. You are going to live a life of misery. You'll always be wondering and worrying. And imagine what it will be like if you have children! Girl, if that's the way you want to live your life I think you're absolutely crazy."

"Maybe he had a puncture! Maybe he called in to his parents. He might have had an accident. You don't know, Laura!" Cassie said agitatedly.

"Stop it! Stop making excuses for him," Laura said angrily. "You're just like his mother, making allowances and excuses. She's never made him face up to his responsibilities and neither have you. You've taken him back time and again. Face the facts, Cassie—Robbie's let you down yet again and that's all you can expect."

"What makes *you* such a bloody expert on everything?" Cassie snapped. Laura with her perfect romance. Laura who was going to marry Saint Doug and live smugly ever after.

"Cassie, I've got a brother just like him. You haven't the monopoly on alcoholic men, believe me," Laura said gently. "I've seen exactly the same thing happen at home. I've seen Mick's girlfriends in tears. I've seen Ma make excuses for him. Why should he change? Mick can behave like a lout and get away with it because he's always going to be taken back and he knows that."

Aileen arrived in with coffee for the three of them. "Here, Cassie, get that inside you, and whatever happens,

Laura and I are always here—don't forget that."

"I know that," Cassie smiled, "and it helps an awful lot."

They drove out to Port Mahon in silence, each lost in their own thoughts. Cassie had bought the Oxford Lunches. She had insisted on paying for them and she was dreading having to tell Nora about Robbie. She had always hidden his drinking from her mother; in fact only Laura and Aileen knew of it.

"Why didn't you tell me about this before? Oh Cassie, I'm your mother. You shouldn't have kept something like that from me," Nora exclaimed in dismay.

"I know...I know...It's just when he joined AA, I thought he'd be fine. I thought he wouldn't drink again."

"Sure maybe he isn't drunk, pet. Maybe there's a good reason," Nora said reassuringly.

Cassie's face crumpled and tears slid down her cheeks. "I know he is: I just know it," she sobbed.

"Ah Cassie, don't cry. It will be all right," Nora drew her daughter close and held her tightly as Cassie cried like a baby. Later, when Cassie had calmed down, Nora arrived into the kitchen carrying two Christmas cakes.

"Forget about those Oxford Lunch things. Wasn't it lucky that I was a bit organised? I made these last weekend for the ladies' club draw. I'll ice them and make two new ones tomorrow. Laura will have her wedding cake. Go into the pantry now like a good girl and get me the icing sugar and the almond essence. We'll have them iced in a jiffy. What colour is the bridesmaid's dress until I see if I have a nice bit of ribbon to match?"

"Oh Mam, you're a brick," Cassie hugged Nora.

"I'm your mother. Why wouldn't I be?" Nora replied, busy getting out bowls and sieves. But Cassie knew she was pleased all the same. It was so reassuring to come home knowing that her mother was there as she always was and that home never changed. She watched as Nora measured her ingredients.

"Cassie, did I put almond essence in already? Honest to God, my memory isn't what it used to be!" Nora frowned.

"You did," she reassured her mother.

"Last week I was making bread and I put bread soda in twice and I had to throw the loaf out it was so green," Nora grumbled. "I must be getting old!"

It was true that Nora had slowed down a bit, but she still looked a fine healthy woman and Cassie smiled. "If I look as good as you do when I'm your age I won't be complaining."

"Go on with you. Here's a bit of almond paste. It was always your favourite when you were a child," Nora said fondly as she began to roll out the almond icing.

They were layering the white icing on the sides of the two cakes when the phone rang. Cassie felt herself tense up.

"Do you want me to get it?" Nora asked sympathetically.

"No! No! I'll get it," she said hastily. Was it Robbie? Had he called to the flat with the cake and seen her note? It was nine-thirty. He was terribly late. He'd better have a damn good excuse. God, please let it be him. Taking a deep breath she picked up the phone. "Hello?"

"Hi, Cassie. Will you tell Mam I'm staying the night at Jenny's and I'll see her tomorrow?" It was Irene.

"Yeah, sure, Irene. How are you?" Cassie struggled to keep the disappointment out of her voice.

"I'm a bit pissed off, actually. I've been called for the County Council earlier than I thought. I wasn't supposed to be going for another six weeks and I'd planned to visit

Dorothy in the States. I'm awfully disappointed," her sister sighed.

"That's a shame all right," Cassie murmured. Honestly, Irene was away with the birds. Instead of being delighted to have got a job months after leaving school, she was moaning. Cassie knew full well that it was Nora who would have been paying for the holiday in America, Irene's only source of income being the few pounds she earned from her part-time job in a boutique in the town.

"I'll see you tomorrow, then." Irene was clearly in a hurry.

"OK. Bye." Cassie hung up and rubbed her eyes wearily. She dialled the number of Robbie's apartment and listened to the phone ringing, willing it to be answered. It just rang and rang. In desperation she dialled his parents' number, to be told by his mother that Robbie hadn't been in contact over the weekend. "He's gone to Drogheda, isn't he?" enquired Mrs MacDonald.

"I was expecting him back today," Cassie said. "I thought perhaps he might have called in home."

"No, dear, he's not here. No doubt you'll see him tomorrow," her future mother-in-law said cheerily. Cassie did not share her optimism.

"Any sign or any word?" Laura asked the following morning when Cassie delivered a perfectly iced wedding cake. Nora had done a very professional job on it and Laura was thrilled. Cassie shook her head.

"Nope."

"I'm sorry, Cassie," Laura said gently.

"Well, at least you've got a cake." Cassie feigned cheerfulness. She wasn't going to spoil her best friend's wedding by going around with a face on her. "Will I deliver this to the hotel for you or what do you want me to do?"

"Oh, would you, Cassie? And if I give you the list

would you make sure the seating arrangements are the way I've organised them?"

"Sure I will," Cassie replied firmly, glad of something to do. It would keep her occupied. She had phoned the apartment twice already this morning to no avail and then she had phoned Drogheda to be told that Chef O'Halloran had still not made an appearance. There was no doubt about it in her mind. Robbie and his friend were well and truly on the batter.

❧

Four hours later Cassie watched as Laura and Doug Donnelly become man and wife. She had been so looking forward to this wedding, and now here she was alone, listening to the priest performing the same marriage ceremony that in the not too distant future she and Robbie would have been sharing. Now what lay in store for her? She was utterly confused, hurt, angry and sick at heart. As she heard Laura pronounce her vows clearly and confidently, a lump rose to her throat and in spite of herself she started to cry. Beside her, Aileen, who had quite a good idea of the emotions her friend was feeling, having suffered a broken heart herself, rooted in her bag and found a tissue.

"Here," she whispered.

"Thanks," sniffed Cassie, feeling an awful fool.

"Do you want to go out?"

Cassie shook her head. "I'll be fine in a minute. If I could get my hands on Robbie, I'd throttle him, wherever he is."

Join the queue, Aileen thought grimly, but she said nothing, not wishing to upset Cassie any further.

Cassie found the day endless. Every minute she expected Robbie to appear shamefaced and repentant through the door.

"Where's Robbie?" all her friends wanted to know.

"Sick, stomach bug," she lied, protecting him as usual. It was a great relief when Laura and Doug made their way through cheering friends to where Aileen and she were standing as they waited to see the newly-weds off. Hugging her tightly, Laura whispered, "Chin up, Cassie. Thanks for everything."

Cassie returned the hug. "Have a wonderful honeymoon, Mr Donnelly and Ms Quinn. See you when you get back." Laura had decided to keep her maiden name. Then Laura and Doug were gone and Aileen and Cassie were left looking at each other.

"Well, at least one of us has had some luck in love," Aileen said glumly. She wasn't having the time of her life, either. She'd been thinking about Liam all day. "Come on, Cassie, to hell with the buggers. Let's go and have a drink before they close the bar."

As she lay in bed wide-eyed and sober despite Aileen's best efforts to get her drunk, Cassie knew she was going to have to make a decision about herself and Robbie. She was going to have to accept his drinking and put up with it or else break off their engagement and cut him out of her life. Whatever she decided, the future looked anything but good.

❦

"Don't do this to me, Cassie. I promise it will never happen again. Please, Cassie, stick by me and give me a chance to prove myself." Robbie looked so woebegone that in spite of herself Cassie's heart went out to him and she found herself wavering.

It was a week after Laura's wedding and she had just given him back his engagement ring. The day before, she had met her old friend and boyfriend of many years past, Donie Kiely. She had stayed friends with him through his years in the seminary and had felt proud and happy for him the day of his ordination to the priesthood. Donie was sympathetic but blunt.

"If you marry Robbie, thinking you can change him, you're making a grave mistake," Donie warned her after listening to her try and come to some resolution about her future with Robbie. "Maybe he *will* stop drinking; many alcoholics do. You've got to decide if that's a chance you're prepared to take. But you have to make the decision to stay with him and then accept responsibility for that decision. If he continues to drink, you can't hold it against him because you knew before you got married what you were letting yourself in for. It's a decision only you can make, Cassie, and though you know I'll support you whatever you do, I won't advise you one way or another. You and you alone have got to make the choice."

He was right, she acknowledged, as she sat by herself in Bewleys having a second cup of coffee. Donie had had to go to fulfil another engagement. The ball was in her court and she had to decide if she could cope with a lifetime of experiences like Laura's wedding débâcle. Deep down, Cassie knew Robbie didn't have it in him to give up the drink. He would be fine for months but when the pressure was on he would turn to the bottle for solace and to escape his responsibilities. Cassie knew that no marriage was a bed of roses and that there would be plenty of pressures in the coming years. Was she prepared to accept that Robbie would never cope with the pressures on his own?

Robbie begged her to understand. "Please, Cassie. It's the first time I've been on the sauce in ten months. That wasn't bad going."

"That's not the point, Robbie," she yelled, all her anger bursting out of her. "That's not the point at all. You let me down and you let Laura down and you didn't give a damn about the consequences of your actions. Do you think it was easy getting another wedding cake at such short notice on a bank holiday? Do you, you selfish bastard?" She was so angry she wanted to pummel him.

"Calm down, Cassie," Robbie said, placatingly.

"I will *not* calm down. How dare you tell me to calm down, Robbie MacDonald. You've such a fucking nerve." Cassie was shaking. "Where's Laura's cake, anyway, or did your so-called mate even bake one?"

"It's in the boot of my car," Robbie said sullenly.

"Since when?"

"Friday week," Robbie retorted.

"That's the place for it, indeed," Cassie said in utter disgust. "Look," she said, calming herself—shouting wasn't going to get them anywhere—"I've thought of nothing else, nothing, Robbie, for the last week, and I just can't go on living my life like this. I *won't* go on living my life like this." Cassie stood up, put her key to his apartment on the coffee-table and walked out the door.

"What about the cake?" Robbie yelled after her.

"Eat it yourself and I hope it chokes you," she retorted bitterly.

Two days later Robbie's mother phoned her to tell her that he was in hospital. He had tried to commit suicide.

"You've got to see him, Cassie, please. He keeps asking for you. Look what you've done to him, Cassie, look what you've done!" The woman sounded hysterical.

Cassie nearly fainted. "Jesus," she whispered. Judy,

who was in the flat with her, took the phone from her and made her sit down.

"What's wrong? What's happened?"

"Oh God! Oh God! Robbie's tried to commit suicide. I've got to get to the hospital."

"Here, I'll drive. Come on. You're in no fit condition." Cassie couldn't remember the journey to the hospital. All she could grasp was Judy saying over and over, "He'll be all right, Cassie. He'll be all right."

They got to Eccles Street and Cassie ran up the Mater steps as fast as she could, with Judy hot on her heels. The first person they met was Lillian, Robbie's sister.

"Oh God, he's dead, he's dead!" Cassie sobbed in despair.

"He's not dead, Cassie, and you're going up to see him over my dead body—"

"Oh I know you must hate me, Lillian. I can—"

Lillian stared at Cassie in amazement. "Hate you? Why on earth would I hate you? I've always liked you, Cassie." Comprehension dawned. "Oh I see. You think I hate you because Robbie's tried to kill himself." She gave a dry, unamused laugh. "It's not you I hate, for goodness sake. I hate that good-for-nothing taking up a bed in casualty, a bed he has no business being in. Listen to me, Cassie," she said urgently. "Robbie is just trying to manipulate you. He's given himself deeper nicks shaving, believe me. When I heard my mother on the phone to you I nearly went mad. Cassie, if you go to see Robbie, you'll be doing exactly what he wants you to do. Listen, he's never ever going to kill himself—he's far too much of a coward. That's why he's pulled this stunt, because he wants you to feel so guilty you'll take him back and then he won't be on his own any longer. He's afraid of being on his own. After all, you've been his crutch for how many years? Don't be a fool, Cassie. See this for what it is, a pathetic attempt to get you back. I like you too much not to tell you how I see it. And don't mind Mother. Robbie is her little boy still and always will be. If she phones you again, just hang up."

Cassie felt her world spinning about her. She had no reason to doubt Lillian's word. But would Robbie do that to her? *Could* Robbie do that to her?

"I don't know what to do. Are you sure? Maybe I should go up for five minutes..." She didn't know whether she was coming or going.

"Cassie, do yourself a favour. Maybe you'll be doing Robbie a favour too. Go home. Your life can only get better."

Cassie stood as though rooted to the spot. Go? Stay? She didn't know what to do.

Judy made up her mind for her, in a way that was totally unlike her usual placid self. Taking her by the arm, she said in a voice that brooked no argument, "The girl has just given you the best advice you're ever going to get. Come on, Cassie, you're coming home."

Cassie looked from one to the other. Then she turned on her heel and walked from the hospital, feeling like Judas Iscariot.

CHAPTER TWENTY-EIGHT

"Underground map, keys, credit card," Cassie muttered to herself, making a final check to make sure that she had everything she needed before leaving the flat to meet Aileen in Mayfair. She smiled to herself. It sounded so strange to be planning to meet in Mayfair in London, rather than in Grafton Street or outside Clerys in O'Connell Street in Dublin.

How drastically her life had changed in just over three months, since the break-up of her engagement to Robbie. Here she was in London, single and free, pursuing her banking career and about to meet Aileen for a night out. Her thumb rubbed the bare space on the third finger of her left hand. She still hadn't got used to not wearing her engagement ring. Cassie sighed. She was really trying hard to put the past behind her and being in a strange new city helped, especially a city as exciting and glitzy as London. Here she had no memories shared with Robbie; here she could be as anonymous as she liked and just get on with living. If she had still been at home she would have gone crazy altogether. It was so difficult working with people who knew them both and couldn't understand the reason for their break-up. It was nerve-wracking every time the phone rang; she dreaded picking it up in case it were Robbie. Judy, who had been a real brick throughout, had always answered it for Cassie if she were there, but Robbie had continued to pester her at work until Cassie had finally agreed to meet him. He had pleaded with her to take him back but Cassie had stood firm and told him on no account was anyone to get in touch with her if he decided on another suicide attempt. She had been almost suicidal herself by the time Christmas was over and it had been a great relief finally to get on the plane to London, knowing that at least it was a chance for a fresh start.

So far it was working, she decided, as she locked her flat and ran down the stairs of the large house on Holland Park Avenue in which she lived. The house was owned by the bank and was laid out in six small self-contained flats. Hers was on the first floor at the rear of the house, overlooking the gardens shared by several other houses. Sometimes it made her feel slightly claustrophobic being so close to the other houses. At night if the curtains weren't drawn, you could see right in people's windows. But then space was at a premium in London and accommodation expensive. She missed the garden in Ranelagh. Although she'd probably go sunbathing in the big park down the road, it wouldn't be the same. Still, the flat itself was very comfortable. She had a sitting-room cum dining-room, decorated in cream and coral, with high ceilings and a tall window, and a sofa that converted to a bed for visitors. There was also a tiny kitchenette. A small, blue-tiled bathroom and a cheery lemon-painted bedroom which contained a double bed, built-in wardrobes, a dressing table and a little desk, completed her living accommodation.

The joy of it all was that she was only a brisk twenty-minute walk from her job in Kensington High Street. It had been a great stroke of luck for her to get the flat. The girl who was leaving it had been transferred to the Liverpool branch, and two of the people who had the option to take the flat already had accommodation that they were happy with. Not having to commute made life so much easier. Lots of people she knew had to get up at six or earlier to be in time for work in the city. Even Aileen, who lived in Wembley and worked in Mayfair, had to be up early to travel into the city by tube each day, although, as she had explained to Cassie, she was on the Bakerloo line and she didn't have to change trains to get to her destination.

Cassie, whose nearest station was on the Central line, was going to have to change to the Jubilee line at Bond Street to bring her to Green Park station near the Ritz Hotel. It was here she was meeting Aileen. It was going to be a new experience because she had never changed lines before. The tube was very handy, but because she had been in London only just over a month, she still didn't know where she was going half the time and lived in fear of her life of getting the wrong line. Going tubing, as she called it, was still an adventure! Aileen, of course, knew her way around like a native.

It was great having Aileen here, Cassie thought, as she walked towards the tube station. It was a dark miserable Friday night and the rush-hour traffic was still heavy although it had eased off considerably from its peak. Come the spring, she was going to buy a bike for herself and cycle around London to get to know it. She had been studying her map of the city and saw that on a bike she would have a pretty direct journey into Oxford Street via Notting Hill Gate and the Bayswater Road. Then she could shop and sightsee to her heart's content. Most of the famous-name shops were in Oxford Street: C&A, Selfridges, Debenhams, John Lewis, Top Shop. What a time she was going to have, ably abetted by Aileen, who adored shopping. Or else she could cycle along Kensington Road and on through Knightsbridge, around Hyde Park Corner and along Constitution Hill to Buckingham Palace. There were lots of places she wanted to see and so much she wanted to do. The thing was to keep herself busy so she wouldn't have a minute to think about Robbie.

What was he doing now? Was he out drinking with his mates or had he gone back to AA? A shroud of loneliness enveloped her, loneliness that pierced her heart and made her want to weep. Had she walked away from him in his hour of need? Had she let him down when he needed her most? Should she have gone to see him in the hospital that time?

Stop it! she ordered herself sharply as she stood on

the platform waiting for the train. He let *you* down so why should *you* be feeling guilty? Typical! Well, she lectured herself sternly, you're not going to ruin your night out with Aileen, weeping and wailing. She had taken this path and that was that. There was no looking back, no guilts, regrets or recriminations. She had to get on with it and make the best she could of her life and if she didn't start concentrating on where she was going she'd miss her stop.

When the train arrived, it was packed, so she caught hold of a strap and stood swaying in the crowded aisle trying to read her small underground map. She had only five stations to go; her stop was the one after Marble Arch.

After the relatively easygoing pace of city life in Dublin, the rush and frenzy of London still took Cassie's breath away. It amazed her to watch people running up and down escalators, the speed of the trains slamming in and out of the stations, the never-ending traffic. It was all go, go, go. And there were people of so many different cultures: Asians, Arabs, West Indians with their dreadlocks and fabulous reggae music. Cassie loved watching the Indian women in their lovely exotic saris and their children who were so beautiful. Everything was fascinating to her, from the bowler-hatted businessman standing beside her reading his neatly folded paper, despite the swaying of the train, to the young Japanese girl on the other side of her who had the shiniest silkiest black hair that Cassie had ever seen.

She came to herself with a start. She had been so busy watching her neighbours she'd forgotten to look out at the passing stations. Was the last one Queensway or Lancaster Gate? They whooshed into Marble Arch and she knew that the next stop was hers. She could

have got a taxi, she supposed, but that would have cost
a fortune and besides it was the coward's way out. If she
were going to live in London she'd better get to know it,
and getting used to the tube was one of her main
priorities.

❧

Cassie was feeling quite proud of herself as she walked
up the steps of Green Park station a short while later and
headed in the direction of the Ritz, following the
directions Aileen had given her. It was just a couple of
minutes' walk and Aileen was waiting for her in the
magnificent foyer of the famous hotel.

She looked stunning! Her auburn tresses were pulled
back off her face in an elegant chignon and she wore a
sophisticated black dress that showed off every curve of
her shapely figure. Her make-up was, of course, flawless.
Cassie had to admit she had never seen her friend looking
so well. Training to be a beauty therapist and coming to
work in London had been the making of Aileen. She had
been working late and that was why they had arranged
to meet at the Ritz as it was just five minutes from where
she worked.

"You look terrific!" Aileen exclaimed, as she gave
Cassie a hug. Cassie was glad she had gone to a bit of
trouble with her appearance. She hadn't taken too much
notice of it since she had broken up with Robbie, but
coming to London and seeing all the beautiful clothes
in the boutiques in Kensington High Street had aroused
her interest in spite of herself. Then the offers in the
January sales had been more than a mortal could resist.
The previous weekend Cassie had got her hair cut in a
becoming bob and gone on a little spending spree. She
had treated herself to a new pure wool coat in a gorgeous

royal blue. Around her neck she wore a beautiful silk Hermès scarf that had cost a small fortune, but she didn't care! A soft Italian black leather bag and expensive suede shoes added the finishing touches to the ensemble. Underneath she wore a glamorous pink angora jumper and a pair of tailored trousers that fitted her like a glove and looked the height of elegance.

"Isn't this posh?" Cassie gazed around in admiration as a smiling waiter glided silently towards them to take her coat. As she walked with Aileen towards one of the grey marble-topped coffee-tables Cassie understood for the first time what it felt like to sink into a carpet up to your ankles.

"I thought we'd have a couple of drinks here to start off with, just to put us in the humour. They'll cost an arm and a leg, but who cares? This is our night out. Then we'll go to another lovely hotel just across the road which won't be quite as expensive, but Cassie, the food there is absolutely mouth-watering."

"Suits me!" Cassie grinned, beginning to perk up.

"What are you going to have?" Aileen was busy perusing the drinks list. "I think I'll have a kir royale."

"I've never tasted kir," Cassie admitted.

"Oooh, it's lovely! You'd like it. Have the royale, it's got champagne in it. I'll treat you. I got a big tip from some Saudi sheik's wife today," she added with satisfaction.

They ordered their drinks and sat back in their comfortable dusky-pink chairs, enjoying themselves. In the background someone was softly playing a piano, and Cassie, who loved examining décor, gazed admiringly at the huge sparkling gilt-edged mirrors and the gold-filigreed ceiling, which was supported by magnificent marble pillars. The walls were decorated in a honey tone which gave an air of warmth and brightness that was most appealing although the room was huge and ornate.

"Wouldn't Barbara give her eye teeth to be here?" Aileen smiled wickedly as she began to make inroads into the bowl of savoury nuts the waiter had brought them.

"Could you imagine the detective here?" Cassie grimaced. "What she sees in him, I cannot imagine."

"Well, you know, they say opposites attract," Aileen said seriously, as she sipped the drink that had just arrived. "You know she's so...so...opinionated and so eager to be heard, and trying to get a few words out of him is like drawing blood from a stone. It's like Judy and Andrew Lawson. She's so gentle and placid and not very sure of herself and he's so flamboyant and arrogant and self-assured."

"Judy's cracked about him," Cassie observed.

"I know, and it worries me," Aileen sighed. "Do you think Barbara and Sherlock will make a go of it?"

Cassie laughed. "Don't ask me, but they've been together a good while now. She's even doing his washing for him."

"Is the woman mad!" Aileen exclaimed in disgust.

"You know Barbara!" Cassie said drily. "I went home one Friday and I wanted to do a bit of washing in a hurry and I couldn't get near the machine. She was washing his sheets, his duvet-cover and about forty shirts. Using *our* powder and *our* electricity and *our* washing-machine—"

"Typical!" interjected Aileen.

"Well, of course, when I pointed this out to her and told her I hoped it wasn't going to become a regular occurrence, she got into a magnificent huff." Cassie grinned at the memory. "Do you know what my dear sister said to me?"

Aileen arched a wing-tipped eyebrow. "What?"

Cassie took a sip of her drink. "She said, 'It's not my

fault if you can't keep a man and I can, so don't go taking it out on me.'"

Aileen's eyes widened. "The little bitch! God, what is it with her! She's had a chip on her shoulder as long as I can remember her and *that's* going back. What makes her say things like that?"

"I don't know! You know her when she gets miffed! There's just something in her make-up. Some people are born nasty and she's one of them. She's writing this gossip column now for the paper she's working for, and the things she writes about people! Of course she's got that Noreen Varling one egging her on and feeding her juicy titbits. You should see them in the Shelbourne drinking champagne. They're so pretentious. And Noreen's so big and stout and Barbara's such a skinny little beanpole, they're like Little and Large sitting there taking people apart. It really is outrageous the way they take away people's good names with their innuendos. One of these days they're going to be sued!"

"God help whoever is suing Barbara," laughed Aileen as she drained her drink. Cassie caught the waiter's attention.

"We'll have two more, please."

It was after nine when they left the Ritz to stroll back along Piccadilly to Half Moon Street, where they were having dinner in Fleming's Hotel. It had stopped drizzling and the sky had cleared and the pair of them were quite ravenous.

"Just look at the chandeliers in here. Aren't they magnificent?" murmured Aileen, as they entered the plush hotel. It was much more intimate than the Ritz and Cassie thought the peach-and-green decor was superb. Opposite the reception desk she noticed an ornate gilt mirror and an exquisite marble-topped table, upon which was placed the statue of a black stallion. Although the Ritz had been sumptuous with its marble pillars and huge yucca plants, she far preferred the classical elegance of this smaller hotel.

"This is lovely and you're right about those chandeliers—they really sparkle," she said to Aileen.

"Oh this is a real find. I've booked a table for us tonight. Wait until you've tasted the food. And the staff are lovely. I've been here several times." Aileen led the way to the dining-room.

"With anybody special?" Cassie smiled.

Aileen laughed. "What do you think I am? A glutton for punishment? No! Madame Lefeur, the woman I work for, has a nephew Pierre, who is, as you can guess, French. He comes over to London on business quite regularly and he stays with Madame Lefeur. They have this huge apartment over the salon. Talk about posh, Cassie! Anyway, he kind of fancies me, the fool! And he's taken me out and we've had dinner here a few times."

"What age is he?" Cassie asked, intrigued, as they were shown to their table.

"Thirty and unwed," Aileen laughed. "And unwed he'll stay if he keeps on showing an interest in me. I'm not getting involved again for a while."

"Me neither," Cassie said glumly.

"Ah, come on, let's not get depressed," Aileen said hastily. "Here, read this menu. It would raise anybody's spirits!"

Aileen hadn't lied about the food. After a delicious five-course meal, they were fit for nothing. Stuffed to the gills, they walked out into the night air and back towards Piccadilly Circus tube station.

"Would you like to go to a nightclub?" Aileen enquired. "We could go to Stringfellows or Jocelyns? I know people who work there so there won't be any problem getting in."

Cassie laughed and yawned. "I shouldn't have drunk that brandy. All I want to do is go to sleep!"

"Me too," confessed Aileen. "It's been an awfully long day and my feet are killing me."

"A right pair of ravers *we* are. Barbara would be disgusted with us!" Cassie yawned again. "Tell you what, to hell with the tube. Let's do it in style and get a taxi home. I love those black cabs. I always feel like the queen when I'm travelling in one of them."

"You're on!" Aileen flagged one down. They drove back to where Aileen lived in Wembley, as Cassie was spending the weekend with her. It was all hours before they got to bed, because once they got back to Aileen's and had coffee, they were revived and stayed up half the night chatting.

They spent a lazy weekend together and both of them enjoyed catching up on all the news. Aileen was staying with an aunt who lived in a large redbrick house in Stanley Avenue off the Ealing Road. Her aunt was a jolly woman in her early sixties and she was delighted to have Aileen staying. She had turned over the first floor for her niece's use as she suffered from respiratory problems and preferred to stay downstairs; so to all intents and purposes Aileen had a self-contained flat.

They had had a lovely lie-in and then breakfasted on juice, croissants, muesli and freshly ground coffee before going out for a stroll. Aileen liked Stanley Avenue. With its tree-lined street and redbrick houses, it reminded her of Griffith Avenue in Dublin. There was a large Asian community so they meandered into some of the colourful Asian shops on the Ealing Road, looking at the saris in the clothes shops and all the exotic fruit and vegetables and spices in the vegetables shops. Cassie bought some star-fruit and passion-fruit and some chillis and a host of different spices. She was definitely going to experiment with her cooking and Aileen was invited to partake of a meal the following week. Then they went up to Wembley High Street and had a ball as they dawdled around Marks & Spencers, C&A and their favourite, Boots. It was all still new to Cassie, and all still a treat. They spent ages in Boots looking at the make-up and toiletries before going to McDonald's for a Big Mac.

That night they set off again, this time to a cinema on the Tottenham Court Road. They were going to see *Star Trek, The Motion Picture* and they were so looking forward to it. Having thoroughly enjoyed *Star Trek* in their youth, like all loyal trekkies they were dying to see the movie.

They enjoyed it immensely, apart from being disgusted that the film-makers had changed the layout of the *Enterprise* completely. The new bridge was a disaster and the new uniforms didn't show off Captain Kirk's sexy bum the way the old one did. They munched popcorn, ate chocolates and drank Coke and felt fifteen again—only Laura was missing to complete the evening.

The next day, Sunday, was lashing rain and they bought all the Sunday papers and sat curled up in front of a roaring fire reading them. Aileen, whose culinary skills had not improved, was delighted when her aunt invited them to Sunday dinner, roast beef with all the trimmings.

It was a lovely weekend and it had cheered her up no end, Cassie reflected, as she got back to her flat on Sunday evening and began to press her uniform for work the following morning. Just as well she was walking to work, she thought; she'd be putting on stones if she wasn't careful. For the first time in ages she fell asleep almost as soon as her head touched the pillow and she slept soundly.

CHAPTER TWENTY-NINE

Gradually Cassie began to settle down to life in London. Her work was engrossing and challenging and she continued to study for her banking exams. She made new friends and she had Aileen, but still at times she would feel a terrible emptiness in her life. Robbie was never far from her thoughts and it annoyed her so much that she wasn't strong enough to banish him from her mind. Whenever old anniversaries or special days like Valentine's Day came up or she heard a song that had meant something special, the old feelings would come flooding back and she would get depressed. Then, no matter how much Aileen told her that things would get better—and wouldn't Aileen know, hadn't she gone through it herself—Cassie would despair.

It was in such a state one evening that she was flicking through one of the evening papers when she saw an advertisement for a new course in interior design. She cut it out and kept it. After she had finished her banking exams, she might like to try something different and she had always been interested in design.

She worked hard at her studies during those first few months in London, achieving honours in her banking exams, much to her satisfaction. But once her studying was completed and her exams were over, she felt very much at a loose end. Cassie knew she could start a management course in September if she wanted and that would really give her career a boost, but the thought did not greatly appeal to her. She felt restless and she wanted to do something not connected with work. Remembering the little cutting about the interior design evening course that she had kept, she sent away for the prospectus. Cassie liked what she saw and decided that her next goal would be a diploma in interior design. It was something she had always wanted to do, ever since she was a schoolgirl, and she looked forward to it immensely.

In the meantime she was kept busy with visitors from home. Her mother and Irene arrived for a long weekend and thoroughly enjoyed themselves, despite the fact that Cassie and Irene had got separated from Nora in Harrods. Their mother had been in an awful state when they found her because, for the life of her, she couldn't remember Cassie's address.

John arrived with his new girlfriend, Karen, and Cassie liked her enormously. John was really working hard setting up his fruit and vegetable farm and Cassie thought a little sadly how proud Jack would have been of his elder son. They spent the weekend seeing the sights and John and Karen had a ball. Cassie was delighted. Her brother deserved a break. He had always been a hard worker and once the business got going he would have precious little free time.

Martin and a friend of his arrived later in the year and the pair of them spent their few days visiting every pub in London. Martin, who was an apprentice electrician, told Cassie that he was about to move into a flat and that Nora was going mad about it.

"I'm twenty, Cassie. I want to lead my own life. I know she'll be on her own with Irene but I'll call and see her and John calls in every day and cuts the grass and things for her."

"Get your flat, Martin," Cassie advised her younger brother. It was hard on her mother, she acknowledged, that all her chicks were leaving the nest but that was life, unfortunately, and Nora was lucky to have had her children living with her for so long.

Barbara phoned one week angling for an invitation for herself and Ian, and Cassie's heart sank. Whatever about putting up with Barbara for a few days, she was not looking forward to having Ian Murray under her feet. She couldn't really refuse, though. After all, she had had John and Karen and Martin and his mate so she couldn't plead shortage of space. Reluctantly, and lying through her teeth, she told Barbara that she and Ian were welcome. They stayed a week and by the end of it Cassie was fit for an asylum. Ian was the laziest, untidiest man she had ever met.

"Maybe I'm being totally unreasonable but he's driving me nuts!" she wailed to Aileen, who was on a day off and whom she met for lunch in a little wine-bar off Kensington High Street. Aileen laughed as she took an appreciative sip of the Sauvignon Blanc recommended by the waiter. Cassie, who had to go back to work, was sticking to Perrier, although she felt like drowning her sorrows.

"You've to put up with them only for another four days. Cheer up!" Aileen encouraged as she tucked into a slice of garlic bread.

"If *that's* the best you can do, it's no help," Cassie muttered glumly. "Barbara wants to go to the Ritz tonight and the Savoy for afternoon tea on Saturday so she can spoof about them in her column when she gets home. She wants to see some famous faces so she can name-drop and pretend she's on intimate terms with them. For a grown woman did you ever hear anything so childish? And people believe every word she writes and read her pieces avidly."

"I can't see Ian enjoying the Ritz. It's not really his scene, is it?" Aileen said doubtfully.

"Oh, he wants to stay at home tonight to watch a match. He'll have beer-cans all over the place. That's why Barbara decided it would be a good opportunity to see the Ritz. Research, she calls it. I hope she's on expenses!" Cassie said tartly.

"I'll tell you what: I'll come with you to the Ritz tonight, and I'll tell her about all the famous people, the film stars, the TV personalities to whom I've given beauty treatments. Would that keep her happy?"

Cassie smiled at Aileen. "Spoken like a true friend, O'Shaughnessy. Always there when the chips are down."

The redhead laughed and ordered another half-carafe of wine. "I'd better fortify myself, so!"

It actually turned out to be a very enjoyable evening. The girls left Ian lounging in front of Cassie's TV with a six-pack of beer and peanuts and crisps and took a taxi to Mayfair. "We don't want Babs to have to slum it on the tube," Aileen whispered. Barbara was in her element and trying hard not to be impressed. She had bought herself a cream linen suit in Aquascutum in Regent Street and a bag, scarf and jewellery accessories in Jaeger and thought she was gorgeous. She couldn't wait to write next week's column. Dressed to the nines in her new outfit, which, she confided, she also intended to wear to the next Brown Thomas fashion show, Barbara loved sipping kirs in the Ritz. She was fascinated by Aileen's descriptions of the rich and famous who came to the plush Mayfair salon where she worked.

"I could stick you in if I get a cancellation while you're here. You could get your eyebrows done or a manicure or whatever," Aileen offered generously. Cassie could have kissed her. Aileen was a gem. Heaven knows Barbara didn't deserve such kindness. She had been quite rude to Aileen during their spats when they lived together. But then, Aileen was not one to hold a grudge over anything. Actually she found Barbara and her notions highly entertaining and roared laughing at her gossip column, which Nora sent to Cassie with the papers every week.

Barbara was in the seventh heaven at the offer, and when they took her to Langan's Brasserie for a meal—Cassie had just got back-money—and she saw Michael Caine and his wife Shakira dining with Roger Moore and his wife, she was ecstatic. The fact that they got a table at the famous restaurant because Aileen knew someone there made her rise notches in Barbara's estimation and she fawned over her for the rest of the evening, much to Aileen's amusement.

"Cassie, I had a wonderful time," Barbara enthused, as she bade her sister farewell at Heathrow a few days later. "I'll have to do it again soon. It's so handy having a base here. I could do all sorts of features on London; I must speak to my editor," she bubbled excitedly. "Didn't you enjoy it, Ian? Maybe we could come and do our Christmas shopping."

"Er...yeah...great," muttered the stocky detective. "See ya at Christmas!"

"No way!" muttered Cassie two hours later as she flung open the windows of her sitting-room and sprayed air freshener around to get rid of the smell of cigarette smoke. There were peanuts down between the cushions of the couch and she got out the hoover and began vacuuming with a vengeance. She had done her duty by Barbara. Once was enough to be landed with Ian Murray. She'd make some excuse!

A week later Nora forwarded *The Irish Mail* with Barbara's column on London. Cassie and Aileen nearly split their sides laughing as they read how Barbara, after champagne cocktails in the Ritz, had bumped into old friends, Michael and Shakira Caine, while dining in Langan's Brasserie, one of her favourite London haunts. The Caines were with their VBFs (very best friends), the Roger Moores. The following day while having a head-to-toe body treatment in a plush Mayfair salon—Aileen shrieked at this—Barbara had bumped into "old gal pal," Lady Diana Spencer, who was currently the subject of intense media speculation concerning her relationship with the Prince of Wales. "Watch this spot!" wrote Barbara dramatically.

"Isn't she just incredible?" Cassie laughed. "And the thing is, people actually believe her! Since she's started writing 'Barbara's Brief,' the circulation of the paper has taken off and is increasing all the time. They're very impressed with her, or so she says."

"She should win an award for her fiction-writing, that's for sure!" Aileen grinned.

❦

Cassie had so many visitors that the summer was over before she knew it. She and Aileen spent a ten-day holiday driving around the South of France and then she took a week's leave and went home to Nora, who was delighted to see her. Cassie spent a few days at home in Port Mahon helping her mother to re-tile the bathroom and from there she went to Dublin to spend the weekend with Laura and Doug.

She had never seen Laura so contented and happy. Marriage really suited her, although she was finding her job pretty hard going. She told Cassie it was difficult to be taken seriously because she was one of only a few women in a large law firm that had the reputation of being sexist, but she was beavering away. She and Doug hadn't two pennies to rub together, with all his money going into the business and her salary just a pittance. But the business was slowly but surely taking off; they were happy together striving to reach their goals and Cassie couldn't help but envy them.

How she would have loved to be married to Robbie and making plans for the future. On her last night with Laura, her friend told her that she had seen Robbie in a pub one night. Cassie felt a sharp stab of loneliness tinged with guilt.

"Was he drinking?"

Laura nodded. "He'd had a few all right! He tried to get me to give him your London address and phone number but I wouldn't give it to him. He wanted to pay me for the wedding cake. I told him to give it to charity. Cassie, you're well out of it, honestly, no matter what you feel now," her friend said bluntly.

Cassie bit her lip.

"Oh Cassie, I'm sorry! I didn't mean to make you cry," Laura exclaimed in dismay as a big tear plopped on to Cassie's lap.

"It's OK, Laura, it's just...Oh it hurts...it still hurts like hell!"

"Isn't it getting any better?"

Cassie wiped her eyes. "It helps being in London, everything is so new and the job is so demanding, but there are times when I get so lonely for him, I'm sorely tempted to pick up the phone."

"Don't!" warned Laura. "Haven't you gone out with anyone at all since you went over? It's what, almost eight months now?"

Cassie shook her head. "I'm in the social club at work and I play basketball and go bowling and swimming and I've been asked out a few times but my heart's not in it and I say no. I'm going to study interior design in the autumn—that will keep me occupied for a while."

"Hey, that's great news. You've always wanted to do something like that. You can decorate our place, whenever we get a place of our own," Laura exclaimed delightedly.

"And when will that be?"

Laura threw her eyes up to heaven. "God knows!"

That autumn, Cassie often thought of Laura's future home, as she sat at her newly purchased drawing-board, which had parallel motion and a stand, practising her technical drawings. She had started her evening classes and was doing seven subjects: materials, history of interior design, draughtsmanship, design, colour, furniture and fittings, and construction of interiors. She loved it. It was no hardship after a busy day's work to go to college and have classes from seven until ten and then go home and do her assignments. Unleashing her creativity was very satisfying. She could immerse herself in a project and spend hours on it and not feel the time passing. She spent hours at the weekend browsing in antique shops and home-design stores. She practically lived in Habitat and Laura Ashley and had enough swatches of material and samples of wallpaper to fill a sack. Her favourite place of all, the General Trading Company Ltd in Sloane Street, was practically a home from home to her with its household furnishings, china, glass, linen and antiques and oriental items. She scoured the markets, nipping up to the one in Shepherd's Bush on her bike, usually arriving home with some find, an antique vase or an old wooden carved letter-holder that she would clean and French-polish and restore to its former glory. For the first time since her break-up with Robbie, she was happy.

With the blessing of Aileen's aunt, she redecorated Aileen's sitting-room and bedroom, using inexpensive materials and the sponging and stencilling techniques that she was learning. Aileen was delighted with the result, especially with the kelim, the flat-woven tapestry rug with its brilliant colours and bold pattern that Cassie had used as the focal point in the sitting-room. A couple of Japanese fans that she had picked up for a few pounds in a flea-market had very much the same colouring and these provided a decorative toning feature on the walls. It was the first example of her work to go in her portfolio and she was very proud of it.

It led to other commissions. A friend of Aileen's was so impressed that she asked Cassie to do a job on the hall of an old house that she and her husband had bought. It was in a right state and Cassie felt a surge of enthusiasm when she first saw it. She couldn't wait to get her teeth into it. The four of them spent a weekend scraping off the old flock wallpaper and chipped paint before she could get to work on the transformation. The following weekend Cassie bonded and treated the walls before applying several coats of a warm buttermilk shade of paint. She used eggshell paint on the dado rail and skirting-board and then papered the dado in a William Morris design wallpaper which she first sealed and then glazed with transparent oil glaze, tinted with artist's oil paint. Finally she stained the floorboards and stairway and covered them with an Eastern runner carpet. The result was elegant simplicity and warmth and light, a complete contrast to the dingy hole it had been. Aileen's friends were thrilled with it, as was Cassie. Nothing that she had ever done in her life before had given her such satisfaction.

When a class tutor told them that their classes in second year would include some courses on setting up their own consultancy and design business, she actually found herself daydreaming about leaving the bank and setting up a business herself. Now that would be a dream come true! In the meantime she kept studying and practising different decorating techniques and spent a fortune on glossy home-design and decorating magazines.

CHAPTER THIRTY

"Cassie, you're looking much better in yourself. I was terribly worried about you there for a while. This time last year you were like a ghost," her mother remarked on Christmas Eve, as they prepared the stuffing for the turkey.

Cassie paused in the chopping of her onions. The thought of Robbie still hurt, there was no doubt about it, but she *did* feel much more optimistic, especially since she had started her course. Compared to last year, when all she wanted to do was run away and hide from everyone, this year she was actually looking forward to seeing old friends and celebrating Christmas with her family.

"It's probably my hair. I got it styled before I came home." She smiled at Nora, who was chopping parsley to add to the breadcrumbs.

"It's more than that, pet. You know, I think you made a very wise decision not to marry Robbie. I never worry about you the way I worry about Irene. You have a core of strength, Cassie, that will always see you through. Irene will always need to lean on someone. I'm worried about her. She hates her job. Maybe she should give it up and try and find something nearer home," Nora said worriedly.

"Mother!" Cassie said firmly, trying to keep the annoyance out of her voice. "Irene will have to learn to stand on her own two feet! You're not always going to be here for her to lean on. She can't give up a good job, at least not until she has another one to go to, and I don't think she's going to get anything in Port Mahon that will have the advantages of the one she has in the County Council. And if she's not careful, she's going to get the sack with all the sick leave she's taking." Irene had been out of work for the previous week with a chest infection.

"The child is not well!" objected Nora, rising to the defence of her youngest as she always did. "She's always been frail, Cassie, not like you and the rest of them." Cassie said no more. Where Irene was concerned, her mother never allowed any criticism.

John and Karen arrived home shortly afterwards and Cassie, observing them smiling at each other, knew that they were a match. She was glad for John; he deserved something good in his life and Karen was a lovely girl. Nora was very fond of her and, watching the way she took off her coat, rolled up her sleeves and started washing the dishes, Cassie could understand why. John had just made a pot of tea and buttered a plate of scones for the lot of them when Barbara and Ian arrived. Typical, thought Cassie in amusement. The work was all done and the supper was just ready. Barbara had always been the same; her timing was impeccable. She was looking particularly well tonight, Cassie reflected, as her sister divested herself of her well-cut herringbone coat.

"Welcome home, Cassie," Barbara smiled. She waved her left hand at Cassie. "Well, what do you think?"

It took Cassie a minute or two to figure out what her sister was on about and then she noticed the engagement ring. Cassie's eyes widened. Barbara and Ian were engaged!

"Congratulations," Cassie managed to say, giving her sister a hug. Nora gave a gasp of surprise. Barbara smirked.

"We waited until you came home so you could be here as well to share the good news. I'm just so happy, I'm over the moon!"

"That's great, Barbara. I hope you'll always be as happy," Cassie said warmly.

"Well, congratulations, Barbara and Ian. I'm flabbergasted!" laughed Nora, getting up to kiss her daughter. Ian stood, hands in his pockets, his face suffused with red.

"Thanks, Mrs Jordan, I'll look after her," he muttered in some embarrassment. Cassie caught John's eye. Her brother threw his eyes up to heaven and grinned at Cassie. He was as impressed with their new in-law-to-be as she was.

"When are you getting married?" Nora asked.

"June," Barbara replied airily, handing Ian the plate of scones.

"Merciful hour!" exclaimed her mother. "That's only six months away! I'll have a lot to do between now and then! Get me a page and pen until I write down my list. If I don't write things down, I forget them."

Cassie got her mother the page and pen. She could see Nora was in her element. Planning a wedding was just the sort of thing she liked to get her teeth into. She had been cheated out of planning Cassie's so she could only hope that nothing would go wrong between Barbara and Ian.

Nothing went wrong between the engaged couple but Nora was not getting her own way as regards the planning of "The Wedding," as Cassie privately called it. When she was back in London, her mother often phoned her to moan about the way things were going.

"Barbara wants to get married out of Ranelagh church and not in Port Mahon. Did you ever hear the like? What are the neighbours and relations going to say!" Nora exclaimed in dismay one Saturday she phoned Cassie to pour out all her troubles. Knowing her sister so well, Cassie had already realised that she'd never settle for a Port Mahon wedding. Barbara would have to swank it in Dublin and besides, the aisle in Ranelagh church was much longer than in the church in Port Mahon.

"Look, Mam, why don't you just let her get on with it and don't be worrying your head over it," Cassie advised.

"But Cassie, it's the first wedding out of the house and I wanted it to be just right. I wish your father were here to advise me," Nora said plaintively. Cassie's heart went out to her mother. Whatever chance she would have had arranging Cassie's wedding—and Cassie would have let her mother have her own way in a lot of things— with Barbara, Nora would have very little say.

"I'll tell you what, Mam," Cassie said reassuringly. "I'll come home at Easter and you can tell me what you want done in the house and we can go shopping for your outfit and we'll make the cake. How about that?" As soon as she got off the phone to her mother she was going to ring Barbara and point a few things out to her.

"Thank you, dear, that would be lovely. Do you think we should invite Judy O'Shaughnessy?"

"Why shouldn't we?" Cassie asked, mystified.

"Well, she's gone off living out of wedlock with that Lawson fellow she's been dating. It's simply scandalous," exclaimed Nora, who was utterly shocked at the ways of the young girls now.

"Now, Mam, that's Judy's business, and it's not up to anyone to judge her. Of course you must invite her to the wedding. She's Barbara's best friend."

Nora was not to be mollified. "Some friend! Leaving Barbara to manage that flat on her own. I hope to God she won't have the nerve to go to Communion and her in a state of sin. Goodbye, Cassie. Take care of yourself."

"You too!" Cassie sighed in exasperation as she hung up the receiver. If only Nora knew that Judy had more or less had to leave the flat because Ian had taken up residence. It wasn't only Judy who was living out of wedlock with a man. But, of course, Barbara was so cute Nora would never get wind of it.

She dialled her sister's number and heard the familiar voice with its recently acquired genteel accent.

"Yaw? Barbara Jordan on the line."

Give me a break! thought Cassie. "Yaw" indeed! No common or garden "yes" for Barbara. No doubt Noreen Varling said "yaw" as well. And why couldn't she just say hello? Barbara Jordan on the line!

"Hi, Barbara, it's me. I've just been speaking to Mam and she's not very happy about a few things. Maybe we could have a chat about them and try and come up with something that will suit everybody." Cassie was trying to be very diplomatic but wanted to get right to the point as well.

"Listen, Cassie, don't you start interfering," Barbara retorted angrily. "It's *my* wedding and I'm going to organise it exactly the way I want it. If Mam doesn't like it, that's just too bad."

"I'm not interfering; I'm just trying to help," Cassie said, controlling her temper with some difficulty.

"Cassie, I'm not getting married in Port Mahon. I don't live there any longer and I want a hotel in the city centre so all my colleagues and friends will be able to come without having to go to the trouble of travelling."

"And what about putting Mam to the trouble of travelling, not to talk about the relations?" Cassie said tightly.

"Well, that's just tough!" Barbara replied sulkily.

Diplomacy flew out the window! "Now you listen to me, lady!" Cassie exploded. "If you were paying for this wedding yourself, I couldn't care less if you had it on the moon, but you're not! Mam's paying for it and that means, whether you like it or not, she has some say in where it's going to be held and you'd better remember that. For once in your life don't be so bloody selfish!"

Barbara was sizzling at the other end of the phone. "Fuck off, Cassie Jordan. It's just sour grapes because I'm getting married and you're not. I suppose you'd have paid for your own wedding, you're such a great one. Well, Mam *insisted* on paying for the wedding, so don't expect me to feel guilty."

"I bet you put up *such* an argument against it too," Cassie snapped. "You're dead right, Barbara. I *would* have paid for my own wedding and I'd have listened to what Mam wants. She deserves *that* much at least—"

"Oh, miss Goody bloody Two-Shoes. You're such a pain, Cassie, always doing the right thing. Well, I'm me and I'm going to do things *my* way!" Barbara declared. "And if that doesn't suit you, go sit on a nettle!" The click at the other end of the line told Cassie that her sister had hung up.

Cassie was still furious when she met Aileen for lunch a few hours later. "God Almighty, but that one would put years on you! It's easy for her to call me Goody Two-Shoes. Does she have any idea how hard it is doing, as she calls it, 'the right thing?' Someone's got to do it! Mam did her best for us and I know she has her faults but she's still our mother and she deserves a bit of consideration," Cassie fumed. "God, it's such a pain being the eldest sometimes, I get all the moans. Irene is over there sitting on her arse, out sick from work again. Some help to Mam she is! Oh I could scream!"

"Wait until we get to the park, dear. It might not go down too well right here in the restaurant," advised Aileen soothingly.

Cassie laughed in spite of herself. "Families!" she exclaimed.

"Don't talk!" Aileen said wryly. "Mother's convinced she's on the verge of a nervous breakdown after she read an article in *Woman's Way* that described perfectly what she imagines her symptoms to be. She's gone into hospital for a rest."

"Oh, I'm sorry to hear that," Cassie said sympathetically.

Aileen laughed. "Don't be a bit sorry. She's having a ball in there, being waited on hand and foot, doctors and nurses dancing attendance and the VHI paying for it. Mother is enjoying herself immensely, according to Judy, who *will* have a genuine nervous breakdown from traipsing half-way across the city every night to go and visit her! *And* she's coming over to me to recuperate. Oh don't talk to me about families—I know all about them. Did you hear about Laura's brother?"

Cassie shook her head. "I haven't got a letter from her for a while."

"No wonder. Judy told me about him when she phoned last night to warn me about Mother coming for a visit. Seemingly he owes a moneylender a large sum of money. You know he was always a gambler as well as a drinker?"

Cassie nodded.

Aileen nibbled an asparagus tip. "Some heavy gang beat him up and broke his arm because he hadn't paid what he owes. He asked Laura at the weekend if she could give him the money. She's going mad about it all!"

"I wouldn't blame her!" sighed Cassie. "We all have our troubles, don't we?"

"Yeah, well, let's forget ours for a while. Pierre is over and he wants to go to the racing at Cheltenham. Are you on?"

"You bet," laughed Cassie, banishing the thought of Barbara and "The Wedding" to the deepest recesses of her mind.

CHAPTER THIRTY-ONE

Barbara Jordan Murray (how she loved her just hours-old newly acquired double-barrel surname) sat at the top table, a faint frown furrowing her made-up brow. There were gales of laughter emanating from Cassie, Aileen and Laura, who were seated at a table in the centre of the plush room where her wedding reception was being held, and these were causing her annoyance.

It was a bit much, really. *She* should have been the centre of attention, not that lot. She hadn't particularly wanted to invite Laura and Aileen but Nora had expected her to, and besides, she couldn't resist having them present to show off to them her exquisite Pronuptia gown and glamorous friends. Noreen Varling was looking a million dollars in a creation by Marc Bohan of the House of Dior that she had *actually* bought in Paris. Barbara was deeply impressed! She watched in annoyance as Cassie laughed heartily at something that Aileen was telling her. Her sister looked really stunning and she had seen Ian's detective friends eyeing her appreciatively. Honestly, she would have thought that Cassie would have kept a fairly low profile considering her broken engagement and the fact that she had no prospects. But no, her sister had arrived at the wedding in a royal-blue silk dress that made her look unmistakably sexy. Andrew Lawson, Judy's boyfriend, couldn't take his eyes off her.

Aileen was wearing an exotic sarong-type dress with a little black jacket. Trust her to wear something outrageous—although Barbara had to admit the oranges and yellows really suited her colouring.

Laura, as usual looking like a model, wore a stylish pink-and-navy suit and a navy hat with matching pink trim. She was always the same, of course, the height of elegance, and Barbara was sorry she had invited her. Ian's friends were paying more attention to the three of them than they were to her. Another shriek of laughter erupted at the table. Just what the hell were they laughing at? They were always the same when they got together! And Laura the only one among them who had a man by her side! Neither Cassie nor Aileen had bothered to bring a companion. Despite her view of herself as a liberated woman of the Eighties, Barbara wouldn't *dream* of attending a wedding without a man at her side. What was more, you would think that Cassie would at least have had the decency to be annoyed at not being asked to be bridesmaid. Barbara had been so furious with her older sister for poking her nose in where it wasn't wanted and trying to tell her how to organise her wedding, that she had decided there and then to have Irene as bridesmaid. Irene was thoroughly enjoying herself in her full-skirted aquamarine dress. And Cassie? She hadn't been one bit annoyed that she wasn't given the honour of being bridesmaid. In fact, Barbara felt she was quite relieved!

Well, at least Barbara had got her way about the church and the hotel. She had got around the problem of the family travelling back to Port Mahon from the Dublin hotel after the reception by hiring a mini-bus. Barbara knew that if her newspaper and society friends had had to travel out to Port Mahon for the wedding, they probably wouldn't have come.

The hotel she had booked was as posh as they come and the Anna Livia Suite with its views over the city was perfect for the reception. No hick country wedding for her. Barbara Jordan Murray had an image to maintain. She and Ian had bought an apartment in Mount Merrion. Ian hadn't been too happy about it (he had wanted somewhere on the northside near his work), but Barbara had insisted on living on the southside. If one wanted to be taken seriously and maintain an upwardly mobile image it would be disastrous to live north of the Liffey. Anyone who was anybody in Dublin lived on the southside, at least in Barbara's book. Northside was "non-U," according to "Barbara's Brief," so how would it look if she ended up living there? It was unthinkable and she had put her foot down, ignoring Ian's moans. Fortunately her husband was on a good salary and with his practically permanent overtime and the rent from his flats he was well able to afford the mortgage. She needed most of her salary to buy clothes and the like. After all, a certain standard was expected from such a highly respected columnist. She was trying to wangle a bigger allowance from her editor, but so far to no avail. He told her she was lucky to have the expense-account she had for her modest entertaining. And modest was the word, compared to some of the gossip columnists she knew. Well, she'd keep after him. After all, since "Barbara's Brief" had started being a talking-point, the newspaper's circulation had increased dramatically. By the time she was finished, *The Irish Mail* would be the biggest-selling paper in the country.

She saw two of Ian's friends make a move towards the girls' table. Honest to God, she might as well be a ghost at her own wedding for all the notice anyone was taking of her. Barbara turned to her husband.

"Ian, I think we should get on the floor because no one else can dance until we start."

"Oh, Bar, do we have to? You know I hate dancing and this get-up is too tight on me," Ian said glumly. He was quite happy to sit there sipping his pint and watching everyone else get on with it.

"You look dishy in your tails," Barbara assured her husband, leaning over and giving him a peck on the cheek.

"Barbara! Not in front of the lads," Ian muttered in horror. He'd be the laughing-stock of the station.

"If you don't get up and dance, I'll kiss you again," Barbara warned tartly. Deciding on the lesser of two evils, Ian Murray walked reluctantly to the dance-floor and took his wife in his arms. The guests cheered loudly as the band swung into action and began to play "When I Fall in Love." The cameras clicked as people took photos of them and Barbara felt like a film star! Encircled in her husband's arms, knowing she was a vision in white and the centre of attention at last, Barbara smiled happily, even when Ian, who was no Fred Astaire, stood on her toe. It didn't matter; today she was the happiest woman in the world. Her wedding had been everything she had wanted, although a few well-known people she had invited to the afters had not yet turned up. But the night was young and besides, if they didn't turn up they might get a nasty surprise some time when they read her column. Nobody snubbed Barbara Jordan Murray and got away with it! Barbara smiled to herself as she planned a few nasty little items about the unsuspecting non-arrivals!

❧

She would be glad when it was all over, Nora thought a little wearily as, beside her, her sister Elsie sermonised about the amount of money being wasted on Barbara's reception. Privately, Nora agreed. It was outrageous the amount of money it cost to get married in Dublin and of course it didn't help that Barbara had wanted as grand a wedding as possible, white Rolls-Royce, red carpet, the lot. Not that she minded paying for the wedding. Jack, God bless him, had left her comfortable and the income she got from renting the farm supported the family. A wedding in Port Mahon would have been well within her means, but this shindig had cost an awful lot more than Nora had anticipated. As well as which, when Irene and Cassie decided to get married, they would be perfectly entitled to have as big and grand a wedding as their sister. Nora knew that Cassie would never allow her mother to be put to the expense that Barbara had put her to. Nevertheless, it didn't do to make fish of one and flesh of another!

She'd have to get used to the idea of weddings, she supposed. John had told her quietly that he and Karen were going to get married but they weren't saying anything for the time being so as not to encroach on Barbara's limelight. John said that it would be a fairly small wedding and that he and Karen would be paying for it. Nora was delighted for John all the same. He couldn't have picked a nicer girl than Karen. She was very fond of her daughter-in-law-to-be; there were no airs and graces or nonsense about her, unlike the girl her younger son was seeing.

Martin's girlfriend was called Jean Allen and Nora felt her son was getting too serious about her. To be honest, she found it hard to take to her. Maybe she was being unfair to the girl, maybe she was shy rather than stand-offish but Nora had the sneaking suspicion that little Miss Jean Allen was looking down her aquiline nose at them, sitting there when she visited with Martin, saying very little, but taking it all in.

It was strange to think that all her children were adults now. It seemed like only yesterday that she had had a houseful of children who looked to her for the final word on everything. Well, she had done her best to rear them well. She had put her trust in God; it was all she could do. And it was all she could do now. All in all, today had gone well enough except for that awful moment she forgot Ian's surname when she met his parents at the church. It was mortifying. She was standing at the entrance to the church when they arrived and held out her hand to greet Ian's mother. "Hello, Mrs..." But it had just gone; for the life of her she could not remember her future son-in-law's surname. Fortunately, Cassie had covered it up very quickly by saying, "Welcome, Mr and Mrs Murray." Just thinking about it gave Nora a hot flush of embarrassment. Her memory wasn't at all as good as it used to be. It was probably the stress of the wedding. She was going back to London with Cassie for a few days to have a little break after all the excitement and she was really looking forward to it.

Cassie was very good to her; indeed all her children were. John had been so kind to her today, making sure that everything was running smoothly. He had given a lovely speech on behalf of the family, seeing as Jack, God rest him, was not there to do it, and she was very proud of him. And they all looked so well. Even Martin had made the effort to please his mother and had got a suit and cut his hair and Irene, her baby, oh she looked lovely, a vision in her bridesmaid's dress. Nora smiled as she watched Irene dancing with the best man. Just then, John came and held out his hand.

"Mam, would you do me the honour?" He smiled down at her.

"I'd be delighted, son," Nora smiled back, allowing him to lead her onto the dance-floor to join her daughters in the first dance of the wedding.

❧

Judy O'Shaughnessy felt a horrible prickly heat suffuse her body and she broke out in a sweat. Excusing herself from the table she slipped quietly from the function room and went into the ladies' rest room. A quick glance around showed that she was the only one there. Entering one of the cubicles, she vomited as quietly as she could. It was her third time today. When it was over she bathed her face in cold water and rested her hot forehead against the cool tiles.

As far as she could make out, Andrew had not noticed her indisposition. He was having a ball! The life and soul of the party as usual. Her boyfriend really had a great capacity for enjoying himself. But then, he was such good company, so attractive and self-assured. Sometimes Judy wondered what he saw in her. She knew he loved her naturally blonde curling hair and he loved the reaction of other men when they walked into a function arm in arm. He enjoyed the fact that other men desired her. It was a turn-on for him, he admitted. Andrew told her once that she was very soothing to be with; he hated argumentative women. Judy had been terribly flattered.

They had been together for over two years now and she had been living with him for the past six months, although her mother would have another nervous breakdown if she knew that. It was very wearing on the nerves, actually. Mrs Jordan had been very cool to her and Judy suspected that Barbara had spilt the beans about her co-habiting with Andrew. It was a bit mean of Barbara. If Ian had not moved into the flat, Judy would have been quite happy to stay there but it had been downright embarrassing at times walking unsuspectingly into the sitting-room and finding the pair of them mauling each other and kissing and cuddling. In the end, she had spent most of her time up in her bedroom and one night she had been moaning to Andrew and he had suggested she move into his penthouse in Sutton. She loved that penthouse with its huge airy rooms and spectacular views over Dublin Bay. Andrew was an extremely wealthy young man. He came from an affluent background, his family were bankers and he himself owned and managed a very successful PR firm.

Andrew was always entertaining clients and because she was well used to meeting people through her job, Judy had no difficulty mingling and making small-talk and occasionally acting as his hostess. Andrew was most generous and lavished gifts of clothes and jewellery on her, despite her protests.

"You're mad! Let him give you presents and take them while the going is good," Barbara said enviously when she tried on the emerald-and-diamond dress-ring that Andrew had given her last Christmas. Judy nearly died but Andrew just laughed at her protests and said that was one of the things he liked about her, that she hadn't a mercenary bone in her body.

Judy looked at the ring on her right hand, glinting under the fluorescent light. It might be the last present he'd be giving her the way things were going, and Angela O'Shaughnessy would no doubt suffer the mother of all nervous breakdowns if past behaviour was anything to go by. Sighing deeply, Judy retouched her make-up and sprayed some Magie Noire on her neck and wrists before rejoining the celebrations.

❦

Laura Quinn was really enjoying herself at this wedding, so unlike her own stressful day two and a half years before. It was great not to have to worry about wedding cakes and seating arrangements, and she had been looking forward to this occasion ever since the invitation had landed through her letterbox. Just as well it was being held on a Saturday, though. She would have had a hell of a job getting a day off from work. Just thinking about work made her blood boil.

It was an understatement to say that Laura was not entirely happy with her apprenticeship in William Bennett Solicitors. The men who had been taken on with her had cushy numbers while she spent her time running around like a lunatic making sure everything she did was perfect and that she always met her deadlines, no matter how unreasonable. The partners in charge of each of the different sections where Laura spent some time were much tougher on her and the other female apprentices than on the men. There was a saying that women had to be twice as good as men to succeed, and it was certainly true of her job.

But today wasn't the day to be thinking of work. She was having far too much fun. It was great to see the girls again. She had missed them so much. Cassie was looking terrific, so different from the pale, drawn depressed person she had been after she broke off her engagement with Robbie. She was so much more confident and in control of things. This interior design course she was doing had given her a whole new lease of life. And Aileen too was in tip-top form, back to her zany, bubbling self and *so* glamorous. They were going to have a night together before the girls went back.

Laura sat back comfortably in her chair and sipped her Bacardi and Coke. Doug was up dancing with Mrs Jordan. He was really good like that and she loved him for it. Doug had a caring considerate side that few saw except herself. She was very happy being married to him. She had never thought marriage could be so totally satisfying. Theirs was a real partnership. Doug was as anxious for her to succeed as she was for him. And succeed she would. Laura Quinn would carve out a successful legal career for herself, come hell or high water.

"Cheer up! You're at a wedding, not a funeral!" her husband remonstrated, interrupting her reflections. "I know, you're afraid I'm going to start an affair with Mrs Jordan. You're jealous!"

"Idiot!" laughed Laura.

"Would you care to dance with an idiot?" Doug teased, his eyes warm as he gazed at his wife with unconcealed admiration.

"I'd love to dance with an idiot," Laura said huskily. He took her into his arms and held her close as the music changed to a soft, romantic song and they danced cheek to cheek.

CHAPTER THIRTY-TWO

"Are you OK, Mam? Would you or Aunt Elsie or Mrs Saunders like another drink?" Cassie asked her mother as she took a breather from the dance-floor.

"Maybe I'll have another Babycham and you could get a glass of lemon and lime for your aunt and a sherry for Mrs Saunders." Nora smiled at her eldest daughter. "Do you think it's going all right? Did everybody get enough to eat, do you think?"

"Everybody had plenty and it's going fine," Cassie reassured her. Personally she felt that the food in the Port Mahon Arms was just as good and it would have cost only half the price. But Barbara had wanted her posh Dublin hotel and, being Barbara, she had got it!

Mind, the wedding was much better fun than she had anticipated. Cassie grinned to herself. Of course when she, Aileen and Laura got together what else could they have but fun? When they got to the church and saw Ian in his top-hat and tails, the three of them had got a fit of the giggles which was not helped when Aileen whispered, "Tom Selleck, eat your heart out." She had kept up a whispered running commentary from the moment Barbara had arrived at the church in her white frills and flounces.

Of course, Cassie wouldn't hurt her sister's feelings

for the world but when she saw the dress for the first time that morning she thought to herself, Uh ooohh! It was way over the top with its ruffles and flounces, and Barbara, who was small and skinny, was quite lost in it. But she loved it and she was the one wearing it, so Cassie kept her mouth shut. Irene looked a dream in her ballerina-length bridesmaid's dress, with her long blonde curls entwined with flowers.

Nora, too, looked very chic in her yellow-and-black two-piece with a little veiled hat perched jauntily on her head. Cassie and she had taken a day in Dublin when she was home at Easter and searched from one end of the city to the other before settling on the outfit that had caught her eye in Madame Nora's. After buying the bag, shoes, and hat in Clerys, they had had a celebratory lunch in the Gresham and Nora had enjoyed her day in town immensely.

Cassie knew today was a hard day for her mother. The first wedding in the family and Jack not there to share it with her. And Aunt Elsie sitting there moaning about everything. Although now in her seventies and getting frailer as the years went by, Elsie still had an indomitable spirit and a voice to speak with, a voice she used many times that day until Cassie and John were nearly ready to strangle her. Cassie had offered to drive her home after the meal if she didn't want to sit and listen to the band but Elsie was having none of it.

"Here I am and here I'll stay. It would be the height of bad manners to leave before the bride!"

Cassie felt her aunt was enjoying herself thoroughly. She got the drinks that her mother ordered and went back to join the girls. At least Mrs Saunders, a great friend of her mother's, was there to give Nora a lift. The relations were all coming to greet her, so she wasn't too

worried about her being short of company. Poor Mr and
Mrs Murray, Ian's parents, were totally overawed by the
whole occasion and Barbara wasn't making much of an
effort to mingle with his family, being too concerned
with dancing attendance on Noreen Varling and her
cronies. Well, Cassie decided, it wasn't her problem and
she was going back to the girls to have a bit of a laugh.

Laura's husband had just asked Aileen to dance.

"Poor Doug!" smirked Aileen. "He really got the rough
end of the stick having to do these duty dances with his
wife's poor spinster friends. He's a real gentleman!"

Doug guffawed. "Some spinsters, and every man in the
room drooling over the pair of you. Get out there,
O'Shaughnessy, and let's show these people how to dance."

Aileen sashayed on to the dance-floor and began to
boogie.

Laura burst out laughing. "Would you look at that
one! She hasn't changed one bit from when we were in
Saint Imelda's."

"Thank God," laughed Cassie. "We need someone
like Aileen around. Speaking of Saint Imelda's I met Sister
Eileen the other day. She's still the same as ever. She was
a dote, wasn't she?"

Laura nodded. "We had great fun there. It was a good
old school all the same, in spite of Mother Perpetua. We
gave her an awful time, didn't we?"

Cassie laughed "Yeah, we sure did. We were little
horrors and we thought we knew it all. Remember that
priest who had the misfortune to give us a retreat?"

"An experience the poor man never forgot, I'd say,"
smiled Laura as Aileen danced her way over to the table.

"Come on! Stop sitting there like two ould wans
having a natter and get up and dance. Doug says he's
man enough for three of us!"

"Is he, now?" grinned Cassie. "Come on. Laura. let's get out there and strut our stuff!"

"I've never danced so much in my life," she confessed about two hours later, as she and Aileen went out on the balcony to get some air.

"So I noticed!" grinned the redhead. "You're getting on very well with Anthony Wilson," she added slyly. "Are we going to have another detective in the family?"

Anthony Wilson was a detective friend of Ian's, and Cassie and he had hit it off.

"Don't be daft! And besides, you can't talk. *You're* getting on very well indeed with Detective Hammond, if I'm not mistaken."

"Hmm," agreed Aileen, "he's a bit of a dish, isn't he? Six foot two, eyes of blue and gorgeous chestnut hair and you know how I like manly men? And Cassie, you know something else? He's got a hairy chest! What more could a girl want?" Aileen giggled. She was ever so slightly tipsy.

"How do you know that?" Cassie laughed.

"Well, he took off his tie and opened his top two shirt buttons and I could see a gorgeous dark shadow of brown hair. Oooh, I can't wait to get my hands on it. Who would have thought that Ian Murray would have such good-looking friends? Come on, let's get back, in case Noreen Varling and her band of admirers snaffle them."

"There you are!" a familiar voice said above Cassie's left ear and she looked up to see Andrew Lawson, Judy's boyfriend, smiling down at her. "Would you care to dance?"

"Sure," smiled Cassie. "Where's Judy?"

"She wasn't feeling too good—a stomach bug—so I got a taxi for her and sent her home."

"I would have brought her," Cassie said in dismay.

Judy had been awfully quiet in herself today and a bit pale-looking.

"She didn't want to make a fuss and spoil the wedding. She'll be fine, honestly. It's probably a twenty-four-hour flu."

"She should have told me all the same," Cassie frowned.

"She'll be fine," Andrew assured her as he put his arms around her and started to dance. "You look terrific today. Living in London obviously suits you." He smiled down at her.

"Thank you," Cassie said lightly. There was no doubt about it, Andrew Lawson was a very charming man. He had all the social graces and was very successful to boot. Judy was crazy about him.

He guided her skilfully around the floor. "Judy tells me you've taken up interior decorating in your spare time."

"That's right. It's something I've always wanted to do, so I've been making the most of my time in London by studying for a diploma," Cassie smiled.

"Maybe you could do something with the penthouse some time you're home," Andrew suggested. "It's about time I had it redecorated."

"Well, I could come and have a look at it certainly," Cassie agreed. She'd been in the penthouse a couple of times and thought it was perfectly fine. The music turned into a slow set and to her surprise, Judy's boyfriend drew her closer. She hadn't really expected this. He was holding her very tightly, intimately, and to her dismay Cassie realised that he was having an erection.

"Andrew, if you don't mind, I'd like to sit this one out," she said coolly. He wasn't drunk or anything like it—not that that would have been an excuse. Anyway, she was damned if she was going to stay dancing with him.

"This is nice. Aren't you enjoying it?" he murmured, nuzzling her ear, his hands sliding down over her hips. "I thought maybe when the wedding was over you and I could get together. You're a very desirable woman, Cassie. I've been watching you all day and I really like what I see. I think we should get to know each other. You like me too, I can tell."

Cassie couldn't believe her ears. "Let go of me, Andrew Lawson!" she snapped. "That is the most despicable thing I've heard in a long time. I hope Judy finishes with you because you certainly don't deserve her. Any man who could make a pass at a friend of his girlfriend is a creep!"

Andrew gave a short laugh. "What a remarkably old-fashioned way of looking at things. You surprise me! You're living in the nineteen-eighties now, you know, not the eighteen-eighties. Judy and I don't feel we have to be imprisoned in our relationship. Both of us are free to do our own thing."

"How convenient for you, Andrew," Cassie said drily. "But if it's all the same to you, I don't want you doing 'your own thing' with me." She turned on her heel and walked away in disgust, leaving him alone on the dance-floor.

What a rat, she thought indignantly. It was quite obvious Andrew Lawson had not the slightest intention of being faithful to Judy and she would be mad to stay with him. Although she was tempted, she decided not to tell Aileen and Laura of what had just occurred. There was no point in ruining their enjoyment of the reception. Besides, Aileen might go for Andrew baldheaded. She had a very hot temper when roused.

The incident spoiled what was left of the evening for

her as she argued with herself about whether or not she should tell Judy. It was a difficult one, really. Judy would be devastated by Andrew's behaviour, as indeed would Cassie if she were in Judy's shoes. If she didn't tell her, she was letting a cad deceive a dear friend. Cassie wondered if Judy had any idea that Andrew chatted up other women. Maybe she did; maybe she just turned a blind eye. It left her in a dilemma. Why did these things always happen to her? She had been minding her own business, enjoying her sister's wedding. Well, blast Andrew Lawson anyway!

"Everything OK? You look as if you'd like to do somebody an injury," Aileen remarked, as Cassie sat down at the table.

"Oh...everything's fine," she lied. "I was just wondering what time Barbara's going to leave. I think Mam and Ian's parents are beginning to wilt. It's after midnight."

"Knowing Barbara, she'll hang on as long as possible," Aileen retorted. She was dying to get the dishy Detective Hammond to herself for a while but she couldn't be ill-mannered and leave before Barbara. Not that she cared a whit about Barbara's feelings but she wouldn't be rude to Mrs Jordan.

"Oh...hold on, I think she's making a move," Cassie noted with satisfaction. By the time Barbara had changed into her going-away outfit and said her goodbyes, Cassie was dead tired, and in the end it was a relief to wave the pair off on their honeymoon to New York. Having accompanied her mother and Aunt Elsie home and made tea for them, it was bliss to go and snuggle down in her childhood bed and forget about Judy and Andrew and everything else and just fall asleep.

❦

Irene lay in bed, wide-eyed, going over all the events of the day. Once the church bit was over, she had enjoyed being a bridesmaid. She had never had so many compliments in her life and her feet were aching from dancing. She had liked some of Ian's detective friends, especially the one Aileen had been with. She liked older men, she decided; they made her feel protected.

What Irene craved more than anything else in the world was security. The thought of being alone and fending for herself filled her with dread and always had. When she left school and went into that dreadful job in the County Council she realised immediately that she was trapped, owned body and soul by the system, from nine until five every single day, five days a week.

It had been a dreadful shock to her, having to sign in at nine each morning and sit under the gimlet eye of her supervisor, typing boring old letters until lunchtime, to have only an hour of freedom and be held at the desk again until five.

When that horrible man in personnel, Timmy O'Dwyer, called her up to his office and told her that her sick-leave record was unsatisfactory and that they were going to stop her increment and postpone making her a permanent and pensionable officer in the Council, she had been almost relieved. Timmy O'Dwyer would have made a great Nazi, with his crew-cut and hard, sneering face. A rude, arrogant bully with absolutely no tact, he was hated by the entire department. Personnel officer, how are you! He hadn't a clue. She was only sorry she hadn't puked there and then, just to show him that she was really sick. Sick of him and the job and terrified even at the prospect of having to work until it was time to collect a pension.

Irene sighed. She couldn't understand the attitude of

her friends and colleagues, who looked upon their careers as a challenge. She felt a bit out of it, really. Did anybody else feel as she did? What Irene wanted was to marry a nice rich man who would look after her and protect her from the big bad world.

How she dreaded getting up for work in the mornings, knowing that if someone didn't marry her she was going to be stuck in her job until she was sixty-five. Just thinking about it made her heart beat faster and her stomach clench with tension. If only she weren't such a scaredy-cat. More than anyone, she admired her sister Cassie, living on her own in London, doing all kinds of courses and not worrying about whether she ever got married. Cassie didn't mind the idea of working at all.

It wasn't exactly that she didn't like *working*. She had enjoyed her part-time job in the boutique in Port Mahon. It was the fact that from nine to five she had no control over her life that depressed her. Her bosses told her what to do and how to do it. Even going to the loo was a big deal. It was this type of control that Irene found so stressful. At least, if she were married, she could stay at home and look after her children and do her work how and when she wanted. She would be her own boss!

She wondered if Barbara and Ian were making love in the honeymoon suite of the International Airport Hotel where they were staying. She had a suspicion that Barbara was not a virgin. Once, when her sister was home for the weekend, she noticed a packet of little white tablets sticking out of her toilet-bag. It had the days of the week marked on it, and Irene surmised that it was a month's supply of the contraceptive pill. She wished she had taken the giant step herself. At least when you had done it once, you would know what to expect and not have to worry about it. After all, she was nineteen, probably the oldest virgin in Port Mahon.

Turning on her side, Irene hugged her old brown teddy. At least she didn't have to go to work the next day. It was such a sweet thought. One of these days, her knight in shining armour would come along and rescue her from her job in the County Council and that little weasel Timmy O'Dwyer. Irene fell asleep composing her letter of resignation.

❧

Martin handed his girlfriend a cup of coffee and sat down beside her on the couch. He was staying the night in her parents' house and he knew he'd be lucky even to get a kiss. When they were in her home, Jean was very circumspect.

"Barbara knows quite a few well-known people, doesn't she?" Jean remarked as she sipped her coffee.

"She meets them through her job, I suppose," Martin yawned. Frankly he thought Barbara's cronies were a pain in the neck but Jean seemed to enjoy their tittle-tattle and gossiping.

"It was a really nice wedding," Jean said wistfully, cuddling up against her boyfriend. Warning bells rang in Martin's ears. Jean had been going on a lot lately about weddings and houses and settling down, and Martin was beginning to get just a bit panicky. He really liked Jean; she was a young lady with a lot of class. He had known that from that first date when he had been trying it on and she told him she was not that sort of girl and to keep his hands to himself. Martin, who was a popular guy with the girls, had not got that type of reaction before and it piqued his interest. And his interest continued to be piqued as Jean stayed very cool in the face of his growing ardour. This woman was getting under

his skin and he was quite enjoying it. But now she had
started going on about weddings and how she looked
forward to settling down some time.

"What's the rush? You're only twenty," he said lightly.
He was just a few months older, and he had no intention
of settling down for years.

"I want to be young to enjoy my children. I want to
create a lovely home. I like the idea of marriage very
much," Jean told him in her breathy whispery voice, as
she smiled into his eyes. Martin had the strangest feeling
that somehow he figured strongly in these plans.
Barbara's wedding had not helped one bit.

Jean tucked her arm in his and gazed wide-eyed at
him with her big Bambi eyes. "If you were getting
married, what kind of wedding would you like?"

"I think I'd like to elope," Martin said hastily, as he
planted a kiss on his girlfriend's cheek and extricated
himself. "I'm really whacked, Jeannie. I think I'll head
on up to bed. See you in the morning." He practically
took flight up the stairs, leaving the petite blonde sitting
alone on the sofa, a pout of dismay on her face.

Upstairs in the guest-bedroom Martin loosened his
tie. He put his hand in his breast pocket and took out a
letter. It was from a company in Baghdad saying that his
application for a job as an electrician had been successful
and wondering when it would be convenient for him to
start work.

The sooner the better, he thought to himself. He
wasn't going to make the same mistake as a mate of his.
His friend had got the job and was all set to go for a two-
year stint, his visa approved and everything, when his
girlfriend of only two months had informed him that
she wouldn't be around when he got back. Because he
was besotted by her, he decided not to go for the time

being. The romance had ended and he had applied again for the job but had been refused a visa. He had eventually gone to work in Germany, but he had really lost the chance to make big money in the Middle East.

Well, Martin wasn't going to make the same mistake. If Jean issued any ultimatums, he wasn't going to let them stop him. He had sounded out Cassie about his plan and she had thought it was a great idea. Cassie was a good old stick, really. She had been very helpful the time he went to London to do the second interview with the oil company. She did a mock interview with him and pressed his recently purchased Louis Copeland suit and sent him off looking very smart indeed. Left to his own devices, Martin preferred jeans and sweatshirts. He'd set his heart on getting that job, and when he got the good news he was so excited that he wanted to tell everybody. But Cassie had asked him not to tell their mother until Barbara's wedding was over, as Nora had enough on her plate to worry about. He had agreed, but the wedding was over now and tomorrow he was going to write to the oil company and tell them he was available immediately. Then he would tell Nora…and Jean.

❧

John cuddled Karen in his arms and smiled at her. She smiled back, almost asleep. They had just had a very sexy time although, at Karen's wishes, she was staying a virgin until her marriage. He really loved this girl so much and the sooner they were married the better, but he knew that financially they were not in a position to marry for the time being. One thing he was sure of. Their wedding was not going to be anything like the wedding he had been at that day. What a waste of his mother's money! It was far from red carpets and Rolls-

Royces they were reared. He knew a wedding was supposed to be a girl's happiest day and finest hour and all that but Barbara had gone a bit overboard—as usual.

Well, he and Karen were going to pay for their own wedding and they had agreed that it was going to be a very small, intimate occasion. They had applied for planning permission to rebuild the farm-labourer's cottage he had bought and he would be doing a lot of the work himself, to save money. They would have to live in a mobile home for the first few months of their marriage, but Karen was quite prepared for it. As long as they were together, she told him, she didn't care. She was totally supportive of all his plans and he knew that he was very lucky to have found her.

It was great that his mother and Cassie liked Karen as well. John knew that Nora had been very pleased by the news of their forthcoming engagement. He had also told Cassie in confidence and she was equally pleased for him. Cassie had looked great today, much better than she had looked for ages—indeed since her split with Robbie. Whatever she did, whether she got married or developed her career or started her own interior design business, which was a dream of hers, he hoped that Cassie would be as happy as he was now. She deserved it.

❦

Cassie opened her eyes with a start. She had been dreaming that she was getting married and that when she got to the top of the aisle the man who had turned to face her was Andrew Lawson. What a nightmare! She stretched luxuriously in her bed. It was pitch dark outside, the only sound the whisper of the breeze in the trees and the rhythmic pounding of the surf against the shoreline. The never-changing sounds of home, so different from the constant noise that she had got used to in London.

Imagine dreaming she was marrying Andrew Lawson! It must have been after the incident at the wedding. God help whoever married that swine. A thought struck her. It hadn't been Robbie at the altar! She had actually dreamt about another man. A first since her break-up with her fiancé. The thought cheered her considerably, even if it *had* been Casanova Lawson.

Cassie had been quite proud of herself at the wedding. She had got through the whole day without once thinking of Robbie. That was a real step forward because she had actually felt apprehensive about how she would feel at the wedding ceremony, wondering if her thoughts would turn to what might have been if she had married him. Thanks to Laura and Aileen, she had a much jollier time than she expected and for the first time she felt free of her past. It was a good feeling, she decided, as she turned over and began to drift into sleep. At least she wouldn't have to worry about attending weddings any longer—she knew she could cope with them. From the way things were going in the family, she'd be attending another one in the not too distant future.

❦

Robbie MacDonald was feeling very sorry for himself. Today he had seen Cassie and he knew without a doubt that he was still crazy about her. He had dated a few women since their split but none of them had understood him the way she did.

He had heard on the grapevine at work that Cassie was back in town. He'd known Barbara was engaged to be married; he'd read it in the social and personal column in *The Irish Times*. Typical of Barbara to tell the whole world about it. When he'd heard Cassie was home, he guessed it must be for the wedding.

It had been simple enough to find out where the wedding was being held. Barbara had been giving boastful briefings in her newspaper column about the arrangements for what she called "one of the social events of the year" and he had purchased *The Irish Mail* every day once he knew of his ex-fiancée's return.

That morning he simply went to the hotel and sat in a secluded corner of the lounge. As luck would have it, his seat had a view of the entrance to the hotel and the grounds where some of the wedding photographs were being taken.

When he'd seen Cassie he felt as though he'd been hit by a tank. She looked sensational, a real knock-out in that royal-blue dress and the black high heels that made her legs look even longer and sexier. She'd done something different to her hair. It was longer, glossier, and it really suited her. He couldn't believe how well she looked, laughing and joking with Aileen and Laura. Robbie had cherished the hope that Cassie might look miserable and unhappy, a hope that was now shattered.

He was sorely tempted to go up to Cassie but somehow he didn't think she would be too welcoming. No, he had a much better idea, a foolproof plan to get them back together. Come Monday morning, he was going to set in motion the train of events that would make his dream come true, the dream of making Cassie Jordan Mrs Robbie MacDonald.

CHAPTER THIRTY-THREE

"He's what!!" Cassie exclaimed, aghast.

"He's taking over from Brian Mooney in Corporate Finance, UK," Miranda Dillon said calmly.

It was a Monday morning, four months after Barbara's wedding, and Cassie had just come back from Port Mahon after attending her Aunt Elsie's funeral. She was shocked to hear that Robbie had applied for a position in Allied Isles' UK headquarters and that in less than four weeks he would be there in that very building just three offices down the corridor from where she was now sitting.

It was bad enough having to leave after the funeral, which had been most upsetting for Nora, and also hearing the disturbing news that Judy was pregnant and planning to marry Andrew Lawson. But to come back to this! She felt anger ignite in her. How mean of Robbie. Just when she was starting to get herself on an even keel again, he was coming to London to work in the same place as her. A thought struck her.

"Where's Brian going?" she asked Miranda, as she poured herself a cup of coffee before starting to deal with the mountain of computer print-outs on her desk.

"He's transferring to Jersey, lucky bugger. You know, Jersey is crawling with millionaires. Why couldn't they send *me* there?"

"Will Robbie be getting Brian's flat?" Cassie asked grimly.

"Oh I'd say so, Cassie. He's assured of it if he wants it. His grade entitles him to that."

Oh God, why are you picking on me, Cassie not for the first time rebuked the Almighty. If Robbie were taking over Brian Mooney's flat, not only would he be working in the same building as her, he would also be living on the landing above her in Holland Park Avenue. Robbie MacDonald was going to be back in her life on a business level if nothing else, and there was nothing she could do about it. "Oh yes, there is!" she muttered determinedly as she dialled the personnel department in head office.

❧

Three weeks later, Cassie was installed behind her new desk at her new job in the Customer Services Department at Allied Isles' main Liverpool branch. Sitting in her sixth-floor office, gazing out at the famous Albert Dock on one side, the Royal Liver Buildings, that great Liverpool landmark, on the other, and the river Mersey straight ahead of her, she almost had to pinch herself to make sure she wasn't dreaming. Everything had happened so fast that it was unreal.

Cassie had spoken to the personnel manager and explained that because of her broken engagement to Robbie she would prefer not to be working with him and that she was wondering if she could have a transfer. The personnel manager was most understanding and told Cassie she would see what she could do. Two days later she phoned Cassie to say she could have a transfer to Customer Services in Liverpool or to their Financial Services Department in Cork.

Cassie had chosen Liverpool mainly because she wanted to continue studying and working at interior design. Having secured her diploma just a couple of months previously, she felt there was more scope in the UK. Cassie also knew that, despite the fact that the Irish Sea separated her from her mother, it actually took her only an hour and a half to fly home and drive to Port Mahon, whereas if she transferred to Cork, it would mean a four-hour drive or train journey. Besides, she had never worked in Customer Services before and she thought she might like it.

The more she concentrated on her interior design, the less ambitious she was becoming at her job in the bank and this worried her. A new job in a new department might be the kick-start she needed to get back on her career track again.

It was the most impulsive thing Cassie had ever done in her life and what a big change she was setting in motion. New job! New city! New place to live! Maybe she was a fool for running away and letting Robbie disrupt her life completely. Lots of people would see it that way but Cassie had decided that she just wasn't prepared to cope with Robbie in her life again. Besides, she felt she needed the shake-up. She had a nice cocooned life in London and it would be very easy to meander along like that for another few years. Her move to Liverpool would be sure to benefit her in some way.

Hadn't Aileen felt the very same just recently? She had begun to get restless, telling Cassie she was fed up massaging the double chins of the rich old trout who came religiously to the salon once and sometimes twice a week to have their facials, their manicures and pedicures and the like. A friend of hers who worked as a continuity girl for a film company had told Aileen that there was a vacancy coming up in the make-up department shortly and urged her to apply. Aileen jumped at the idea and did a dazzling interview, emphasising that she had had lots of dealings with showbiz personalities in the Mayfair salon and that she was well able to cope with temperamental prima donnas if the need arose. She was also a very good make-up artist and was most interested in learning about special-effects techniques, something usually mastered on the job.

Who could resist Aileen when she was at her bubbly best? She had got the job, handed in her resignation to a most disgruntled Madame Lefeur, and a week later she was on location in Cairo! She was ecstatic. This was the break she had been waiting for and she knew she was going to love the life.

Cassie had been delighted for her friend. It really was the perfect career for Aileen, travelling the world, meeting people, using her artistry. Just as she had discovered a whole new lease of life when she had released her creative talents with her interior designing, so too would Aileen.

But she'd miss her around, miss their lunches and their shopping jaunts. Aileen was still using her aunt's place in Stanley Avenue as a base. She would often be working in London, especially when films were being shot at the studios, but she would be doing a lot of jetting around and they certainly wouldn't be seeing as much of each other as they were used to.

So Cassie left London without any huge sense of regret. After almost three years of living there the glitz and excitement had worn a little thin for her. Tubing had long since lost its thrill. She had seen all the sights, gone to the hot nightspots with Aileen, and the constant noise and traffic and fast pace of life had begun to pall. In Liverpool, she'd be less than an hour's journey from the sea, which would be a big plus. And she had heard that the Wirral was a lovely place. When she told people at work that she was going to Liverpool, they all assured her that she would love it. If she had not finished her interior design diploma she would not have considered leaving the capital, but now fresh pastures beckoned and Cassie began to look forward to the change with optimism.

❦

Almost from the moment the train slowed to a halt at Lime Street station and Cassie emerged on to the street, she felt positive about her move. A lovely taxi driver with his distinctive Scouse accent unburdened her of her luggage and said, "Welcome to Liverpool, luv. Where to?" This was her first taste of the famed Liverpudlian friendliness and warmth; she knew she had done the right thing and that she was going to like Liverpool. The bank had arranged for her to stay in a guest-house until she found accommodation, so she gave him that address. Friends of hers in London had offered to store her possessions until she got a place of her own. Two weeks later, Cassie had a flat off Chaloner Street opposite the Queen's Dock, fifteen minutes' cycle from her office. She had her belongings freighted up by train and once she had arranged them in the flat, she felt more settled.

She had no idea what Robbie had felt when he arrived in London to discover that she was no longer there. All she knew was that she was glad she had made the move.

Customer Services was a much more people-orientated job than her previous work with computers, and Cassie enjoyed it. The other people in the office were extremely friendly and helpful and before long she had completely settled in. She became particularly friendly with two of her colleagues, Pauline and Ann, who shared a house in West Kirby on the Wirral peninsula. They invited her out to stay with them one weekend and she thought it was *such* a scenic place. Their lovely redbrick town house was only minutes from the sea and on the Saturday morning after a scrumptious breakfast the three of them had gone for a long walk down by the sea-front. It was a windy November day but the sun was shining and the

skies were blue and as the breeze whipped her hair around
her face, Cassie sniffed the fresh salty air appreciatively
and thought what a nice place it would be to live. Coming
over to West Kirby on the train, she was quite surprised
at how rural the peninsula was, once they went under
the Mersey tunnel and left the suburbs. It was an eye-
opener and the journey had been only half an hour. She
began to think about moving out of the city to live on
the coast. New Brighton and Wallasey were other picturesque spots that she liked. After Christmas, she decided,
she would start looking for accommodation by the sea.

Pauline and Ann had driven her to Chester that
afternoon and Cassie really fell in love with the
magnificent old city. This was a place she was going to
have fun exploring at the weekends, especially the
antique and bric-à-brac shops. That night the girls took
her to a restaurant in West Kirby called What's Cooking
and they had a superb meal, which Cassie insisted on
paying for. They both had been hospitable to her and
had helped her settle in quickly at work.

Pauline was blonde, bubbly and vivacious, reminding
Cassie somewhat of Aileen, while Ann was dark-haired,
elegant and had an air of serenity that was in complete
contrast to her flatmate. Both of them were in their late
twenties like Cassie and, like her, the girls were moving
up the career ladder with Allied Isles so they had a lot in
common. The atmosphere in the office was jolly and
relaxed, in contrast to the rather brisk, efficient air she
had been used to in the London office. But then, for
customer services, a jolly, relaxed atmosphere was just
what was needed!

The week before she was due to fly home for Christmas
Cassie clattered down the steps of the office block with
the intention of heading to George Henry Lees, the superb

department store that was a landmark in Liverpool and only a few minutes from Lime Street station. She still had a few Christmas presents to buy and she had seen a few nice things there that would suit her purposes admirably. Liverpool was crowded with Christmas shoppers over from Dublin and during the week when she went shopping in her lunch-hour she felt she might as well be at home in Henry Street there were so many familiar accents from all sides. Special shopping trips were organised by the car-ferries and hotels and doing the Christmas shopping in Liverpool was an annual event for a lot of Irish people, and much looked forward to by the shop and hotel owners. Barbara had been terribly disgusted that Cassie had moved from London. Shopping in Liverpool definitely hadn't the social clout of shopping in the capital. Barbara was not inclined to visit her sister in Liverpool, and Cassie was just as glad.

As she reached the bottom of the steps, a man stepped in her path and Cassie came to a halt. "Hello, Cassie," a familiar, heart-stopping voice said, and Cassie got the shock of her life as she stared up at Robbie.

"What are you doing here?" she gasped, stunned.

"I came to see you," Robbie smiled down at her. "You shouldn't have left London and run away. Surely you don't hate me that much."

"I didn't run away!" Cassie retorted, stung by his accusation. "And I don't hate you," she added wearily. "I just want to be in control of my life and I never was with you."

"Cassie, I'll make it up to you, I promise. I'm really sorry for the way I've treated you. I'm off the drink for good this time," he said eagerly, grasping her by the arm. Under the streetlight, Cassie noticed that he had aged since she had last seen him; his hair and beard were lightly flecked with grey and the lines around his eyes had deepened. Her heart softened and for a moment she was tempted to put her arms around him. Robbie was like a little boy, really. He thought by saying he was sorry that he would make it up to her and wipe the slate clean. How many times had he said those words to her? It dawned on Cassie that Robbie really had no conception of the grief and pain he had put her through.

"Robbie, I'm very glad that you've stopped drinking and I'm delighted you've got the job in London. It's a great career move and I hope you do well out of it. But it's over between us and nothing is going to change that!" she said quietly, firmly.

"But, Cassie, I came over to London to be with you. To show you I've changed. I couldn't believe it when they told me you'd been transferred here!" Robbie protested.

"I asked for the transfer when I heard you were coming, Robbie. I didn't want you in my life again," Cassie said bluntly as she struggled to suppress the shock and anger his surprise visit was causing her.

"I never realised you were so hard, Cassie."

"That was something I learnt from my time with you, Robbie,' Cassie retorted bitterly. "It's called self-preservation!"

"You're telling me it's over then, definitely over?" Robbie said slowly.

Cassie drew a deep breath. "Yes, Robbie, it's over. I'll always remember the good times and try and forget the bad. I suggest you do the same." She started to walk away.

"Couldn't we at least have dinner together or something," Robbie urged. "I've travelled all the way from London to see you."

"Where are you staying?"

"Well, I was hoping I could stay with you," Robbie said wryly.

"I'm sorry, Robbie, that's out of the question! Look, here's the name and address of a good guest-house." She scrabbled in her bag for a pen and paper. "Give me an hour and a half and I'll meet you there and we can go and have a bite to eat."

"OK," Robbie agreed glumly, taking the piece of paper from her. He couldn't get over Cassie. She was so decisive and sure of herself and *much* more independent than when she had been with him. For the first time since they split, Robbie began to face the fact that Cassie was serious about wanting him out of her life. It was a thought that could put a man back on the beer! He hailed a taxi and Cassie watched him go.

Maybe she shouldn't have agreed to have dinner with him, but it was the civilised thing to do. After all, it was better to part as friends. God, she had got a shock to see him standing there. He didn't play very fair, though, she reflected, as she marched along towards the city centre. She had decided to walk instead of getting a bus, as she needed to clear her head.

It was the strangest thing. She *had* run away by leaving London; deep down she acknowledged that. But, after facing Robbie five minutes before, Cassie knew she would never again have to run away from Robbie or her own feelings. When she said it was over, she had finally known it herself. Finally accepted it without pain. Looking at the man she had once loved and been passionately intimate with, her strongest feeling was one of pity. It shocked her, but it liberated her. At long long last, Cassie was free of her past. It was a turning-point in her life.

CHAPTER THIRTY-FOUR

Two years later Cassie had bought a house in West Kirby and was inundated with commissions for her interior design skills. She was part of a great social scene at work, engaging in lots of sports, including windsurfing, which she had taken up when she moved out to the peninsula. She was also pursuing a course in fine arts one night a week. She was having the time of her life. Moving to Liverpool was the best thing she had ever done, and she had been told by her superiors that she was in line for promotion.

Buying the house in West Kirby was a very positive step that had really enhanced the quality of her life. It happened almost by chance the spring after her encounter with Robbie. Ann had mentioned that the house next door to her was up for sale and she was wondering who would buy it and what their new neighbours would be like.

"I wonder how much it will go for?" said Cassie. The sum that Ann mentioned was not outrageous. In fact with the special low-interest mortgage from the bank that was available to all employees and the few thousand pounds that Aunt Elsie had left to Cassie in her will, it was quite within her range.

She had heard about Elsie's bequest only when she went home the Christmas after Barbara's wedding. Her aunt was a shrewd woman and had played the stock-exchange with no small success. She had left each of her nieces and nephews three thousand pounds, and a larger sum to her sister Nora. Her house and its contents were to be sold and the proceeds to go to the church. Barbara had been disgusted at that and urged Nora to contest the will, but Nora had sent her daughter off with a flea in her ear. The rest of them were all delighted with their windfalls, and because of Aunt Elsie's generosity, Cassie felt that the time had finally arrived to become a woman of property.

With Pauline and Ann egging her on, Cassie made an appointment to view. The house had exactly the same layout as theirs. A small entrance hall opened into a living-room, off which was a good-sized fitted kitchen. Upstairs there were two bedrooms and a bathroom. It was an ideal size and Cassie couldn't help getting excited. The thought of redecorating it to her own taste was exhilarating. A whole house to work on. What a treat for an interior designer! It was the garden that clinched it for Cassie: a long, shrub-filled lush-lawned oasis that reminded her of the garden she had shared with Aileen and Laura so long ago in Ranelagh.

"Buy it! Buy it!" the other pair urged. "And then it won't matter if our parties get a bit noisy because *you'll* be at them."

If she bought it, of course, it would mean she had to commute. But that would be a small price to pay, and besides, the train journey from West Kirby to Liverpool was little more than half an hour, through very picturesque countryside. And the big big plus was that she would be living only minutes away from the sea and she could walk along the prom and down by the Marine Lake daily if she wanted.

Cassie put in her offer with enthusiasm and endured a few nail-biting days before hearing that it had been accepted. From then on it was all systems go. A Cassie house-moving weekend was organised by her friends at work, and before she knew it, she had been shifted lock, stock and barrel from her little flat in Liverpool to her spacious new home. She wasn't sorry to leave the flat. It was not as comfortable as her London one and, although she had done her best with it, it had been faintly musty and too old for her to effect much improvement.

Sitting on the stairs of her new home with half a dozen friends and colleagues, munching pizza and drinking wine, Cassie couldn't keep the grin off her face. This was an achievement to be proud of. Her own place at last. It gave her *such* a sense of satisfaction. She wasn't even thirty yet and she had got a mortgage on her own. Independence tasted very sweet. Barbara, from her smug eyrie of marriage, was always dropping barbed little remarks about spinsterhood and being left on the shelf. But Cassie was undisturbed. If she *were* to die unwed she would do so happily, rather than marry a lazy lout like Ian Murray. As far as she was concerned she couldn't be happier with her life at the moment. She had everything going for her: a good career, a great social life, her independence and her beloved interior design. For the first time in her life she was doing what she wanted, without having to worry about anybody else. She could come and go as she pleased; she had no commitments to anybody. It was the best of times. There would never again be a year like 1984.

Nora had been delighted for her. Cassie went home for John's wedding the summer she bought the house and, knowing how stuck for money John and Karen were, and that they had not planned a honeymoon for the time being, she gave them the keys of her house, told them to get the ferry to Liverpool and stay there for a week. She spent the time with Nora, giving the house a good clean-out for her mother, who wasn't able to look after the place as well as before.

Honestly, thought Cassie, as she hung the fireside

rugs on the line and whacked the dust out of them, Irene was absolutely hopeless around the place. The idea of giving the rugs a beating or hoovering the cobwebs from behind the wardrobes would never dawn on her. Her latest notion was that she wanted to resign and use Elsie's bequest to go to the USA, where their wealthy cousin Dorothy lived. Because it was what her baby wanted, Nora thought she should do it, even though it would mean that she was finally alone in the house.

"And what happens when she runs out of money?" Cassie enquired of her mother when she heard this news.

"Don't be like that, Cassie. Let her do her own thing. After all, you did yours and the rest of them have done theirs!" retorted Nora.

"True!" agreed Cassie and said no more. Irene was a big girl now. Let her run her own life.

Barbara was six months pregnant, much to her chagrin. Everyone had been surprised to hear about it. It didn't go with the image of a diarist, as she preferred to call herself, because it had a much more up-market ring than "gossip columnist." Having a baby would certainly clip Barbara's social wings.

Judy, who was now the wife of Andrew Lawson and the mother of a baby boy, seemed to be settling into her role as mother and chic wife to the wealthy Andrew. She confided in Cassie that she was sure that Andrew would dump her when he found out she was pregnant, but he had been delighted and when she had a baby boy he was over the moon. He wanted plenty of sons, Judy said drily, but what he wanted and what he got were two different things and one pregnancy was enough to endure for the moment. Her mother was still not speaking to her!

Laura and Doug were working day and night, but

Doug's business was expanding all the time and Laura was getting her teeth into some meaty business at work. She had been given more responsibility in the property section of the firm and was actually closing deals.

Martin came home from Iraq for John's wedding and Cassie had never seen her brother look so well. He was tanned and healthy-looking and making money hand over fist, he confided. He was going to renew his contract for another term and then come home and set up on his own. She was very pleased for him. Martin had always felt a bit guilty that he wasn't interested in the market-gardening the way John was, so it was nice to see him doing his own thing. It was a bit of a surprise when he invited Jean Allen to the wedding. Cassie had thought that romance was all over when he went to Iraq.

It was nice to get home for the week, but she was glad to be going back to her own house. She had a lot to do with the place and she was anxious to continue her decorating.

When Ann's and Pauline's landlady, Winnie, saw Cassie's redecorated house, she was so impressed she asked her to do her sitting-room and bedroom. Then a friend of Winnie's had asked her to do a job on her child's nursery and it just seemed to go on from there. There was never a time when Cassie was not doing a designing and decorating job for somebody and she was in her element. Once or twice, things didn't work out quite as well as she hoped. She remembered with a shudder a lilac bathroom that she had to redo completely. But on the whole, Cassie was very satisfied with the way her life was going and with all that she had achieved.

❦

Nora was driving herself up the walls! She knew she had BiSoDol indigestion tablets somewhere but she was damned if she could remember where she had put them, and her indigestion was getting worse. She just couldn't shift it. She had tried bread soda, Andrew's Liver Salts, everything. It was most annoying. She had planned to make her Christmas cakes this evening. After all, it was the beginning of November and she'd want to be getting a move on. This was going to be a special Christmas. Irene's last one at home and the first for her brand new grandchild. Barbara's baby was a little beauty and Nora was thrilled with her. She just wished Barbara would visit with her more often. Nora had been a bit shocked to hear that Barbara had no intention of giving up her job to look after the baby. Even Judy O'Shaughnessy, who had not become a mother in the most desirable of circumstances, had stayed at home to rear her child. Not so Barbara. She was going to pay a woman to come in and clean her apartment and take care of her daughter.

Nora thought it was a terrible state of affairs. To have another woman coming in to your house to do your cleaning and rear your child was in her eyes a sign that you had completely failed in your role as a woman. In her day a woman was expected to keep the home running smoothly and raise the children to the best of her ability and leave the man to bring in the money. All this modern stuff was not working. One had only to look at the broken homes, the violence of society, the lack of respect of young people towards their elders to see that something was very wrong. If Barbara called her old-fashioned for her ideas, she didn't care. Nora knew she was right. She'd like to have seen Jack's face if she had announced she was off out to get a job. Maybe she was odd, but she had never felt she was in any way inferior by staying at home to take care of the domestic side of things. Nora had always taken great pride in keeping her house spick-and-span, in cooking tasty meals for the family, and in watching her children grow up happy and healthy. She had her charity work and community involvement and ladies' club to stimulate her and she never felt deprived because she had not had a career outside the home.

Of course, Barbara had never been the most domestic of girls, Nora had to admit. Now she was going so far as brazenly writing in her column that a "housewife" she would never be! In Nora's eyes this was nothing to brag about.

Irene would love to be a housewife. She'd love to be married and have children of her own and not have to go out to work. Maybe on this trip to the USA, she'd find a nice man and settle down. Nora dearly hoped so. She would like to see her youngest daughter taken care of.

For Cassie she had no fears. Cassie would cope with anything that came her way, although it would be nice to see her married. She was thirty next year, getting on a bit, especially if she wanted to have children. But you couldn't rush these things. If they happened they happened and since Robbie Cassie showed no signs of wanting to settle down with anybody.

God, she wished this pain would go away. Her chest was getting very tight, as if there were a heavy band around it. She was definitely never eating brown bread and bananas again, after this dose of indigestion. Nora sat down in Jack's chair. Irene would be in soon. She'd get her to go to the chemist and buy some antacid tablets. In the meantime she'd just sit down for a while and rest. Time enough to do the Christmas cakes later. All of a sudden the pain got worse. With a little gasp, Nora slumped over in her chair just as Irene put her key in the front door.

CHAPTER THIRTY-FIVE

"When did she have it?" After hearing the news John had just told her on the telephone, Cassie was shocked and terribly anxious about her mother.

"Calm down now, Cassie," John said reassuringly. "She had a *mild* heart attack earlier this evening. She's in hospital and she's under observation."

"I'll get the first flight home I can. It will probably be tomorrow, though."

"Look, don't be worrying, Cassie. She's sedated now, asleep a lot of the time, so even if you were here she wouldn't be very aware of it. Ring me tomorrow and tell me what time your flight gets in. Karen or I will collect you from the airport."

"I'll see you tomorrow, then," Cassie said, hanging up the phone. Her poor mother. Nora had never been in hospital in her life, not even to have her babies. She had all her children at home. She'd hate it!

Nora looked very pale and grey when Cassie finally arrived at the hospital, but her eyes lit up when she saw Cassie and she gave her daughter's hand a squeeze. "There was no need for you to come home, pet. It was just a bad attack of indigestion. I'll be fine. There's no need for me to be in this place at all. Tell them I want to go home."

"Now, Mam, just do what the doctors tell you," Cassie warned her mother. The doctors confirmed that Nora had suffered a heart attack and that she would have to lose weight and take more exercise. Cassie knew Nora was going to find the former very difficult. Her mother had a terrible sweet tooth and was always baking tarts, scones and cream sponges, most of which she ended up eating because Irene and she were the only ones at home.

She was hospitalised for eight days and Cassie took three weeks' special leave to be with her but she felt that Nora would need a little more time to recuperate. Irene was all for resigning her job and looking after her mother, but the heart specialist was horrified when he heard this plan.

"Your mother will make an excellent recovery as there was very little damage to the heart muscles. Resigning is much too drastic a step to take," he said firmly to Cassie. "Tell your sister to take some leave for a fortnight or so, that's all she'll need. I insist you don't treat your mother like an invalid because she *isn't* one. She's responding very well to treatment."

"I can't take leave," wailed Irene. "I haven't got any holidays left, and if I take any more sick-leave I'll end up on half-pay. Why can't I just resign and go on the dole? I'll be going to America in the spring, anyway."

"Look, Irene, if Mam thought you'd resigned the job because of her she'd be awfully upset. I really think you should hang on!" Cassie said firmly.

"Well, I think it's a good idea," interjected Barbara, who was party to the conversation. "*I* certainly can't look after her. I've got my hands full with the baby."

"Nobody is asking you to, Barbara," Cassie said shortly, irked by her sister's attitude. Honestly, you'd think she was being asked to make a huge sacrifice.

"Well, Karen has offered to come in every day for a few hours and cook Mam's dinner. We'd have her to stay with us if that were possible but I don't think the mobile would be such a great place in the winter," John said. "She's begged me not to let her be sent to a nursing home. She really hates hospitals, God love her."

"I can't take any more unpaid leave," said Cassie. "I've got a mortgage to pay at the end of the month. I wonder would Mam come and stay with me for a while?"

"Perfect idea!" Barbara said with satisfaction and Cassie couldn't help but be amused. Her sister's selfishness was mind-boggling.

"I don't want to be a nuisance to you, pet. Sure I'll be fine at home," Nora exclaimed when she heard Cassie's proposal.

"Ah come on, Mam, we'll have a bit of crack and you've never seen the house. I know you'll love it," Cassie wheedled.

"And what about Christmas? I haven't a thing done. And what about Irene? She can't stay here on her own."

"For goodness sake, Mam, Irene's not a baby. She's a grown woman. And don't worry about Christmas! You can spend Christmas with me and Irene can fly over when she gets her holidays," Cassie said firmly. "Please, Mam, I'd love to have you."

"All right then, Cassie, as long as I won't be putting you out!" Nora agreed.

Nora loved Cassie's house and her guest-bedroom decorated in restful greens and cheerful Laura Ashley prints. Nora thought the matching curtains and bedspread so very fetching that Cassie told her that for her Christmas present, she'd buy her a set for her own room in Port Mahon.

Mindful of the doctor's advice, Cassie kept a sharp eye on her mother's diet and cooked only the healthiest of meals, although as a treat she took her to What's Cooking once a week and let her have a gooey dessert. Once Nora got back on her feet, they went walking along the prom every evening unless it were raining. Cassie felt a huge sense of satisfaction as she saw the colour return to her mother's cheeks. Every day before she went to work, she gave Nora her breakfast in bed and brought her a daily paper. She left a light lunch prepared for her in the fridge, and then when she came home, she cooked dinner. At the weekend she drove her mother all around the Wirral and brought her to Chester, Birkenhead and Liverpool to do her Christmas shopping.

Although her social life was dramatically curtailed, Cassie did not begrudge the time spent with her mother. She liked giving her little treats, Nora was so appreciative of everything Cassie did for her and it was nice showing her around the places that she had grown to love. Nora enjoyed going down Banks Road to do a bit of shopping. There was a hardware store there that she loved browsing in. Then she would go down into West Kirby itself and into the bookshop by the station or over to Boots or to the flowershops. Cassie was glad she had started going out on her own. Her mother had got terribly nervous as she got older and she was petrified she was going to get lost. Cassie had photocopied a map from the Wirral A-Z atlas and marked Nora's route in red biro for her and that had eased her mother's fears somewhat.

One evening Cassie arrived home from work to find a terrible smell of burning. Nora was out in the kitchen, almost in tears.

"I'm awfully sorry, Cassie. I put on a stew for the dinner and I forgot all about it. I'm afraid the saucepan's burnt."

"Don't worry about it, Mam!" laughed Cassie. "I'm always doing the same thing myself."

"I wanted to have a nice dinner ready for you as a treat," Nora said in disgust.

"Ah come on, we'll go out on the town," Cassie decided cheerfully, giving her woebegone mother a hug.

Christmas came and went. Nora was delighted to see Irene and the three of them had a jolly little Christmas together but she was sad watching her daughter leave to go home. She told Cassie that she felt much better and that she missed Port Mahon and wanted to go home soon. Cassie persuaded her to stay until January was over but she could see that Nora was fine again and she was fretting and looking forward to going back.

The night before she left, as they sat watching *News at Ten,* Nora turned to her daughter. "Cassie, you've been very good to me recently and always have been, and I'll never forget you for it." She leant over and gave Cassie a hug.

Cassie hugged her back. "Don't mention it, Mam. It was nothing!"

"Oh it was, dear. I know you've not been able to do the things you would usually do because of me. But, Cassie, I was so glad to get out of that hospital and I dreaded the thought of going to a nursing home. Those places put the fear of God in me," Nora confided. "I hope to God I never have to have any truck with them again. All those tubes and machines and things. I was afraid of my life." She seemed to get very agitated at the memory. Taking her daughter's hand she stared at Cassie. "Promise me, Cassie, if anything ever happens to me you'll never put me in one of those nursing-home places. I want to die in my own bed."

"You're not going to die, for heaven's sake, Mam," Cassie laughed.

"Please, Cassie, promise me," Nora urged her daughter.

"Of course, I promise, Mam. Now would you not be worrying about things like that!" Cassie said gently.

"It's something we all have to face some time, pet," Nora sighed.

"I know, Mam, but don't be worrying about it. You're

not going to end up anywhere you don't want to be,"
Cassie reassured her.

Nora smiled at Cassie. "You're the best daughter a
mother could have, and these past two months you've
done more than than anybody has a right to expect."

Cassie looked at the white-haired woman at her side.
The heart attack had taken its toll and she looked her
age, although she seemed far better than she had done
two months before. Cassie realised with a sharp sense of
shock that her mother was getting old. It was a dismal
thought and she banished it quickly from her mind.
Leaning over, she held Nora close. "Mam, it was a pleasure
to have you here and you're very welcome to anything
I did for you because I love you very much."

"And I love you, dear," Nora said, with a smile of
pleasure.

❦

It was great to be home, Nora smiled to herself, turning
her face up to the watery light of an early February sun.
It had been a mild winter and already the crocuses were
beginning to burst out of the ground and, if she weren't
very much mistaken, the buds were beginning to appear
on the cherry-blossom trees.

Today she was going to perform a very important
task. She had been thinking about it lately, since those
funny little episodes began. She'd been having them for
a long time now and it was very frustrating. Something
was not quite right; she couldn't put her finger on it, but
she just *knew*. The heart attack hadn't helped either. But
it *had* helped her make up her mind about what she was
going to do, and the sooner she did it the better. Although
she loved all her children, and Irene, her baby, a little bit
more than the others, Nora knew that it was Cassie she

would always turn to in her hour of need. She realised that it wasn't very fair always to expect Cassie to come to her aid but, in all honesty, she knew she couldn't turn to Barbara. It pained her to admit it but her second youngest daughter had a woeful self-centred streak that had *not* disappeared as she had got older.

As for Irene, poor lovey, she just wasn't able for hassle. She had gone into hysterics when Nora had the heart attack and the doctor had to give her something to calm her down. Irene would always fall to pieces in a crisis.

No, it was Cassie who would cope as always and that was why Nora was taking the step she was taking. She had put on her best suit, the one Cassie had bought her in Liverpool. She went out the gate and headed up the town.

❦

Cassie sat beside her mother at midnight Mass. It was Easter and the Easter Vigil was drawing to a close. Nora had always loved the Easter Vigil but this year she was uncharacteristically down in herself. In fact Cassie was quite worried about her. She seemed almost to be in a world of her own and was very absent-minded. In spite of her brave words, she had taken Irene's going very badly. Irene had left for Washington the day after Saint Patrick's Day and her mother was missing her sorely.

Cassie didn't seem to be able to cheer her mother up at all. Nora hadn't even noticed that she had given the house a hell of a spring-cleaning, something that was badly needed. She had never known her mother to be sloppy about her housekeeping, but under the sink in the bathroom and the pipes behind the toilet-bowl were in need of a good clean. And so was the fridge; in fact there was a smell from it, and on further investigation Cassie had discovered two sausages that were green. And what was her mother doing buying all those teabags? She had half a dozen boxes in the cupboard. When Cassie asked her about it, Nora had stared at her blankly. "What teabags are you talking about, pet? I don't remember buying any."

"Mam, I was just thinking, why don't you get someone in for a few hours a week to help you look after the house. It's a big place to be looking after by yourself now that everybody is gone and I'm sure you could afford it!" Cassie suggested, as they walked home underneath the starry sky after midnight Mass.

"I can do my own housework, Miss, thank you very much!" bristled Nora.

"It was only a suggestion, Mam," Cassie said mildly as they went into the kitchen.

"Well, you can keep suggestions like that to yourself. Who do you think I am? *Barbara!*" Nora retorted tartly with a touch of her old spirit, as, chuckling, she made a pot of tea for them.

By the time Cassie was leaving, Nora was more like her old self but Cassie worried about her although she knew John and Karen called in every day without fail.

In the meantime, she was looking forward to Laura coming over to her for a weekend in the early summer. Aileen, who expected to be back in London for a while, was going to come and join them in the Wirral. Aileen had stayed with her a few times and they had had some great laughs but with Laura coming over to join them it would be perfect, just like old times.

❦

On the Friday evening of Laura's arrival, Cassie drove out to Liverpool airport to collect her friend. The weather was gorgeous and expected to remain so. There was going to be some serious sunbathing done and some mega-serious gossiping! Cassie couldn't wait. And then, the most exciting thing had happened at work that day, and it was so fitting that the girls would be the first to know about it.

"Oh Cassie! Cassie! Cassie! Isn't this great?" Laura was giddy with delight and anticipation as she hugged Cassie in the arrivals hall. "What time is Lady Muck arriving?"

Cassie grinned, hugging her back. "In about an hour and a half's time. We'll drive directly to Lime Street to pick her up; it will save her having to change trains to get to West Kirby."

"I'm dying to see her!" exclaimed Laura, who was looking bandbox-fresh after her flight.

"Me too," said Cassie as she led the way out of the airport to where her car was parked. They hardly drew breath on the trip into Liverpool and when Aileen's train arrived and she saw her two best friends waiting for her she gave a shriek of delight. There was a flurry of hugs and kisses before they left the station and drove under the Mersey towards West Kirby.

"Do you want to go out on the town, or what?" Cassie asked as they got near home. Aileen and Laura shook their heads.

"I've got a litre bottle of Bacardi from the duty-free!" Laura grinned.

"And I," announced Aileen, "have a bottle of Veuve Clicquot."

"What the hell is that? It sounds a bit vulgar to me," giggled Cassie. She didn't need alcohol. She was getting high just being with the girls.

"You philistine, Cassie Jordan!" Aileen guffawed. "I'll have you know it's the best of champagne given to me by none other than the director of the film I've just worked on. And guess what? I might be working on a film with Anthony Hopkins! Oh joy!"

"*Anthony Hopkins!*" shrieked the others. "Wow!"

They stopped at Cassie's favourite haunt, What's Cooking, and had a very tasty meal over which they lingered for ages, enjoying one another's company as they caught up with the backlog of news. They then adjourned to Cassie's house and Laura went into ecstasy at the décor.

"I love the mirrors on the curve in the stairs. They make the whole place seem much bigger," she enthused. "And did *you* do those stencils along the stairway?"

Cassie nodded, smiling.

"Oh Cassie, it's fabulous. You must be dead chuffed with yourself."

"As a matter of fact, I am, and not only with the house." Cassie was so thrilled that she could keep her news to herself no longer. "Guess what happened today?"

"What?" they chorused.

Cassie did a little twirl of delight. "I got promoted. I'm an assistant manager!"

"Yippee!" yelled Aileen, as Laura thumped Cassie on the back.

"That definitely calls for champers. Come on, let's get tiddly!" Aileen ordered.

It was five in the morning before the three friends called a halt and retired, very tiddly indeed, to bed.

Despite their late night, they had an early start the next day. Cassie was determined to show Chester to Laura and Aileen, and they spent an enjoyable few hours shopping in the picturesque city. They returned home after a madly satisfying spree and headed for the back garden wearing their bikinis. Lying in the warm sun, Cassie floated contentedly off to sleep, and was soon joined by her companions. They snoozed happily for a few hours. By the time they had their tea and showered and dolled themselves up, they were raring to go for a night on the town. Cassie took them to the bank's social club and introduced them to Pauline and Ann and the rest of her friends. They all decided to go to a nightclub and it was the early hours of Sunday morning before their heads hit the pillows.

A lie-in was definitely on the next morning and they slept like logs until midday. After a huge breakfast, they went for a long walk down by the Marine Lake. It was a very pleasant day and the lake was full of windsurfers.

"It's a lovely place, isn't it?" Laura observed. "I can see why you're so happy living here."

"Mmmm," agreed Aileen. "Much and all as I like London, I could quite fancy living here myself."

"I do love it: I've made some great friends; I'm doing well at work; I get a lot of interior design bits and pieces to do and I love my house. I can't see myself coming home for a long time. I never thought I'd say this but this is home for me now," Cassie confided as she pointed out Hilbre Island and the Irish Sea to her right and the coast of Wales and the river Dee to her left.

She wished the girls could stay longer but Laura was flying home that night and Aileen was leaving the following morning.

While they got in another few hours' precious sunbathing, Cassie prepared a delicious salad to accompany her Chicken Kievs and carried the food out to the garden on trays.

"This reminds me of that first picnic we had in Ranelagh. Do you remember?" smiled Aileen.

"They were great carefree days, weren't they?" Cassie said, as she poured the chilled wine.

"And we've come a long way since then," added Laura, raising her glass and clinking with Aileen.

They were just having their coffee when the phone rang. It was John, and as she listened to her brother's news, Cassie felt her knees go shaky. She was as white as a ghost when she came back out to the girls. "Mam's had an accident. She crashed the car and she's in hospital. John thinks I should come home, the sooner the better." She tried to keep her lip from trembling.

"I'll phone and see if there's a seat on my flight," Laura said briskly, springing into action.

Aileen put her arms around Cassie. "I'll pack for you and drive you to the airport and I'll tidy the house and leave it spick-and-span when I go away in the morning. Don't worry, Cassie, your mother will be all right."

Cassie swallowed hard. "John said she wasn't in danger or anything but he just felt I should come home. Something's wrong that he's not telling me about, I just know it. He sounded dreadfully upset on the phone although he was trying to hide it."

Laura emerged on the patio. "I've booked you a seat on my flight. Come on, let's get packing.

In the rush to get ready, Cassie didn't have time to think, but as they sat on the short flight over the Irish Sea, she felt knots of fear and tension inside her.

"Take it easy," Laura urged sympathetically.

"I'm trying to, Laura, but I feel awfully scared. Something's wrong, I just know it. There's something really wrong with Mam!"

❧❧❧

Book III

1985–1990

CHAPTER THIRTY-SIX

"Alzheimer's disease! Oh God, John! Are they sure?" Cassie thought she was going to be sick as she sat in the car with her brother *en route* to the hospital from the airport.

"Well, that's what they think it might be, Cassie. All her symptoms point in that direction. They're just making sure it isn't hypothyroidism or vitamin B12 and folic acid deficiency. It will be a while before they can make a firm diagnosis and confirm what really *is* the matter but they say her symptoms are very indicative of Alzheimer's and to be prepared for that possibility."

"What symptoms?" Cassie said tremulously. Her heart was racing, her palms were sweaty and she felt nauseous. John sighed.

"The memory loss, the mood swings and depression, the confusion. Mam's short-term memory is gone to pot. She can't even remember having the accident. The guards think she put her foot on the accelerator instead of the brake."

"But when did all this happen? I know she was a bit down in the dumps when I was home at Easter, but this all seems so sudden."

"Mam hasn't been herself for a while now, Cassie, you know that, and since Irene left, she really went in on herself. She started to do some really strange things, ordering groceries, things that she didn't need, two and three times a week. She had this irrational fear that she was going to go hungry. She locked herself out many times because she'd forgotten her keys; I was always having to come up and get in the window. The consultant said the Alzheimer's has been developing slowly over the years but sometimes a shock or an upsetting event can hasten its development. He thinks that Irene's going to Washington could have been a factor and then the accident really brought on an acute attack. Cassie, she was completely confused, she didn't know us, didn't know where she was or what had happened. And she wasn't concussed or anything."

"This is unbelievable!" Cassie shook her head in shock and yet, as she reflected, she could see how Nora's behaviour had changed over the years: the gradual onset of forgetfulness, the disimprovement in her house-keeping, even in her appearance. Nora had always been neat as a pin, with her hair done every week, but Cassie had noticed, especially the last time she was home, that her mother was much less inclined to go to the hairdresser or keep herself smart and tidy. She remembered the episode with the teabags. She should have realised then that all was not well with Nora, she chided herself. What this all meant for the future, she dared not think.

They arrived at the hospital and Cassie tried to compose herself. Alzheimer's disease. Some people called it the living death, and the doctors thought her mother could have it. She wanted to cry, to howl her eyes out and shriek abuse at the Almighty and even at Jack. How could he have let this happen to his wife? The dead were supposed to watch over the living. If that were the case, her father hadn't done a very good job of it!

"Mam is sedated so she might not recognise you," John warned as they walked down the long hospital corridor, Cassie's high heels echoing hollowly, breaking the silence. It was the same hospital that Jack had died in, and the antiseptic smell was enough to turn her stomach. When they reached her mother's bedside, she saw with dismay that the rails around the bed were up.

"In case she wanders." John sighed deeply. "She wants to go home. She gets very agitated at being in hospital so they had to sedate her."

Nora lay doped to the eyeballs. There was not a flicker of recognition as her daughter lowered the rails and bent over and kissed her mother on her waxen cheek. Sitting down beside the bed, she took Nora's hand in hers and rubbed it between her own.

"I'm here, Mam. You'll be all right. Don't worry. Cassie and John are here."

"Where's Barbara?" Cassie wearily asked John.

"She was here this afternoon, then she had to go off to some gala. She said she'd ring you tomorrow."

"What about Irene and Martin? Have you told them?"

Her brother shook his head. "I wasn't sure whether I should or not. I wanted to tell you first and see what you had to say. What do you think?"

"I suppose we might as well wait until we see how it goes. Irene will only get hysterical. She can't handle things like this at all. And there's no point in having Martin worrying until we know a bit more." Cassie wished someone else could make these decisions but knew that, as the eldest, it would be left to her.

"That's what I was thinking too," John nodded his agreement.

"How's Karen?" Cassie enquired, as she stroked her mother's hand.

John smiled. "She's fine, Cassie. She's the best in the world, you know."

"I know that, John. You were dead lucky to find her."

"You can say that again. She's at home in Mam's, airing a bedroom for you, and giving the place a bit of a tidy-up. She calls in every day and does a bit for Mam ever since she started to—well, you know..." John couldn't bring himself to say "go a bit peculiar."

"I hope she's not overdoing it, John. She has enough on her hands," Cassie said in concern. Her sister-in-law was heavily pregnant with her first child, and Cassie knew that she and John were very anxious to have the house finished before the onset of winter. Karen also helped John with the paperwork of the business, so giving Nora a hand was more than kind of her.

"Does Barbara visit much?" Cassie asked. She knew that Nora was thrilled with her little grandchild. Maybe if her mother had someone like the baby to focus on a bit more it might help her condition.

"You know Barbara!" John said wryly. "As far as she's concerned, Port Mahon is a no-go area, the sticks! She visits about once a month. Irene writes every week. She loves Washington. She's staying with Dorothy and of course money's no object there and Irene's having the time of her life. She's minding Dorothy's baby, but as far as I can gather, there's a live-in nanny as well, so I don't think she has to work too hard."

"Well, she can't do that forever; her money isn't going to last. What's she going to do then?" Cassie snorted.

"Search me!" John grinned. "Meet a millionaire and marry him as fast as she can—I think that's the plan."

"That's as good a plan as any, I suppose," Cassie retorted drily. They sat silently for a while, lost in their own thoughts, with just Nora's breathing breaking the silence. Cassie felt a lump rise to her throat as she saw how vulnerable her mother looked in her hospital bed. What was to become of her? It was obvious that Nora could no longer live on her own. There was no point in asking Irene to come home; *she'd* never cope with an ailing Nora. Barbara and John were married and had commitments, although Cassie knew that John and Karen would bend over backwards to help out. That left her and Martin. And though he was scheduled to come home by the end of the year, Cassie just couldn't see him agreeing to come back to Port Mahon to live with his sick and ageing mother.

That left her! Whatever way she looked at it, it was always going to be *her*. Barbara wouldn't look after Nora, Cassie just knew it. Irene couldn't. If John and Karen had their house built, Cassie felt that they would. But why should Karen have to take on the responsibility of her mother-in-law, when Nora had three daughters of her own?

Why should you have to shoulder it either, she argued fiercely with herself, feeling utterly trapped, very resentful and terribly guilty for harbouring such selfish and disloyal thoughts. But God, things had been going so right for her: the house, the promotion, the interior design, getting on her feet after Robbie. And she had worked hard for everything she had achieved. She had studied hard and it had paid off. And now, when she was relaxing and enjoying the benefits and having fun in her life, this!

"Maybe we could get someone in," she spoke her thoughts aloud.

"What?" John looked at her enquiringly.

"Sorry, I was thinking aloud," Cassie explained. "I was just thinking perhaps we should get someone to keep house for Mam when she gets home."

"Well, you know *we'd* take her if we had the place fixed up," John declared.

"I know that but that's not very fair on Karen, and besides Mam would be better off in her own home. Later on, if she gets really bad, she'll have to come and stay with me, I suppose. Barbara won't take her and Irene would be useless."

"Mmm," John agreed, "but that's not very fair on you either, is it?"

Cassie shrugged her shoulders. "Who said life was fair? It stinks, if you ask me, but John, when any of us were in a fix Mam always helped us out. I'm not going to turn my back on her in her hour of need. I just wish I didn't feel so goddamned resentful and angry about it. I feel like a lousy daughter and I hate myself."

"Cassie, you're only human, and you deserve the most out of life the same as any of us. You've nothing to reproach yourself with. I think we should look at all the possibilities before you commit yourself to anything," John said firmly. "We'll talk to the doctor again tomorrow."

A nurse came in and took Nora's pulse. She had cracked a couple of ribs and broken her wrist in the accident but apart from that she had got off lightly.

"I think you should leave now," the nurse said. "It's been a long day for you and, as you can see, your mother is quite peaceful and she'll sleep for the rest of the night!"

Cassie looked at John. She hated leaving her mother on her own. Just say she woke up and was looking for them. "You go," she said. "I'll stay here for a while longer. Laura told me I could stay the night with them if I wanted and she's given me a key."

"Are you sure, Cassie? It's just that I've got to check up on the temperature in the glasshouses."

"Go on, John. Tell Karen I'll see her tomorrow some time," Cassie ordered crisply.

When he had gone, the nurse offered to get her a pot of tea, and Cassie gratefully accepted. It seemed ages since she'd had a cup with the girls after dinner at home. As she sat sipping the welcome brew, her mother stirred and muttered something inaudible. Cassie flew over to her.

"It's all right, Mam, I'm here," she whispered consolingly as she tucked the sheets around her mother. Nora's eyes flickered open for a moment.

"Cassssie," she slurred, and gave the tiniest smile before drifting back to sleep. Cassie felt a fierce surge of joy. Nora had recognised her and been aware she was there. Thank God she had stayed just for that precious moment. She sat with her mother until long after midnight and then at the nurse's urging she ordered a taxi to Laura's apartment, comforted by the fact that Nora was fast asleep and in no distress.

Although it was the small hours, and Cassie was very careful to make no noise as she let herself into the apartment, Laura had obviously been listening out for her because a few moments later she emerged from her bedroom, pulling on a negligee, and joined Cassie in the lounge.

"Well?" she enquired anxiously.

Cassie burst into tears.

"Oh Cassie! Cassie!" Laura drew her sobbing friend to the sofa and put her arms around her. "What is it? Tell me what's wrong with your mam."

"Laura, they think she might have Alzheimer's. Oh God, what's going to become of her? How do you cope with something like that? I just can't bear the thought of it."

"Oh, Christ above!" Laura exclaimed. "Oh, Cassie, I don't know what to say." She couldn't imagine strong, outgoing Nora Jordan losing her mind to dementia.

Cassie rubbed her eyes fiercely. "Oh Laura, I don't know. It's going to come to the stage that Mam will need a lot of caring and attention and I feel such a bitch because I know it's going to be left to me and I just resent it so much. Barbara couldn't even stay at the hospital until I came. She had to go off to some gala or other. Irene will fall to pieces when she hears and probably get an asthma attack. I can't see Martin coming home. I know John and Karen will help out, but they don't even have a proper house so that just leaves me." Cassie shook her head, desperation written all over her beautiful face. "God, I get so fed up of being the strong, dependable one. It's not fair, Laura. It's just not fair! And I feel disgusting and despicable for thinking such selfish, mean, ungrateful thoughts. Mam did everything for us, but there's more than me and John in the family. The rest of them share the responsibility as much as we do." She looked at her friend through blurry eyes. "Do you think I'm a selfish bitch?"

"Don't be daft, Cassie, you haven't a selfish bone in your body!" Laura retorted. "You're just being very human, and if you ask me you've always taken on more than your fair share of family responsibilities. Don't take this on. You've been promoted, you've a life to live in Liverpool, you have commitments the same as the rest of them. Don't make the mistake of thinking *your* commitments are any less important than any of theirs. Believe me, Cassie, going on their past behaviour, Martin and Irene and most certainly Barbara will be perfectly happy to let *you* take on the care of your mother. You've *got* to be strong. You've *got* to put your foot down this time. You've *got* to think of yourself and your own future. I really mean it, Cassie!" Laura warned as she poured out two glasses of brandy. "Here, drink this, it will help you relax."

Cassie sipped the warming spirits and stayed talking to Laura for a little while before finally going to bed. She found it difficult to sleep and she tossed and turned restlessly, trying to come up with a solution to their dilemma that would best suit her mother and the family. The best she could come up with was that Nora should eventually come and live with her in Liverpool and the others could contribute to having someone come in during the day to keep an eye on their mother. Exhausted, Cassie finally slept.

CHAPTER THIRTY-SEVEN

"Oh noooo!" Barbara gave a groan of dismay as the insistent wail of a baby disturbed her sleep. Ian was on a drugs stake-out somewhere so she'd have to get up to Britt herself. She'd called the baby Britt after Britt Ekland, whom she'd always thought exceedingly glamorous and to whom she fondly fancied she bore a striking resemblance.

She was absolutely whacked. She'd been to a charity gala organised by Lorna Smythe, the social queen of the country. If you were invited to one of Lorna's dos you automatically went on to everyone else's guest list. Oh yes! Barbara was on the "A" list now, after years of brown-nosing and sycophantic toadying to all the right people, even though at times it had nearly killed her. She had finally made it! And she intended to stay on there. She was going to write a wondrously glowing report about Lorna's gala and all the high-society movers and shakers who had attended. About some of them, of course, she would write a barbed comment or two, like Mike Boyle, who was the greatest male chauvinist going and who thought he was God's gift to women. Pulling "birds" was all he could talk and think about. Thinking about it was probably all he could actually do. A fat, florid, heavy drinker, Barbara doubted if he had made love to a woman in years despite his boasting. That was a good caption. "Boyle's Boasts!" Yes, she'd do something with that in the morning.

If only Britt would stop bawling so she could get some sleep. Wearily she dragged herself from the bed and went into her daughter's bedroom. Britt's cheeks were roaring red and she was wet; she was getting teeth. Barbara changed her nappy and gave her a spoonful of Calpol, and when there was no sign of an end to her howls, she went with bad grace to the kitchen to make up a bottle.

She wondered if Cassie had got home. This thing with her mother was very disturbing. Barbara was shocked to hear that Nora might be suffering from senile dementia or whatever the hell name they were calling it. She hoped to God it wasn't hereditary. She'd have to be very careful too that word of it didn't leak out to anyone she knew. If any of her rivals got wind of it it would be a disaster. She was already conducting a feud in print with Kristi Killeen, chief hackette of a rival newspaper. Kristi, in Barbara's opinion, should win the Booker Prize for fiction, for fiction was all she wrote, pretending to have been at this bash and that do. At least Barbara wrote about things she *went* to, even if she did a bit of embroidery at times. They had been sniping at each other for ages now but Barbara had really seen red when the bitch wrote about a certain "big-ears busybody" who was spotted buying babygros in Dunnes. Surely, said Kristi, someone on her supposedly fabulous salary could afford to shop in BT.

It was unmistakably directed at her and Barbara didn't know whether she was more annoyed with the crack about her big ears or about shopping in Dunnes. And wouldn't she love to know just who had seen her in

Dunnes! Mind, Barbara got her own back magnificently, writing about "a big-bottomed bore," infamous for free-loading—hence the weight problem—who had told people she was going on a very expensive island-hopping cruise in the Mediterranean on a yacht belonging to a Greek tycoon. Fortunately for Barbara, Noreen Varling, who also happened to be on holidays in the Greek islands, had spotted her protégée's arch-rival, looking hot and sweaty and lugging her own luggage up the gangplank of a tourist ferry-boat. Noreen had been so excited at her discovery she had phoned Barbara from Greece and urged her to use it in her column the next day. Barbara, of course, needed no second urging and it had been the most gratifying filleting job of her journalistic career so far!

It had caused orgasmic delight among the glitterati, most of whom couldn't stick either Barbara or Kristi, and had been the talk of the town for ages. When Kristi returned home and found out what Barbara had written about her, she had practically lost her tan with fury! The knives were out between them, much to the delight of their respective editors, who both foresaw a gratifying increase in circulation.

If Kristi ever found out about Nora...Barbara went into a cold sweat thinking about it! She gave Britt the bottle and to her great relief the child fell asleep. How lovely it would be to have a live-in nanny! That was one of her dreams and that was why Barbara Jordan Murray was about to embark on the writing of a novel! That's where the money was to be made! It was going to be an Irish *Gone With the Wind* but more literary! After all, she was looking towards the Booker Prize!

Barbara got back into bed, burrowed her head under the pillow and tried to get to sleep. But sleep would not come. No doubt Cassie would be annoyed that she had left John alone in the hospital with Nora and gone to Lorna's gala. Cassie wouldn't understand that Barbara had gone to *work*, not to *enjoy* herself. Cassie was always so bloody holier than thou, doing the right thing. Well, this would be her chance really to do the right thing by looking after Nora. After all, she hadn't the responsibilities Barbara had: a husband and child, a demanding career. Barbara couldn't possibly take care of her mother, and besides, it was only a two-bedroomed apartment. She just hadn't the space! When she met her sister tomorrow she would say that if she had an extra bedroom, Nora would have been very welcome to come and stay with them. Cassie couldn't argue with that!

❦

Irene sipped her Dom Perignon as she listened attentively to the grey-haired man at her side. He was a US Senator and Dorothy had told her that he was a millionaire. Dorothy was throwing a party and Irene was quite enjoying the interest being shown in her as Dorothy's "Irish cousin." Senator Dean Madigan was a fascinating man who had suffered a great tragedy. His wife had been horse-riding on their sprawling Texas ranch when the horse had taken fright and bolted and she had been thrown. She had suffered a head injury which had left her in a coma for the past year and it looked as though she was never going to recover from it.

Irene thought it was the saddest thing she had ever heard. Life could be so cruel. Didn't she know it? If she hadn't got out of her job in the County Council and away from that bastard Timmy O'Dwyer she knew she would have ended up having a nervous breakdown. The stress of her last few months of work was something she would never forget. Irene had really thought she was going to crack up, especially when the personnel officer had told her she was on her last chance.

Well, that was all behind her now, thanks to Aunt Elsie's bequest and the five thousand pounds her mother had given her and told her to say nothing to the others about. She missed Nora. Her mother understood her better than anyone. God, she'd got an awful shock that day she had gone home to find her mother having a heart attack. She'd been more afraid than ever before in her life and had really panicked.

In a way she was glad she wasn't at home now. Her nerves would be gone, wondering if and when it might happen to her mother again. Here in Dorothy's she had nothing to worry about; she was waited on hand and foot and all she had to do was mind the baby for a while in the mornings and afternoons. Dorothy was delighted to have her stay, she had assured Irene. She loved having someone from home, and besides, it was great to have someone to go shopping with. And boy, did Dorothy love to shop!

Dorothy had told her that she would introduce her to some nice eligible men, but so far the nicest man she had met was Senator Madigan. What a pity he was married! Still, she would write to Nora and tell her all about the party. Her mother would be delighted to know that she was enjoying herself.

❧

Martin hung up the phone with a frown. He couldn't figure it out; he had been trying all day to get in touch with his mother to tell her his news and no one was answering the phone. He had tried John and Karen's as well and there was no reply from them. Maybe there was just something wrong with the lines. He often had trouble ringing from Iraq.

He hoped Nora would be pleased for him. It was a bit of a surprise, he supposed. In fact, he had surprised himself by asking Jean to marry him, but now that he had done it he was starting to get excited about it.

They had gone on holidays together three weeks ago. Jean had flown out to Rome and he met her there and they went to the Italian Riviera for a week before heading over to Capri. It was a great holiday; they had really enjoyed themselves and Jean had let him sleep with her for the first time. She had told him tremulously that she was a virgin and he had been very gentle and patient with her. It had touched him deeply that she had given herself to him and he had felt very protective of the petite blonde, who obviously cared for him a great deal.

When he proposed marriage on the spur of the moment, Jean squealed with delight, fluttered her huge eyelashes and flung her arms around him. Before he knew it, they had bought the ring and she wore it proudly, admiring the flashing diamond every five minutes. She was so excited going home that he had almost wished he were going with her.

Now that he had finally committed himself, Martin knew that he would have to come home for good. Jean would never cope with conditions in Baghdad. Well, he had made his money there, enough to set himself up in business in Port Mahon. To tell the truth he was sort of looking forward to going home to proper food and a decent pint of Guinness. He'd had enough home-brew to last him a lifetime! His mother would be delighted to hear his news and to know that he was coming home...if only he could get in touch with her. Well, never mind, he'd try again tomorrow. Whistling to himself, he poured himself a glass of the dreaded home-brew and sat down to write a letter home to Jean.

❦

"Hello, Barbara," Cassie greeted her sister and held out her arms to take hold of her baby niece. Britt beamed at her auntie and Cassie smiled as she held the baby close and gave her a cuddle. Between them, Barbara and Ian had produced a gorgeous child with big blue eyes and soft curly blonde hair that was so fine and downy it looked like spun gold. Barbara smiled proudly as Britt made a grab for Cassie's earring. They had all arranged to meet at the hospital to have a chat with the consultant in charge of their mother's case, and to try and come to a decision about Nora.

"Were you up with Mam?"

Cassie nodded. "She's very dopey and she seems to think the nurses are trying to poison her. But I managed to calm her down and she told me she wanted to go home."

"Well, at least she recognised you," Barbara said with relief. "She hadn't a clue who I was yesterday. Or John. It was really scary. She kept saying, 'Tell Jack I want him,' as if Poppa were still alive; it was awful." In spite of herself, Barbara's lower lip trembled.

"Barbara, if you start crying, I'll start crying," Cassie said, her voice going a bit wobbly. It had been terrible to see her mother so agitated; it made Cassie feel utterly helpless.

Barbara managed to compose herself. "Sorry! It's just I can't believe this is happening. Have you got in touch with Martin and Irene yet?"

"No. Have you?" Cassie shot back. Barbara looked surprised at the idea.

"I was waiting for you to come home," she said defensively.

But of course! thought Cassie. Let good old Cassie look after things. Remembering Laura's stern lecture to her last night, she faced her sister squarely.

"What are we going to do about Mam?"

Barbara looked at her in amazement. Why was Cassie asking *her*? Barbara had been full sure that Cassie would take command and make some decision. Now she was asking *her* what they were going to do as if she expected *Barbara* to have some plan.

"I...I...don't know,"she stuttered.

"Well, surely you must have some idea?" Cassie pressed. Barbara was not going to get off so lightly and neither for that matter were Martin and Irene. She was going to get in touch with them immediately and put the facts straight in front of them. It was a decision they all had to make and Cassie had decided that she wasn't going to make it easy for any of them. She knew in her heart and soul she would see that her mother was taken care of, but, as Laura had pointed out, she too had a life to lead!

"What do *you* think we should do?" Barbara asked, trying to hide her dismay at Cassie's uncharacteristic indecisiveness.

"I haven't a clue," Cassie told her sister calmly. Barbara's heart sank.

"Well, *I* can't take her. *I* don't have the room," Barbara said in desperation, and then could have bitten her tongue. That wasn't the way she had meant to say it at all. She had meant to imply that if she had another bedroom, of course she'd take her mother. It was just that Cassie always put her on the defensive, and always had, ever since they were children. It was infuriating.

"We'd better see what the others have to say about it," she babbled.

"We'd better," agreed Cassie, taking a perverse pleasure in Barbara's discomfiture. It was quite obvious from her sister's reaction that Barbara had expected Cassie to provide the solution.

John and Karen arrived and Cassie gave her heavily pregnant sister-in-law as much of a hug as her rotundity would permit. Karen looked tired, but when Cassie asked her how she was feeling, she assured her she was fine.

"We'd better not keep the doctor waiting," John reminded them, leading the way to the consultant's office.

They listened to the tall, slightly stooped man tell them that of course they could get a second opinion if they wished but that in his opinion, from his observations and from what John had told him, Nora was displaying the characteristic signs of Alzheimer's disease, although the disease could be confirmed only by post-mortem. He told them kindly but bluntly that the cause of the disease was not known, there was no known cure or even satisfactory treatment, that it could strike anybody, man or woman. Alzheimer's was no respecter of class or creed. Cassie knew he was trying to prepare them for the worst. Anger, fear, grief, pity, fought for supremacy within her. Barbara was white-faced and John and Karen sat holding hands tightly.

Cassie took a deep breath. She knew what had to be done and who had to do it. "I think the best thing, then, is for Mam to come and live with me in Liverpool and for us to pay someone to be with her while I'm working during the day."

Barbara looked relieved that Cassie had recognised that she was the only one who could possibly look after their mother. After all, she was single and free, not like her married siblings. And if Nora were in Liverpool, that bitch Kristi Killeen would never get to hear about their mother's frightful disease.

"Cassie, I think that's a terrific idea. Mam's always been very close to you and of course you do have the space for her. Naturally we'll help out financially, won't we, John?" Barbara appealed to her brother.

"It's very generous of Cassie to offer, but I don't think it's fair on her to have to carry the responsibility."

"We will be helping financially, John!" Barbara interjected sharply. Why couldn't he just shut up and accept Cassie's offer gracefully like she had.

The consultant watched this exchange. He had seen this scene played out so many times before as families squabbled over taking responsibility for their poor demented parent. The trouble was that there were no adequate back-up services to assist and support carers. And usually the unfortunate carer who ended up looking after the sufferer lived through hell on earth, sometimes for many years, as they watched their loved one become a total stranger to them, regressing almost to a childlike state. He had seen love turn to hate; he had seen anger and resentment build up until the carers themselves were close to breakdown. The frustrating thing for him as a physician was that he could do nothing except prescribe tranquillisers to both the carer and the cared-for.

He pitied the lovely girl seated in front of him, who faced the truth unflinchingly and who took the responsibility on her shoulders. People like her were the unsung heroines and heroes of this life. The other one, the one with the baby and the hard face, couldn't wash her hands of her mother quickly enough. It was something he understood very well. If he were in the same position, knowing what he knew, he would be very tempted to do the same.

He turned to Cassie. "I'm afraid, Miss Jordan, that moving your mother to Liverpool would be one of the worst things you could do for her."

Cassie's mouth opened in surprise and the consultant felt a brief, totally unprofessional flicker of satisfaction, as he saw the other woman's jaw drop with shock. Life isn't that kind and easy, ma'am!

"Why?" Cassie asked in dismay.

"The thing to do with a patient like your mother, Miss Jordan, is to keep her in her own familiar surroundings, where she has a life-pattern that she has carved out for herself over many years. Her home is unthinkingly familiar to her, yours is not. You must not add to her confusion by bringing her to a strange place where she has to learn a whole new routine, new kitchen layout, new bathroom and so on. Your mother is losing her ability to remember and learn. Do you understand, Miss Jordan? The longer she is in her own surroundings the better for her. After this particular acute episode wears off it is quite possible that your mother will cope for the time being with just someone to do her shopping and help her cook a meal. The thing is to give the patient as much independence as is possible and reasonable, and also," he added quietly, glancing at Barbara, "to treat her as a human being who is entitled to her dignity at all times." He smiled at Cassie. "Don't make any dramatic change in your life yet. See how things progress. We'll keep your mother in for a few days to get a better picture of her condition and to allow her physical injuries to heal. Needless to say, she will not be driving again, so I suggest you keep the car keys in a safe place. I will be writing to your GP and he'll take over from here."

They filed from his office in various states of emotion. Cassie was faintly relieved that the doctor had told her not to make a dramatic change in her life. It was a reprieve of sorts, for however long. Barbara was grim-faced as she realised that the problem which she had thought so satisfyingly and neatly solved was in no way solved. John was wondering if he should give up the thought of building his house and instead suggest that he and Karen move back to Nora's house in Port Mahon. He knew his wife would probably agree as she was a very selfless person, but he didn't want to place the burden of his mother on her shoulders either. After all, soon she'd have a baby to look after, and, besides, if they lived in Nora's house he would be three miles away from the glasshouses and that would be a hell of a nuisance as regards checking the heating and temperature.

Well, whatever they decided to do, they were going to have to make a decision soon, the sooner the better, really.

"I think we should make an appointment to see Doctor Tyne pretty quickly and see what he has to say," Cassie suggested.

"Good thinking!" agreed John.

"I think that specialist was *most* unhelpful," complained Barbara.

"He told us the truth, fair and square, and he didn't give us any false expectations. I thought he was very honest," Cassie reflected quietly.

"Well, what are we going to do?" demanded Barbara whose nerves were beginning to give way under the strain.

"I don't know about you, Barbara, but I'm going to do whatever I have to do to deal with this situation and that means not letting Cassie carry all the burden!" John declared.

"That goes for me too," Barbara added hastily.

In spite of herself Cassie smiled. Poor Barbara; life was rearing its ugly head and intruding on her airy-fairy, trivial attitudes. There were times she felt the teeniest bit sorry for her younger sister. Her life had no real substance, as far as Cassie could see. John's words had lifted her spirits. He, at least, would always stand beside her. Whatever hard times were to come, she wouldn't have to bear them alone.

"Well all I know is I'm dying for a cup of tea. Come on, let's go get one," Cassie suggested. In every crisis in her life she had turned to the teapot for comfort. There was no reason for it to be any different today.

❦

Barbara felt like bursting into tears. Nothing had gone right at all so far that day. Britt was like a little she-devil, although at least she had behaved when she took her in to Nora. Her mother's eyes had lit up at the sight of the baby and Barbara had suffered a horrible twinge of guilt that she hadn't brought her daughter to visit her grandmother more often. The nasty feeling would not go away and it was making her feel quite miserable. She did her best, God knows. She had a career, a husband to look after, an apartment to take care of and a baby. Once a month was all she could manage to visit.

As she drove into the car-park of her luxury apartment block she saw Anthony Wilson and Pete Hammond sitting in an unmarked squad car. They must have been dropping Ian off.

She switched off the ignition and reached into the back for the baby.

"Barbara!" Anthony had come up beside her, followed by Pete. They had a funny look on their faces.

Barbara stared at the two detectives.

"What's wrong?" she said, shakily standing up. She knew by their faces that something was up. Something that she wasn't going to like.

"Ian's had an accident, Barbara. He's in hospital, the Mater. You'd better come with us!"

Barbara heard his words from a distance. She felt as though she were in a horrible nightmare. First her mother, now this. She wanted to ask if it were serious. A brief image of herself in widow's weeds flashed across her consciousness, and then she fainted.

CHAPTER THIRTY-EIGHT

Barbara stared aghast at her husband. "Early retirement on medical grounds and a pension! But you're only thirty five!" These last two weeks had been an absolute horror. Not only was Nora still in hospital, having got a chest infection a day before she was due to be discharged, but her husband, Ian, was lying strapped in a plaster cast. His back had been broken when he was pushed over a balcony in a mêlée with some drug-pushers he and a colleague were trying to arrest. How was it troubles always came together? He had been told he would have to have several operations on his back and would never be fit to return to work in the police force.

"Take it easy, Bar!" her husband admonished. "It's not as bad as you think. I'll be getting a lump sum, a pension and I'll be able to put in a claim for compensation. I'll come out of this very well and we still have the income from the flats." Once he'd got over the trauma and discomfort of the accident, Ian was not at all distressed by the news that he would never have to go back to work. He was having a great time in hospital, fussed over by all the nurses, who were treating him as a bit of a hero. He was getting the best of grub and was able to watch sport all day on TV. If he had a few pints of Guinness he wouldn't have asked for anything more.

Barbara digested her husband's news. Put like that, she supposed it didn't sound too bad at all. Actually it might prove a blessing in disguise. She wouldn't need any longer to have a woman in to look after Britt. That would save them a fortune, and she'd also be saved the worry of trying to get a babysitter at night when her and Ian's schedules clashed.

An even more welcome thought struck her, although for a moment she had the grace to feel ashamed...but only for a moment. If Ian were unable to work and were going to be having operations, there was no way that Barbara could be expected to look after Nora now or in the future. A disabled husband was enough to have on one's plate.

It was very true that old saying that every cloud has a silver lining, Barbara reflected, as she drove to the hospital where Nora was. Cassie would be there so she could tell her of Ian's fate. Driving into the hospital grounds, Barbara composed her expression into a suitable one for the distressed wife of a disabled husband. Mind, Cassie might give out about her for not giving the time to Nora that she should, but at least she wasn't as callous as Irene. When Cassie told her the news, her younger sister informed them she wasn't going to come home from the States to visit their mother. Even Barbara had been shocked by her younger sister's unbelievable selfishness. Martin had promised he'd get home just as soon as he could get his exit visa. But Irene was staying put! Barbara felt quite saintly compared to Irene.

❦

Irene was terrified. From the moment she had got the horrifying call from Cassie telling her about Nora, she felt as though her world had collapsed around her ears. She had refused outright to go home. After what Cassie had told her, she couldn't bear to see Nora, her strong, supportive, protective mother who had always been the pillar of her life, in the pitiful, frightening state that Cassie had described. It was a terrifying thought, one that made her heart beat so fast and her palms sweat, and butterflies as big as eagles flutter wildly in her stomach. She had been in such a state that Dorothy had insisted on calling the doctor, who had prescribed tranquillisers for her.

Senator Madigan, who had called her several times after the party, had been very kind when he heard her tragic news. He brought flowers and chocolates to try and cheer her up and when he discovered her sitting out in Dorothy's arbour crying her eyes out one day soon after she had heard the news, he had put his arm around her in the most comforting manner and told her that she was right not to go home until she was a bit stronger in herself and more able to handle the shock. She had nestled into his shoulder, feeling greatly comforted, almost like when she was a child and her father had soothed away her fears.

Wasn't it strange, Dean said, how much they had in common, each of them having a loved one mentally incapacitated in tragic circumstances? To cheer her up a little and take her mind off things he had suggested that she and Dorothy and Dorothy's husband, Jim, join him for a few days' cruising in the Caribbean.

It had been a delightful experience, as long as she was able to push the thought of Nora's illness to the deepest recesses of her mind. If she thought about it, the fear took over and she would start to cry.

One evening, about two weeks after she had heard the news about Nora, she was sitting on deck trying to count the stars—an impossible task, but something to do to try and stop her thinking about her mam—when Dean joined her. For a man in his early fifties he was exceptionally good-looking, tanned, craggy-faced. He hadn't an ounce of superfluous flesh and his salt-and-pepper hair, cropped close to his head, was still springy and thick. Dorothy and Jim had retired to their cabin, so they were alone together.

"Honey, can I get you a drink?" Dean asked.

Irene shook her head.

"Are you thinking about your mom?"

Irene nodded, a lump in her throat. Dean sat down beside her and put his arm around her.

"I just feel so alone. Mam always took care of me. I can't imagine her being...being the way she is."

Dean sighed. "I know, Irene, it's a tough thing to deal with, but don't feel alone. You've got Dorothy and Jim," he smiled down at her, "and you've got me." Bending his head he kissed her gently. Irene returned his kiss. She liked this strong, sympathetic man; he made her feel cherished and protected. All her life she had been searching for a man like him. What a pity he was married. Mind, he might as well not be, with his wife lying in a coma and unlikely to recover. A lesser man might have divorced and left her, but Dean had told Irene that he would not desert his wife.

"I've been so lonely," he whispered against her earlobe. "And now you have come into my life and it seems like fate that we should be together to comfort each other in our hour of need."

He stood up and held out his hand to her and Irene knew he was going to lead her to his state-room.

It was like what he said: "fate." The time had come for her to make a decision. She could chicken out as she usually did or she could grasp this chance with both hands. Maybe Dean was her future. His wife couldn't survive in a coma for ever. Nora would be disgusted if she knew what Irene was thinking of doing, but Nora wasn't there any more. By getting this awful illness, it was as if her mother had betrayed her. Irene had to look out for herself now, something she had never foreseen. Dean seemed to be willing to take on the role of protector. And, what was just as important right now, the thought of making love to him didn't scare her as much as she had anticipated. Dean would be gentle with her. Irene just hoped he wouldn't be disappointed when he found out that she was a virgin!

❧

"Lord, Barbara, I'm really sorry to hear that!" Cassie said in concern, as her sister gave her the latest news on her husband. "God, what's happening to the family at all?" As if things weren't bad enough, now Barbara had to cope with this. Nora's chest infection had been an unforeseen setback and she was still convinced that the nurses were trying to poison her. She would eat her food only if Cassie served it.

Cassie had spoken to Doctor Tyne, Nora's GP, shortly after their conversation with the consultant and he had been extremely helpful. He had agreed with the consultant's advice that Cassie should not make any big change for the moment. He too felt that Nora would be able to come home for the time being if she had some good home-help. He assured Cassie he would keep a very watchful eye on her. He also recommended a woman who was a retired nurse and interested in part-time work. Cassie and John met this Mrs Bishop, who seemed very nice and ideal for the job. She agreed to come to Nora for a few hours every day except Sundays. John and Karen said they would look after Nora for that day.

Both Martin and Irene had been told the news and Martin, though shocked, had promised to get home as soon as he could. Irene had gone to pieces, as Cassie knew she would. In fact, she had been a touch hysterical and when Cassie suggested she fly home to visit Nora she had refused outright. Cassie had not been as upset by Irene's behaviour as the others were. Knowing her sister, she understood her fears. It was Nora's cosseting of Irene that had made her the way she was. All the same it just wasn't good enough. There were times when you had to put your own fears and worries behind you and think of other people. Irene had never been able to do that. Her concerns were always for herself, and Nora was a lot to blame for her attitude. Irene had never grown up enough to stand on her own two feet; she was always going to have to depend on someone, always going to duck her responsibilities. No wonder she was terrified to come home to see Nora in the condition she was in. Irene wouldn't be able to cope at all, and though her sister had always taken the easy way out, Cassie thought there was something pathetic about the younger girl's behaviour. There was no point in having her coming home if she were going to have hysterics; they had enough to deal with. Nevertheless, Irene's behaviour was self-centred in the extreme and Cassie was sorely tempted to get on the phone and give her sister a good talking-to. John persuaded her not to do it for the time being.

Cassie had felt some relief that decisions had been made and acted upon but she was too much of a realist not to know that Mrs Bishop was only a short-term solution. The consultant and Doctor Tyne had both been quite frank with them: as time went on the situation would become harder. Residential care was a solution both men had advised but residential care was extremely expensive and Cassie could not forget how Nora had pleaded with her never to put her in a home. Cassie had made a promise to her mother. Keeping it was going to be one of the most difficult challenges of her life.

❦

Just how difficult, Cassie could not have imagined. She realised this ruefully ten months later as she began to think about making arrangements to put her house in the hands of an estate agent and say goodbye to her friends in Liverpool, for how long she did not know.

Mrs Bishop had taken very good care of her mother from the time of her discharge from hospital and Nora had been glad to get home. She had shown a marked improvement once she got into her own familiar surroundings and a much-relieved Cassie had gone back to work in Liverpool.

Then Nora's condition had begun to deteriorate. When Cassie came home for Christmas, she could see that her memory was slipping. Her mother's short-term memory was hopeless. She could not remember things she had done an hour beforehand, or the day before. But she still had good recall of far-distant events in her life.

By Easter, Cassie knew the time was approaching when she would have to decide to come home. Mrs Bishop told her that her mother was getting very distracted as regards time and place. She was beginning to wander and was confusing day and night. There had been several incidents when she had been found walking along the streets of Port Mahon in the early hours of the morning, "on her way to Mass." She needed much more care than Mrs Bishop could give and Cassie reluctantly began to consider taking leave from work to go home to Port Mahon.

There was no other option as far as she could see. She spent nights tossing and turning trying to come up with a solution that would suit everyone, a solution that would mean she could retain some control over her life. The truth was that Cassie did not want to leave Liverpool. She didn't want to leave work, where she relished her new role as assistant manager, making decisions and following them through. It was hard work and entailed a lot of responsibility but it was well within her capabilities. It was what she had trained and studied for, and when she was working she was able to concentrate on her job and put all her other problems to the back of her mind.

More than anything, she did not want to leave her house. She had spent so much time scouring the antique and bric-à-brac shops, to get just the right piece for each room. She had rag-rolled, and marbled and sponged and stencilled to get the desired efect on her walls, and had turned her house into a light, airy, welcoming abode that had earned much praise from those who had seen it. As a result, she always had a decorating project on the go. Her last scheme had been to redesign and decorate the foyer and reception area of a local law firm. She had been thrilled with that, even though it took up all her evenings and weekends for several months. It was a nice change to move out of the domestic market. The carpenter, electrician and painter whose services she used for her various projects had been as pleased as punch; it was a big job. It had turned out very well indeed and consequently she had been approached by a Birkenhead businessman to do a similar job with his offices.

Reluctantly, Cassie turned him down, and it had really been a big disappointment to her because it would have been great experience and an important addition to her already crammed portfolio. She guessed she would be going home and, as it was a big job, she felt it unlikely that she would have completed it before she left for Port Mahon. In spite of herself she felt angry and resentful at what she was giving up.

Nor did she want to leave her friends and excellent social life. When she wasn't doing her interior design work, Cassie spent her spare time at the social club. She windsurfed, she swam and she still played basketball occasionally. Her life was very full and active and her heart sank at the thought of going home to Port Mahon. She knew nobody there now; all her schoolfriends had moved away or married and she had long since lost touch with them.

"Tell Irene to get her ass home from America!" Aileen said grimly one evening as they strolled down around the Marine Lake, enjoying the breeze blowing in off the sea. She had come to spend a weekend with Cassie, having just flown in from the South of France, where she had been on location. Tanned and glowing, loving her job and her life of exotic travel, Aileen knew she would never be able to make the sacrifice Cassie was considering. She felt desperately sorry for her friend but also a bit angry. In Aileen's opinion, Cassie always had to cope for the rest of her family; they expected far too much of her. She should put her foot down.

Cassie sighed. "Aileen, there'd be no point in Irene coming home. She'd go to pieces. She's afraid of her life to come home even for a visit."

"Yeah, well, that's very convenient—if I may say so!" Aileen snorted. "Imagine if *you* decided you couldn't cope and were going to fall to pieces. Then what would happen?"

"I suppose John and Karen would have to do something about it."

"Well, let them get on with it. They live there, they wouldn't have to uproot themselves like you do."

"They would do it, I know that. It's just they've a new baby to look after and John's doing his best to get the business going. It's practically a twenty-four-hour job and I don't think it would be very fair," Cassie argued.

"Well, *I* don't think it's very fair that *you* have to give up career, house, friends, just so as the rest of them won't be discommoded," Aileen retorted, tossing her auburn hair out of her eyes and scowling ferociously. "What about Martin and Jean? Couldn't they move into your Mam's house when they get married and keep Mrs Bishop on during the day? I presume Barbara isn't going to make any offers."

Cassie looked at her friend and laughed drily. "You presume right. Now that she's got an 'invalid' for a husband, in her eyes that lets her off the hook entirely. But I never thought of Martin and Jean coming to live in the house. That's an idea. I wonder would they be willing." She felt a flutter of hope. Maybe, just maybe, that might be the solution to all their problems. Martin and Jean would have somewhere to live. They could keep Mrs Bishop on and they'd have to take care of Nora only at night. Trust Aileen to come up with a brainwave.

"You know, Aileen, I think you might have something

there. I'll hop over next weekend and see if we can sort something out. O'Shaughnessy, you're a genius," Cassie smiled happily at her friend.

"I know!" smirked Aileen modestly.

Cassie felt quite buoyant during the following week. The more she thought of Aileen's solution, the more perfect it seemed. Maybe she wouldn't have to give up her job to go home; she'd be able to do the office commission and her lovely life could continue as it was.

CHAPTER THIRTY-NINE

"Ah...yeah...sounds reasonable to me," Martin nodded reflectively, "as long as everyone continues to contribute to Mrs Bishop's salary. Barbara's a wagon for not paying up on time."

"I'll speak to her," Cassie said grimly. "Of course, we'll continue to pay the salary; take that as agreed. Martin, I'd be so grateful. I'd come home for all my holidays to give you a break and you and Jean could have the use of the house in Liverpool any time *you'd* like a break." Cassie felt almost lighthearted as she sat in the kitchen sipping tea with her brother. Martin was laid-back about things, and had always been good to their mother. Nora was watching Terry Wogan on TV and having a spirited conversation with him. She thought he was speaking to her personally. Through the open door Cassie could hear her.

"And another thing," she was saying, "you should tell that one beside you to put something else on other than her nightdress. It's very immodest for a young girl to be showing her bosom and wearing a nightdress in public. You tell her now, like a good man. Do you hear me?"

"God, it's awful, isn't it?" Cassie's mouth quirked in a smile in spite of herself.

"Do you know what she did yesterday?" Martin chuckled. "You know that writer David Williams, who lives up the road?"

Cassie shook her head. She knew the man only vaguely. He had come to live in Port Mahon several years back, and was a well-known biographer.

"Well, seemingly, Mrs Bishop was on the phone to Karen and Mam slipped out and went up and knocked on his door and told him she knew he was digging a tunnel from his house to right under her bed, but she'd be waiting with a poker for him so he'd better watch out!"

"You're not serious!" exclaimed Cassie, half-amused, half-horrified. "What did he say?"

"Well, he was very nice about it. He promised her he'd stop tunnelling immediately and then he brought her home. He obviously knows Mam's not well; everybody does at this stage. The butcher brought her home the other day. She was trying to buy a half-pound of sirloin with three pebbles. He gave her the steak, too, and wouldn't let Mrs Bishop pay for it!"

"Ah, wasn't that nice of him!"

"Look, I'll head off to Jean's and see what she has to say. I'll probably stay the night in Dublin, seeing as you're home. Would you mind?"

"Of course I wouldn't mind. I think I might take Mam for a walk. She finds the sea soothing and it might tire her out so she'll sleep better tonight," Cassie said.

"No way!" expostulated Jean, when Martin put Cassie's proposal to her.

"But Jean, it would mean we wouldn't have to buy a house for the time being, so I could expand the business a bit more. And Mrs Bishop would be there to take care of Mam during the day and she looks after the house as well, so you wouldn't even have to do much housekeeping. I think it's not a bad idea at all. I'll look after Mam at night; you won't have to get up. I'll see to that."

"Martin, I want a house of my own, I've seen the perfect house in Skerries. You've plenty of money for the business that you earned abroad. I don't want to live in Port Mahon."

"But Jean, someone's got to look after Mam, and if Cassie has to do it, she's going to have to give up her job and come home from Liverpool. After all, I'm here, I *am* her son and Karen and John are perfectly willing to help out. Won't you even consider it for a year or two?" Martin pleaded. He hated the idea of disappointing Cassie. He had really thought that Jean wouldn't mind. She always seemed so sympathetic about Nora and she was very good to her own mother, who was a widow. Jean always had him cutting the grass or clearing the gutters, despite the fact that Mrs Allen had two married sons of her own.

"Look, Martin, Cassie isn't married; she isn't even going out with anybody. She can always buy another house some time. Even Barbara was saying the other day that Cassie's got no commitments like the rest of us and that she should come home."

"Well, Barbara *would* say that. She's not prepared to lift a finger to help out!" Martin scowled.

"Martin!" exclaimed his fiancée. "Barbara's got an invalid for a husband. Poor Ian's back will never be right after that terrible incident. She's the breadwinner, so how can you expect her to take care of your mother? It's bad enough that she has to pay towards Mrs Bishop's salary; she told me that it leaves them quite short," Jean said sympathetically. Barbara and she got on very well.

"Invalid, my foot!" Martin said scornfully. "He's well able to elbow his way through a crush at the bar to get his pint. And that fellow's rolling in money. He has a house let in flats and he's going to get a whopping sum in compensation. So don't give me any more of that crap."

"Martin Jordan!" Jean sniffed primly. "Kindly don't use that sort of language in front of a lady! The answer for once and for all is no! I am *not* going to live in your mother's house and if Cassie doesn't like that, there's nothing I can do about it!"

❧

"I'm sorry, Cassie, Jean wasn't happy about it. She has her eye on a house out in Skerries," Martin confessed.

Cassie felt her bubble of hope burst. She was so disappointed she actually had a lump in her throat. She swallowed hard.

"Maybe we could think of something else," Martin suggested. "Why don't we all get together tomorrow afternoon before you go home. I'll ring Barbara now and we can tell John this afternoon when he comes over."

"OK," agreed Cassie as lightly as she could, knowing her brother felt bad about Jean's response. She supposed she couldn't blame the girl. Not many would want to take on the responsibility of a senile mother-in-law. Cassie had been clutching at straws. There was nothing else to be said; she'd just have to pack up and come home.

❧

"We could sell the farm and get twenty-four-hour nursing care for Mam!" John suggested as they sat in the lounge of the Port Mahon Arms Hotel the next afternoon. Karen had offered to look after Nora, and Cassie, Barbara, John and Martin were sitting in a secluded corner of the lounge trying to thrash out a solution.

"What!" Barbara choked on her G&T.

"That's a bit drastic, John. What happens if Mam lives to be ninety and runs out of money?" Martin murmured.

"Precisely...precisely!" Barbara twittered. God, if they sold the farm to pay for round-the-clock nursing, there'd be nothing left!

"And the market is very depressed at the moment. Land is going for nothing," Martin added. He didn't like the idea of selling the business. He was ashamed to admit he had had the same mercenary thought as Barbara, but the market *was* depressed, no doubt about it, he comforted himself. Even if they waited until prices rose...

"What do you think, Cassie?" John asked.

"I think it's an excellent idea," Cassie said evenly. "It would mean Mam would have the best of care, she would still be in her own home, which is what she always wanted. It's *her* business. I don't see why she shouldn't sell it and reap the material benefit. After all, that's what Poppa would have wanted for her. Let her use her money to make her life as easy as possible and to hell with what's left!"

"She'd never be able to sell it in the state she's in. I'm sure a senile woman can't legally sign contracts," Barbara objected.

"That obstacle could be easily overcome," Cassie retorted.

"How?" challenged Barbara.

"Get Mam made a ward of court or have one of us made guardian. I'll do it."

"Over my dead body," snapped Barbara.

"*You* be her guardian then," Cassie snapped back. "I don't care who it is as long as Mam's looked after."

Barbara digested this. If *she* were Nora's guardian, then *she'd* control the purse-strings. It wasn't such a bad idea at all. Yes indeed. It wasn't that she'd fiddle anything, but at least she'd be in charge of the cash, and nobody would be able to fiddle *her*.

"Right, I will then!" Barbara announced.

"Over *my* dead body," declared John. "Barbara, you haven't lifted a finger to help Mam. Why do you want to be her guardian all of a sudden? The mind boggles."

"You shut up!" Barbara rounded on her brother. "You know very well I have my hands full with Ian, the baby and my job. I'm as concerned about Mam as you are, so don't take the high moral tone with me, mister!"

"Keep your voice down, Barbara. We don't want to be the talk of the town," Cassie ordered.

"Huh!" hissed Barbara, "It's all right for you. What commitments do *you* have? You're terrified you're going to have to come home and leave your lovely cushy life. No wonder you're so anxious to sell the land. That would make life *very* simple for you, wouldn't it? Well, I think you're being pretty selfish!"

"Barbara, cut that out!" John gritted.

A red mist exploded before Cassie's eyes as fury surged through her. She itched to give her sister a good hard slap on the jaw and it was only through iron determination that she managed to control herself. It really infuriated her that people thought she had "no commitments," just because she wasn't married. It was *so* unfair. What was she, a second-class citizen, with no rights at all?

"Barbara, one more crack like that from you and you'll be mighty sorry, believe me," Cassie warned.

Barbara got to her feet. "I can't stay here jabbering all afternoon. I've got to go to the airport to do an interview for the diary with Maureen O'Hara. I strongly oppose selling the business. If that's the best idea you can come up with, it's pretty pathetic."

"You come up with one then!" John growled. "Are you willing to increase your payments to cover the salary for a night-nurse?"

"Dammit, John! You *know* my situation. You *know* I can't!"

"Right then!" John said decisively. "Cassie and I are agreed that we should sell the business. You and Martin disagree. I'm going to telephone Irene. If she agrees—and she'd bloody well better seeing that she hasn't even bothered her arse to come home once—that will be a majority of three to two. The business will be sold! And if you don't like that, Barbara, that's just tough. Mam's going to get the best of care. She doesn't want to go to a home so she shouldn't have to, and Cassie shouldn't have to make any sacrifices that the rest of us aren't willing to make as well!"

❧

"By God, we'll see about that!" Barbara muttered furiously. "Sell the business, indeed, just because Cassie is too mean to come home and look after Mam! And who does John think he is, speaking to me like that? Why can't he and Saint Karen take Mam, if he's *so* bloody concerned?" She careered around a corner, her tyres spitting up gravel, as she drove towards the main Dublin–Belfast road. John would probably persuade Irene to agree to have her mother made a ward of court or have Cassie made guardian so they could sell the land and glasshouses. It was galling, so galling to be over-ruled. Barbara overtook on a single white line and gave the two fingers when an oncoming driver tooted angrily at her.

I should phone Irene myself, she thought, as she sped towards the airport and her interview with the famous film star.

"I bloody well *will* ring her!" she exclaimed in triumph. "I'll call into the office when I've finished with Maureen O'Hara and make the call from there." No point in running up my bill at home, she decided, extremely pleased with her brainwave. She'd do it as soon as possible too, to get in before her brother. John and Cassie needn't think they were getting away with selling off their heritage and probably lining their own pockets at the same time. Barbara didn't trust anyone when it came to money. She smiled to herself. "I'll tell Irene *exactly* what's going on. Ha! Soon they'll be selling the home from under her if she's not careful!"

When she reached the airport, she was still planning what she would say to put the wind up her younger sister.

❧

Martin sat in Kennys pub. John had taken Cassie home but he had decided to go for a pint. He was annoyed at the way the family meeting had gone. Trust Barbara to fly off the handle and cause friction; she had managed the whole affair very badly, although he had to agree with her, selling Jack's market-garden was a very drastic step. It was prime land with well-maintained glasshouses. The neighbouring farmer who leased it from Nora was making a very good living out of it. He had been trying for years to persuade Nora to sell him the farm but Nora had always refused. It was Jack's farm and as long as she were alive it would remain Jack's farm. If only Jean had agreed to come and live with his mother, all this would have been avoided. Nora would have been looked after, the business would have been there for them when she was gone and that would have been the end of it. He supposed he was being a bit selfish, but Nora had always said they were to get equal shares in her estate when the time came. If the market-garden were sold in such a bad recession, Martin knew the full value would never be realised and he could see the money dwindling if his mother lived for a long time, as was quite common with Alzheimer's victims.

He'd always thought of his share of the estate as his bulwark against hard times. That was why he was able to take the risk of setting up his own business as an electrical contractor. And Jean had her heart set on this big house in Skerries. Mind, it was a fabulous four-bedroomed detached house with sea views. He'd liked it very much himself and it would be a great place to bring up children. It was handy enough for work too, because he'd based himself in Port Mahon and he worked all over north County Dublin.

If Irene agreed with the sale of the property, there wasn't much he could do about it, but if she didn't, it looked as though Cassie might have to come home. He knew it was tough on her. The only thing was that if she *did* come home, at least she'd be secure in the knowledge that eventually she'd get her share of the estate. No matter what she said now about spending it on her mother, she wouldn't hand her share back when she got it! It was easy for her, with her permanent and pensionable job and her low-interest mortgage, to talk about selling the business. The same went for John: in a few years' time he would be established as a market-gardener. He had no mortgage; he had built the house in stages according as he had the money. They weren't all as well set-up.

There was no point in asking Jean again about coming to live at home. She told him that if he mentioned it once more he could have his ring back, and she was very sparing with her affection at the moment. She always used sex to reward or punish and he was getting rightly punished. For such a delicate little thing, Jean could be very stubborn, he reflected, as he ordered another pint. She didn't like the smell of beer off his breath, either. Well, tonight she could moan about it; it wasn't as though he were always drinking. A man was entitled to a pint now and again, especially after the family hassle this afternoon.

❦

"Oh my God, Barbara! Selling up the farm and maybe the house!" Irene couldn't believe her ears. "And it's up to me? Oh dear! Oh Barbara, what should I do?" Irene wailed. Things must be really bad with her mam if all this was going on.

Irene started to cry. She was so lonely for Nora she'd give anything to be able to go home to her mother and feel her arms around her and have her take care of her the way she used to.

"Come home and look after Mam! Me?" Irene echoed her sister's words down the phone. "Oh Barbara, I'd be dead scared. Just say she had a heart attack like before. It was terrible! You don't know what it was like." She listened to Barbara going on and on about how important it was that she say no to John about selling the land, and when her sister finally got off the phone she felt utterly drained.

It was not a good time for Irene to be thinking about troubles at home; she had enough problems of her own. Her period was ten days late and she was petrified she was pregnant. When she started her affair with the Senator, he had used condoms, but as time went on he suggested she go on the pill or get the cap. The pill made her fat and sick so she had come off it and had gone to be fitted for a cap. She didn't really like using it but Dean much preferred making love without a condom and she wanted to please him in every way. In his arms she felt very safe and protected and he was kind and generous to her, giving her beautiful gifts of jewels and clothes.

Dean liked to see her looking glamorous. A few weeks before he had bought her a Bob Mackie outfit that cost a fortune, with lots of tassels and sequins and cut-away bits at her boobs and midriff. Irene thought it made her a bit tarty but Dorothy had said she looked swell and Dean had liked it so much he got very randy and couldn't keep his hands off her. They had been attending a party at another senator's house and Dean took her out to a part of the garden hidden from view of the house and made love to her standing up against a big oak tree. He was so passionate and excited it was very sexy, and then on the way home in the car he pulled off the freeway and told her she looked so damned sexy in that dress he was so aroused he was going to explode! He had made frantic love to her in the car! The only thing was...they hadn't taken any precautions, and now, all because of Bob Mackie and his provocative dress, her period was ten days overdue.

A dozen times she had walked into the drugstore to buy a pregnancy-testing kit and hadn't had the nerve. She'd bought conditioning creams and shampoos and make-up remover pads, things she didn't need at all. But she'd just have to take her courage in her hands.

She wondered what Dean would think. The Senator had one son from his marriage and he was very proud of him. But Irene went into cold sweats thinking about all the pain and discomfort of pregnancy and childbirth. It seemed like the most awful experience and there was nothing you could do about it. It took control of you, whether you liked it or not. And then, imagine telling them all at home that she was going to be an unmarried mother. Even Dorothy might not take too kindly to the idea, although she wasn't a bit put out that Irene and Dean were having an affair. She was rather pleased, in fact.

She wished Barbara hadn't phoned. It was all too much to cope with. It had always been a comfort to her to know that some day she would inherit money from her mother's estate and now it looked as if there might be nothing to inherit—if Cassie and John had their way.

It was a bit selfish of Cassie, in a way. After all, she *was* the eldest and Nora had always depended on her. And anyway, Cassie was good at nursing and house-keeping, much better than Irene. She always used to look after Aunt Elsie when she got poorly on her visits to their house. If Irene saw anybody getting sick she nearly got sick herself and once she knew someone was ill she felt very apprehensive in case they had an attack of some sort.

She *was* doing her bit for Mam. As well as taking care of Dorothy's baby, she was working a couple of hours a week doing secretarial work for Dean and he paid her a very generous salary. She sent her money towards Mrs Bishop's salary home every month religiously. If they wanted to increase the contributions, she could manage that, but she didn't want them to sell the farm. There must be some other solution. Selling the business was taking the easy way out, just because none of the others would put themselves out. After all, *she* was thousands of miles away so she couldn't do much. But John and Barbara and Martin were all living at home, and Cassie was only a hop, skip and jump away in Liverpool. Surely they could work something out between them without having to resort to selling off the inheritance.

The more she thought about it the more determined she became to tell John that her answer would be no. Maybe it was just as well that Barbara had phoned to forewarn her; otherwise she might have been in such a tizzy when John telephoned that she would have allowed him to sway her into agreeing to the sale. Well, her answer would be no and that was that. With a very heavy heart, Irene began yet another trip to the drugstore to purchase the dreaded test-kit.

CHAPTER FORTY

"I don't know, Cassie. It's hard to believe that they're kicking up about selling the farm. Irene wouldn't agree, either, so it looks like we're outnumbered."

"It would probably take too long the way things are going," Cassie said glumly as she drank the mug of tea her brother handed her. "To hell with them all, anyway—I'll come home and look after Mam. At least I'll be able to look myself in the face when she dies!" She was angry, very angry at the attitude of her siblings. Their selfishness astounded her. She couldn't care less if she never got a penny from the estate. It was Nora's, as far as she was concerned, and should be used to get the best care for their mother. Obviously the attitude of her two sisters was that Cassie had no real commitments and that she should come home. She was tempted to get on the phone to Irene and give her a piece of her mind. The nerve of her to oppose selling when she hadn't even had the decency to come home once. Oh no, far better to act the ostrich in America! Well, that was one thing, but the least she could have done was agree to the sale of the business. Really, in her own way Irene was as selfish as Barbara.

John stayed for a while and told her he would drop her to the airport at the crack of dawn the next morning for her flight. It would be her last flight east across the Irish Sea. Her next trip would be her journey home. Nora was wandering around looking for Jack, and Cassie's heart went out to her. "Let's go for a walk, Mam," she suggested and Nora smiled happily.

"That would be nice, Elsie," she agreed. Sometimes Nora knew her children and was quite lucid. At other times, she was off in a world of her own and Cassie could be anybody from Elsie to her grandmother, or even a stranger.

It took a while to get Nora organised as she was having difficulty with buttons, but eventually they set off. Turning on to the sea road, Cassie could not even find solace in the setting sun that was turning the sky and sea to flame. She had always looked forward to spending a few days at home, enjoying the picturesque beauty of Port Mahon, but at this moment she felt as if she were about to become a prisoner. From now on she would no longer have a life of her own. She would be there to take care of Nora, and from the few books she had read on dementia and Alzheimer's, things would get much worse as time went on. How long it *would* go on was anybody's guess.

They walked along slowly, Cassie accommodating her steps to her mother's shorter ones. A man walking a glossy cocker spaniel came towards them and smiled as he passed by.

"Good evening," he said pleasantly and Cassie responded politely. He seemed vaguely familiar and he had a lovely mellifluous accent. Oh Lord, yes! It was that Welshman, David Williams, that Nora had accused of digging a tunnel under her bed. Maybe she should have apologised. Oh well, he was gone now. No doubt she'd see him again some time when she was back for good.

Later, when Nora was in bed, Laura phoned. She was disgusted when she heard Cassie's news.

"They should be ashamed of themselves, the selfish buggers!" she exclaimed.

"I suppose in a way I always knew I'd have to come home. If I were the only one in the family, it wouldn't upset me so much; it's just their attitude that I've no real responsibilities or any right not to be inconvenienced that bugs me. That's the way it is with families, though, isn't it? There's always one who's left to deal with the problems. I just wish it weren't me."

"Cassie, I've been reading up about this disease, and I came across a book that gives some very sound advice for the carer," Laura said briskly. Cassie smiled to herself. How typical of her friend to be so practical.

"Now, the thing is," Laura explained, "you must build up a network of support. You must allow time for yourself and you must let others share the load. Are you listening?"

"Yes, Laura," Cassie said meekly. Laura was always in her element when she was organising and planning.

"Now, you'll have Mrs Bishop. Keep her on, for God's sake. Then you'll have John and Karen. You'll have Martin—forget Barbara—and you'll have me! Cassie, on no account are you to give up your interests. You must enrol in a class or take up some activity to get you out of the house so that you'll have time to yourself. Right?"

"Right," agreed Cassie.

"And," ordered Laura, "you have to come over to me once a week for a meal and a chat and to unburden yourself—and of course to have a bit of a laugh, knowing us. I really mean that now, Cassie. One night off a week is something you've *got* to insist on. The rest of them can take turns to sit with Nora. I'll come over to you as well. So don't feel too lonely, Cassie. Don't worry, I'll be here any time you need me."

Yeats's lines flashed into Cassie's head.

Think where man's glory most begins and ends,
And say my glory was I had such friends.

"Are you there, Cassie?" Laura said anxiously, when there was no response at the other end of the phone.

"I'm here, Laura," Cassie assured her, swallowing the lump that rose to her throat. "And I'll be over for dinner once a week, never fear. And thanks for all the advice."

"Just take it!" Laura said crisply.

It was pretty sound advice, Cassie reflected, as she sat on the flight back to Liverpool the following morning. Now that she had made her decision, she was going to have to make the best of it and not go around acting the martyr! One of her great faults was taking everything on herself. Well, this was one thing that was too big to handle alone, however much she might think she could cope. Cassie was going to have as positive an attitude as she could, because she realised that it would be the easiest thing in the world to despair because of the situation in which she now found herself.

The first thing she had to do was to tell her employers, and then she was going to have to make a decision about the house. Personnel were exceptionally kind and refused her resignation, telling her to take unpaid leave of absence for as long as she needed. Knowing that she didn't have to burn her bridges gave her a great boost, she told Pauline and Ann over dinner that night. Her two neighbours and colleagues were very upset that she was leaving and considering putting the house up for sale.

"Look, my cousin Trish is getting married," said Ann, "and she and Mike haven't bought a house yet and they're looking for a place to rent. Why don't you rent your house to them? They'll take good care of it and the rent would pay your mortgage; so at least you'll still have the house when you come back to work."

It was an excellent idea. Cassie had hated the thought of selling the house but she knew she wouldn't be able afford the mortgage if she weren't working. Ann's suggestion was perfect, and she arranged to meet Trish and her fiancé. They were a likeable young couple, excited to be getting their first home. They loved Cassie's house and agreed terms quickly. She felt relieved that it would be in good hands.

John arranged to come to Liverpool with his van to take home her clothes, books and interior design equipment. The evening before she left she went for one last walk around, out of Madeley Drive, where her house stood in redbrick neatness in its well-kept little court, across Hilbre Road and down Victoria Road to Banks Road. She'd miss Banks Road. She'd always enjoyed the walk from the station on her way to and from work and

Saturday morning was often spent browsing in the shops. She'd really miss What's Cooking too! Cassie had become one of their best customers. A minute later she was down on the South Parade, strolling along the Marine Lake, where she had spent so many happy hours windsurfing. She walked right around the causeway, breathing the sea air, watching the lights of Wales across the river beginning to twinkle in the gloaming.

Far away to the right, she saw a cargo-ship gliding serenely across the Irish Sea. This time tomorrow, she'd be home! She walked past the boat-yard, listening to the breeze tinkling the riggings. It was a sound she would always associate with this peaceful place where she'd been so happy. Reluctantly, Cassie took the road home. She didn't sleep well that last night in her own house.

John and Cassie arrived in Dun Laoghaire at six the following evening. Watching the Irish coast come into view, she felt many emotions but most of all apprehension. How was she going to cope with what lay ahead?

That's enough of that! she told herself sternly. You've made your decision. No more feeling sorry for yourself. Just get on with it!

When Nora's tired, befuddled eyes lit up with recognition as she walked through the door, Cassie felt a heel for being so self-pitying.

"I'm home, Mam!" she hugged her mother. "Don't worry, Cassie will take care of you."

CHAPTER FORTY-ONE

"Haven't you got the life of Reilly, all the same?" Cassie heard someone say as she sat in the garden, sipping afternoon tea with her mother.

She managed to curb her irritation and reply as pleasantly as possible, "Hello, Mrs O'Connell, how are you?"

Maggs O'Connell got off her bike and looked as though she were prepared to stay for a good long chat. "Oh I'm fine myself, thank God, no complaints. I just came up to see how poor Nora was."

Of course you did, thought Cassie sourly. Maggs was currently president of the Port Mahon ladies' club and loved a bit of gossip. She would relish going back to the rest of the ladies and telling them, yes, it was really true, poor Nora Jordan had gone completely gaga and Cassie had come home to look after her.

"It's a warm day, all the same. It's nice drinking tea in the open—very refreshing."

"Very refreshing," agreed Cassie, ignoring the other woman's broad hint. If it had been anyone else, she would have offered them a cup of tea immediately.

"And how *is* poor Nora?" Maggs lowered her voice conspiratorially.

"Oh, Mam's fine, thank you!" Cassie responded, smiling at Nora, who was gazing into the distance, oblivious of her visitor.

"But how's her memory?" Maggs was not one to take a brush-off as readily as that. Honestly, Cassie Jordan had no manners. She wouldn't even ask if you had a mouth on you. Here she was gasping for a cup of tea after cycling all the way out of the goodness of her heart to see how Nora was.

"Like us all, good days, bad days," Cassie said off-handedly. She was determined *not* to get into a discussion with this woman about her mother's memory problems.

"Are you the queen?" Nora turned around and stared at Maggs.

Maggs's jaw dropped and she turned to Cassie in confusion.

"How very nice to meet you. We've been expecting you," Nora said, holding out her hand. Maggs shook it with an expression of shock. She hadn't realised things were this bad!

"I'll just go and see that your room has been prepared," Nora said grandly, heading up towards the house.

"Excuse me, Mrs O'Connell, won't you?" Cassie said politely, getting up from her seat. "Thank you for calling."

"Oh, a pleasure...I mean...I mean you're welcome!" Maggs stuttered. *Wait* until she told the rest of them about this. It was very sad all the same to see Nora Jordan end up this way. She was the best president the ladies' club had ever had and had raised more money for charity in her terms of office than the previous three presidents put together.

Cassie followed Nora up to the house. Maggs O'Connell had certainly got what she came for! Cassie smiled, remembering the other woman's shocked expression. Ever since Nora had seen a programme about the queen and the royal family a few days before, she had got it into her head that they were coming to visit her in Port Mahon, and there was nothing Cassie could do to persuade her otherwise. In the end she had stopped trying to reason with her mother. Over the past couple of months she had found it was the easiest way to deal with her. Whatever notions she got, she let her have them. If she called her Elsie, or Irene, or another name, Cassie didn't argue. If Nora set the table for Jack's tea, she let her. When she accused John of being an IRA man come to shoot her, she just told her brother to go home and come back a couple of days later, by which time

Nora would have forgotten the accusation.

It was so hard to accept that her mother's mind had gone completely. There were times she didn't know who Cassie was; at other times she would get terribly abusive, accusing Cassie of hatching all kinds of plots against her; and then there were times like this afternoon, when she was quite placid, content to sip tea in her garden, lost in her own little world.

It was a disturbing experience watching her mother turn into a stranger who sometimes didn't know her, and Cassie had to fight the tendency to get depressed. Her life had changed so completely. She took Laura's advice, though, and decided to do a correspondence course. Fine arts and antiques was the one she had finally selected. She could do it at her own pace. She'd be learning something new and studying would keep her brain sharp.

Once a week, John spent an evening with Nora while Cassie went over to visit Laura. Mind, it was an hour and a half's drive there and back, so she had only about three hours with her friend, but it was a break, and Laura always went out of her way to cook a nice meal.

Cassie had joined a gym in Port Mahon as soon as she returned home, and when Mrs Bishop came in the mornings, she usually slipped off to the gym for a workout. She really looked forward to the hour or two in the gym. It was a way of working off her terrible frustration.

As soon as she came home, Martin had moved out. He and Jean had bought the house in Skerries, and although they weren't getting married for another few months, Martin explained that he didn't like the house to be empty. Cassie had been a bit annoyed, to say the least. It was as clear as day; now that she was here to look after Mam, the rest of them could get on quite nicely with their own lives. Only John and Karen made any real effort to help out so that Cassie could have some kind of life.

It was never knowing what to expect with Nora that caused the major strain. She was dreadful for wandering off, particularly at night. Nora was always restless; she would wander around the house, unable to sleep, and Cassie spent many an exhausted night making sure that she came to no harm.

One lovely warm August evening shortly after Maggs O'Connell's visit, Cassie and Nora were having their tea in the garden. Cassie had been up three nights on the trot and was exhausted. Her mother was flicking through a magazine. Cassie bought her plenty of magazines; Nora liked the pictures in them and they would keep her occupied for an hour or two.

Soothed by the rustle of the breeze through the trees, and the shushing rhythmic sound of the sea, Cassie felt herself relax as she sat in the deckchair, catching a few rays. Her tan had come up magnificently, she had to admit, looking at her golden limbs. She and Nora spent a lot of time sitting in the garden; it seemed to give Nora solace and ease her restlessness, and Cassie had always loved the outdoors. The scent of the roses and the flowering shrubs was heady and Cassie gave thanks for this few hours of pleasant serenity. She was dreading the winter, when Nora would be forced to remain indoors.

Assured that for the moment Nora was quite happy, Cassie lay back in her deckchair and raised her face to the sun. Sunbathing was one of the most relaxing and pleasurable treats to indulge in, and now that she had the chance she might as well take it. She had put her shorts on earlier in the day, and she slipped off her T-shirt and lay in her strapless bikini-top, enjoying the heat of the sun on her bare skin. A lovely lethargy enveloped her. It was just past six; she'd get another hour's sun at least.

She awoke to find a strange man shaking her shoulder and Nora standing beside him, the bottom half of her dress soaking wet.

Cassie didn't know where she was. She sat up, rubbing her eyes, blinking against the sunlight. "I must have fallen asleep," she murmured, trying to drag herself back to consciousness.

"I brought your mother home. She was sitting on the sand down by Cockleshell Bay letting the waves flow in around her. I saw her as I was walking the dog," the man explained, and Cassie recognised the accent. It was the Welsh writer, David Williams.

Scrambling up from her chair she said hastily, "Thanks very much. I'm terribly sorry you were put to trouble, I must have dozed off for a few minutes. And...I'm sorry about the time Mam accused you of tunnelling under her bed."

The man smiled. "Don't worry about it at all. These things happen. I had an aunt who accused her next-door neighbour of having an affair with her husband. All of them were in their eighties at the time!"

Cassie laughed as she put an arm around her mother. "I'd better go and get these wet clothes off Mam. Thanks again," she said.

"You're welcome," he replied, calling the cocker spaniel to heel. "Goodbye, Mrs Jordan," he added politely.

"Are you the king?" Nora asked brightly, oblivious of the fact that she was standing there dripping wet.

"I'm afraid not," her neighbour laughed. "I'm just a

lowly writer." He smiled again and walked down the garden path. Cassie urged her mother indoors. Nora was covered in sand as well as being wet and Cassie reflected that with the way Nora behaved, it was sometimes like having a four-year-old child in the house.

She helped her mother bathe and dry off, hoping she wouldn't catch a chill or a kidney infection. Then she made her some hot chocolate. When she was tidying up the bathroom, she caught sight of herself in the mirror and realised that she was still in her bikini-top and shorts. What that man thought of her she could not imagine. A fine sight she must have looked, sprawled out on her deckchair snoring her head off while her mother went rambling around the country. She wasn't being very effective as a carer, she thought glumly. She'd have to be careful about that in the future.

It must be nice being a writer, she reflected, as she tried to get rid of the sand in the bath. Imagine being able to come and go as you pleased, write when the mood took you and your creative juices were flowing. Cassie imagined that it must be like the high you got when you designed the perfect room after spending hours at the drawing-board. This man had the most wonderful voice. Cockleshell Bay sounded so exotic the way he pronounced it.

She went into the kitchen to find Nora eating the cat's Whiskas. "Oh Mam!" she groaned, grabbing the dish from her. If that man Williams were a fiction writer, he'd get plenty of material right here in this house!

❧

David Williams walked back along the sea road, a frown furrowing his brow. He had gone for a walk in the first place because he was suffering a terrible writer's block and had written only a half a dozen or so pages that day. It wasn't that he didn't have the information he needed— indeed, he had plenty. He had researched Indira Gandhi until he was blue in the face, travelled to India and spent over two months there, less than six months after her assassination by her trusted Sikh bodyguards. He had been writing the book for over a year, so at this stage he was quite sick of it.

David had certainly never envisaged that he would become a bestselling biographer. He had been quite happy working in the background as a senior editor with a prestigious publishing house until one of his authors, Rory Callan, died while writing a biography of Harold Macmillan. Deeply involved with the project, and having done his doctoral thesis on the unfortunate Prime Minister who had had to resign because of the Profumo scandal, David had been the obvious choice to take over the writing of the book.

At the start of the new decade, the Eighties, a whole new career opened up for him at the age of thirty-six. The biography of Macmillan won critical acclaim. Another publishing company, much impressed by the fair but incisive way he had tackled his subject, asked him to write a biography of de Gaulle. It had taken him three years, during which time his marriage broke up. His French wife, Danielle, was unable to cope with the demands made on him by his work. To be sure, she had enjoyed the research trips to Paris and Algiers, and basked in his fame; but she loved socialising and had *not* been able to endure her husband's retreat from the world during his writing periods.

David sighed, his brilliant blue eyes clouding over at the memory. It had been a terrible time, and after what Danielle did to him, he knew that he would never trust another woman. Finding his best friend in bed with his wife was an experience that had turned David into a loner. Oh, he had his relationships. He was a normal healthy man and the existence of a monk did not appeal to him. But he kept the barriers up and never allowed himself to get close to anybody again. Although he had been able to take advantage of the new divorce law enabling couples to end a marriage after one year of separation instead of three, and he had been divorced for almost two years now, the wounds were still raw.

After the break-up of his marriage he had to get away, out of London. He went back to Wales, to Fishguard, his home town. But he couldn't settle. He often thought of driving aboard the car-ferry for Ireland, but he never got around to it. Life in Fishguard revolved around the arrival of the car-ferries from Rosslare Harbour. As a boy he had watched the *Saint David* and *Saint Andrew* arrive with their cargo of travellers and his father and he would count the cars disembarking.

"A good haul today, boyo," his father would say, puffing contentedly on his pipe. His father had gone to war on the *Andrew*. Despite the fact that she was a hospital ship and lit from stem to stern, she had been bombed and battered regularly. Her sister-ship, the *Saint David* had been sunk, but his dad's ship had sailed on. David never tired of his father's reminiscences, especially his stirring tales of the Battle for Anzio and Salerno, and his account of the invasion of Sicily.

It was his father who suggested that they both go off on a trip across the Irish Sea. "You've got to do something about that long face of yours, boyo. This moping around is no good for you or me. Come on, let's go across and have a bit of a holiday for ourselves."

His suggestion had taken David completely by

surprise. His father was not one for uprooting himself. But since his mother's death, his father had been lonely, and David, preoccupied by his writing and his marital troubles, had not made the trip from London to see him as often as before. Maybe making the three-hour journey to Ireland and doing a bit of touring around would do them both good. It would be nice to spend some time in his father's company, just like the old days.

Sailing past the Tuskar Rock lighthouse, the sunset dappling its white-painted exterior with red-gold rays, David and his father leant over the rails of the ferry and watched the emerald fields and cliffs of Rosslare Harbour come into view. As he inhaled the bracing sea air, David felt his lethargy and depression lighten. He needed a holiday, needed to get his life together and decide what he was going to do with himself now that his marriage was over and he was awaiting a divorce. Maybe he would sort himself out on holidays with his father.

It was the first of many trips to Ireland, but on that first visit, he never dreamt that after his father's death he would uproot himself completely and end up living there. He was now working even harder than before, as his reputation as a biographer grew and he was offered more and more commissions.

When Indira Gandhi was shot dead in 1984, David was once again on holiday in Ireland, recharging his batteries after the de Gaulle biography and trying to come to terms with his divorce. His publishers had immediately written to him and asked him to do a biography of the late Indian premier and, following that, a biography of Margaret Thatcher. It was a lucrative contract but at the time David had been reluctant to sign it. He wanted a complete break. He had earned a substantial amount from his first two biographies; he wasn't ready to face another long slog. He had gone to New Zealand and Australia to continue his holiday, ignoring the pleas of his English and American publishers, and the outraged howls of his agent, who saw her dream of retiring to Barbados disappearing down the Swanee. The following March found him in India, researching.

Right now, he was more than sorry he'd ever started the damn thing. It was always like this when he was immersed in a biography. Cabin-fever set in! No matter how hard he had tried today, he just could not put his mind to it. The sun was shining and he wanted to get out. He had cut the grass and painted his gate and gone in again to try and organise himself to write. Usually he was very disciplined, but today discipline had gone out the window. He strolled down to Port Mahon with Prince, his cocker spaniel, toyed with the idea of a workout in the gym, decided against it and had a bite to eat in Tum Tums instead, watching the world go by.

On his way home David encountered his unfortunate neighbour sitting at the edge of the beach, letting the tide surge in around her. He was a bit apprehensive about approaching her. Their last encounter, when she accused him of tunnelling under her bed, had been a bit of a shock. The girl in the bikini-top must be the eldest daughter, who had come to take care of her mother. David was kept abreast of the doings of the denizens of Port Mahon by his daily, Mrs Kelly. He felt sorry for Mrs Jordan's daughter. It was obvious from the dark circles around her eyes that her nights were disturbed. No wonder the poor girl had fallen asleep in the sun. Seeing Mrs Jordan really put things in perspective. He was lucky he had only a deadline to worry about.

Mrs Kelly had informed him that Cassie Jordan had given up a very good position in the bank to come home to take care of her mother. He thought it was an admirable thing to do and he could understand why she did it. If his father had needed him, David would have taken care of him, but God had been kind. He died of a massive heart attack one day while sitting out on top of the cliff, smoking his pipe and watching the ferry from Rosslare Harbour docking. For his father it was the perfect way to go. He would have coped badly with any long-term illness, his son knew that for sure. Now David had only himself to look out for. All in all, he had a very good life. He had his cottage in Port Mahon, he had money in the bank, no commitments to anyone—and that was the way he intended to keep it. Whistling to himself, David opened the gate to Hawthorn Cottage, the framework for a new chapter beginning to present itself to his mind. Maybe he'd just try a few more pages to see how he got on.

Down the hill he could see the lights being switched on in his neighbour's bungalow. He hoped Mrs Jordan would suffer no ill-effects from her outing on the beach. Maybe the fresh air would tire her out and her daughter would get a night's sleep. A very attractive young woman she was, and she had brains as well as beauty if Mrs Kelly were anything to go by. Not that it mattered to him; she could be Miss World and he wouldn't pay the slightest heed. Involvement with a woman was something that was definitely *not* on David Williams's agenda.

CHAPTER FORTY-TWO

Cassie was like a demon as she cycled into Port Mahon to do a workout in the gym. She was tired, upset about her mother, and she had a strong urge to strangle Barbara.

At about five o'clock that morning, a resounding crash woke her. She got up in panic to discover Nora trying to make porridge in the kitchen. The floor was covered with oatflakes and, even worse, sugar. Her mother had dropped the sugar-bowl, and as well as broken crockery, there were gritty particles of sugar everywhere.

"What are you doing?" Cassie yelled at Nora, who started to cry. She instantly felt a heel. She had raging PMT and was wired to a very short fuse, but that gave her no excuse to take it out on her mother.

"It's all right, I'm sorry. Cassie's sorry." She put her arms around Nora to try to comfort her. "Are you hungry?" she asked her mother, who was now clinging to her like a child. Nora nodded, big tears running down her worn cheeks.

"Oh Mam, don't cry, I'm really sorry." Cassie started to cry herself. It broke her heart to see Nora just like a child and she was in a bad enough state without Cassie shouting at her. The two of them stood weeping in the middle of oatflakes and crockery and gritty sugar until Cassie pulled herself together, cleared a pathway for her mother, brought her to the bathroom and washed her feet. Nora was terrible for walking around in her bare feet unless Cassie were there to insist on slippers.

She cleaned up the mess in the kitchen and made some creamy porridge, toast and tea for the two of them. Now that Nora was awake and up, there wasn't much chance of getting her back to bed. Maybe she would sit and listen to some music—she liked that—and Cassie could get some of her correspondence course done. It was at odd hours like these that Cassie managed to do some studying. There were no terms as such, so she could pace herself as she pleased, but it took her mind off things. It was a course that would be very helpful if she ever pursued a career in interior design, and at least she felt she was not stagnating.

Just before nine, Barbara phoned. Ian was in hospital having his disc fused and she was wondering would Cassie take Britt for the weekend as she had been invited to a very swanky do in Ashford Castle, the *crème de la crème* of hotels. It was a two-day event and her regular babysitter couldn't oblige. This was the third time Barbara had pulled a stunt like this. As far as Cassie could see, Barbara thought that Cassie sat like a lady doing nothing all day, because she had Mrs Bishop in for a few hours. The last time she was over, she had made a sarcastic comment about Cassie's glowing tan and Cassie had to suppress the urge to let fly. She felt fragile enough without having a major row. With Barbara it was always as if she were treading on eggshells. Still, it never stopped Barbara from asking Cassie to take care of Britt when the need arose.

Much as she loved her little niece, Cassie had been exhausted the two previous weekends she had looked after her. A fretful child was no joke; a fretful child *and* a senile mother was enough to tax the patience of a saint, and right now, with the state of her hormones and Nora's increased restiveness, Cassie decided that enough was enough. If she didn't put her foot down with Barbara, she'd be minding Britt practically every weekend for the next few months, as Ian was going to have to spend weeks in hospital and he would be in no condition to mind a child after he came out. But this was a problem Barbara was going to have to handle herself. God knows, she had been quick enough to wash her hands of Nora once Cassie arrived to take over responsibility for her.

"I'm sorry, Barbara, I just can't help out this weekend.

Mam's very agitated; she's up at all hours and I'm getting very little sleep. I have my hands full, I'm afraid," Cassie said firmly.

"But can't you give Mam some more tranquillisers, for heaven's sake? Britt will be no bother. All she needs is feeding and changing!"

"Barbara, I don't want to be pumping Mam full of tranquillisers; it's not fair. A time will come when I'll have to give her more than she's getting now. I'm being guided by Doctor Tyne about it. I'm sorry, I just can't take the baby this weekend. Why don't you ask Noreen?"

"Noreen can't stand children," Barbara said sulkily.

"Judy?" suggested Cassie, trying to keep the note of impatience out of her voice.

"She's gone to Madrid for a few days with Andrew!"

"Maybe Jean would mind her." Barbara and Martin's girlfriend had become very friendly. They both loved high fashion and mingling with the glamorous set. Jean was terribly impressed by Barbara's exciting job and lifestyle and Barbara loved impressing the younger woman.

"I couldn't ask Jean; she'll be up to her eyes in wedding preparations."

"Sure, that's not for weeks yet!" Cassie retorted.

"Believe me, a bride has an awful lot to do before her wedding. *I* know, I've been there," Barbara declared loftily, the implication being that Cassie in her spinster state had no conception of what was involved. "I wouldn't *dream* of asking Jean!"

But you don't mind asking me, Cassie thought resentfully. I have damn all to do here. "I'm sorry, Barbara, I can't do it. I've got my hands full with Mam," she said flatly.

There was silence at the other end of the phone.

Then, "Well, thank you. I hope you're never in need of a favour, Cassie Jordan!" Barbara snapped before hanging up.

Cassie slammed down the phone. That girl was incredible. She had no idea of what Cassie was going through and she always made herself out to be the injured party. As long as Cassie could remember, it had been the same. Anger and resentment surged through her. She felt like hitting someone or smashing something into smithereens. For some reason she had a strong urge to hurl a cup through the TV set. It was PMT on top of everything that made her like this. When she went into the sitting-room and found her mother with her head stuck up the chimney carrying on a conversation with someone, and soot everywhere, she let out a string of curses that would have put any man to shame.

By the time Mrs Bishop arrived, she had cleared up the mess and was washing Nora's hair, much to her mother's disgust. There was water everywhere as she struggled against her daughter. Taking one look at Cassie's face, Mrs Bishop put on her apron and said, "I'll finish that. Get off down the town with you. I don't want to see you for the rest of the morning!" Gently but firmly she took hold of Nora and ordered, "Be good now, Nora, and I'll give you a nice cup of tea and some chocolate biscuits when your hair is washed." Nora's struggles subsided and she submitted to Mrs Bishop's ministrations with hardly a murmur. Cassie decided to go while the going was good.

Although it had just turned September, it was like a midsummer's day. Maybe she'd go for a swim on the way home. It would be very refreshing to feel the cool water against her skin and it might clear her head a bit. Yes, she decided, she'd do her shopping, have her workout, go for a swim and perhaps she'd be in a better frame of mind when she got home.

Cycling along the sea road with the warm breeze blowing her hair off her face, Cassie wondered if Barbara had found someone to mind Britt. If she thought her sister were really stuck and that it was for something urgent, she would probably have taken her niece. But for Cassie, a weekend in Ashford Castle, wining and dining, and mixing with this celebrity and that celebrity did not constitute a crisis. When she got on the machines in the gym, she worked out with a vengeance, banishing thoughts of her family from her mind and just concentrating on what she was doing. If she didn't have a safety valve like this, she would probably have gone mad long ago.

She supposed she was really one of the lucky ones. After all, she had Mrs Bishop; she had John and Karen; she had a couple of hours of freedom every morning and a night off every week. There were a lot of people in her situation who had no support at all. She knew of one woman in Port Mahon who had had to care for her husband for ten years. She had done it all by herself as she had no family to rely on and her husband had been terribly abusive to her. The poor woman had died of a heart attack, and the husband was still alive in a home. He was well into his eighties but he had the constitution of an ox. Imagine if her mother lived into her eighties! She could have years like this ahead of her. Cassie shuddered to think about it.

Stop it, she ordered herself, as she stood under a hot shower, washing off the sweat of her exertions. But the blues would not lift and she dreaded the thought of going home. She dressed and collected her belongings, smiling goodbye at a girl she had spoken to in the gym earlier on.

"Hello!" said a vaguely familiar voice at her side. She turned to see her Welsh neighbour walking down the corridor beside her.

❦

David Williams had gone to the gym feeling very pleased with himself. The chapter that had caused him so much trouble had been completed at three o'clock that morning and the end of the book was in sight. Another six weeks' hard work should do it. Of course the manuscript would have to be edited, typeset and proofread, but the worst would be over. Then he'd be off on the publicity trail. The celebrity launch, TV talk-shows, newspaper and magazine interviews, signing sessions, the whole palaver. Criss-crossing the UK, and then a repeat of the whole thing in the USA and Canada. It was hard work, no doubt about it, and once he had completed the Thatcher biography he was going to review his options. Still, today he felt good and he had enjoyed his workout.

After his divorce, he had let himself go. With lots of booze and living on take-aways he'd put on two stone in no time. After buying the cottage in Port Mahon, he had turned his back on his old life. Now he took plenty of exercise, ate properly and didn't bother much with booze. A couple of pints now and again, but no hard stuff. He hadn't felt so well in years!

He had been on the rowing-machine when he noticed the Jordan girl arriving. He could see the strain etched on her face. She was in terrific shape, though, he observed, admiring her long tanned legs and her shapely figure in a pink leotard. She had been lost in a world of her own for her entire workout and had not noticed him at all. He felt a little put out, for some reason. What did he care whether she noticed him or not? He wasn't interested in women any longer, he told himself sternly.

He had a relationship of sorts with a woman from the PR firm who handled his books. Carla was a lovely, go-getting woman who was advancing up the ladder of success at a great rate. A husband and children did not figure in her dreams and in that respect she and David were perfectly matched. She always accompanied him on his publicity tours. They had been attracted to each other and had started an affair on a publicity trip to Edinburgh. It was very pleasant and suited their needs perfectly. When David was in London they got together, and occasionally she flew over to Ireland for a weekend. It was undemanding for both of them and that was what they wanted— so why was he feeling miffed because he hadn't been noticed by a complete stranger, albeit a very attractive stranger? "Keep rowing, Williams!" he muttered, taking his eyes off the woman in the pink leotard and putting his all into his rowing exercises.

It was just by chance that they both came out of the shower-rooms together. Again, she didn't appear to notice him. She strode down the corridor and before he knew it, he had lengthened his stride to catch up with her and found himself saying hello.

❧

"Oh! Oh hello!" Cassie came out of her reverie.

"How's your mother?" her neighbour was asking her.

Cassie grimaced. "Not the best," she admitted.

"She didn't catch cold, did she?" he asked in concern.

"Oh no, nothing like that. It's just...it's just that she's a bit restless..." She couldn't really say that her mother was driving her round the twist at the moment.

"I see," the Welshman murmured. Cassie looked at him, really looked at him and noticed him. She had been too occupied with her mother to do so the day he had brought her home from her escapade on the beach.

He was in his forties, she guessed, of medium height, a head taller than she was. He was wearing a white T-shirt and jeans and she could see the well-developed muscles of his chest and arms. His face was tanned. He had a good strong jawbone, a nice straight nose, a firm well-shaped mouth and the clearest, bluest eyes she had ever seen. He wore his greying hair cut short and it suited him.

"I'm David Williams, by the way. We've never been formally introduced."

Cassie smiled as she felt her hand taken in a firm grip. "And I'm Cassie Jordan. Thank you for looking after Mam the other day."

"It was nothing at all. I'm sorry to hear she's not too well. You must find the going very tough sometimes."

The genuine sympathy in his voice was Cassie's undoing. To her absolute horror, a lump as big as a melon rose to her throat and tears welled up in her eyes. Bowing her head, she managed to mutter, "Yes, yes...I must go now." She turned away, mortified at her behaviour. Imagine bursting into tears in front of a perfect stranger. She knew her hormones were awry but this was a bit much. She was going to live on vitamin B6 and evening primrose oil from now on.

"I'm terribly sorry. Please don't rush away like that. I didn't mean to upset you." David hurried along beside her, his face creased with concern.

"Oh, no, *I'm* sorry. It's not *you*. *Please* don't think that," Cassie sniffed, desperately trying to regain her composure.

"Maybe you'd like to have a cup of tea and talk about it. It helps just to talk sometimes," she heard him say sympathetically. Cassie stopped short, and blinked the tears away from her eyes.

"Not at all, David, I'm fine. Things just got a bit on top of me today for some reason. I don't usually carry on like this."

"Of course you don't," he smiled, and Cassie noticed that the smile made his eyes crinkle up and his face seem very kind.

"I'll tell you, there were a few days last week that I felt exactly like you do," David joked, "and if someone had asked me to go for a cup of tea and offered to listen to my woes, I'd have gone like a shot! Come on," he said persuasively. "I'd only be worrying about you if you went home like this and it would interfere with my creative processes. So, really, I'm being quite selfish."

Cassie laughed. She liked his sense of humour, and, despite the fact that they were virtual strangers and she had just disgraced herself by bawling in front of him, she felt very comfortable in his company.

"Well, I suppose I couldn't have that on my conscience," she agreed. "But I look a sight, I'm not really dressed up for going for tea." She was wearing jeans, worn sneakers and a lemon T-shirt.

"You look fine," he said, as they continued down along the corridor.

They emerged on to Main Street, and he quirked an eyebrow at her. "The Port Mahon Arms, The Sea View, Tum Tum's, Mrs Hardy's teashop? Where would you like to go?" Before Cassie could reply she heard a plummy voice and her heart sank. Mrs Carter, the gossip to beat all gossips, was bearing down on her.

"Good morning, Cassie, and how are you? I haven't seen you since you came home. And how is poor Nora keeping? It's a very sad thing."

"Hello, Mrs Carter. Mam's fine, thank you," Cassie said crisply.

"Aren't you lucky all the same that you have Mrs Bishop to help out, so you can get to your keep-fit with Mr Williams here?" Mrs Carter smiled coquettishly.

Cassie was speechless. David, standing slightly behind Mrs Carter, tried to keep the amusement off his face. She turned her attention to David. "I suppose you feel the need some days to get out from behind your typewriter."

"Oh indeed," he agreed. "I like coming into town; you meet some real characters." Mrs Carter looked slightly affronted at this. She wasn't quite sure but she felt she had just been insulted.

"Yes, well, good morning to you both!" she sniffed a touch frostily, and carried on down Main Street with her nose in the air. Bloody foreigners buying into Port Mahon. Why couldn't they stay wherever they belonged? *Characters* indeed. And that Jordan one was no better than him, with her high-and-mighty airs. Sure, the whole town knew Nora Jordan was gone senile. I was only enquiring after her health, she thought self-righteously, as she spotted the bank manager's wife and waved at her. Just wait until Lizzie heard about Cassie Jordan and the Welsh writer! She'd be amazed. Thrilled with her scoop, Mrs Carter crossed the street to impart the exciting details to the town's second biggest gossip!

"It's a pity," said David, as he watched Mrs Carter march down the street, "that I'm not writing fiction, I'd get plenty of material from the likes of her."

Cassie laughed. "That's funny—I had exactly the same thought about you the other day. You *do* realise it will be all over Port Mahon that we were seen coming out of the 'keep fit' club together!"

"And if we have tea in any of the hostelries, our

reputations will be ruined. You'll just have to come back to my place, and when news of that gets out there'll be wigs on the green!"

"I've got my bike with me," Cassie said.

"No problem. I'll dump it in the back of the station-wagon." He indicated a somewhat battered red Peugeot that was parked just down the road. "That's if you want to come, of course," David added.

"That would be very nice, David, thanks," Cassie smiled. "Whenever I go anywhere in town, everybody wants to know about Mam. I know they mean well but it gets a bit wearing."

"Well, that's settled then. How would you fancy a few potato-cakes, I'll get some from the bakery; they're second to none."

"Mmm," grinned Cassie, who was beginning to feel more cheerful. After being stuck at home for the past few months, seeing just the same old faces, it was nice to meet someone new and interesting.

"Don't expect too much of the cottage," David warned as they drove along the sea road with her bike in the back and a bag of fresh potato-cakes on her lap. "I've done very little with it since I moved in, I've been too busy writing. One of these days I must get down to it."

"You could do so much with it," Cassie enthused as she looked around the small cottage. "I *love* Agas!" she exclaimed, when she saw the gleaming stove in the kitchen. Already she was working out designs and décor in her head. "This kitchen would be lovely done in pine and if you had terracotta tiles on the floor, it would look very rustic, very Mediterranean."

"That sounds nice," David agreed as he cut some brown bread, heated up the potato-cakes and placed pickles, beetroot and a variety of cheeses on the table outside the back door.

"Don't go to any trouble!" Cassie protested.

"It's no trouble. I always eat a bit of lunch at this hour of the day and the brown bread is fresh."

"It's gorgeous!" Cassie declared five minutes later, as she tucked in. David had poured her a glass of wine and, feeling utterly decadent and to hell with the worldish, she was enjoying it. He was very easy to talk to and she could listen to his beautiful accent forever. As they ate the simple but delicious repast, they chatted freely, and Cassie found herself telling him about her mother and how she had yelled at her, about Barbara and how angry she was with her. It was a relief to talk and he was a very good listener.

"Lordy, I'm telling you all my secrets. It's a good job you're not writing fiction," Cassie said, a little embarrassed. Then she laughed when she realised that she had repeated David's own remark almost exactly.

David's eyes crinkled up in a smile. "I might write your biography one day though, and your sister might not like it!"

"Oh she doesn't mean it. Barbara never stops to think!" Cassie said hastily, afraid she had been too disloyal about her sister.

"I don't know how you keep sane at all," David remarked as he poured Cassie another glass of red wine. "If my father had gone like your mother I'm not sure that I would have coped. Danielle, my ex-wife, took her father into our home a few weeks before he died and I spent a lot of time with him, but it was only for three weeks or so and I was quite wrecked after it. I couldn't write at all. You must make sure that the rest of your family take on their responsibilities too," he said gently. "You don't want to get burnt out."

"I know," she agreed, thinking to herself that it was

easier said than done.

They sat under the shade of a glorious honeysuckle, eating their meal, sipping their wine and watching the sun sparkling on the sea. "I was going to go swimming!" Cassie said, patting her full stomach. "I feel like such a glutton. That bread was lovely and I've eaten half the loaf." She glanced at her watch and shot out of the chair. "Cripes, it's nearly three o'clock," she exclaimed. "Mrs Bishop will think I'm lost and you've missed a morning's writing."

"Oh, but I've enjoyed myself." David stretched as he stood up. "I'll spend the rest of the day writing."

"I think I'll do a design for your kitchen. That would give me something to do. I love planning new rooms." She had told him about her experience in interior design.

"Do that! I'll frame it. It will be a Cassie original," David smiled as he got her bike out of the back of the car. "Are you capable of cycling, seeing as you're under the influence, or will I drive you home?" he teased.

"Not at all, I'll freewheel down the hill. It's only a pity Mrs Carter won't be here to see it," Cassie laughed, getting on her bike. She held out her hand. "David, thank you for lunch, I enjoyed it. I hope I didn't moan too much."

"You didn't moan at all and I enjoyed it too. I'll tell you what. If I set myself a goal of a chapter completed by this day next week and achieve it, would you come for lunch again after the gym?" he asked, as he shook her hand. "It would be a great help to me because I'd have something to look forward to, so I'd make myself work?"

Cassie's eyes twinkled. "Only if you get your chapter finished by then!"

"Right, and you've got to have your design done."

"OK," Cassie smiled as she got up on her bike and cycled towards the gate, with David's cocker spaniel running beside her just like Spock in the old days.

"You don't look too unsteady from here. I'll see you this day week in the gym." David stood watching her as she cycled on to the road and took off down the hill.

She turned for a second and waved and he waved back and then she set her face against the breeze and cycled down towards the bungalow, feeling extraordinarily refreshed and energised. It had been such an unexpected encounter. She was dying to get to work on the design of David's kitchen, and she was looking forward to this day next week. Whatever happened at home, she'd have that to look forward to. And Laura was coming over to spend a day with her next week as well, as she had some leave to take and wanted to visit her own mother in Port Mahon.

She must telephone Martin about getting the central heating installed before the winter, she decided, as she walked to the shed and put her bike in. She was afraid of Nora with the fire. God knows what she might do with herself. It shouldn't be too much of a job to convert from back-boiler to oil and Nora had more than enough money in the bank to cover the expense. As her guardian, Cassie would have access to the money to pay for the conversion. It would be nice getting up to a warm house in the mornings and not having to light the fire to get the heat going. She'd phone Martin this minute!

Nora was sitting under the oak tree watching the seagulls circle a trawler. She looked old and tired and Cassie felt a terrible guilt rise up in her for the way she had yelled at her that morning.

"I'm sorry, Mam, I really am. I love you very much!" Cassie sat down beside her mother and hugged her tightly. Nora, content to be held within the circle of her daughter's arms, sat quietly gazing into the distance.

❧

David cleared up the dishes after lunch and shook his head. He had really surprised himself today. Several times! Being miffed because Cassie had not noticed him, deliberately catching up with her so he could say hello and then asking her up to the cottage for tea, a tea that had turned into a long, lazy lunch.

He wasn't used to strange females bursting into tears in front of him and he thought he had handled the matter very well. Asking Cassie to have a cup of tea was the least he could do. It was quite obvious that the poor girl was under enormous stress. And no wonder! Some of the things her mother got up to were incredible. The sister, Barbara, sounded like something else. He had read a few of her columns in *The Irish Mail*, courtesy of Mrs Kelly, and thought they were hilarious. Mrs Kelly told him that Barbara was a celebrity now and wouldn't give Port Mahon the time of day. She didn't have much time for her mother either, it seemed. And as for the one in America, although Cassie hadn't said much about her, David sensed that she was even less helpful than the so-called celebrity.

He liked Cassie, he had to admit. She was good company and he enjoyed her sense of humour. She'd got really animated about the cottage and it would be interesting to see what designs she came up with. David didn't invite many people to his home and he hadn't enjoyed a meal so much in ages. Next week he'd cook one of his specialities, a pasta dish. He enjoyed cooking for company and it would certainly give him the incentive to complete his chapter on time. Whistling to himself, he dried the last dish and strode into his study, sat down at his word processor and began to write.

CHAPTER FORTY-THREE

"He's a gorgeous cook!" Cassie informed Laura a week and a day later, as they sunbathed together on the lawn, making the most of the magnificent Indian summer.

"Get to know him, girl, he sounds like a dreamboat!" Laura laughed. Cassie needed something good in her life right now and this man sounded very nice. Laura didn't know how her friend was managing. She had been really shocked at Nora's deterioration. Nora hadn't a clue who Laura was and had asked her several times if she were Elsie's daughter. To Laura's certain knowledge, Cassie's Aunt Elsie had never been married, let alone had a daughter, but to soothe her friend's mother, she agreed that she was who Nora said, and Nora seemed content with that.

"I wonder why his wife left him," Laura said, shifting to find a comfortable spot. She was three months pregnant and not having it too easy.

"She couldn't cope when he had to lock himself away and spend months writing. David says it's the most anti-social of occupations. I felt very conscious that when he was entertaining me yesterday he was away from his word processor. He assured me that he'd finished the chapter he had set himself and he was entitled to a little treat. It's not like our jobs where you're finished when you leave the office; it's a twenty-four-hour thing really. I always thought the life of a writer would be heaven, but this sounds like a bit of a drag to me!" Cassie observed.

"Huh! I'm bringing home work all the time now," moaned Laura. "It's the only way I can see to get on. Increase my workload, get it done efficiently and show up my rivals. You know something, Cassie, I'd love to set up an all-female practice where we could all get promotion on merit. It really *is* a man's world."

"I was lucky in the bank, I guess," Cassie said. "They were enlightened."

It was lovely having Laura over for the afternoon. She'd been looking forward to it for ages. Nora was placid for a change. All she had done today was to get into the bath with her clothes on. Now she was sitting peacefully under the tree and the girls were relaxing and having a good gossip, just like the old days. The longer the good weather lasted, the better, for both her and her mother.

She had thoroughly enjoyed her lunch with David the day before. The week had seemed to crawl by, probably because she was looking forward so much to meeting him. She had met him in the gym, they had worked out, and on the way home, he had suggested a swim in Cockleshell Bay. Cassie needed no second urging. She had popped in home, changed into her bikini and they had a lovely swim. Because it was September and they had had a hot summer, the water was warm and it was bliss to stretch out and float, feeling the sun on her face. Both of them were good swimmers and they raced each other to the point, with David winning by just a head. They arrived ravenous at the cottage, and while Cassie changed, David served the most scrumptious pasta and chicken dish. This time she had brought the wine and they sat eating and chatting and enjoying themselves. David was enthusiastic about the design she had drawn up for the kitchen. For a few hours, she was able to forget completely about her normal, stressful life.

She and Laura were sipping iced tea and eating some cake that Laura had brought when Cassie thought she heard the sound of a car on the front drive. A few minutes later, Barbara appeared and surveyed the scene.

Cassie's heart sank. Her one afternoon with Laura, and her sister, who rarely set foot in the place, had to arrive and spoil it.

"Well, that's what *I* call living," Barbara declared crossly. "I wish I could take things as easy."

"Change places with me then," Cassie said, not even trying to keep the sarcasm out of her voice. Typical of Barbara to arrive when Nora was quiet and Cassie was able to relax for a few hours. No fear of her arriving when Nora was being difficult, or covered in soot or standing in sugar and oatflakes at five in the morning.

"Would you like some iced tea?" Cassie asked, as politely as she could.

"I'd prefer a cup of coffee," Barbara sniffed.

"Sit down. I'll go and make one. Go over and say hello to Mam."

"Sure, what's the point? She won't know who I am. The last time she kept calling me Nellie, whoever the hell *that* is," Barbara retorted. It really annoyed her that her mother didn't recognise her.

Cassie, cursing under her breath, made her sister's coffee, located another deckchair and went back out into the garden.

"Here you go, Barbara." She tried to keep her tone pleasant. "What are you doing in this neck of the woods?"

Barbara took the coffee and selected a slice of cake, the biggest on the plate, Cassie noted, disgusted with herself for her pettiness.

"I was in Malahide looking at a site so I came on up. Ian and I are going to sell the apartment and build a house when his compensation comes through. Noreen was telling me about a site near her, so I went to have a look at it."

"I never thought you'd come back to live on the northside, Barbara," Laura murmured.

"North *County* Dublin actually," Barbara corrected. "The apartment was fine when there were just the two of us, but Britt needs somewhere to play and I don't think apartments are ideal for children."

"I'll be in the same boat, I suppose," Laura confessed, patting her slightly rounded tummy. "We'll cross that bridge when we come to it."

"When's the baby due?"

"February. It seems like an age."

"Why don't you look for a secondhand house instead of going to the trouble of building?" Cassie enquired, surprised by Barbara's news.

"Ian has a friend who knows a builder who'll do the job at a good price. I'll be able to design the house the way I want it. I'm going to get a conservatory and a utility-room and a patio and have it exactly the way it suits me!" Barbara informed them.

"It will be very handy your living in Malahide. You'll be able to let Cassie have a break the odd weekend and she can come over to me for a rest," Laura said cheerfully.

"A rest!" Barbara arched a quizzical eyebrow and glanced around meaningfully. "Hmmm." She took another slice of cake and asked, "What are all the pipes at the side of the house? I noticed them when I was coming in."

"I'm getting oil-fired central heating put in before the winter," Cassie replied.

Barbara's eyebrows shot heavenwards. "How much is *that* going to cost?"

"A contact of Martin's is installing it and Martin will be doing all the electrical work so the quotation is very reasonable," Cassie answered. It was really none of Barbara's business, anyway.

"What's wrong with the central heating from the back-boiler? It was always good enough for the *rest* of us!"

"I'm afraid Mam will get burnt at the fire. She's got a fixation about the chimney; she's always talking to people up there," Cassie explained, as patiently as she could.

"Put a fireguard up," Barbara suggested, unimpressed by Cassie's argument.

"Barbara, any time you feel you want to take care of Mam, go right ahead. If you want to risk her getting burnt, fine! I won't, and if *I'm* taking care of her, I'm having the heating installed. OK?" Cassie spoke sharply. She knew well Barbara was insinuating that she was spending Nora's money on getting the heating in to suit herself.

"You know best," Barbara said drily and stood up. "Well, unfortunately, I'm not a lady of leisure. I've got work to do, so I must be off," she announced. "Thanks for the cake and coffee." She walked across the lawn and never even said hello to her mother.

"Bitch!" swore Cassie,

"Wagon!" spat Laura.

"Have you ever met the like of her? I know she thinks this is all I do and that I'm getting central heating installed to make life easy for myself!" fumed Cassie.

"Ignore her, for God's sake!" ordered Laura. "Did you see the face of her when I said she'd be able to give you a break when she comes to live in Malahide? She nearly had a fit."

Cassie laughed. "She's going to have an even bigger fit when she finds out that I'm going to buy a tumble-dryer for the winter. I have to change Mam's clothes so often that I'd never get them all dry. Sometimes she doesn't make it to the toilet in time," Cassie confided and her lip trembled. "Poor Mam, all her dignity as a human being is gone. It's awful, Laura; it's so cruel to see her like this." She started to cry. The tiff with Barbara had upset her, and the fact that her sister had completely ignored her mother had upset her even more.

Laura put her arms around her. "Cassie, your Mam will always have her dignity. She's very lucky to have you to look after her. When people see her, they see a neat, clean, fresh person and the fact that she is like that is a great tribute to you. They don't realise all the work that goes into keeping her like that, the constant washing and changing. Cassie, you're magnificent. Don't let Barbara upset you. You've got more humanity in your little finger than she has in the whole of her body."

"Oh, Laura, I'm no saint. There are times I get so frustrated with Mam I feel like strangling her. It's such a struggle not to shout at her sometimes. Just as soon as I've cleaned her, she'll go and mess herself up again."

"Of course, you always expected perfection of yourself. It must be an awful shock to realise that you're a mere human like the rest of us," Laura teased.

Cassie wiped her eyes and gave a watery smile. "Thank you, Laura," she said.

"Oh, you're welcome. Any time you need a bit of philosophy, I'm your woman."

Cassie laughed. Laura was a great old buddy, no doubt about it. She'd be lost without her.

❧

Barbara drove towards Dublin in a mighty bad humour. Honest to God, Cassie was as cool as a cucumber. No wonder she was mahogany—able to lie out in the sun in the middle of an afternoon while everybody else had to work.

Cassie looked fabulous with her lean, tanned stomach. Easy knowing she'd never gone through a pregnancy. Barbara was covered in stretch-marks and she had fat around her waist that she just couldn't get rid of after having the baby. And all she ever did was go pink and burn if she showed her skin to the sun. It grieved her.

As far as she could see, there was no need for them all to be paying Mrs Bishop a salary; Cassie should be well able to manage on her own. Oh she might not be able to sunbathe as much. And wouldn't that be tough! Why should the rest of them subsidise Cassie to live like Lady Muck when they could all do with the money in their own pockets? She was sure Jean would agree with her. After all, she and Martin were saving to get married and had just bought a fabulous house in Skerries. Mind, by the time Barbara had built the house of her dreams, designed by herself, it would be hard to beat. She planned to invite some of the women's magazines to feature it in their "house of the month" section. Kristi Killeen, eat your heart out!

And who did Cassie think she was, getting the central heating in without even a by-your-leave from the rest of them? There wouldn't be a red cent left by the time Cassie was finished squandering her mother's money. Barbara had known that would happen once her sister became Nora's legal guardian. Of course the rest of them were too cowardly to say anything. Irene was hopeless, Martin was too easygoing and John and Saint Karen would let Cassie spend every penny and not say boo.

Well, *she* wouldn't. From now on, Barbara was going to keep a strict eye on things, and from now on, she most definitely was *not* going to contribute another penny towards Mrs Bishop's salary. Let Cassie get up off her ass and do something instead of acting the lady with Laura Quinn!

CHAPTER FORTY-FOUR

"Are you all right?" David put his arm around Cassie's shoulder as she stood looking out over the lights of Dublin Bay. Cassie turned gratefully towards him.

"I'm fine. I was just thinking of Mam and how she always enjoyed weddings—except Barbara's, that is!" They were standing in the big bay window of the ballroom in Sutton Castle Hotel, where Martin's wedding reception was being held. "I'm really glad you came," she said. David smiled, his eyes crinkling in that sexy way that she loved.

"I'm glad I came, too. Otherwise, I'd never have got to meet all these family characters I've been hearing about. I'm *definitely* writing a novel the next time," he teased. "And I think Barbara just *has* to be the heroine," he added, laughing.

Cassie laughed with him. She had long ago given up any pretence about the rest of the family with David. He knew what Barbara and Irene were like; he knew that Martin wasn't much help either, because Jean made such demands on him, but that John and Karen were the salt of the earth and did their best to help Cassie out.

Over the months a great friendship had developed between Cassie and David, a closeness that sustained

her through her troubles. Now that he had finished his
Gandhi biography, he had time to spend with her and
together they were decorating his cottage to her design.
His kitchen was transformed, with warm terracotta tiles,
pine dresser and matching table and chairs. David loved
it and Cassie had enjoyed herself immensely overseeing
the redecoration. The precious few hours a week she
spent with him always rejuvenated her. She could moan
about her siblings in comfort; she could relax completely
and engross herself in redesigning his rooms. Sometimes
they just sat in front of a roaring fire listening to the
wind blowing down the chimney and the rain lashing
against the window-panes. When the winter arrived, she
had given up driving over to Laura once a week. Karen
and John and the baby sometimes stayed on a Saturday
and she went to visit her then. Mostly she stayed at
home, except for her hour or so in the gym twice a week.

Barbara had stopped contributing towards Mrs
Bishop's salary so Cassie had been forced to make up the
amount from her mother's income. Barbara was furious
when she heard this but Cassie, backed up by John, had
told her to go to hell. Martin kept his own counsel but
Cassie got the impression that he wasn't in favour, either.
As far as she was concerned, that was *his* problem. She
wasn't going to be walked on. Nora was as much the
others' responsibility as she was Cassie's and if Cassie
had to spend her mother's income to give her proper
care, well, that was exactly what she was going to do.

"Dance with me, *caryiad*?" David held out his hand
and she stepped into the circle of his arms. He was a
graceful dancer and she loved having his arms around
her. For the first time since she finished with Robbie,
she was attracted to a man and it was a heady feeling.

Laura and Doug had very kindly offered to take care

of Nora so that Cassie could attend the wedding. They made her book a room in the hotel so she wouldn't have to come home and so that she could have a decent night's sleep for the first time in months. Irene was home, so she could look after her mother during the night.

The dance turned to a slow, romantic waltz and David held her close, his cheek against hers. "This is lovely," he murmured.

"Mmmm," she agreed.

"Do we have to stay until the bride and groom go?" He nuzzled her earlobe.

Cassie laughed. "Yes, we do!"

"Spoilsport," smiled David.

"Where were you thinking of going, anyway?" Cassie asked.

"Anywhere I could have you to myself for a while." The dance ended and they stood looking at each other. It was as if everyone else in the room had disappeared.

"Come back to the cottage with me when this is over." David's blue eyes were passionate as he stared into hers.

"I'd like that very much," Cassie replied, reaching up and kissing him softly on the mouth. Staying with David was so much better than a hotel room on her own! Barbara, walking by, gave a "tsk" of disgust, to David's amusement.

❦

Barbara, dressed to the nines in a purple Basler suit, was swanning around Sutton Castle, impressing Jean's family no end. She had really been looking forward to this wedding of Martin's. She was glad it was a winter wedding, as tans weren't a must. Mind, the week after Christmas was a bit difficult for her as there were so many functions she had to attend. Still, she was managing fine, as usual, thanks to impeccable organisation. It made life so much easier that Ian wasn't working.

In fact, she was really in brilliant form tonight. She had just been promoted to editor of the women's page, so that, as well as writing "Barbara's Brief," she was responsible for women's features and all book, film and music reviews. It would be a lot more work but the prestige of the position more than compensated for it and, besides, she would be able to commission work from freelance journalists. There were quite a few who had got up her nose in the past and they wouldn't be getting any work from her. But she had her pals and they would be well rewarded.

She couldn't get over Cassie and that Williams man. To think that her sister had been associating with a very well-known biographer—a celebrity—and she had known nothing about it! Why, David Williams was as well known and respected as Melvyn Bragg or Antonia Fraser.

And he was perfectly gorgeous! Those eyes. Barbara gave a little shiver. The man just *oozed* sex appeal. Trust Cassie to nab someone like him. She could tell he was very impressed by *her*, especially when she told Cassie of her promotion in his presence. Obviously, intellectual, go-ahead career-minded women appealed to him. He had held her hand for far longer than was necessary when they were introduced. And what strong, firm hands he had! Barbara had read an interview once where a politician's wife said she had been attracted to her husband because of his "maleness." That was precisely what one could say of David Williams, Barbara decided, as she slipped into the ladies' to retouch her make-up. David Williams was a very "male" man indeed. What he saw in Cassie she could not imagine. Her sister led a deadly boring life. She wasn't an "interesting" woman any longer. All she had going for her was her figure and her long legs. But David Williams would need more than a woman with a good figure—Barbara was sure of it.

She wondered whether he was interested in having an affair. Because really, right now, she wouldn't mind one. All Ian was good for these days was lowering cans of beer and smoking fags in front of the TV. A woman had needs, especially one as smart, glamorous and intelligent as she was. To tell the truth, Ian wasn't great in bed. Just thinking of David Williams and those fabulous, hooded eyes that had looked her over from tip to toe made her quite randy. Practically everyone Barbara socialised with was having an affair. It was very common among the glitterati and nowadays they didn't come any more *glittering* than she did. Imagine Kristi Killeen's chagrin if Barbara and David Williams became an item! All she could manage was an affair with some two-bit politician who was no oil painting and who had more interest in the whiskey bottle than he had in Kristi.

Adding a touch of lipstick and another spray of Youth Dew to her wrists and ears, Barbara glided out of the ladies' and went back upstairs, to find David and Cassie kissing on the dance-floor.

❦

Martin guided his new mother-in-law around to the music and wished to God she would stop whinging. Now she was moaning about the band being too loud. Earlier on she'd been giving out about the saucy telegrams. If there were one thing that had nearly put him off getting married, it was this whiner in his arms.

He wished Nora had been there. She used really to enjoy a good wedding. All day long he couldn't get her out of his mind. Despite the fact that the rest of the family was there, he had felt very alone in the church. He had called in to see her that morning, all dressed up in his wedding gear, but she hadn't recognised him and thought he was a waiter and ordered a pot of tea. He had actually felt like crying. And it took a lot to make Martin Jordan feel like that. It didn't help either to have Irene bursting into tears every five minutes.

Of course, seeing Mam like that was an awful shock to her. She had been away from home nearly two years. The rest of them had seen Nora deteriorate gradually and had got used to it—well, not got used to it exactly, but it wasn't as shocking to them as it was to Irene. Martin was surprised his younger sister came home for the wedding. He thought Cassie had something to do with it. Cassie was a pretty determined lady when she got going. According to Barbara, she was spending Mam's money hand over fist. Central heating, tumble-dryers, aluminium doors and windows. He'd been a bit dismayed about the last lot; they'd cost a fortune. But Cassie said she needed doors and windows that were more secure in order to stop Nora from wandering. Seemingly she hated to be trapped inside and much preferred to be out of doors.

"Be careful, Martin! That's the second time we crashed into another couple!" His mother-in-law poked him in the ribs.

Ah shut up, you old bat! he thought savagely. Much more of this and he would seriously consider getting well and truly drunk. Of course, Jean would never forgive him and no one could put a man in the doghouse like Jean!

Martin was feeling most unhappy even though he was at his own wedding and he was mightily relieved when the dance ended. He headed up to the bar and ordered a double Scotch!

❦

Irene looked with disgust at the members of her family on the dance-floor. John and Karen were giggling away at some private joke; Martin was dancing with his bride; Barbara was flirting with a friend of Martin's, and Cassie— Irene was so shocked—Cassie was actually smooching with her new boyfriend, David Williams. They all looked to be having such a wonderful time. How could they, with Mam at home in the state she was in? Irene almost started crying again at the thought of it. Her mother didn't know her from Adam and sometimes she just sat staring into space as if Irene weren't there. It was unnerving. And she hardly slept at all. Cassie was up at all hours with her. Poor Cassie, she had gone to skin and bone. Still, she was very angry with her eldest sister. If it weren't for her, she would not have come home. Cassie had insisted that she do so, saying that Martin would need all the family support he could get on his wedding day, in the absence of their mother.

"The least you can do is come home for Christmas and the wedding. Stop being so selfish!" Cassie said crossly. Even Dean thought she should come home and bought her ticket for her.

It had been a mistake to come home, a big mistake. All her old terrors had come rushing back, especially when she saw Nora. Irene knew it was God's way of punishing her for living with a man out of wedlock, and a married man at that. And for that unmentionable thing she had done!

She wished Dean were there to soothe away her fears. She wished she were sitting in her spacious bedroom looking out over Washington while Dean worked on his papers until he were ready to make love to her.

He was very kind. He had bought her the most gorgeous condo and given her credit cards and a car and to all intents and purposes they might as well be man and wife. She accompanied him to all his social functions. At first she had been a bit uncomfortable going out in public with him, especially with his wife lying in a coma in a Texas hospital, but nobody else batted an eyelid and Dorothy told her that everybody in Washington was having affairs and not to worry her head about it. To Irene's amazement, Dorothy confided that she herself was conducting an affair with a handsome young congressman. Dorothy had been thrilled when Dean bought her the condo. Whenever Irene and the Senator were away on a trip, she was able to take her congressman there without fear of being discovered.

Oh yes indeed, Irene was being well and truly punished for her decadent life, but if her mother hadn't gone all funny, she wouldn't have had to adopt this kind of lifestyle. She wanted to shake Nora and yell and shout at her, "It's me! It's Irene. Stop doing this. Stop pretending you don't know me. You must know me! I'm Irene!"

Tears welled up in her eyes. She couldn't *possibly* stay alone with Mam tonight, no matter how badly Cassie needed a night's sleep. John could stay with her; Karen wouldn't mind.

She brushed away her tears and searched in her handbag for her tranquillisers. The doctor had given them to her when she pleaded with him before she left the States. They really were great things. They took the edge off your fear, and although you knew it was there, it couldn't really touch you. She put two of the miracle tablets on her tongue, took a sip of champagne to swallow them and waited for them to work their magic.

❧

"Mrs Jordan! Mrs Jordan, you have to come in. It's raining." Laura shivered. It was bitterly cold and the rain was beginning to fall steadily. Laura had gone to the loo for five minutes and Doug had been on the phone reassuring Cassie that everything was fine, when Nora disappeared. They had found her at the end of the garden hanging rashers and sausages on the clothes-line.

"Come on in, Mrs Jordan," Laura coaxed. "You'll get your death of cold." Doug was retrieving the rashers and sausages but when he gently took Nora by the arm she gave a yelp of terror and ran away. It took them an hour to get her into the house and by the time they managed to bathe her and get her dry and dressed in fresh clothes, Laura was exhausted.

Her baby kicked and she rubbed her bump soothingly. Only a few weeks to go. To think that she was bringing a baby into the world and it could end up like Mrs Jordan. To think that *she* could end up like Cassie's mother. Laura suddenly felt terribly depressed. She was almost sorry she had offered to stay with Nora, but Cassie had been so grateful. She enjoyed getting dolled up and she looked lovely in a cream Regine dress that she had bought in Roches for a fraction of the price Barbara had spent on her "Basler." Her purple suit had cost a fortune, or so they'd all been told. "It's a Basler. Do you like it?"

Laura, who had felt queasy for her entire pregnancy, had whispered to Cassie, "Pass me the sick bucket. I'm going to puke!" Cassie had burst out laughing. She had actually looked happy going off with David. *I'd* look happy going off with David! Laura grinned to herself.

David was a very nice, very sexy man. If she weren't a happily married woman she might have lustful dreams about him. And she was not the only woman to find him attractive: Barbara was obviously smitten as well.

Two hours later Cassie phoned again. "Is everything OK, Laura? How's Mam?"

"Your mam's fine!" Laura assured her. "Are you having a good time?"

Laura could sense that Cassie was smiling at the other end of the phone. "Oh Laura, I'm having a ball!"

"Well, carry on, Cinders, and don't worry about a thing! Just make the most of Prince Charming!" Laura instructed, thanking God that Cassie couldn't see her mother sitting on the kitchen table, refusing to budge!

❦

Cassie awoke with a start, ears straining for her mother.

"Go back to sleep," David murmured softly against her ear. Cassie snuggled in closer to him, remembering where she was. It had been wonderful making love with David, like a dream she wanted to go on for ever. He was such a caring lover and it had been so long since she was in a man's arms. She had never thought she would fall in love again after Robbie and here she was, head over heels in love with David.

What had started out as an easy friendship and turned into a great companionship had, last night, ended up as a wild, passionate, sexy love affair. Cassie ran her fingers through the hair curling on David's chest, smiling as she remembered how Aileen had always loved older men and hairy chests. David would suit her down to the ground! She followed her fingers with her lips.

"Guess what?" she breathed, reaching his mouth and giving him a deep kiss. "I don't want to go to sleep."

"Neither do I," David murmured huskily, his hands curving around her, sending tingles of hot wet desire flooding through her as he caressed her eager body.

CHAPTER FORTY-FIVE

Twelve months after Martin's wedding, Cassie knew she would never have remained sane had it not been for David and the stalwart support she had come to rely on. Not only had she her mother to take care of, she also had Barbara, Ian and Britt living with her. It was supposed to have been for a week at the most, while they were waiting for the builder to finish their mansion in Malahide, but the week had turned into a month and then two and she was at the end of her tether.

Christmas had absolutely finished her, and if Ian Murray weren't careful, he was going to end up as a murder victim.

He was driving her crazy. Never in all her life had she met a man so absolutely lazy as her brother-in-law. And slovenly was his middle name. Ian would go out to the kitchen to make himself a snack, throw the buttery knife in the basin, leave crumbs all over the counter-top and, when he was finished, leave his cup and plate under his chair. He never cleaned the bathroom after him. Cassie invariably found herself wiping dribbles of toothpaste off the washbasin and taking hairs out of the bath. He was incapable of replacing the cap on the toothpaste and as for putting the lid of the toilet-seat down...forget it!

He spent his morning flicking channels on the TV, and in the afternoon, he would put Britt in her pushchair and head off to the pub for a couple of pints. He and Barbara and the child lived on pizzas and take-aways.

"Maybe I'm a nitpicker, maybe I'm prissy and turning house-proud in my old age. I try to ignore it but I can't! Aileen, if they don't go soon I swear I'll end up in an asylum!" Cassie wailed. Aileen was home for a week and they were sitting in Tum Tums eating cherry log with their mugs of steaming coffee.

"In the name of God, what possessed you to allow them to stay in the first place?" Aileen asked. She thought Cassie looked dreadful, haggard and very tired.

Cassie sighed. "It was supposed to be only for a week and Barbara is pregnant and I sort of hoped that maybe she might see what I have to put up with with Mam. I thought it might make her a bit more understanding of the situation," she finished mournfully.

Barbara had phoned out of the blue, to say that they had to be out of the apartment by the agreed closing date at the end of the following week, and as their house was not quite ready to move into, she wondered if they could stay with Cassie for a while.

"It will be only for a week, Cassie," Barbara promised. Cassie agreed, even though David told her she was making a big mistake. After that he'd had to go to London to research the Thatcher biography.

"I've a brilliant idea!" declared Aileen, eyes sparkling. "Why don't you and I take off somewhere for a few days, anywhere you like, and leave Babs and Ian to look after your mother? They'll be gone the minute you come back, I guarantee it!"

"Oh I'd love that!" Cassie exclaimed, her eyes lighting up at the idea. Then her face fell. "I couldn't, really. I couldn't leave Mam to Barbara's tender mercies. She has no patience at all with her."

"Christ, Cassie, what about *you*? You definitely need a break. Look at the state of you!" Aileen argued.

"What's wrong with me?" demanded Cassie.

"You're about a stone too thin! You're as pale as a ghost! Your hair is lacklustre and you've circles as big as hula hoops around your eyes!" Aileen retorted.

"Did you ever think of writing a novel? 'Circles as big as hula hoops'!" snorted Cassie.

"The truth always hurts!" Aileen said primly.

They glowered at each other and then started to laugh.

"Look, tomorrow night is Saturday. Just take one night off and we'll go over to Laura's for the night and goo and gaa over the baby. I'll drive, you sit back and relax and we'll come home early the next morning so you won't be worrying about your mother. How about that?" Aileen urged.

"If Barbara agrees, nothing will stop me!" Cassie promised.

❦

Barbara was not a bit happy about the idea but she couldn't very well say no. There was no sign of that damned house being finished and staying with Cassie was saving them a fortune. Otherwise they'd have to rent a house at enormous expense.

Their first builder had gone bankrupt, the second had put their roof on so badly that it leaked and the one they were currently employing to rectify the mistakes was costing them an arm and a leg and taking his time at it! And Ian was not being one bit helpful; he was leaving all the dirty work to her. All the stress was showing on her face.

Kristi Killeen had made a crack in print the other day about several of her so-called rivals who were supposed to be younger than she was but who had to trowel on the foundation to hide the wrinkles, while her creamy skin was flawless and untouched by the surgeon's knife. She was, said Kristi about herself, a woman in her prime! Well, just that morning, Barbara had penned her response. The next edition of "Barbara's Brief" would include an item on a well-known dirt-disher who was recently seen purchasing a *corset*, something that was mandatory for all women of a certain age—and weight! Let Kristi Killeen put that in her pipe and smoke it!

As well as all these problems, Barbara was three months pregnant. This time, it had been planned. Pregnancy was the "in" thing at the moment; everybody who was anybody was having a baby. And Kristi, who was husbandless and long past her childbearing years, was definitely out in the cold, much to Barbara's satisfaction. Of course, Kristi pretended she preferred to be as free as a bird. Ha! Barbara knew better than to be taken in by that. No woman, despite her protestations, wanted to be free and single forever, especially a woman of Kristi's advancing years! Barbara was reserving a few razor-sharp barbs for when the muck-throwing got really nasty. Once, she had called Kristi a "spinster of the parish" in print and she heard afterwards that her arch-rival was so furious she had got a picture of Barbara and stuck it on a dartboard and spent hours flinging darts of fury at it. Barbara was chuffed; she loved getting under people's skin.

This was definitely the last child, though! After this one, she was getting her tubes tied! Ian refused to have the snip, afraid of his life to get a needle. How he ever became a detective mystified his wife! Fortunately, she had to admit, she was feeling fine, but the drive into Dublin and back daily left her very tired and she was making just brief appearances at the functions she had to attend, so she could see who was there and who wasn't. Spending a precious Saturday night looking after her mother was *not* what she had planned.

Cassie was much better able to take care of Nora. Barbara found herself getting irritated. It was so hard to believe that that strange old woman who could do nothing for herself was their mother. Barbara just left Cassie to get on with it. She was rarely at home anyway and she was just as glad. If only they had their own house finished. The way things were going, all Ian's compensation would end up in builders' pockets and they'd be left on their uppers!

Aileen was collecting Cassie. She looked stunning these days, with her permanent tan and mane of tumbling red hair. That was the life, travelling all over the world, hopping from one exotic location to another. Who the hell did she think she was, Isadora Duncan, Barbara thought sourly, as Aileen roared up the drive in her mother's pristine Starlet and strode to the front door, hair blowing wildly in the wind.

❧

After the two months had passed, Cassie had given up hope that she would ever see the back of her unwelcome guests. The plumber who was installing the central heating in the Malahide house had made a complete hash of positioning the boiler, and Barbara and he were in dispute over payment. Cassie was terribly tired and her nerves were frayed. David insisted she go to the doctor, who was very kind to her and put her on iron tablets and a tonic. He also suggested a mild tranquilliser to help her for a short period. Cassie was very loath to take the tranquilliser; she was afraid of getting hooked, although the doctor promised her he would not let that happen. She had a sneaking fear that by taking the tranquillisers for even a short period, she was losing control and admitting she was not able to cope. Nora had become very withdrawn and was dependent on Cassie for everything. She had even forgotten how to feed herself.

One Sunday afternoon, Jean arrived to visit Barbara. It was a habit she had got into. Martin was left at home to wash up after the dinner he had cooked and he usually spent the afternoon enjoying the peace and watching sport. Cassie found herself very resentful of these visits. It was as if her house were invaded. Barbara and Jean would natter away in the sitting-room, ignoring the fact that Cassie might have wanted to look at a film on TV or just lie down on the sofa to try and snatch forty winks.

When her sister-in-law had first started coming, Cassie felt constrained to offer her tea. Jean was more than content to sit back and act the lady and be waited on hand and foot until one Sunday Cassie just had enough. She pointed Jean in the direction of the kitchen and told her to help herself, then she went off for a walk. Both Barbara and Jean were very frosty on her return.

Rather than have to put up with the two girls this afternoon, she decided on the spur of the moment to call on David and see if he would like to go for a walk on the beach. She usually didn't disturb him without a prior arrangement, respecting his need for solitude to work.

They went for a walk and ended up having a row. David had been encouraging her for ages to tell Barbara and Ian that they would have to get alternative accommodation. He knew Cassie wasn't able to cope.

He had watched her get more and more irritable as the months went on and had himself suffered a few times from the sharp edge of her tongue, although she had always been quick to apologise.

"For Christ's sake, don't *you* start!" Cassie snapped, when he again urged her to do something about the situation.

"Well, I'm browned off listening to you moaning every time we meet. And you won't take my advice," David snapped back.

"I can't just throw them out on the street!"

"Don't be so dramatic, Cassie! You're not throwing them out on the street; they'll just have to go and rent a house somewhere." David viciously kicked a can along the beach.

"I am *not* being dramatic, David Williams. Why don't you just go home and write your damned book and leave me alone!" Cassie exploded.

"Right, I will, if that's what you want!" David glared back at her.

"That's what I want!" Cassie turned on her heel and marched down the beach, leaving David to stand and curse at the inconsistencies of women.

Tears smarted in Cassie's eyes as she jammed her hands in her pockets, letting the wind whip her hair around her face. Some help he was! Men, she'd never understand them! She walked as far as Cockleshell Bay and then turned around and walked home. Jean was still there, she and Barbara deeply engrossed in the latest society gossip. There was no sign of Nora and Ian was slumbering on the sofa. Britt was playing in Irene's old room.

Cassie walked down the hall to her mother's room. When she tried to open the door she found that it was

locked. Barbara must have locked it! Cassie felt fury
envelop her. How dare she! How *dare* she! Never in all
the time she had been minding Nora had Cassie locked
her mother in her room. She went in to Nora, who was
sitting whimpering on the floor.

"Mam! Oh Mam, it's all right, love." She helped her
mother up on to the bed and sat cuddling her for a while
and when Nora relaxed in her arms she left her propped
up against the pillows and walked down towards the
sitting-room.

She stood at the door and stared at Barbara and
actually felt hatred for her sister. "What's wrong?" Barbara
asked, slightly unnerved by the strange look on Cassie's
face and her sister's unusual pallor.

"You're what's wrong!" Cassie's voice was shaking.
"You're what's wrong, you bitch. How dare you lock
Mam in her room? How *dare* you? This is *her* house. Are
you listening to me, you...you!" Driven beyond reason,
Cassie made a lunge at her sister, tears streaming down
her face.

Barbara gave a shriek of horror. "Ian! Ian! Get her off
me. She's gone mad. Get her off me." Cassie was clawing
at Barbara, Jean was white with fright and Ian, woken
out of his sleep, didn't know what was going on.

"I'll kill you! You selfish little bitch," Cassie shouted
hysterically, as Ian lumbered to his feet and grabbed her
from behind.

"Calm down!" he ordered.

"Let go of me, you lazy fat lump," Cassie struggled
furiously against him. "You creep, you parasite! I want
the two of you out of this house *now*," Cassie yelled.

"Don't *you* talk to my husband like that!" screamed
Barbara, outraged. "I'll sue you for assault, Cassie Jordan.
Attacking a pregnant woman! You're mad! Jean will be

a witness. Won't you, Jean?" she appealed hysterically to her sister-in-law.

"Aaah…" stammered Jean, who was quaking in her shoes. She had never seen anything like this.

"You get out too, Miss. Who do you think you are sitting in my mother's house and allowing her to be locked in her room so that your precious gossip won't be disturbed. *Out!*"

Jean took to her heels and ran out the front door as if all the demons of hell were after her. She nearly knocked down David, who was just arriving. He had come to make amends with Cassie.

"What's wrong?" he demanded of Jean. He had heard the sound of raised voices from the driveway.

Jean burst into tears. "You'd better get in there or Cassie's going to kill someone. She's gone mad!"

"Jesus Christ!" David muttered, as he ran through the door to see Cassie screaming and struggling in Ian's arms and Barbara holding a bloody nose and screeching that she was bringing Cassie to the highest court in the land.

"Let go of her!" ordered David in fury, as he wrenched Cassie out of Ian's arms. "What the *hell* is going on here?"

"She tried to murder me!" Barbara bawled.

"It's a pity she didn't fucking succeed," David exploded. "Come on, Cassie, come outside and cool off. You two!" He pointed a finger at Barbara and Ian. "Get your things together and beat it!"

"You can't talk to me and my husband like that!" Barbara gasped in disbelief.

"Watch me, lady! Out!" David's eyes were ice-blue flints. He put his arms around Cassie, who was pale and trembling, and led her out the front door.

"It's OK, you're OK now, Cassie!" David reassured her, as he walked her down the steps to the garden.

"Oh David, I'm going to be sick!" Cassie doubled over and threw up in the shrubbery. David held her head and when it was over gently wiped her mouth with his handkerchief.

"She locked Mam in her room, David. It just freaked me out," she wept brokenly, her body shuddering with sobs. "I can't cope any longer. I don't know what's wrong with me. I feel so scared. I lie awake at night and my stomach is in knots and my head feels as if it's going to explode and my mind is racing and I can't seem to get a grip on things. What's wrong with me? Am I going mad?"

"No, you're not going mad at all, Cassie, you're just exhausted!" David soothed. Privately, he was horrified at the state Cassie was in. He hadn't realised she was this close to a breakdown. "Just come over here and sit down on the garden seat for a minute. I just have to fix something up inside."

Too weary to argue, Cassie sat down on the seat and tried to stop crying.

Back inside, David lifted up the phone and rang the doctor. He glared at Barbara who was holding a towel to her bleeding nose. "I'm ringing the doctor for Cassie. She's very close to a nervous breakdown. You can get him to look at your nose if you want. What's John's number?"

Barbara ignored him.

"It's in the little book by the phone," muttered Ian, completely at a loss. His wife glowered at him for assisting the enemy. David gave John a brief rundown of the incident and told him he should get over to the house as quickly as he could. He, Karen and the doctor arrived at the same time and David explained the situation to them all.

"I'll just check Barbara out, seeing that she is pregnant," the GP said. "Although I'm sure she'll be fine," he added reassuringly when he saw the looks on their faces. "Go and take care of Cassie until I'm ready to see her."

When Cassie saw John she burst out crying again. "I'm sorry, John, I'm really sorry. I don't know what came over me," she sobbed.

Her brother put his arms around her. "Shush, Cassie! It's all right. Don't worry about a thing!"

"Barbara's fine!" the doctor announced rather grimly when he saw Cassie's stricken face a few minutes later. Privately and unprofessionally, he was only sorry Cassie hadn't given her sister a black eye as well as a bloody nose. He brought Cassie into her bedroom and conducted a quick examination, and then told her he was giving her an injection and that she might feel a bit woozy after it.

"What about Mam? She needs to be changed. You know she's incontinent," Cassie said agitatedly, struggling to get up.

"Lie still, Cassie, like a good girl!" Doctor Tyne said, easing her back against the pillows. "Karen's here. She'll look after Nora. Now, let me give you this shot!"

"OK," she whispered, defeated.

The doctor stayed with her until the drug took effect and when he saw that she was quite sedated he closed the door gently and went out to David and John, who were in the kitchen.

"I've sedated her but she's going to need a complete break for a couple of weeks. You've got to make some arrangements. I can have your mother put in residential care until Cassie's capable of taking care of her again. I'm going to send Cassie into a nursing home this evening,"

"Mam would fret in a home, wouldn't she?" John said worriedly.

"Well, she's in an advanced stage of Alzheimer's and it's hard to know, but she probably wouldn't react too well to a strange environment," the doctor agreed.

"Look, Karen's agreed that we'll move up here for as long as Cassie needs and Mrs Bishop will be in during the day. I think Cassie might be easier in her mind if we did this. She'd be upset if she thought Mam was in a home; she told me she promised her never to put her in one," John said.

"Well, whatever you want, John, that sounds fine. I'm just going to make the arrangements to get Cassie into the nursing home. Maybe Karen would put together whatever she'd need for a couple of weeks."

"Of course." John went off to talk to his wife.

The doctor turned to David. "Mr Williams, would you like to come with me when I bring Cassie in?"

"I would! She *will* be all right, won't she?" David asked anxiously.

"Ah, she'll be fine. Cassie's a great coper. She just needs to recharge her batteries for a while!" the doctor told him kindly. "That pair will have to go, though!" He jerked a thumb in the direction of the sitting-room, where Barbara and Ian were ensconced.

"You can say that again!" David growled.

❦

Once she had got over the shock of it all, Barbara was furious. Cassie had *really* gone too far. It was galling to have the doctor arranging for Cassie to go to a nursing home, and not a word about *her* or her unborn child. God knows what trauma the baby had suffered as a result of her aunt's deranged attack. She was going to *insist* on having a scan.

God Almighty! All she had done was lock Mam in her room for an hour or two so she wouldn't be wandering around getting into mischief while Cassie wasn't there to keep an eye on her. It was Cassie's own fault, anyhow, for gadding off with that Williams skunk. The cheek, the unmitigated cheek of him to speak to her and Ian like that. In her own home. The bloody nerve of him. Well, she wasn't going to stay here and be accused of causing Cassie's so-called nervous breakdown. She'd be gone in the morning. If that was what they wanted, fine. Let them throw her and her family out on the street. She'd never forgive them. By God, she'd get her own back on them. She'd sue Cassie for assault and David Williams…his time would come. Oh yes, Barbara would deal with him in her own special way…

CHAPTER FORTY-SIX

After ten days, Cassie was feeling a whole lot better. She had been heavily sedated for the first few days of her stay in the nursing home, sleeping for most of the time. By the end of the first week her drug dosage had been much reduced. Reassured constantly by John, Karen and David and the doctor that Nora was being well taken care of, she gradually began to relax as her body caught up on some much-needed rest.

She badly wanted to phone Barbara to apologise for striking her but the doctor would not allow it for the time being. John told her that the Murrays had moved out a few days after the incident and rented a house in Swords until their own place was ready.

"And about time too! Don't feel bad about them, now, Cassie," John declared.

Nevertheless, Cassie was agitated about it, so Doctor Tyne finally allowed her to phone Barbara. She immediately hung up on Cassie.

"That's her problem now, Cassie. Forget about it, OK?" David ordered when he heard the news. "She drove you to it!"

"There was no excuse for what I did!" Cassie said miserably.

"Cassie, forget it! I mean it; she deserved everything she got," he grinned. "I can only say I don't know how you waited so long to sock her one! It's a pity Kristi Killeen wasn't on hand to witness it!"

"Oh David!" exclaimed Cassie, laughing in spite of herself. He had been so good and kind to her, making her feel loved and cherished. She would never forget the support he had given her in her hour of greatest need.

She returned home after two weeks of rest, able once again to pick up the reins and carry on, relieved that Barbara and Ian were gone, sad that her sister would not respond to her efforts to apologise. She cared for her mother with all the love she had to give her and tried as best she could to keep her own spirits up.

And then, several months later, when she went into Nora's room to check her early one morning, she knew that there was something different about her. Her mother's breathing was very slow and, as she bent over her in concern, Nora's eyes flickered open briefly. They focused clear and unclouded on her daughter.

"Cassie," Nora whispered, giving a little smile and

then, gazing at something in the distance, she murmured "Jack" and sighed softly. Cassie knew that her mother was dead.

❧

Cassie stood dry-eyed at the graveside, watching her mother's coffin being lowered into the ground. "Thank you, thank you, God, for giving me that little miracle," she whispered. To have her mother recognise her after all this time had given Cassie such joy. She knew her father's spirit had been in the room with them and that he had been there to bring Nora on her last journey.

She had sat silently in prayer over her mother's body and a great feeling of peace had enveloped her. She knew Nora and Jack were with her, she could sense their presence so strongly, and from that moment she lost her fear of death.

Afterwards, of course, there had been much to do. She phoned the doctor and John immediately and then David. John took care of the funeral arrangements and David spent his time making tea and sandwiches as required. Doctor Tyne had been very consoling and said that the massive heart attack that had caused Cassie's mother's death was a blessing in disguise.

Barbara had not spoken to Cassie at all! She completely ignored her sister, much to David's fury. He wanted to say something to her, but Cassie forbade it. "Not now, David. I don't want Mam's funeral to turn into a slagging match, and besides, she looks as if she's going to have that baby at any minute!"

Jean said nothing to Cassie either, in solidarity with her friend Barbara, and Cassie felt hurt and worried. Had neither of the other two women realised at all the immense stress she had been under? Were they going to hold a grudge for the rest of their lives? At this stage it looked like it. Cassie, who had never held a grudge against anyone, could not understand them.

Irene came home for the funeral and was hysterical with grief. She stood beside Cassie at the graveside, sobbing her heart out. Cassie put a comforting arm around her.

"Mam knew me when she died, Irene. She was her old self and it was very peaceful for her," she whispered, consolingly.

"It's all my fault!" sobbed Irene. "You don't understand! It's all my fault. I had an abortion and God is punishing me."

Oh God! thought Cassie in dismay. How on earth was she going to handle this?

❧

Irene lay in bed in her old bedroom and felt that a great load had been lifted from her shoulders. When it burst out of her about the abortion she was sure Cassie would be disgusted and call her a murderer. But her sister just took her home and put her to bed and told her that she was no judge of anyone and that Irene had done what she felt she had to do and that God was understanding and did not go around punishing people by letting their mothers die of Alzheimer's disease, however much it might look like it.

Every since she went to that clinic and terminated her baby's life, Irene had felt guilty and frightened. But there was no other option available to her. It was Dean who had organised and paid for the abortion. If she kept the baby she would have lost him and the security he represented. She knew she couldn't take care of a baby. She'd be scared out of her wits by a tiny thing like that and by all the responsibility and worries that having a child entailed. And she was petrified at the thought of childbirth. At the time, termination had seemed like the best idea, but looking back now Irene wondered if it had been a mistake. Maybe she would have coped better than she expected. Cassie would have been there. Cassie would never turn her back on anyone.

Irene buried these thoughts. Maybe now that Mam was dead, she would come back home and live with Cassie. Cassie would take care of her the way Mam had! Maybe that's what she'd do, she thought, as she drifted off into a Mogadon-induced sleep.

❦

Barbara was on the horns of a dilemma! After the funeral, there had been tea and sandwiches for the mourners in the Port Mahon Arms Hotel, although Cassie had taken Irene home first as she was dreadfully upset. Now practically everyone was gone and she couldn't decide whether to go back to the house or not. There were a few items there that she had her eye on. Surely she was as much entitled to them as anyone else in the family. Her mother's ivory jewellery-box for one, and that gorgeous filigree brooch that Jack had bought her for one of their wedding anniversaries.

It was a bit awkward not talking to Cassie, from that point of view. But she had vowed never to speak to her sister again and she wouldn't. It was upsetting Cassie, Barbara noted in satisfaction. Maybe she *wouldn't* go back, just to annoy her. She'd tell Irene what she wanted and make her get it for her. No, she wouldn't go to the scene of her assault. Let Cassie stew in her own juice for a bit longer.

David Williams had been glaring at her throughout

the funeral but she had just ignored him. Rather than put her off, his macho behaviour had only increased her interest. Although she was furious with him and hated him, she couldn't forget the way his eyes blazed with fury the day of the row and how he *ordered* Ian to let Cassie go. Oh, to have a man act like that for her. And Ian, the wimp, did as he was told and never said boo.

Barbara didn't know if it were due to her hormones going awry in the ninth month of her pregnancy, but all she could think about was sex. And not with her husband. Oh no! Ian was a dead duck as far as sex was concerned. When she went to bed at night she had the wildest fantasies of David Williams taking her by force, as she cursed and struggled with him and finally surrendered to his passion. For the first time in her life Barbara was having a wonderful sex life…except that, unfortunately, it was all in her mind.

❧

Aileen and Laura sat in the kitchen they both remembered so well from their schoolgirl days. Cassie was talking to relatives, John was talking to David, and of Barbara and Martin and Jean there was no sign.

"She's a bad bitch, isn't she, not to come home on the day of her mother's funeral!" Laura said in disgust.

"I wouldn't expect any better from her. How she survived so long without someone socking her in the jaw, I don't know!" Aileen sipped her tea and stretched out her legs. "I wish I'd been there to see it! Barbara with a bloody nose would have been a sight for sore eyes."

"Shhh," whispered Laura, "Cassie was very upset about it."

"More fool her! I hope she gave her a kick in the ass, too!" Aileen muttered.

"Cassie looks awful, doesn't she? I hope she takes a break before going back to work," Laura mused. "I'll miss her when she goes back to Liverpool."

"Is she going to go back?" Aileen asked. "I didn't get much time to talk to her. I only got here this morning."

"I think she will. Her house is there."

"David's here," Aileen murmured.

"True," Laura nodded. "I'd forgotten all about that. I wonder what she'll do."

"Well, she'll have to get the will settled and out of the way first, I'd imagine. I hope every t is crossed and i dotted, especially with the likes of Barbara. You know the troubles wills can cause," Aileen whispered, as a neighbour came within earshot.

"Tell me about it!" grimaced Laura. "I'm a solicitor!"

CHAPTER FORTY-SEVEN

"Oh my God! The fat's in the fire now!" Cassie muttered in shock, as she read the document in front of her. It was a copy of her mother's will that had just arrived in the morning's post. No doubt the rest of the members of the family had got a copy too. Barbara wouldn't be one bit happy when she read it! Sighing, Cassie went to phone David and tell him the news.

❧

John came in for his breakfast and saw the letter propped up on the mantelpiece. Karen was dishing up rashers and sausages and John was starving. He'd been in the glasshouses since six o'clock. "What's this?" he asked cheerfully, planting a kiss on his wife's cheek.

"I didn't open it. It's addressed to you," Karen smiled. "And if it's a bill, it's *definitely* nothing to do with me!"

John read the letter and document in silence and a big grin spread across his face. "Good girl, Mam! Here, Karen, read this. Barbara will go bananas!"

❦

Irene was doing her last-minute packing. She was flying back to Washington early the following day and Cassie had been really kind and brought her up her breakfast in bed. There had been a letter on the tray and Cassie had explained that she had received an identical letter. It was a copy of their mother's will. With tears in her eyes, Irene read Nora's last will and testament. She felt a bit hurt. She had always thought she was Nora's pet, but it was Cassie who was being favoured in the will. Well, at least, Cassie would always make sure Irene had a home, so maybe it wasn't the worst thing to happen. All the same, it wasn't what she had expected of her mother. Irene felt quite disappointed.

❦

"Well, honestly, Martin, were *you* expecting this!" Jean pointed a perfectly manicured finger nail at the section of the document that had been totally unexpected. "Well, what are you going to do about it?" his wife pressed.

"I don't know. I'll have to see what the others have to say first," Martin growled. He hoped his wife wasn't going to start nagging. She was three months pregnant and got a bit hyper sometimes. He just had to be careful of her. Jean was a delicate little thing, easily upset, and she had never got over that incident when Cassie had ordered her out of the house during the spat with Barbara.

"Well, I don't know about you, but I'm going to ring

Barbara. I bet *she'll* have something to say about this!"
Jean declared.

ও

"The sneaky cow!" Barbara shrieked as she read a copy
of the same document in her home in Malahide. Upstairs
her new baby son howled, wanting to be fed. Barbara
was oblivious of him.

She waved it under her husband's nose. "Look at the
date of that will, February 1985. *I* remember, that was
just after Mam came home from staying with that sly
bitch in Liverpool. It's obvious that she put pressure on
Mam to change her will. Well, by God, she's done it
now! She's not going to diddle the rest of us out of what
is rightfully ours. Oh the hypocrite. Miss Goody Bloody
Two-Shoes! I *knew* she'd pull a stunt like this. I just *knew*
it! Well, she's not getting away with it. If I have to drag
her through every court in the land, I will. She got away
with assaulting me but she's gone too far this time!"
Barbara was so overcome with emotion she burst into
tears, much to Ian's dismay. He hated it when women
got emotional!

ও

"Mam's left the house to me, David! She made a new
will that nobody knew about after her heart attack. In
her old will the house and farm were to be sold and the
money was to be divided equally between us all. Now I
get a share of the farm *and* the house. She said it was
because I was the one who always took care of her. Oh
David—" Cassie started to cry. When she thought of all
the times she had felt so resentful of her mother for
being the cause of her having to give up her lovely life.
When she thought of the times she had yelled at her

during her illness and not been as gentle as she might have been because she was tired and stressed, Cassie felt overcome with guilt. Now, as a reward, her mother had left her the house, which was worth sixty thousand pounds or more.

She couldn't quite believe that her mother was dead. At night, Cassie still slept lightly, waking often, listening for her mother and then remembering that she was gone.

It was strange having time to herself. She had been wired up for so long, looking after Nora, that she didn't know what to do with herself. So she began a frenzy of housework, much to David's annoyance; he was trying to get her to relax now that she had the chance.

She was going through Nora's personal possessions and they brought back heartbreaking memories. Although Cassie knew that for her mother death was a merciful release, it didn't stop her grieving. She comforted herself with the memory that at least Nora had known her for that one brief moment to say goodbye. The rest of her siblings had not been so blessed. Nora had thought so much of her that she had left the house to her. Cassie was deeply touched, not at the material gain, but at the thought behind it.

Knowing the dissent it would cause, she would have been just as happy to go by the original will.

❦

"You'll do no such thing, Cassie Jordan!" David exclaimed, when he heard Cassie say that for the sake of peace and family harmony she was proposing to abide by the terms of the original will.

"Your mother must have had some premonition of the sacrifices you were going to have to make and this is her way of making it up to you. Your mother is giving you the chance to reclaim your life. Sell the house, use the money to do something you've always wanted to do. Grab this chance with both hands, Cassie, and make her smile in heaven!" David argued passionately, holding her very close.

She raised her face to his and said, "I love you so much, David. You'll never know how much."

"If you love me, then accept your mother's will in the spirit it was made. After all, it was what she wanted," he advised.

❦

John said exactly the same, as did Laura and Aileen. Irene told her to do what she thought was best, which was no help. Martin said he wasn't happy about it and wanted to talk to her and Barbara sent a solicitor's letter stating her conviction that the will was null and void due to the mental incapacity of her mother and that if Cassie were not prepared to accept the terms of the first will, Barbara would see her in court.

CHAPTER FORTY-EIGHT

"How would you describe your mother's state of mind when she came to stay with you after her heart attack?" The barrister who was questioning Cassie on Barbara's behalf smiled suavely at her.

"She was tired. She had hated hospital, but once she started getting back on her feet we had some good laughs, and I think she enjoyed her stay with me very much." Cassie said quietly, facing her tormentor.

"Did you notice memory loss?"

Cassie sighed. "Well, it wasn't something I was really aware of at the time, but looking back, yes, my mother's memory was not as good as it had been. I had to give her a little map when she went down the High Street, and she was cooking a dinner once and forgot about it and burnt the saucepan."

"So you would agree, Miss Jordan, that your mother had Alzheimer's disease at that point."

"I would say," said Cassie, "that my mother was in the early stages of the disease, yes, but that she was by no means incapacitated."

"My question was: had your mother got Alzheimer's disease when she was with you in December 1984 and January 1985. Yes or no!" he shot back.

"Yes," Cassie said, lifting her chin and staring the obnoxious man straight in the eye.

Facing her, Barbara smiled triumphantly. On the same bench, Jean and Martin stared stonily ahead. Glancing a little to Barbara's left, she saw John and David sitting together. David gave her an encouraging wink and she knew that whatever happened here, he and John would be waiting for her. It was because of them that she was sitting here today fighting for her mother's wishes, although, if Nora had known the family was going to be so bitterly divided, maybe she would have left things as they were.

"I will repeat the question!" the barrister barked, as Cassie forced her thoughts back to the present moment. "Would you say your mother was more suggestible than usual during the period when she was staying with you immediately after her heart attack?"

"I wouldn't ever say Mam was *suggestible*. She had a mind of her own," Cassie retorted. Who did he think he was, talking so knowledgeably about *her* mother.

"But did she agree to do things she normally wouldn't agree to? She did spend a long time with you. Was that of her own choice?"

"If you're implying I kept Mam in Liverpool by force..." Cassie said furiously.

"I am not implying anything. The facts will speak for themselves." The barrister was coldly courteous.

Don't get rattled; he'll try to rattle you, her own barrister had warned. Keep your cool. Cassie took a deep breath. "It was the middle of winter, my mother had had a heart attack, she needed someone to take care of her. Barbara wouldn't," she glared at her sister, "John and Karen weren't in a position to, Irene and Martin were abroad, so that left me. Mam agreed to come to Liverpool with me. By the end of January she was feeling much better and anxious to get home, although I would have preferred for her to stay a little longer."

"I see!" Barbara's barrister drawled. "I put it to you, Miss Jordan, that in the time she was in your..." he paused and glanced around the court, "care," he paused again and looked at the judge, "you persuaded your mother to make a new will leaving her house to you, a house, I may add, that was recently valued at seventy thousand pounds."

"That is *not* true!" Cassie said heatedly.

"Well, how do you explain the fact that your mother changed her will and made a new one within days of coming home after staying with you in Liverpool!"

"I have no explanation for it!" Cassie said firmly.

"Oh come now, Miss Jordan. You surely don't expect the court to believe that."

"It's the truth!"

"I'd like, if I may, to move on to the period when you were at home in Port Mahon taking care of your mother."

Oh must you, Cassie thought wearily, wishing this whole ordeal could end.

"During this time you purchased a tumble-dryer. Is that correct?"

"Yes! My mother needed several changes of clothes and in the winter it wasn't always possible to get her clothes dry, so I bought the dryer," Cassie explained.

"And paid for it out of your mother's income. Isn't that the case?"

"I had no income of my own, I had given up my job. So it had to be out of Mam's money."

"And did you use this tumble-dryer for your own clothes?"

Cassie gave the barrister a scathing look. What the hell did he think, that she left her own clothes out in the *rain* to dry! "Of course I did."

"And you found it convenient?"

"Very!" she gritted.

"I see!" Cassie wished he'd stop saying "I see" in that sceptical drawl. He really was a loathsome man, Laura had warned her about him when she heard the name of the barrister Barbara's solicitor had instructed.

"You installed oil-fired central heating in the house despite the fact that there was a perfectly good back-boiler system in operation already. This was also paid for out of your mother's income. Why?"

"I was afraid that my mother would get burnt at the fire. She was fascinated by the chimney. She thought people were talking to her down it. I was afraid she would get burnt."

"Did your sister, my client, Mrs Jordan Murray, not suggest you install a fireguard?"

"Yes."

"Why didn't you?" he probed. "Surely it was the

obvious solution."

"I didn't want to take the chance."

"And central heating is so much more convenient than having to light a fire every day, isn't that so?"

"Yes," Cassie agreed wearily.

"So it was for the convenience as much as anything else."

"My mother's wellbeing was my prime concern," Cassie snapped.

"You spent several thousand pounds having aluminium windows and doors installed."

"Yes."

"Again paid for out of your mother's income?"

"Yes."

"What's your..." he smiled insincerely, "explanation for this?"

"Mam was always wandering. She climbed out the windows a few times. The doors and windows I had fitted had excellent locks."

"Couldn't you have changed the locks on the doors and windows? Wouldn't it have been far cheaper than spending your mother's income on a whole new set?"

"I could have done that, yes. But the existing doors and windows were quite old. The man who installed the heating told me that in the long run it would be a saving to get double-glazing, as otherwise I was going to lose a lot of the heat because of draughts."

"Best for *you*, you mean," Barbara's barrister accused.

"Look, I didn't know Mam was going to leave me the house. I thought her estate was to be divided equally and therefore whatever improvements I made would increase the value of the house and benefit everybody."

"Instead it benefited you!"

"I didn't know it was going to do that!" protested

Cassie, nearly in tears.

"I submit to this court that, having in the most devious way persuaded your mother to make a new will in your favour, you then in the most calculating way set out to improve the value of the property by spending your mother's income while she was alive, knowing that it would all accrue to you in the end. I submit, Miss Jordan, that you are a calculating woman, who would swindle your own brothers and sisters out of their just inheritance. And I submit that this will was made while your mother was suffering from Alzheimer's disease and was mentally incapacitated and is therefore null and void."

"No! *No!*" Cassie protested.

"Your Honour, I have no further questions for this witness." The barrister swept away. Barbara was over the moon with his performance.

❦

"Look, calm down, Cassie," John comforted her. "Doctor Tyne has to give his evidence and Mam's solicitor, and the witness to her will. You know that Mr Kenny has told us that Mam was perfectly clear about what she wanted to do the day she made her will and that in his view it's legal. So stop worrying."

"Did you hear the way that man twisted everything I said and made it look as though I were out to line my own pocket. I'm sure the judge will believe him. The way that barrister put it the evidence is overwhelming. He doesn't know me. I'm sure things like this *do* happen and people are manipulated to change wills. He probably thinks I'm one of those manipulators, especially since Martin is siding with Barbara. I can't believe Martin would think I'd do a thing like that to Mam and the family!"

"It's that Jean. She and Barbara are as thick as thieves!" John said in disgust.

"Come on, Cassie, eat a bit of something," David urged as he noticed her pushing her plate away without touching her food. They were having lunch at a hotel near the court. It was the final day of the hearing.

Cassie smiled at him. "I'm sorry, David, I'm not hungry. Maybe when it's over."

"It will be over soon," David promised, squeezing her hand.

❧

Barbara tucked into a plateful of mussels in garlic on a bed of pasta. She was starving. And very hopeful. Miles Regan had *crucified* Cassie on the witness stand. No one in their right senses could fail to doubt that her sister had indeed persuaded their poor addled mother to change her will. God, she hadn't even shed a tear at the funeral, while she and Irene had been in floods. Oh, Cassie was as cute as they come despite her saintly demeanour. And she was not the only one who thought, so; Martin and Jean were firmly committed to proving the same point. Jean had proven herself a gem in this case. She had been as angry at Martin's being done out of his inheritance as Barbara had been on her own account.

The judge would *have* to rule in her favour. Ian had told her it was practically a foregone conclusion. He had seen enough court cases to know how it was going. By tonight Barbara would be a wealthier woman than she was this morning.

"This is lovely, isn't it, Jean?" she smiled at her sister-in-law, who was relishing her plate of smoked salmon.

"Very nice indeed, I must say," the other woman agreed. "Martin, eat up; the food is very tasty!" she admonished her husband.

"I'm not hungry," Martin said glumly.

"Well, *I* certainly am!" laughed Barbara. "Here, pass it over to me."

❦

"It is clear to me," said the judge, smiling at Cassie, "that Miss Jordan acted in her mother's best interests at all times in a very kind and caring manner. From the evidence presented to me by Mrs Jordan's solicitor and GP, I believe that, although in the very early stages of Alzheimer's disease Mrs Jordan made her will under no duress and was quite clear and specific about her wishes. And her wishes were that the business be sold and proceeds divided equally between her children, and that her house be left to Miss Catherine Jordan, her eldest daughter, as a token of her gratitude for the care she has always received from her. Miss Jordan can leave this court with her head held high knowing that she cared for her mother admirably." He scowled at Barbara. "The will is upheld."

❦

"Congratulations!" David swept Cassie off her feet and swung her in the air before kissing her soundly.

John laughed. "Cassie, it couldn't have gone any other way, so put the matter behind you now and get on with your life."

"I will, oh I will!" Cassie vowed. "Barbara has upset me for the last time!"

❦

"We'll appeal it!" Barbara said hysterically. "She's *not* getting away with it!"

Barbara's solicitor looked enquiringly at Miles Regan, the barrister.

"I would have to advise that you run the risk of incurring major losses should you fail to win an appeal against today's decision. Your solicitor and I will, of course, be instructed by you. The decision to appeal is yours. I must repeat, however," he looked straight at Barbara, "that your losses would be quite substantial if you failed in your attempt to overturn today's verdict."

"You can appeal yourself, Barbara. I've had enough!" Martin announced.

"*Martin!*" exclaimed his wife. "You can't leave Barbara in the lurch like that."

"I can and I will. It's already cost me a fortune. I've no intention of throwing good money after bad."

The barrister said snootily, "As you wish!"

"But Martin—" protested his wife.

"The answer is no and that's final. We should never have taken this case in the first place. Cassie would never have swindled Mam or us. And I'm ashamed I was persuaded otherwise. Come on, Jean, we're going home!"

Jean and Barbara stared at Martin in dismay.

"Martin's right!" Ian muttered. "It would only cost us more money. If you want to spend your own money, Barbara, that's up to you. But count me out!" her husband declared, adding, "I'd cut my losses if I were you!" Barbara couldn't believe her ears. She was being deserted by everyone. Only Jean was prepared to stick to the bitter end and she had no money of her own.

Feeling that her world was collapsing around her ears, Barbara turned to walk out of the building only to discover Kristi Killeen smiling sweetly at her from a corner of the large waiting-hall!

CHAPTER FORTY-NINE

It was such a relief to have the court case over. Cassie felt as though a burden had been lifted from her shoulders. It was as if she had been living in a limbo this past year, ever since Barbara had filed a petition to declare that Nora's will was null and void and that Cassie had coerced her into changing it.

Cassie had been *so* shocked at the charge. Barbara refused to speak to her, and when Martin and Jean supported Barbara, she was devastated. How *could* they think she would do such a thing? She was their sister, she had loved her mother. It was incredible.

She had cried for weeks until, in desperation, David suggested that she go back to work. It was a move she had been putting off for ages, but she knew he was right, so she contacted her personnel department to see what the position was.

The dilemma about whether to return to Liverpool or not did not materialise; there was no vacancy in her branch and she could either go back to London or to Head Office in Dublin. She chose the latter.

Getting back into a routine helped a lot, although commuting from Port Mahon was a drag. She didn't want to get a flat so she began to think about selling the house in Liverpool and buying one in the city, but she decided not to make any decision on the matter until after the court case.

About six months before the court case was due to be heard, Cassie was offered a position in Allied Isles' branch in Malahide and she jumped at the chance. It was less than half an hour's drive down the coast from Port Mahon and Cassie liked the bustling seaside town. David sometimes came in and met her for lunch.

It was strange in the empty house without her mother, especially at night, and Cassie found it hard to sleep. For the previous few years, she had been so used to sleeping practically with one eye open that it was hard to remember that Nora was not there to require attention.

When the case was over and the will was settled, the business was sold for a very satisfactory price and Cassie knew it was time to make up her mind about the house. She decided to sell. Her home held too many unhappy memories for her and she wanted to make a fresh start. In December 1989, just six months after the court case, she put the bungalow on the market. She wanted to start the new decade afresh and she had already put a deposit on a house in Malahide.

❧

On the first day of the new decade David cooked Cassie a superb brunch. She had spent Christmas with John and Karen and their two children. This New Year's Day, she didn't want to go home at all. David and she decided to go for a walk along Broadmeadows Estuary in Malahide to work off their meal. It reminded her a little of the Marine Lake in Liverpool, with its sailboats bobbing up and down and windsurfers and waterskiers in the summer. Across the river lay Portrane and, to the right of her, Lambay Island. It was a very picturesque part of north County Dublin, she thought, as they walked the road to Lissenhall and fed the swans and watched the sun glinting between the bare trees on the opposite bank. On the way back to the car, a homemade For Sale sign caught Cassie's eye.

It was a little house overlooking the river and there was something about it that appealed to her at once. She had set her heart on living in Malahide, not far from the bank, and had been very disappointed when the owners of the house on which she had paid a deposit had changed their minds.

"David, look!" She pointed the property out to him. "Isn't it lovely? I wonder if I could have a look around? Maybe it's an omen that I've seen it today. I started a new life in London at the beginning of the Eighties; maybe this is a new start as well!" she said excitedly.

"No time like the present to find out," David, always a man of action, said briskly. He led the way up the winding little path and knocked on the door. A small woman with bright, lively eyes answered.

"I was wondering...I saw the For Sale sign and I was interested. Would I be able to have a look around? I'm hoping to buy a house," Cassie explained.

"Certainly, dear, certainly." The woman stood back to let them enter. She led them through a small hall into the sitting-room. Or, as the old lady called it, the parlour. And a real parlour it was with its Victorian flock wallpaper and faded green pelmet curtains with their swing tassels and the old chairs and sofa with lace antimacassars. A fire blazed in the hearth and the place was very tidy with all the old mahogany furniture polished and shining.

David, seeing Cassie's enraptured face, grinned to himself. He knew exactly what the love of his life was up to; she was mentally redecorating.

"Come along, dear, I'll show you the dining-room and kitchen," the birdlike woman smiled. Her name was Matilda Cox and she was going out to New Zealand to live with her daughter. "I can't wait," she confided. "I've always wanted to travel and see the world but until last November I had to look after poor George." That was her husband, who had suffered a stroke some years previously. Cassie could empathise with the bright-eyed, friendly woman and she found herself telling Matilda about her own mother. The little woman took her hand. "She's in heaven now, dear, and so is my George. But believe me, from now on you will be showered with blessings. I know. It's happening to me already. One night I just decided I wanted to do something different in my life. Rita suggested I come and live with her, and you know something, dear? I heard George telling me to say yes. And do you know something else very strange?" she remarked as she led them through a tiny kitchen and out to a jungle of a garden.

"What's that?" Cassie smiled.

"Would you believe that I put the sign up only five minutes ago? I waited purposely until today. I wanted to start the Nineties in a positive way."

"Me too!" exclaimed Cassie, delighted with this kindred spirit. "That explains why I didn't notice it when we set out. So does this mean that we're your first viewers?"

"It does!" Matilda nodded. "And maybe my last!"

"How could that be?" Cassie asked.

Matilda smiled. "Well, dear, I like you and your beau and if you want the house and you give me my price, you can have it. I don't want any old Tom, Dick or Harry living in my house. I've had a very happy life here and I want to leave it in good hands. I know you two are happy together. I watched you from the window and I felt it in my bones. I said, Matilda, look no further, the answer to prayer has arrived. It's George again, you see!"

Cassie was afraid to look at David in case she started to laugh. The poor dote. Imagine calling them an answer to prayer!

Matilda brought them up to the bedrooms, two cosy rooms with their windows in the eaves and a magnificent view of the estuary. Cassie was hooked! This was the house for her. Maybe Matilda was right. Maybe Nora and George were organising this between them in heaven.

If she bought it, there'd be a lot of re-vamping to do. The kitchen would have to be extended and a new bathroom suite plumbed in, but that would be half the fun. After all, she *was* an interior decorator! She knew the price would be well within her means. It was a small house that required a lot of work; she'd probably be able to buy it for cash.

Matilda named her price, which was far lower than Cassie had expected. "That's much too low," Cassie said firmly, adding another five thousand pounds, to Matilda's delight. David just looked at Cassie as if she had gone crazy altogether. The two women exchanged the names of their solicitors and Matilda promised to set things in motion the next day.

"I don't know which of you was the crazier! Omens! Answers to prayer! Divine intervention! Adding five thousand pounds to the asking price! Women! I'll never fathom them!" he grinned. "And she's mad to let complete strangers into her house."

"*You* wouldn't understand. Matilda and I understood each other perfectly!" Cassie retorted. "Anyway, I wouldn't have been happy to take the house at that price. She was doing herself. Property here is very expensive."

"Cassie, you're going to have to gut that place, you know that. You're too soft-hearted," David responded.

"David, you know as well as I do that if that house had been in the hands of an estate agent, he would have got the price I gave her and more, except that he would have pocketed a tidy sum for himself," Cassie argued.

"You've an answer for everything, woman!" David

laughed, giving her a hug. "Come on; we'll go up to Howth and have a look around." They drove up to the summit and sat overlooking the bay. They could see as far as Wicklow and it was magnificent. The sky was just beginning to redden as the fiery sun dipped behind the hills. Driving down the village to go for a walk along the pier they stopped to let people cross the street to the DART station.

"You know I've never been on the DART," Cassie mused. "I must, some time. It goes right out to Bray."

"*Never* been on the DART? Tut! Tut!" David grinned. "Why don't you start the decade doing something you've never done before."

Cassie stared at him. "You mean, go on the DART right now?"

"Yeah! Right this very minute! We could have a pot of hot chocolate in the Royal Marine in Dun Laoghaire. You haven't lived until you've tasted their hot chocolate." His eyes twinkled.

"Come on, then!" she said eagerly. "There must be one due soon."

David parked the car and hand in hand they walked into the station and bought their tickets. Cassie enjoyed every minute of their train ride, especially after Killester when they passed Clontarf and Fairview and she watched the setting sun turn the waters to flame along the seafront to her left. They crossed Butt Bridge and she saw birds circling the cream-and-black Guinness boats. She loved their names, the *Lady Patricia* and the *Miranda Guinness*. Imagine having a ship named after you!

"Oh look! Look, David, it's Trinity College. We're passing at the back of Trinity," she exclaimed a few minutes later. Cassie was fascinated by the way the city changed character in the space of minutes. After Amiens

Street station they passed through the affluent suburb of Ballsbridge and then they were speeding through the Merrion Gates and the sea came into view with Dun Laoghaire in the distance. Booterstown, Blackrock, it was like a guided tour of the city.

"Oh David, I really enjoyed that," Cassie said as they walked up through the grounds of the Royal Marine Hotel. "It's a great way of seeing the...the living city."

"I know what you mean. You catch glimpses of people's lives through their windows as you speed past. You share an intimacy with them for a second or two and then you're gone! I love train journeys myself!" David agreed. "Maybe we'll go on the Patagonia Express or the Orient Express or even cross America some time!"

"I'd love that," Cassie smiled, snuggling against him. It had turned cold and they drank their hot chocolate appreciatively, sitting beside a big fire, gazing out at the darkening night. It was so delicious that David ordered another pot and they relaxed completely.

"We could have dinner here," David suggested, a little later. "I'm starving."

"Me too!" agreed Cassie happily. They had walked several miles earlier on and dinner would be nice.

The waiter seated them by the window and lit a candle on their table. Behind them the lights of the pier twinkled and in the distance they could see Howth, far across the bay. Their meal was superb and afterwards they went to the bar and had brandies.

"I don't know about you but I'm so comfortable I don't feel like getting the train to Howth and driving all the way back to Port Mahon." David smiled at Cassie, his eyes warm in the lamplight. "How would you like to begin the new decade by making wild passionate love in a hotel room?" he invited.

Cassie burst out laughing. "You devil, David Williams! You had this all planned!"

David laughed. "No, I didn't, honestly; it was you who mentioned the DART. But now that we *are* here, do you want to go back home? If you want to, of course we'll go."

"And miss a night of wild passionate love...not on your nellie!" Cassie teased.

They made love like it was the first time for them both and it was beautiful. Cassie lay with her head resting on David's chest, listening to the slow beating of his heart, and realised that, for the first time since Nora died, she actually felt happy. Yes, today had been a very happy day for her and David. She fell asleep in his arms.

She awoke before dawn. Gently easing herself from David's embrace, she slipped his jumper on and sat in one of the chairs beside the big windows that faced out on to Dublin Bay. They were on the fourth floor and beneath her the lights of the pier shone like stars. Across the bay, the city shimmered and twinkled in the black velvet night. It was a very beautiful sight and she sat quietly enjoying the view.

She felt so serene just now, so different from the agitated, restless woman she had been this past year. Deciding impulsively to buy the house had helped. For the first time since she could remember she had felt in control. It had been so good picturing how she could redesign the house. All the old creative juices had started to flow. She felt excited at the thought of it. God, she had missed her decorating and interior design.

Something David had said to her soon after her mother's death came back to her. "Reclaim your life!" he'd said. "Do something you've always wanted to do!"

Cassie's eyes widened. Why hadn't she thought of

that before! It was perfect! And to think that she had been staring straight at it and not seen it until now!

Hugging her excitement to herself, Cassie slipped off the jumper and slid back into bed, putting her arms around David's broad back and curving against him.

Reclaim her life! Do something she had always wanted! That was exactly what she was going to do. Too excited to sleep, Cassie began to make her plans.

CHAPTER FIFTY

Cassie, dressed in a denim overall, was overseeing the refurbishment of her newly acquired premises on Malahide's main street. She had taken a few days' leave from the bank.

"I think I'll have the reception desk and counter here, and the small sofa and easy chair here for when I'm discussing designs with clients. So could you put some sockets on this wall?" she asked the electrician.

"No problem, Cassie."

"Have you decided what to call it yet?" Brian, the carpenter, asked as he put the finishing touches to the pine ceiling. Cassie was going for a warm rustic look.

She sighed. "Interior Motives? Designs on You? New Horizons? I don't know yet. I'm meeting the girls for lunch over in Breakers. Maybe we'll have a brain-storming session and come up with something," Cassie smiled. "Listen, you guys, I'm off. If you hear wild shrieks down the street it's only four mad women having a reunion so don't panic. OK?"

"OK," they laughed.

Slipping out of her overalls, Cassie grabbed her bag

and ran. She was meeting the girls in five minutes and needed to brush her hair and put on a bit of lipstick. She had told them to meet her in the restaurant. No one was going to see the place until it was ready and she could have a grand unveiling, and that was quite a while off.

She smiled to herself as she walked past her bank. Soon she would be handing in her resignation and doing something she had always wanted to do. Setting up her own interior design business.

Who would have thought eight months before, when she sat overlooking Dublin Bay in the early hours of a January morning, that her dream would become a reality.

First the house, then the business! Saying it like that made it sound easy, but of course it hadn't been. Cassie had bought her little house overlooking the estuary with the money from her share of the sale of the business. There had been more than enough left over to have the place extended and re-vamped. When the builders were finished Cassie intended decorating it herself.

While this was all taking place she had made enquiries about a shop that was for sale on the main street in Malahide. She passed the premises every day on her way to work and noticed it was for sale but never even thought anything of it until that life-changing morning when the idea came to her. But buying the place had been a difficult task. She had made an offer that had not been accepted and had had to go higher.

Then she had to sell Nora's house and the house in Liverpool in order to raise the purchase price of the premises. Sometimes she thought that she would be on bridging finance for ever. The Liverpool deal went fine. The couple who were renting it from her wanted to buy it and Cassie had agreed a price with them. That had lulled her into a false sense of security about selling the bungalow. The first buyer had pulled out before signing the contract, the second had not got loan approval and had been devastated. Finally, the third couple that decided to buy it were ready to close when their solicitor died, causing a further delay. Cassie was frantic because she was afraid she would lose her business premises.

She got her first commission by accident. She was chatting with the hairdresser in Port Mahon while she was getting her hair done. The new proprietors, a husband-and-wife team had remarked that they wanted to give the place a new look. Of course, Cassie had immediately come up with several suggestions, explaining that she had done an interior design diploma. The next time she went in to get her hair done, they asked her if she would like to submit a design. Cassie jumped at the proposal and the result was that Port Mahon had a trendy new-look hair salon, and Cassie was back in the interior design business.

Several other jobs had come her way by word of mouth and once again, as in London, she became a much happier person when her creativity was liberated. David backed her in everything, despite the fact that he was up to his eyes in the Thatcher biography. Cassie often went over to Hawthorn Cottage, cooked him a meal and left it to keep warm on the Aga for him. Their only contact would be her goodnight kiss as she left.

She tried to be as supportive as she could, while looking forward to the day when David's immersion in the book would end and they could have time together. He had vowed never again to sign away his life on a contract and she knew he would be glad to be a free man. That was why she made no complaints when he spent days, nights and weekends at his word processor. The pressure of his deadline was always there and she wasn't going to make his life more difficult by moaning. David had been a tower of strength for her when she needed him most; now she was doing the same for him.

After work and at the weekends she was kept busy with her new commissions, and whatever spare time she had was spent getting the new premises ready. Sometimes she wondered if she had been too impulsive, spending so much money on the house and new business. Would she get enough work to justify going into business? It was a risk, and a big one, but if she hadn't taken her chance, she knew she'd never do it. She would go on working in the bank, and always there would be a sense of regret for an opportunity lost. Whenever she had doubts, she said to herself, "You're reclaiming your life!"

It had been a wrench finally to sell the family home. Irene had nearly gone crazy when she heard that Cassie was planning to sell and this had only increased Cassie's feelings of guilt. In the end she knew that if she really wanted to start afresh it was something she must do. She wrote to Barbara and Martin, informing them of her decision, and offering them the chance to take anything they wanted out of the house. Barbara's response had been a letter from her solicitor with a list of items that she required, including Nora's valuable ivory jewellery-box and filigree brooch, a Japanese tea-set, and the *Encyclopaedia Brittanica* that Jack had bought for them as children.

John had been disgusted by the letter and advised Cassie to tell Barbara to get lost, but Cassie, sick of confrontation, replied to the solicitor saying that Barbara could have what she asked for. Barbara had sent a taxi for the items and that was all the contact the two sisters had had since the court case. Taking a last look around the house that had held such happy and sad memories,

Cassie wept and John had been just as upset, but as she closed the door behind them for the last time she knew she was ending one chapter in her life and opening another. She made a promise to herself never to look back, to try to leave all her regrets behind. Cassie had been reading a little book she had found among her mother's possessions, called *The Game of Life and How to Play It*. Written by a teacher of metaphysics in New York called Florence Scovel-Shinn, it was a powerful little book. As she walked down the garden path of home for the last time, Cassie remembered something she had read in it just a few days previously: "Jesus Christ said behold, now is the accepted time. Now is the day of Salvation." On this the author had commented, *Lot's wife looked back and was turned into a pillar of salt. The robbers of time are the past and the future. Man should bless the past, and forget it, if it keeps him in bondage, and bless the future knowing it has in store for him endless joys, but live fully in the now.* This had made a tremendous impact on Cassie. How true it was. Well, she would bless the past and leave it behind her and start living for now.

Because her new house was not nearly ready, Cassie went temporarily to live with John and Karen. David had wanted her to come to him but, though terribly tempted, Cassie knew she would only be a distraction. When his book was finished and he was his own man again, they would have all the time in the world together. Cassie smiled, thinking of their plans. She knew she and David were destined to be together forever. With him she felt serene and happy, so different from her dark days of anxiety with Robbie.

She was in the ladies' in the restaurant, brushing her hair and making herself presentable, when she heard a familiar giggle and an answering guffaw! Her face wreathed in smiles, she flew out the door and into the arms of Aileen and Laura. It was *so* good to see them. All talking nineteen to the dozen, they sat at their table and grinned at one another. They were waiting for Judy, so they ordered some wine. She rushed in a few minutes later, all flustered.

"So how's the entrepreneur? Tell us all the news!" Aileen was agog. Cassie laughed and brought them up to date on her current situation.

"I think it's just perfect for you, Cassie," Laura announced as the waiter arrived with their menus.

Judy sighed. "I envy you, Cassie. You've done so much with your life and so have Laura and Aileen. All I've done is get married and produce two children."

"I think that's a great achievement, Judy," Cassie responded. "Don't knock it."

"Yes, but it's not enough!" Judy burst out.

Her sister arched an elegant eyebrow. "Get a job then!"

"Oh, Andrew would have a fit, Aileen. He's very much against me working at all. He likes having me there to run around after him. Sure I could have got a job in Marcia Ellis's PR firm but he made such a fuss about it I had to give up the idea."

"I know what I'd do with Doug if he ever tried anything like that!" Laura declared.

"You always *were* too soft," Aileen frowned Judy.

"Would you really like to be working again, getting up early, dealing with the public, having to be cheerful all the time?" Cassie grinned.

"Wouldn't I just!" sighed Judy.

"You're hired!"

"What!"

"I love your style!" drawled Aileen approvingly.

"I need a receptionist/assistant to be there all the

time when I'm out on jobs," Cassie explained. "Someone I can trust, someone who's got a bit of commonsense, someone who's got taste and style, someone just like you!" she smiled affectionately.

"Oh Cassie, I'm speechless!"

"I'm delighted!" Cassie exclaimed. "I knew I'd have to get someone eventually and you've just solved one problem for me. But what will Andrew say?"

"He can say what he likes; this time I'm going to do what *I* want for a change."

"The worm has turned at last," smirked Aileen, downing her second glass of wine in celebration. "Not that you're a worm, Judy," she added hastily, catching sight of her sister's face. "I was speaking metaphorically."

"And I just thought you were plain ol' drunk!" Laura deadpanned and they all burst out laughing. It was a jolly lunch. The food was delicious and Cassie urged them to try the pecan pie for dessert. She had long become an addict. "It's yummy!" she promised them.

"Has Barbara been in contact at all since I was home at Christmas?" Aileen asked, as they sipped their coffee.

Cassie shook her head. "Not personally. Not since the week after the funeral when she found out that Mam had left the house to me!"

"She's a bitter old pill, isn't she!" Aileen mused, adding a heaped spoon of brown sugar to her coffee with never a thought for her fabulous creamy complexion. "Imagine not speaking to you for two years!"

"She's a pathetic person, really," Laura said reflectively. "Going through life with a chip on her shoulder, not being able to forgive and forget, and holding a grudge that will always poison her. Look at what she's lost. Your friendship and John's, and if *that's* not worth having, I don't know what is!"

Cassie smiled. "Thanks, Laura, but to be honest I don't worry about it any longer. I don't hold grudges and I don't dwell on the past," she said firmly. "Barbara will always have a bee in her bonnet about something."

"A hive would be more like it!" snorted Aileen. The others guffawed.

"She's written a novel, you know!" Judy informed them. Barbara and she met quite regularly on the party circuit so Judy was *au fait* with Barbara's latest!

"You're not serious!" exclaimed Aileen. "What's it called? *A Martyr Called Barbara?*"

"I know!" laughed Laura. "I bet she's called it *Return of the Wind.*"

"That sounds as if the heroine had beans for supper!" giggled Aileen, who was deliciously tipsy.

"I'll have you know that according to Barbara it's a serious literary novel set to take the publishing world by storm, and it's called *The Fire and the Fury.*"

The others shrieked with uproarious laughter.

"She's not quite finished it, but next year's Booker Prize is a foregone conclusion according to her."

"I'd give anything to read it!" Aileen wiped her eyes.

"I bet I know who's the bitch!" grinned Cassie. "Me, with Kristi Killeen coming a close second. I'd better tell David to look to his literary laurels!"

"How *is* the sexiest man in the world? You haven't got tired of him by any chance, have you?" Aileen teased.

"'Fraid not," Cassie grinned.

"Oh well, I live in hope! Actually, Pierre and I met up again recently, so we've become an item again!" Aileen informed them.

"Frenchmen are *so* romantic!" sighed Judy.

"Dear, once you've washed a man's smelly socks, it doesn't matter whether he's French, Welsh, or Irish. You can forget about the romantic bit," Aileen philosophised.

"Have more coffee; there's a good girl," Laura urged, winking at Cassie.

"I'd prefer another bottle of wine, actually, if it's all the same to you," joked Aileen.

"You plonker," her friend retorted.

"What are you going to call the business?" Judy asked.

"I don't know yet. There's a name out there waiting to be picked. I'll know it's right when I hear it." Cassie smiled at her friends. She was having a lovely time with these cherished companions who had been at her side all through the years. With friends like these she could cope with anything; Cassie Jordan had already proved that!

❧

What *would* she call her business, she wondered, as she lay in bed that night. She'd had a lovely day with the girls and then David had arrived at her premises completely out of the blue with a bottle of champagne and a lovely bunch of freesias, her favourite flowers. They had gone for a long walk by the sea and made love back at the cottage.

"Stay the night!" David urged and she had been so tempted, but she knew if she stayed, he would write no more for the rest of the evening nor the next day.

"When you've finished this book, I'm going to lock this bedroom door and we're not leaving it for a month!"

"Drat! If I were writing fiction, I could have a tidal wave to drown the whole lot of them or they could perish in an earthquake or a massive fire and I could finish the book tonight!" he said ruefully.

"I don't think Maggie Thatcher would allow a mere tidal wave or earthquake or massive fire to get in *her* way," Cassie teased. "I wonder if that's what happens in

The Fire and the Fury? Fires and earthquakes!"

"*That* I am dying to read!" David chuckled. "With a title like that, Barbara can't go wrong! It's a pity she's not talking to you; she'd have no problem coming up with a name for the business!" David Williams was soundly battered with a pillow, for being such a smarty.

❦

Cassie smiled at the memory. David had phoned just an hour ago to tell her he had written twenty pages after she left him so he was feeling quite chuffed with himself.

She snuggled down into the bed. It was a high old-fashioned beds and had bolsters stuffed with feathers and masses of soft white pillows. Karen laughingly confessed that sometimes she engineered a row with John just as an excuse to spend a night in her guest-room. She and John made her so welcome and she would miss them when she moved into her own house, even though she was really looking forward to that.

Yawning, Cassie picked up her mother's book. She'd just read a few pages before she went to sleep. It was such a positive book and written so simply. She opened it at random and read the chapter heading, "Perfect Self Expression or The Divine Design," under which was written:

No wind can drive my bark astray
Nor change the tide of destiny.

What a lovely line, she thought, as she read on. A piece of paper fell out from between the pages and with a little stab of loneliness, Cassie saw it was covered with her mother's handwriting. "Things to be done before Cassie's wedding." That was going back a good few years, when Cassie and Robbie announced their engagement and Nora said to make sure she had plenty of time to prepare for the wedding, a wedding that was not to be.

Robbie *had* married, though, Cassie heard when she went back to work. He was currently working in the training centre in Ranelagh. Cassie had never seen him again after their meeting in Liverpool, nor had she any desire to. She rarely even spared him a thought. David gave her everything she had ever wanted or needed in a relationship. There was no comparison between their love and what she had endured with Robbie.

Mend the front gate, Nora had written. Buy a new shower curtain. Paper the hall. Get the chimneys cleaned. Put the finishing touches to the front porch. Cassie smiled. Her poor mother. What finishing touches she had to put to the front porch, Cassie had never discovered. Probably add some plants or an ornament or two. As long as she could remember, her mother had been putting the finishing touches to something or other. A dress she was making, a room she was papering, a cake she was icing...It hit Cassie like a bolt from the blue, Finishing Touches! *Finishing Touches!* That was it! That was the name! Nora had provided the means for her to make her dream come true, and now she had provided her with the perfect name. Her mother hadn't left her at all; she was still looking after her. Cassie remembered the little poem she had learnt after Jack's death:

*Death is nothing at all. I have only slipped away
   into the next room...*

That's where her parents were, together in the next room, keeping an eye on her. This was the proof. Comforted beyond words, Cassie switched off her light and pulled the sheets up around her. She knew without a doubt she was doing the right thing.

"**Finishing Touches** it is, then! Goodnight, Mam, goodnight, Pops," she murmured as she fell asleep.

🌟🌟🌟

EPILOGUE 1991

THE PARTY

"Are you right, Karen?" John yelled upstairs to his wife. "Joan's here to babysit!"

"I'm coming. Hold on. I'll be ready in a minute."

John paced the hall. He liked to be early for things and Karen always left at the last possible moment.

He was showered and dressed and ready in twenty minutes, while his wife was still titivating herself after an hour! Karen ran down the stairs in her stockinged feet.

"Did you see that new pair of shoes I bought the other day?"

"We're going to be late!" exclaimed her husband in exasperation.

"In the name of God! How could you be *late* for a party? Would you stop being a Hysterical Hilda and help me look for my shoes!" Karen snapped, equally exasperated. It was always the same when they were going anywhere. Even to Mass on a Sunday!

Mr and Mrs Jordan left the house in silence ten minutes later, waved off by Joan, who was used to the way they went on.

In silence they drove towards the main road. "I'm sorry!" said John, who was feeling better now that they were actually on the way.

Karen sniffed. "You're always the same! You never even noticed my new suit! I might as well be going in a sack for all the compliments I got from you."

"Well, it's the nicest sack I ever saw!" John grinned at his wife.

Karen couldn't keep her face straight. It was so annoying the way he always got out of trouble by making her laugh. He pulled into the side of the road and stopped the car. "What are you doing?"

"Just going to show my approval of your new suit," John declared, putting his arms around her and drawing her close.

"We'll be late, John," Karen murmured ten minutes later.

"How could you be late for a party?" her husband replied, as he continued to show his approval.

❦

Jean added a bit of extra mascara. Not that she was going anywhere special, she told herself. She and Barbara might go somewhere for a drink and when she was with Barbara she always liked to look that extra bit glamorous. Her sister-in-law was such a glamorous person and so well-connected. Barbara knew everybody who counted in Dublin!

She pulled down the skirt of her Private Collection suit a little bit more, conscious that she was not as thin as would like to be. She had caught a glimpse of Cassie in Malahide the other day, dressed in a pair of shorts and a skimpy T-shirt. The tan of her! She looked very well, Jean had to admit sourly. Much better than during the court case, when she had been skin and bone. So well she might, spending the money they should all have shared, and starting up her own business. And from what Jean had heard around, her business was taking off. It was becoming an "in" thing to have your house done over by Cassie Jordan. Half of her north County Dublin acquaintances seemed to be considering taking the plunge.

Well, Cassie Jordan would never again set foot inside her door. Jean still had bitter memories of the day she had been told by her sister-in-law to get out of Nora's house. Jean couldn't care less if Cassie had been on the verge of a nervous breakdown. Anyone with breeding did not behave like that with their family. Well, tonight, Cassie would rue her behaviour. The only members of her family to share her shallow triumph would be John and Karen. Martin, Irene and Barbara wouldn't be seen dead in **Finishing Touches**—and serves her right! Jean sprayed herself with Chanel No 5, told the babysitter that Martin was working late so she should stay the night if she wished, and headed off to meet her sister-in-law, or VBF, as Barbara would say in her column!

❦

Martin finished the job earlier than he had expected and headed back to the office to change. Jean wouldn't be a bit happy if she realised what his intentions were, but he knew what he had to do! It had been on his mind for ages and this was the perfect opportunity. Having made his decision, he whistled lightheartedly as he sped along the Dublin–Belfast road in his van. Tonight he'd sleep better than he had done for years! It was a nice thought.

❦

Irene came through the arrivals hall in Dublin airport feeling nervously excited. She had done it! All by herself. Made all her own arrangements. Flown Concorde across the Atlantic, got a Dublin flight at Heathrow and here she was! It was a heady feeling. She wondered if Dean had got her note yet!

The Senator had been on a business trip to New York and hadn't been sure when he was coming back to Washington, so she just left him a note to say she had to come home to deal with some family matters! That might shake him up. Make him see that she could do things for herself without depending on him all the time. Show him that he wasn't dealing with a bimbo here. Irene conveniently forgot that it was the Senator's money that had funded her credit-card purchase of her flight tickets.

Now that she was here, though, she had no plan. She couldn't go home to Port Mahon; Cassie didn't live there any longer. Should she go directly to Malahide? **Finishing Touches** shouldn't be hard to find. There was no point in going to Barbara's! She wouldn't be a bit happy that Irene had flown from America to go to Cassie's party!

A look of doubt crossed Irene's perfectly made-up brow. Maybe she'd go to John and Karen's. That might be the best idea.

"I don't believe it! Irene Jordan! What are you doing here?" a familiar voice shrieked, and Irene turned around to find Aileen O'Shaughnessy grinning from ear to ear. "Have you come for Cassie's party?"

Irene nodded, delighted to see a face she recognised.

"Oh Irene, Cassie will be thrilled! I've just arrived from London myself. Where are you going? Will we share a taxi?"

"Well, I'm not sure exactly where I'm going. I don't know how to get to where Cassie lives now and I was thinking I might go to John and Karen."

"I'll tell you what!" Aileen's eyes sparkled. "Why don't you come home with me and we won't let Cassie know you're here and we'll give her a great surprise tonight!"

"That's a brilliant idea, Aileen," Irene smiled happily. She didn't have to worry now about where to go or what to do; it was all arranged, thanks to Aileen.

"Come on, let's get a taxi!" Aileen urged, making for the taxi-rank. Irene was quite happy to follow her lead.

"You never told me you were bringing visitors!" Angela O'Shaughnessy moaned after she had shown Irene to Judy's old room.

"Oh Mother! Irene's not a *visitor*, she's Cassie's sister. and it's just for a few hours before we go to the party! Look, if it's too much trouble, we'll just go to Judy's and stay there!" Aileen retorted.

"No, no, it's all right," her mother backtracked hastily. She had been looking forward to her daughter's arrival. The house was so quiet without the girls.

"I'm just going to give Laura a call and tell her the news," Aileen said, breezily waving her left hand in the direction of the telephone.

"Fine, call away. I'll just make a pot of tea." Angela bustled out to the kitchen.

Aileen stared ruefully at the emerald adorning the third finger of her left hand. "And mothers are supposed to notice everything!" she muttered. God knows it was big enough! And Irene hadn't noticed. But she was in such a tizzy about actually being here for Cassie's party. Well, Aileen was going to say nothing to anyone. It would be interesting to see which of her friends or family noticed her engagement ring first.

Aileen looked again at her ring. Even she found it hard to believe that after all these years, she was finally going to settle down with Pierre. He had given her an ultimatum. Marry me or we never see each other again. Put like that, there was no dilemma. The man was crazy about her, and had been, from the first time they met in his aut's beauty salon in Mayfair. They had split up and got together and split up and got together but this time Pierre had had enough. He had ordered her to make a decision, so Aileen had decided to stay.

It was about time she stopped gadding about anyway, she decided, grinning to herself. It was lovely being engaged. It gave her a little warm glow...even if no one else had noticed. It was a pity Pierre couldn't have made it tonight. He was on business in France. Never mind, they'd be together soon.

Humming to herself, Aileen dialled Laura's number.

❦

"Congratulations, Mr MacIntyre. You now own the River View Public House!" Laura handed the keys to her client and shook hands with him and his solicitor. She sighed with relief, tidied up her papers, grabbed her coat and briefcase and flew out the door of the other solicitor's office. She was dead late. Things had got delayed, and her whole schedule was awry.

She had to collect her daughter from the crèche, feed and bathe her and put her to bed. Then get herself ready for Cassie's party and bring a change of clothes over to Doug's office, where she was collecting him because his car was being serviced.

The traffic was bumper to bumper and she cursed long and loudly as she inched her way along Leeson Street. This was the second time this week she would be late for the crèche and they didn't take too kindly to tardy mothers! Laura yawned, as fatigue flooded every muscle. She hadn't had this on her first pregnancy, although she had been queasy, which was worse in a way. She hadn't had to rush around as much or work so hard on her first pregnancy.

Be careful what you ask for—you might get it, went the old saying. Laura smiled to herself. Now that she had her partnership, was it that important? Frankly there were times when she'd give anything not to have to send her daughter to the crèche, so she could spend the whole day with her precious child. She was missing so much of her growing up. She'd never thought she'd feel this way, but the feeling was getting stronger by the day. God knows how she'd feel after the new baby.

Wasn't life strange all the same, she thought, as she swung left and headed along the canal. Look at the way things had worked out for Cassie, when everything had once seemed so bleak. Tonight was going to be a terrific night. To hell with Barbara and the rest of them. Cassie was going to be surrounded by people who really loved her. Wasn't it great about Irene coming home for the party? Laura would never have thought she had it in her. And Aileen had sounded so bubbly on the phone. That one was up to something; Laura knew her friend too well not to know. She was really looking forward to tonight, to seeing Aileen and Cassie and having a few laughs. There was nothing like meeting your best friends for perking a girl up! Nothing like it in the world!

❧

Judy caught sight of the time and gave a little shriek of dismay. She had been visiting her mother-in-law in Saint Vincent's Hospital, because Drew was far too busy to take the time, so she popped over to the Merrion Centre to get some smoked salmon in Quinnsworth. She then nipped into Wordsworth, the bookshop, where she had completely lost track of time. Judy had been looking for a book on assertiveness, and Kim, the attractive blonde proprietress, went out of her way to help. Judy now had three assertiveness books tucked under her arm.

She'd better get a move on if she didn't want to get stuck in the rush-hour traffic. She'd take the East Link and bypass town and be home in no time. Judy headed for her Golf. She was going to read these books and take note of them. Even now, Drew didn't think she was serious about going back to work. And she was starting the following Monday! Well, he'd better get used to the idea! He could huff and puff as much as he liked because back to work she was going! And she was so excited about it!

She couldn't wait for tonight. Drew wasn't coming with her, but Judy didn't care. Her friends would be there, Cassie and Laura and Aileen, her sister. *They'd* give her the support and encouragement that was so lacking from her husband.

"Screw you, Andrew Lawson!" Judy declared assertively, as she swung the Golf out of the car-park and headed in the direction of the East Link Bridge.

❧

Robbie MacDonald ordered another double whiskey. He was fed up. It had been a tough day at work. He was having a row with his wife because he had forgotten their wedding anniversary. And he felt like getting pissed!

He had heard too that Cassie was having a party out in Malahide to celebrate some new business venture she had started. He downed his whiskey in one gulp and ordered another.

Cassie Jordan was the only woman who had ever understood him, the only woman he had ever really loved. And she had turned her back on him, he thought, awash with drink and self-pity. He should have been at her side tonight at this party she was giving, not some flaming Welshman that she was dating. He'd heard about him on the bank grapevine.

He looked at the bouquet of flowers by his side. He

had bought them as a belated anniversary present for his wife, but nipped into the pub for a few quick ones before he went home to face the music. He knew to whom he'd far prefer to be giving them.

His expression became determined and he laughed to himself. Why hadn't he thought of that before? Lurching out of the bar with his flowers, Robbie hopped into a taxi and sat back, feeling very pleased with himself.

❧

Kristi Killeen doused herself liberally with Poison and admired herself in the mirror. She had spent a fortune on this Cerruti white linen trouser-suit and the gold leather Osprey handbag, but it was worth every damn penny.

She couldn't wait for tonight. This would really get up BJM's nose, and heaven knows her nose was nearly as big as her ears! Kristi chuckled at her bitchiness.

Oh yes, these days she had the upper hand on Barbara Jordan Murray. Ever since that court case that she'd had the greatest luck to get wind of, big-ears Barbara had been treading on eggshells as regards Kristi. And if there were one thing Kristi Killeen thoroughly enjoyed, it was a good old family feud!

Would her arch-rival be at her sister's big bash tonight?. Kristi just didn't know, but she intended finding out. Again it had been the greatest piece of luck that she had found out about the party! Andrew Lawson had happened to mention that his wife, Judy, was going to the opening of a new interior design business called **Finishing Touches**, and Kristi had vaguely remembered someone on the circuit mentioning that Cassie Jordan, Barbara's sister, was setting up something similar. A bit of flattery and Andrew Lawson was eating out of her hand. Kristi had got all the information she needed!

Putting on her Ray-Bans, despite the fact that the sun was setting, Kristi strode out to her Alfa Romeo and scorched off in the direction of Malahide.

❧

Barbara was fit to be tied! This very morning her precious novel, *The Fire and the Fury,* had been unceremoniously returned in the post with a bland note from the publishers saying that unfortunately their lists for the next year were full and that they could not publish the novel. They wished her the best of luck in placing her novel elsewhere.

By God, but she wouldn't forget their rejection of her. Any of *their* books that came her way for review from now on would get slated! She had been depending on them to publish *The Fire and the Fury*. They had published some unknown civil servant who had written two blockbusters that had shot into the bestsellers list and made her seriously rich and a media celebrity. It was galling. Barbara's novel had far more class than those two pathetic efforts! Well, the next one was due out soon and by the time Barbara got her hands on it, the author and publishers would be mightily sorry they had ever heard the name Barbara Jordan Murray! Barbara was so furious she had written down some phrases to use when the review copy of the next blockbuster landed on her desk: "fit only for imbeciles"; "one long (very long) yawn"; "mind-bogglingly banal."

She supposed she'd send her manuscript off some-where else, but all the same, it was very disheartening.

She still hadn't made up her mind whether to go to Cassie's party. The only reason she would grace it with her presence was to get a chance to see David again. The man obsessed her; she couldn't get him out of her head. He was just the sexiest man she had ever encountered.

She gave a little shiver as she remembered how she had accused him just before the court case of being in cahoots with Cassie over swindling them out of Nora's house. Very quietly David had told her that if she cared to repeat the accusations he would sue her for slander. His voice had been much more menacing than if he had ranted and roared. It had actually left her speechless and she had walked away!

Many times she replayed that scene in her mind. It always turned her on...She would never ever forgive Cassie, of course. That went without saying!

Barbara sighed. She'd better get dressed, she supposed. Jean was calling and they had arranged to go for a drink. The ice-pink Versace that she had planned to wear was a *bit* too dressy just for going for a drink. But she wanted to keep her options open...just in case. *If* she were going to be seeing David Williams this evening, and it was still a big if, she wanted to look stunning!

Maybe she'd wear her Paul Costello. If he was good enough for Princess Di, he was good enough for her. Barbara went upstairs to her walk-in closet and selected her outfit. She'd see what Jean had to say when she arrived. They could always drive down Main Street, Malahide, and see what was happening; there was no law to stop them doing that! It was a free country, no matter what Cassie Jordan and David Williams might think!

❦

David stood singing under the shower. He was in great form. The Thatcher biography was practically completed. All contracts honoured. No more to be signed. He hadn't given a thought about what he was going to do but there was plenty of time for that.

One thing that was high on his agenda was to spend a lot more time with Cassie. She had been so supportive during his writing period, so different from Danielle, his ex-wife. But then, of course, Cassie Jordan was an exceptional woman! Tonight would prove that. To think she had succeeded in making her dream come true after all she had endured. To think she had even been able to put her hurt and anger aside and invite that bitch, Barbara. David knew there was no way on earth he could ever be *that* forgiving. He didn't know whether he wanted Barbara to show up or not. For Cassie's sake, it would be nice. She wanted to see the members of the family forget their differences. David felt that if he came within three feet of Barbara he'd be tempted to strangle her!

Forget about her, he told himself as he liberally applied deodorant and aftershave lotion. Tonight, when the party was over, he and Cassie would be alone and that was what he desired more than anything. He went into his bedroom and picked up the sapphire-and-diamond ring that he had bought for Cassie. It was an antique with an unusual heart-shaped setting and he hoped she'd like it. He wanted to mark this special night for her. He had ordered roses for her earlier in the day and she had called him in delight to say they had been delivered.

It was a bit like launching a book, he mused, all the fuss and excitement. Well, if anyone deserved it, Cassie did, and he knew she was as excited as a child about it all. Tonight was her night and he was part of it. That made him very happy.

Smiling, David put the ring back in the box and began to dress.

He didn't want to be late. He wanted to share every minute of Cassie's pleasure.

❧

Cassie was trying to stay calm, but it wasn't working! She had been up since the crack of dawn. Her first port of call had been Finishing Touches, to make sure everything was absolutely right. It gave her such a thrill to see the place. It looked superb.

There had been times when she had thought it was never going to get off the ground, especially after the fuss over the fire regulations, when everything had ground to a halt, the pine ceiling had had to be taken down and the place treated with fire-resistant material before she got the all-clear. That had really delayed things and only now, six months later than planned, was she finally ready to move in.

Well, it was worth the wait.

She wondered whether Barbara and Martin would come tonight. She really hoped so. Irene could have phoned to wish her well, or sent a card or something, she thought, a bit sadly.

"Don't think about it; just keep going," she ordered herself, as she drove into Dublin to collect two ceramic urns she had ordered from Flamingos on Capel Street. They had arrived in the shop only the previous evening, but she wanted them. Filled with dried flowers, they would put the finishing touch to her décor.

She parked at a meter on Mary Street, very near a beauty salon owned by a friend of Aileen's. Her eyes glinted. Would she? It was her special day, after all. Why not treat herself? It was early in the morning, so maybe Aoibhinn would have a free session. She'd got her hair done yesterday; she might as well go the whole hog.

Cassie ran lightly up the stairs of the Beauty Shop. She popped her head around the door. "Hi, Aoibhinn! Any chance of a facial and make-up?"

Aoibhinn Hogan, the attractive beautician, smiled in welcome. "Cassie, I haven't seen you in ages! Come in. How's it going? How's that O'Shaughnessy brat?"

Cassie laughed. Aoibhinn and Aileen had trained in beauty school together and Aoibhinn had opened her own salon and made a lovely job of it, Cassie thought in admiration, as she gazed around at the soothing décor. Cassie couldn't have improved on it if she tried!

"Sit here in the chair. We'll have a cup of coffee and you can tell me what you want done," Aoibhinn invited. "I don't have an appointment until ten-thirty. And there's just someone on the sunbed at the moment."

They chatted and drank their coffee and Aoibhinn gave her a manicure and then made up her face beautifully, emphasising her eyes under their arched brows, highlighting her cheekbones with a light shading of blusher, and outlining her lips with a lip pencil before filling in her lipstick. Cassie couldn't believe it was her, she looked so glamorous. David wouldn't recognise her!

Aoibhinn refused payment, despite Cassie's protestations. "Indeed, I'm not taking it. I remember what it was like the first day I opened for business, I was so excited! It's a great buzz and I wish you every success with the venture," Aoibhinn said warmly, accompanying Cassie to the door. "Tell Aileen to get in touch this time."

"I will," Cassie assured her. "She won't be home until later. She's flying in from London, so I won't see her until tonight."

It was amazing what an hour in a beauty salon could achieve, Cassie thought, as she crossed over to Capel Street. She felt like a new woman. Aoibhinn had been very kind.

Her urns were ready and Cassie drove back to Malahide in great humour. It was a lovely day, the sun was sparkling on the sea, and she felt ready for anything. She fixed up her newly acquired pieces, arranged the dried flowers and went back to her house. David was staying for the weekend and she wanted to change the bedclothes and have the place tidy. She was decorating one room at a time, although she hadn't done much lately because of the business, but the bedroom with its big brass bed was finished and Cassie loved it. Decorated in cream and yellow, it was a soothing retreat from the world. The bed faced one of the small windows under the eaves and Cassie loved watching the sun and moon rise over the estuary. It was so peaceful. In this house her spirit was serene.

She'd better get a move on, she decided; the caterers were coming and she wanted everything to be just right. The most important people in her life were going to be there tonight and Cassie wanted nothing but the best for them.

It was almost dark! Barbara and Jean sat in Barbara's car watching the comings and goings just up the street. **Finishing Touches** was a blaze of colour and Barbara had to admit in spite of herself that it looked very, very impressive. She had to admit, too, that she was sorely tempted to go inside and have a look. She and Jean had decided to motor down through Malahide and see what was happening, *en route* to their drinks destination, which they had not yet selected. That was what Barbara liked about her sister-in-law. She had a mind that worked just like her own.

Guests were arriving at a great rate and she and Jean had a comment about everyone. "Oh look, there's Laura Quinn and her husband. She's put on a bit of weight!" Jean announced smugly. "And would you look at that O'Shaughnessy one? Gaudy as they come! And who's the one beside her? Who does she think she is? Ivana Trump?"

Barbara peered forward to get a closer look at the sequinned apparition that was accompanying Aileen and nearly choked! "That's Irene! What the hell is she doing here...the turncoat."

"Omigod! Look! Look!" Jean nearly wet herself with excitement. "Who's that getting out of the taxi? Oh crumbs, he's as drunk as a skunk. Look at the flowers; they're falling to pieces."

"Where? Let me see." Barbara craned her neck. "Ooh, there'll be ructions! That's Robbie MacDonald, who used to be engaged to Cassie. I told you about him already." Barbara was practically rubbing her hands with glee.

"Oh look! Oh look! He's being thrown out. David Williams and John are throwing him out. He hasn't had a chance even to get through the door!" Jean kept up a running commentary, as Barbara devoured her first sight of her idol!

David had Robbie by the scruff of the neck and was telling him a few home truths. John hailed the taxi that had brought Robbie, as the driver was doing a U-turn to head back to town. Almost as quickly as he had come, Robbie was back in the taxi and John was handing the driver some money. Off went the taxi. David and John were shaking hands and laughing before going back into the party.

Barbara was almost quivering with the excitement. David Williams was so masterfull Desire scorched through her. "Will we go in or what do you think?" she asked her sister-in-law, hoping against hope that Jean might say yes.

Jean was sitting like a stone, speechless, pointing her finger. "Look!" she whispered! "How could he! How could he betray his own wife!"

Barbara followed the line of Jean's shaking finger and saw Martin, dressed up in his good Louis Copeland suit, with a huge bouquet of flowers in his arms, walking down the street towards Finishing Touches. Outside he paused, as if taking a deep breath. John and David appeared and Martin shook hands with the two men. Then, smiling as if he hadn't a care in the world, with his brother's arm around his shoulder, Martin disappeared through the door.

"I'm going to leave him," vowed Jean as Barbara sat stunned. "The two-faced rat!"

All the family had turned up for Cassie's party, all of them except her. Had they no *pride*? Barbara thought in disgust.

A familiar Alfa Romeo squealed past from the far end of the street and came to a halt with a screech of brakes.

"Christ Almighty! I don't believe it!" exclaimed a horrified Barbara.

"What?" Jean didn't think anything could be much worse than watching her own husband do the dirty on her.

"It's big-mouth Killeen! Duck quick; she can't catch us sitting here!" Barbara urged frantically.

The pair of them slid down in their seats, as Kristi parked and marched past.

"God, would you look at the rig-out! Look at the sunglasses and it's almost pitch dark! Typical!" Barbara slid cautiously up the seat. "Nosy bitch. I bet she hasn't been invited. Cassie doesn't know her. She's going to gatecrash!" Barbara was furious to think that her arch-enemy was going to be nosing around at Cassie's party.

Kristi waved at someone inside as if she knew them and swanned through the portals of **Finishing Touches**.

"Oh I hate her guts!" Barbara almost wept in rage.

"Oh look, Barbara! Barbara, look, she's coming out. Look at the face on her! Oh they've rumbled her! Quick, duck again!"

They slid down in their seats and heard an angry clip-clop of high heels and then a slamming of a car door. Kristi did a U-turn that would have shamed a grand-prix driver before roaring off into the night.

Barbara and Jean sat back up in their seats, utterly drained by the drama of it all.

❦

Inside, the atmosphere was electric, the gaiety infectious.

"You're engaged, Aileen O'Shaughnessy!" Cassie shrieked, catching sight of Aileen's ring.

"Even the best of us have to go some time!" smirked Aileen, thrilled that Cassie had noticed. Laura and Judy crowded around to have a look. They were so excited and so engrossed they never even noticed the drama at the door. Cassie and Irene hugged each other. Cassie's face was wreathed in smiles. To think that Irene had actually flown home for the party! It was unbelievable and she thought she was going to disgrace herself by crying. Then Martin had arrived with a huge bouquet of flowers and she *did* disgrace herself. "Oh Martin, I'm so glad you came." She buried her face in her brother's shoulder.

"I'm really sorry about everything, Cassie. I just can't tell you how sorry I am!" Martin was nearly in tears himself.

"It doesn't matter! It doesn't matter. You're here now and that's all I care about," Cassie beamed.

Everybody was talking nineteen to the dozen, when David caught sight of a vaguely familiar woman edging her way through the throng. He had seen her somewhere before. Where was it? It clicked. He had seen her at the back of the court on the last day of the hearing. Cassie had told him it was Kristi Killeen, the gossip columnist. He knew Cassie hadn't invited her, so she could be here only to cause trouble.

Before she knew it, Kristi Killeen had been taken gently but firmly by the arm and escorted out the door.

"Family and friends only, I'm afraid," she heard this man say, with an accent that was too divine for words, as she was unceremoniously ejected from **Finishing Touches**. She didn't even have time to find out if Barbara was there or not!

Cassie, oblivious of everything else, basked in the glow of attention from her family and friends. She was so glad that Martin had come and made amends for the unpleasantness about the will. And Irene! Who would believe that she had taken the trouble to come all the way home for her party?

David came and stood beside her and Aileen clapped her hands for quiet.

"I think we should toast Cassie! And wish her great success!" she declared gaily.

A loud cheer went up as champagne glasses were held aloft. Cassie thought she was going to burst with happiness as she smiled at all the people who meant so much to her.

"For she's a jolly good fellow...!" sang David in a deep melodious voice.

"For she's a jolly good fellow..." everyone else took up the chorus.

"For she's a jolly good fe...ell...ow, and so say all of us!"

The roof of **Finishing Touches** was almost lifted by the cheers.

Outside, Barbara and Jean stared at each other as they heard the singing inside and Cassie being toasted.

"I don't really want to go for a drink now, do you?" Jean muttered.

"No!" said Barbara glumly. "Let's go home!"

"I wonder where Barbara is," Laura whispered to Aileen. "She's missing all the fun."

"Who cares?" bubbled Aileen. "She's an idiot."

"Who's an idiot?" grinned Cassie, catching the tail-end of the conversation.

"No one that you know," Aileen laughed. "Are you having a good time?"

Cassie caught David's warm gaze and smiled happily at him. "The best ever. I'll never forget tonight as long as I live!"

☙☙☙☙☙